LAND OF ECHOES

LAND *of* ECHOES

A CREE BLACK NOVEL

DANIEL HECHT

BLOOMSBURY

Published by Bloomsbury Publishing, New York and London
Distributed to the trade by Holtzbrinck Publishers

The Library of Congress has cataloged the hardcover edition as follows:

Hecht, Daniel.
   Land of echoes : a Cree Black novel / Daniel Hecht.
      p. cm.
   ISBN 1–58234–393–4
   1. Parapsychologists–Fiction. 2. Women school principals–Fiction.
3. Spirit possession–Fiction. 4. Indian students–Fiction. 5.
Seattle (Wash.)–Fiction. 6. Navajo Indians–Fiction. 7. New
Mexico–Fiction. I. Title.

   PS3558.E284L35 2004
   813'.54–dc22

                                                    2003017983

First published in hardcover by Bloomsbury Publishing in 2004
This paperback edition published in 2005

Paperback ISBN 1-58234-473-6
ISBN-13 9781582344737

1 3 5 7 9 10 8 6 4 2

Typeset by Hewer Text Ltd, Edinburgh

All papers used by Bloomsbury Publishing are natural,
recyclable products made from wood grown in
well-managed forests. The manufacturing processes
conform to the environmental regulations of the
country of origin.

Printed in the United States of America by Quebecor World Fairfield

This book is dedicated to Ruth Storer and Bob Kirk, for teaching me so much, for feeding me and my family so well, and most of all for being such good friends.

1

S AM YAZZIE, the boys' dorm night supervisor, was in his room reading when he heard an odd sound from the far end of the building. He put down his book and tipped his head to listen.

For a few seconds, there was nothing but the noise of wind in the eaves. Then he heard it again: a forced vocalization of distress. He tried to tell himself it sounded like one of the kids having a stomach problem, heaving up cafeteria food in the bathroom, but he knew better. It was the same sort of noise Tommy Keeday had made that awful night just a week ago.

He laid the book aside, went into the hall, and stopped again to listen. The building was long and narrow, divided by a corridor that stretched its whole length. On the right was the room that served as his office and residence, along with the utility room, two bathrooms, and two six-boy dorms; on the left, the day supervisor's office and four dorm rooms. Sam's impression was that the sounds had come from the far end.

As usual, the corridor lights were off, but night-lights glowed at regular intervals, and the open bathroom doors spilled enough light to illuminate the hall. He walked down to the first door and went into the tiled, fluorescent-lit room. Nobody: no feet visible under the four stall doors, nobody in the showers, nobody tossing it up at the sinks. The ceiling fluorescents blinked irritatingly, and he made a mental note to ask the maintenance staff to replace the tubes.

When he paused in the hall to listen again, everything was quiet, and his tension eased a little. Maybe it was something outside, not a kid after all. Maybe the wind, which was high tonight, bearing in from the north and bringing a chill. More likely a coyote or fox. The two dorms stood apart from the classroom and administration buildings, and the whole school was just a dot in an endless expanse of rolling sagebrush desert. It was big country, sparsely populated, with plenty of wildlife. A couple of times a year, coyotes raided the cafeteria trash bins and made a ruckus. Maybe—

The sound came again, a muffled scream and some garbled words, definitely human. It choked off and left only the midnight silence. A chill crept over Sam's skin as he began to stride down the hall.

It had to be Tommy again. The first time, he'd recovered within half an hour or so, and Julieta and Dr. Tsosie had written it off: bad dream, exhaustion, stress. After the second episode, they'd sent him to the Indian Hospital in Gallup, a four-day diagnostic workup that ended with the doctors pronouncing him perfectly healthy.

Now he'd been back for only two days. If this was Tommy getting sick again, it didn't look good for the poor kid. And it would break Julieta's heart to know her prize new student had some chronic or recurring condition.

Whatever it was. There was something strange about the way Julieta and Joe Tsosie were handling this.

Approaching the north end of the building, Sam stopped at the door to the room Tommy shared with five of his fellow sophomores. Even in the dim light, he could see six beds and six motionless lumps wrapped in blankets, including Tommy, who looked dead asleep with mouth wide open, one arm up above his head on the pillow. None of them moved, and the only sounds they made were the faint wheezes and sighs of their breathing.

Then the stifled cry came again, and the lump that was Tommy moved. It seemed to swell and swarm with bumps that must be knees or elbows but that didn't look right. Sam didn't move. Part of his mind noticed that the lights were fluttering in the second bathroom, too. Tommy's blankets humped and shook, and it occurred to Sam that maybe there were two people in the bed, maybe there was some British boys' school-style hanky-panky going on. But then the mound deflated and he could see it was only Tommy, tangled alone in his blanket, lying on his back. One side of the boy's face was drawn up as if a string was pulling a corner of his mouth toward his ear, and as Sam stood, still unable to move, Tommy's body twisted and convulsed. The whole bed shook with the force of it.

Sam's paralysis broke and he stepped quickly toward the bed. But before he could reach it, Tommy's body went slack.

He stopped again, confused. Tommy now lay fast asleep or unconscious, motionless but for the shallow pumping of his chest. For the first time, Sam noticed that the other boys weren't asleep—how could they be, with the awful noises Tommy made?—but were lying immobile in some kind of semi-conscious paralysis. David Blanco, in the bed next to Tommy's, lay with his eyes slightly open, just glistening pale slits. In the deeper shadow at the far end of the room, Jim Wauneka was sitting up, rigid, motionless. Sam almost called to him but then realized his eyes weren't really open, either—just unseeing slits, like someone anesthetized or dead.

Tommy's chest and stomach and legs began rising and falling, rippling in a series of convulsions. At first, the movements were gentle and rhythmic as ripples undulating in a pond, but they quickly grew faster and more vehement until it looked as if the scrawny body would wrench itself apart. The sheer violence of the movement seemed to knock Sam another step backward. He felt torn between wanting to run and duty to his charges, between terror and a hideous fascination.

This wasn't right, he knew. This wasn't natural. Nothing he'd encountered in the army or as an orderly in the crisis ward in Phoenix had prepared him for this. Abruptly he became aware of the great dark sagebrush plains all around the building, the infinite night sky above hundreds of thousands of square miles of bare red-brown earth, stark rocks, lonely mesas, and shadowed canyons. He remembered the feeling from his childhood, from the times he'd be herding his family's sheep in the evening as the stars pricked through one by one and the sun bleached only the very western edge of night and he could feel in the lonely empty hollow of his gut just how big and incomprehensible the world was. He'd almost forgotten. Now he realized with a sense of calamity that the world he'd disciplined himself to accept, that he'd spent his adult life buying into and working to master, wasn't real after all: The world of white America and science and school, jobs and sports and TVs, didn't have an explanation for this. This was something come out of the world's hidden places, from the old world of the Bible or his grandfather's stories or the dark legends of witches and ghosts that had been whispered from person to person long before human beings knew how to write them down.

Tommy made a quiet, awful sound, as if a full-bellied scream had been throttled by a throat too constricted to allow it to pass. Sam bolted forward, but just as he caught the arching shoulders, the awful tension went out of the boy. One moment Tommy's right arm had started to push forward and then Sam felt something like a shock through his hands and arms, a vortex of sensation that buzzed quickly through his stomach, and the boy's arm snapped back and lay limp on his chest. All Sam held in his arms was a slack, sleeping fifteen-year-old.

Sam felt only an instant of relief as he lowered Tommy back to the pillow. His movements felt as if they were resisted by a powerful force, some warped gravity or a form of magnetism that influenced flesh and bone. The light bleeding in from the corridor was really going crazy now. It strobed as if a string of flashbulbs was going off in the bathroom as Tommy began to shudder and twitch and another wave of convulsions took him.

Julieta McCarty stared across her desk and tried to assimilate what Sam had just told her. He insisted that there was no other way to look at it. It wasn't a prank or even an ordinary seizure. Some kind of disturbance or force radiated from the Keeday boy: The other boys had lain or sat unmoving throughout his battle with Tommy, despite the awful noises he'd made and the thrashing and wrestling. Sam had felt it himself. Now Tommy was in the infirmary, Sam said, doing that thing again like last time, and the nurse had called Dr. Tsosie.

As an afterthought, Sam informed her that he was quitting, effective immediately.

He didn't have to explain why. Sam was forty years old, a reliable staffer who had served in the army, where he'd been trained as a paramedic, and he'd earned a bachelor's degree in social work from the University of Arizona; though he'd been born on the reservation he'd lived a good part of his life elsewhere. But like most Navajos of his generation, he hung uncertainly between the old beliefs and the view of the world he'd absorbed from white America. In Julieta's experience, even the most culturally assimilated Navajo believed that some truth lay beneath the traditional fears of Skinwalkers, Navajo Wolves, spirits of the dead, and the consequences of violating old taboos.

"Sam. You know I'll never be able to replace you." Julieta tried to keep the pleading out of her voice.

"I've had six hours to think about it. I talked to my wife. It scares her for me to be here anymore." He knew what his leaving meant and was clearly feeling bad about his decision, but he left her office with a resolute stride.

Only eight-fifteen in the morning, and she was already confronted with two pieces of very bad news. It was bad enough that she'd just lost a linchpin of her residential staff, a man both she and the students admired. But equally disturbing—no, worse, a sick, strangling fear that clotted in her chest—was that Tommy Keeday had been back only two days and already his troubles had resumed. Why Tommy, of all of them? The first time his bizarre symptoms had cropped up, they had passed quickly, and she and Dr. Tsosie had decided to let it go as some flu symptom, maybe, or a touch of food poisoning. But the second time, the attack had lingered and intensified, and Dr. Tsosie had referred Tommy for an exhaustive diagnostic workup at the Indian Hospital. The problem was that the symptoms had passed before they'd even completed the hour-long drive to Gallup, and after four days of testing that had included CT scans, electroencephalograms, comprehensive blood work, and a battery of psychological tests, the doctors had given Tommy a clean bill of health. He'd shown no cranial abnormalities, no detectable seizure activity, no sign of any illegal drugs in his system. In fact, he'd shown no symptoms of physical illness at all.

"Probably just dehydration," one smug intern had told her. "Sometimes its effects can mimic seizure activity. It's only temporary. Make sure he drinks lots of Gatorade."

Remembering his condescension infuriated Julieta—as if a lifelong resident of the area and principal of a boarding school wouldn't know the effects of the hot, dry climate of western New Mexico on teenagers!—and she mastered her anger with the hard pragmatism her position required of her. She had to think clearly, couldn't let her emotions get in the way.

That Tommy's symptoms had returned meant that he was a child seriously at risk. But how? The hospital couldn't find anything wrong with him. And what was she to make of Sam's claim that the . . . disturbance . . . had affected the other boys?

Two lights on her phone had begun blinking demandingly, and abruptly she realized she couldn't be bothered with whatever it was, she needed to get away from distractions and think this through. She left her desk, stopped briefly to tell the secretary that she was going for a walk, and hurried out of the administration building.

Outside, it was a perfect mid-September day. The strong north winds that had battered the school last night had died out. The sun was halfway up the eastern sky, its heat already a smart slap on her face even though a layer of cool air still hovered above the ground. Arms crossed, chin on her chest, she scuffed across the rear access road to the partial shade of a trellis she'd had set up as a place for staff to take lunch. A sunning lizard darted away as she sat on the picnic table.

It was a good vantage from which to look at the school. With everyone in class now, the complex was quiet: a little cluster of one-story buildings, a gravel-surfaced parking lot, a row of five stubby yellow school buses, a white water tower. The admin, classroom, and dorm buildings were new, built of concrete and surfaced to resemble adobe in gray and pink tones. A large hogan, eight-sided and built of logs, occupied a central spot between dorms and classroom buildings. Set farther back amid some cottonwood trees stood the little adobe bell tower and her own sandstone-block house, which now served as the infirmary until she could raise the money to build another unit.

The school stood alone and diminished by the vastness of its surroundings. To the north and south stretched sagebrush desert, rolling swells of bare soil and rocks in a red-brown, gray-green mosaic only rarely varied by the dark green of a piñon tree; to the west, the land rose and broke into the hills bordering Black Creek. Beyond the school buildings to the east, the view was cut short by a little mesa, its cliffs making a meandering wall that eventually curved out of sight. Far to the north, the horizon was capped by the rugged line of the Chuska Mountains' southernmost slopes. Above, the vault of clean blue sky, streaked today with thin, high clouds.

Not another human thing in sight. Beautiful.

And that's it, Julieta thought desperately. *My life. The one good thing I've ever done. The only thing I've ever done right.*

She looked at the place and loved it painfully, and it seemed the sun stung her eyes and brought tears. Starting this school had been a way not only to give something to the people of the region, it had been a personal crusade—redemption for a life of stupid mistakes, wasted years, squandered self. It was a line she'd drawn in the sand, the demarcation between past and future. Whatever neurotic hopes or submerged long-ings might have shaped her motivations, it had turned into a good thing.

Just starting its sixth year of operation, Oak Springs was the first privately run boarding school for gifted and talented Navajo kids, and it was now weekday home to sixty-seven high school boys and girls drawn from western New Mexico and eastern Arizona, most of them from the rez. Every Friday the buses returned all but ten to their homes in remote trailers and hogans and shacks scattered over an area of fifteen thousand square miles, and every Monday brought them back for another five days of instruction and, she hoped, inspiration. She'd spent all of the money she'd gotten in her divorce settlement, had campaigned hard for the rest from charitable foundations and state agencies, and she'd done it, she'd built it and certified it and staffed it and got it up and going. Every step of the way had been hard, and every step had been wonderful and worth it.

Except that now it was about to fall down around her.

Sam Yazzie's leaving would have ramifications far beyond the need to shuffle staff and advertise for a replacement. If Sam felt he had to get out, it wouldn't be long before other Navajo staff and faculty—virtually every employee at the school—started abandoning ship. And if Tommy Kee-day's problem couldn't be solved, it was a much larger issue than the fate of one very bright, troubled boy. If word of his problem got out into the community, people would stop sending their kids. A vital opportunity would be lost to those who needed it most.

And Julieta McCarty would be left without a reason for living.

Again the jolt of intolerable fear hit her: the prospect of an empty life. She got up quickly and almost ran to the boys' dorm, hoping to catch Sam before he left.

She found him in his room, pulling things off his desk and stuffing them into cardboard boxes. With his barrel-chested build, brush-cut dark hair, and the downturned lips common among older Navajo men, he came across as stern and martial. The look was misleading; Sam was a sweet person, and it had always pleased Julieta to see that dour mouth smile so surprisingly and rewardingly.

She stopped at the doorway. He glanced at her, then opened one of the desk drawers and spent several minutes sorting through it in silence.

At last Sam shook his head, the crescent of his lips tightening. "My grandfather, I mentioned it to him last time, he says not to talk about it. He says if you talk about it, it will come after you. You shouldn't give it a name. He can tell twenty stories about what happens to you. Says he knew a guy up in Lukachukai, couple of months ago, saw something strange way out on Carson Mesa and talked about it to everybody. Next day he got killed in a freak accident. Drove his pickup into the side of an empty stock trailer. Wasn't drunk. The way they found him, he was kind of . . . up under the hood of his truck. It wasn't right. Nobody could figure out what happened."

"People get killed in accidents every day. It isn't supernatural."

"The *other boys,* Julieta! Like, I don't know . . . zombies." Just remembering it put a tremor in his shoulders, and again he shook his head, unwilling to describe the event in any more detail. "You have to see it. Then you'll understand." He gestured with his thumb toward the students' rooms, looking at her with sympathy in his eyes, then went back to packing his things.

"Did your grandfather say what he thought it was?"

Sam took several books from their shelf and then paused. She knew he was wrestling with his reluctance to tell her anything at all, the universal fear that bad things could be contagious and that holding evil in your thoughts brought it upon you.

"You know how the old people talk," he whispered. "It's a chindi. Maybe this place was built on bones, maybe Navajo, maybe Anasazi, and the ancestors don't like the school being here, disrespecting their graves. Or maybe we're doing something else wrong, maybe somebody died in the dorm building, we shouldn't be using it, and the ghost is coming back. More likely there's some witches live near here, want to hurt us or hurt the kids. He said it would come from the north, evil comes from the north? And we had a north wind last night." These explanations seemed to bother him, and he threw down the books in frustration. "Look, Julieta, forget I'm Diné. Last night, I wasn't looking at it from some ethnic perspective, okay? Maybe I smoked too much dope at UA, or maybe some UFO landed near here, there's aliens doing experiments or something to people's minds. I don't care what. I don't want to deal with it."

Again he looked at her with regret and sympathy, and she realized with a pang how much she'd depended on Sam for the last five years.

8

Still she stood in the doorway, unwilling to move yet unable to ask him one last favor.

He couldn't meet her eyes, but his voice was gruffly compassionate when he spoke again: "I know, Julieta. I won't tell anyone what I saw. This place'd be empty by sunset."

When Julieta put her head into Lynn Pierce's examining room, the nurse looked up with a start, and the pencil she'd been writing with snapped in her fingers.

"Any word from Joseph?" Julieta asked.

"He'll get here around eleven."

"How's Tommy?" The blinds over the window to the ward room were half slatted; all she could see was a mound of twisted bedclothes.

Lynn's eyes darted to the window, and she bit her lips. She gestured at the patient voice monitor on her desk. Through the soft hiss pouring from the speaker, Julieta could make out gentle snoring.

"Sleeping now. But it was worse this time. It lasted longer."

"His spine again? The right arm?"

A tiny nod.

"Why didn't you call me, Lynn? I would have—"

"Joseph told me I should let you rest. Unless it was a crisis. Yazzie and I were able to keep him from hurting himself. By the time I could get free to call you, he'd stabilized."

"Is there any point in my going in with him?" All Julieta could think of was to hold him.

"No. Wait until Joseph gets here."

The thought of Joseph's earnest face and skilled, strong hands soothed Julieta a little. It helped that he knew how much this meant to her. That there was someone who knew it all. Surely he'd have some solution, he'd think of the next step.

"Have you talked to his teachers?" Julieta asked.

"I sent out my usual absence notice. I didn't go into details, just said he wasn't feeling well."

"Who else has seen him? Is anybody talking about it yet?"

Lynn would know this was the school administrator turning to damage control, the need to contain superstitious gossip. The nurse was one of the

9

few non-Navajo staff at the school, a solidly built woman in her midfifties with silver hair pulled back into a thick braid that hung down to her waist. She had dazzling blue eyes made more startling by an iridescent bronze fleck in her left iris that was distracting and sometimes made her expression hard to read. She had come to the rez as a VISTA volunteer in the 1970s and had married a Navajo man from the Nakaibito area. Childless, her husband now dead, she seemed to have taken the stream of student patients here as her family. Somehow Julieta hadn't really gotten close to Lynn in her three years here, but right now she took comfort in the fact that the nurse shared her concern and distress.

"Nobody's called me for details," Lynn said, "so if Sam doesn't talk, it'll probably be all right for a few days. Sam says the other boys don't remember anything, but I wouldn't count on that—I don't know what kind of gossip they might be spreading. The teachers will inquire if he doesn't show up in class soon, and his grandparents will need to be informed . . ." Lynn finished with a gesture: *And soon everyone will know.*

Julieta shut the examining room door and leaned against it. "Lynn," she whispered. "What *is* this? Be honest with me. Have you ever encountered anything like this?"

Lynn toyed with the snapped pencil, her fingers drawn again and again to the jagged break. "The brain is a wilderness, the strangest things can happen. All I can guess is that this is a profound neurological aberration. But I can't square that with what Sam says—the way it affected the other boys."

They thought about it for a moment, listening to the deceptively serene noise of breathing coming through the monitor.

"What're we going to do?" Julieta whispered at last. "Where do we go from here?"

Lynn shook her head, and she looked at Julieta with her lopsided, startling gaze, her eyes now moist, nested in wrinkles of worry, and very guarded. "I have no idea."

2

CREE GLANCED up to see that a shape had materialized at the rear of the auditorium. Backlit by the ceiling lights near the entry, at this distance, it was no more than a dark silhouette: no face or features, just the outline of heavy shoulders and a large head so low above the body that it seemed the being had no neck. It loomed low behind the last row of seats like someone crouching or stooping, both menacing and disturbingly familiar.

In the instant it took to place the profile, Cree lost her train of thought. The last echoes of her words rang out over the speakers, and she wished she could somehow retrieve them and discern what she had said only an instant before.

Mason Ambrose. Here in Albuquerque. It had to be.

Sure enough, as she hesitated, another figure took up a post above the man in the wheelchair: Lupe. The ceiling spot haloed her gray hair and gave exaggerated dimension to the sockets of her eyes, her gaunt cheekbones, her thorn of a nose. Lupe, thin as a bone and as hard, not so much Ambrose's eternal personal assistant as his familiar, the sorcerer's mysterious creature companion.

Covering her surprise, Cree cleared her throat and took a sip of water from the glass on the podium.

"Excuse me!" she apologized. She scanned the nearer rows of the audience, located the earnest face of the woman who had spoken, smiled, and found her thought again. "It's hard to explain, but I've been asked that question before and I've given quite a bit of thought to how to answer it. I think I can convey the sensation to you if you'll follow along with me."

Moving to the side of the podium so that everyone could see her clearly, she raised her voice. "Put your index and middle fingers together and place them just under your right ear, where your jawbone meets the muscle that comes up the side of your neck. Got it? Now move the fingers forward, just under the jaw, until you feel them slide into the notch there. About halfway to your chin." Cree tipped her head and tossed her hair back as she demonstrated. *There*. Most of the audience were obligingly putting their hands to their throats, wondering where she was going with this.

"You might have to push fairly hard. But you should be able to feel your carotid artery there—a rubbery cord about as big around as a pencil? You can feel it stiffen and soften with every heartbeat."

She gave them a moment just to feel it.

"You're putting your finger right on your physical life. That throb—it's always been with you. Your heart's keeping you alive without your conscious thought—it's living inside you almost as if it's a separate creature alive in your chest. It does its job day in, day out. Most people don't like feeling it. We don't like to be reminded that there's an automatic part of ourselves, going about its business without our conscious supervision. It's a little creepy, isn't it? Vital, insistent, sort of foreign somehow? Yet of course it's deeply intimate, that pulse—deeply familiar, right?"

The audience was silent; most of them had their heads tilted, hands at throats. Some serious expressions, a few uncomfortable grins. Two hundred people feeling the secret pulsing inside.

"So, to answer your question, that's how it feels. That's how . . . *intimate* it feels. That's how *real* it feels, how disconcerting it feels, to experience a ghost. Both physically and psychologically, that's the closest analogy I can come up with. That's the way experiencing a ghost reminds you of what you really are."

And if you don't like that, Mason, if that's too "spiritual" for you, she thought defiantly, *screw you.*

At the rear, the silhouettes of Lupe and Mason Ambrose hovered, motionless as a trompe l'oeil painted on the back wall.

The woman who had asked the question was clearly among those who were uncomfortable with touching that pulsing serpent. She nodded seriously, two fingers still held against her neck.

There was another moment of quiet, and then Dr. Zentcy, the conference's coordinator, moved from the wings and took over the microphone. He was a pleasant-faced man who struck Cree as rather too young and too informally dressed to be an academic of any kind, let alone head of the psychology department of a major university.

"And I think that should be our last question for Dr. Black today. Thank you, Lucretia, for a provocative talk, and for taking so many questions. You've given us a great deal to think about. And thank you all for coming. Dr. Black's lecture is the final event today, but I hope we'll see you all here tomorrow for the final presentations in this year's Horizons in Psychology seminar."

The wash of applause was genuine, but as the room lights came up Cree didn't feel the gratifying release of tension that typically came after she'd delivered a lecture. Mason Ambrose didn't just casually show up at conferences, and his presence disturbed her. She hadn't seen him in four years, hadn't even spoken to him in perhaps two. If he was here, he had a reason. She realized that her body had something of a Pavlovian aversion to him, derived from the two years she'd spent working and studying with him. It wasn't just his grotesque physical appearance, or that he seemed to relish the more gruesome aspects of paranormal research: Mason Ambrose liked to push you into a learning curve so steep it could give you a nosebleed.

Dr. Zentcy had turned to Cree with a puzzled, pleased frown. He tipped his head slightly toward the back of the hall and asked under his breath, "Is that . . . that isn't by any chance—"

"Why, yes," Cree said, pretending she hadn't noticed earlier. "Mason Ambrose. I believe it is." *Internationally renowned neuropsychiatrist and expert on abnormal psychology, internationally controversial scholar of parapsychology. My mentor.*

"I didn't know . . ." Zentcy tried, "I mean, I had no idea he was actually . . ."

"Still alive? Good point." Cree leaned toward him with a bogus paranoid face and whispered, "What makes you so sure he *is?*"

For an instant, Zentcy's eyes widened, and Cree regretted teasing him— it was an indication of her own uneasiness. Zentcy was a good guy who deserved kudos for putting Cree and her radical ideas on the agenda here. The academic world was simply not ready for the idea that ghosts were real, and that the experience of death—and living people's relationships with the dead—must be central to any theory of psychology. His open-mindedness had no doubt earned him some scorn from his colleagues here at the University of New Mexico, yet he'd treated her with only respect and consideration.

"I'm kidding," she reassured him. "But I know what you mean. With Dr. Ambrose you're never quite certain. I'll introduce you, if you like."

Zentcy nodded with equivocal enthusiasm.

A dozen audience members had assembled at the front of the room, waiting to speak with her: students with theoretical questions, professors with bones to pick, even a few local residents with personal tales of ghosts and hauntings. By the time the last of them left, the figures at the back of the room had vanished.

Cree left the building feeling a mix of disappointment and relief at Mason's disappearance. Why would he have taken the time to attend her talk if he didn't want to meet with her? Just playing Mr. Mysterious, she decided; she'd hear from him again before she left Albuquerque. She drove back to her hotel to find a faxed note that confirmed her hunch: *Take the Sandia Peak tramway at 5:00. See you at the top. Ambrose.*

3

T HE AERIAL car started toward the peak, swinging up the slope and quickly leaving the embrace of the lower tramway station. Cree gripped a pole as she looked out over the heads of the kids who had pressed themselves against the windows. Ahead stretched a steep rocky incline almost bare of vegetation; below, beyond the concrete planes and angles of the station, the flat valley and the streets of suburban Albuquerque began to open and fall away. The southern slopes of the Sandia range came into view, tinged pink by the westering sun, their rocky turrets set against hard shadows.

Space. Light. Rock. Sky.

A grand land, Cree realized. A place of heroic proportion. There were fifteen other excited sightseers standing with her in the car, but their chattering stopped as the ground dropped away and a gulf of air opened beneath their feet. Everyone was experiencing the same awe. For a long moment there was a collective suspension of breath broken only by the hum of the drive machinery. Then the kids' excitement boiled over in exclamations of astonishment, and people started talking again.

The views mesmerized Cree, but she couldn't suppress her apprehension. Drama aside, Mason would have some reason for meeting her on Sandia Peak when any coffeehouse or hotel lobby would have been sufficient. He always had a reason. It no doubt had to do with "instructional value," but Mason's motives were mysterious and would remain so until he revealed them. And then he'd stick it to you hard and enjoy watching you squirm. There was a sadistic quality to Mason and his methods.

So why take the effort to see him?

Actually, the answer was simple. Whatever he had in mind, it would be something eye-opening. Mason Ambrose was a genius, a pioneer in psychology in Cree's estimation as important as Freud or Jung. He was also a brilliant teacher, infinitely giving and subtle and patient despite what could seem a purely self-absorbed and confrontational style. In Cree's case, he'd served as guide, guru, and therapist as much as teacher. He'd had the insight to accept her as his research assistant seven years ago, even though he'd seen her for the damaged merchandise she was. When she'd applied for the internship advertised in the Harvard grad school bulletin, she had been a widow for almost three years, still deeply wounded by the loss of her husband, crazy and sick with it. The grief alone would have undone her, but the way she'd found out about Mike's death—his appearance in Philadelphia at his dying moment, three thousand miles from the Los Angeles car wreck that killed him—had upset all her beliefs about the world. About life. When she'd come to Mason, she'd been lost and frightened, a spiritual seeker floundering and flailing in her quest to find answers to life's mysteries. A swimmer about to go under.

Mason had seen all that in his first glance. He'd spent two years redirecting her anger and fear, merging them with her hunger to learn and helping her focus them on her work. He'd goaded or finessed her into disciplining her talents. He'd helped her accept that her urgent fascination with the paranormal was not compulsion but passion, not useless but crucial. Most important, he'd believed in her and affirmed that the empathic techniques she used to commune with ghosts and those haunted by them were valid and necessary.

But his methods were, as he liked to put it, "rigorous." He'd plunged her into experiences of the paranormal that drove her nearly to insanity. One of the first, long before she was ready for such an encounter, had been the New Jersey motel ghost. She'd lived in the squalid, piss- and cigarette-stinking room for a week as she slowly got to know the revenant of a serial killer whose dying moments consisted of remembering his murders. Mason had seemed to relish every detail, including Cree's terror and distress.

Huge tubes of blue steel intruded suddenly across her field of vision, jolting her out of her recollections. Just as startled, the other passengers gasped and laughed uneasily. The tramcar had reached one of the support gantries partway up the mountain, and as it came to the peak of the first swoop of cables and changed incline it bounded gently, suspending gravity and leaving Cree's stomach hanging. The gargantuan tower's passing revealed how fast they were moving and how high they were.

Below, a vast space had opened between the car and the slope. To the west, the grid of Albuquerque's streets stretched out on a plain so flat it could have been pressed by some titan's rolling pin. Beyond lay a breathtaking sweep of desert, slightly hazy with distance, bounded at the far horizon by purple mountains.

Cree gawked like the rest of the passengers. What was it about the Southwest? Maybe the New Agers of Santa Fe and Taos had it right after all, and it was a magical land, a place of Earth energy convergence. She had spent only a week in Arizona, three years ago, and had never been to New Mexico, yet the place felt familiar, as if the size and smell and feel of it had been latent in her blood for a lifetime. The light was stronger, purer. The sun was more immediate and commanding. Here on the Sandia ridge, the mountains were carved with gullies and clefts as expressive as the lines of ancient faces. Between dense stands of pine, towers of rock thrust naked from the escarpment; you could feel the geology here, millions of years of tectonic and mineral processes exposed to the eye.

That's what it was, she decided: *Time* itself was here. And time was big and there was lots of it. Good to remember.

Cree's ears popped for the fourth time. Another gantry loomed, and again the car did a hydraulic-suppressed lurch before beginning its final ascent. Three minutes later, they swung up into the arms of the receiving station, bumped softly, and eased to a stop. She stepped out with the other passengers onto a platform hung out over the nearly vertical slope. Just above was a small visitor center topped by the huge red wheels of the tram machinery, paused now; to the left lay a series of red-painted wooden decks, joined by stairs and ramps and cantilevered out over the mile-high cliff.

Below was the whole world.

The space and scope and light walloped Cree. She bellied up to the railing, feeling as if she'd stepped out on an airplane wing. When she fought off the vertigo and remembered to inhale, she found the air sweet and crisp and twenty degrees cooler than at the bottom.

The tourists had mostly dispersed by the time she pulled herself away from the rail and scanned the platforms for Mason and Lupe. She spotted them on the farthest deck, past the restaurant, and began walking the meandering ramps toward them. Mason was staring outward at the grand view, but Lupe's round head swiveled as Cree approached. Wordlessly, she turned Mason's chair so he faced Cree.

He looked Cree up and down with eyes disconcertingly quick in his slack, fleshy face. After a long moment he tipped his head back toward Lupe. "I told you she'd ripen well! A fine, lush bit of woman flesh if there ever was one. I am always right in these things. Always." His voice had once been a rich and dignified baritone, but it hadn't survived the ruin of the rest of him.

Lupe regarded Cree disapprovingly, as if blaming her for Mason's lack of propriety.

"Hello, Lupe," Cree said. "Hello, Mason." Some physical contact seemed called for, but Lupe offered no opening, and the thought of touching Mason repelled her. When she put out her hand, Mason brought it briefly to his lips.

He wore an expensive charcoal suit tailored to minimize his growing deformity, but it couldn't hide the deterioration that had taken place since last she'd seen him. Though he was no older than his early sixties and his hair was still mostly black, his big body appeared to be collapsing in upon itself. He lurked deeper in his chair, chin nearly riding on his chest. His high, square forehead and strong jaw were well formed but now only made him all the more grotesque, a parody of the handsome man he'd once been. A thin green cylinder of oxygen was strapped to the chair, Cree noticed, its clear plastic tube and nose feeder looped on one of the handles.

"Your lecture was superb," Mason gurgled. Looking up at her exposed his face to the sky, and the light seemed to give him discomfort. "You struck precisely the right tone for speaking to the great unwashed of academia in terms their rigidly compartmented little intellects could grasp. Yet never the bald, craven appeal to the popular taste we see so much of these days." The big head twisted to the side again and he said to Lupe, as if scolding her, "I told you she would mature. I told you she would shine!"

"So what brings you to Albuquerque? Surely not the conference—"

"I live not far away now—Santa Fe. To the extent that I can be said to *live*." Mason chuckled. "Or to do so in any one place. I am mostly between here and Switzerland. Returning to Geneva tomorrow, in fact. One of the reasons I contacted you. It was most fortuitous, your coming at this time. Still enjoying Seattle? Your little outfit, what's it called . . .?"

"Psi Research Associates."

"—is it doing well? Doing a brisk business in ghastliness?"

"Yes."

"And your partner—the engineer, the physicist . . .?"

"Edgar Mayfield."

"Yes, our good Dr. Mayfield. Has he recorded the irrefutable physical evidence he so ardently desires?" Mason's expression conveyed his low opinion of Edgar's technological approach to paranormal research.

"Physical evidence, quite a bit. Irrefutable—that's up for argument."

"But he hasn't succeeded in winning your heart with his efforts, has he. Because, one can safely assume, you're still searching for your dead husband and remaining chaste as a statue of the Virgin Mary." A glint of malicious amusement lit the hooded eyes.

Cree tried not to stiffen. "You know, Mason, I've never considered your sadism to be your most admirable characteristic."

"And just what would that be, Lucretia—my most admirable characteristic?"

Cree was tempted to say something hurtful. But, as she'd inventoried on her way up, she did admire a great many things about him. Even now, even as he did his best to be offensive, she could feel something noble in him—synesthetically, it came across as a rich crimson-and-peach-toned glow, steady and fine, just visible beneath the blackened, warted surface of his affect. Mason was the ultimate frog prince, always awakening her desire to free him from his enchantment, too ugly to bear to kiss. He was a hideous, aging man being eaten alive by some unknown malady, collapsing upon himself in a wheelchair, and he broke her heart.

In any case, rule one with Mason was you couldn't let him get under your skin. The only way to get by was to stay yourself. Show him you were above his provocations, which, she had to believe, were nothing more than oblique affirmations of affection and intimacy.

She touched his hand. "That you're easily disarmed by candor and affection. It suggests you have a human streak in you somewhere. That you're not the monster you think you are."

Lupe snorted at that, and Mason joined her with a chortle, chin hard against his chest. When he recovered, his big face hardened quickly. "Lupe, I will need a moment to speak with Cree in confidence."

Lupe's mahogany eyes locked accusingly on Cree's before she took her hands from the wheelchair grips and removed herself to the railing.

"If you wouldn't mind, Cree—" Mason gestured toward the far corner of the platform, an acute angle jutting well out over the cliff face.

Cree rolled him away from Lupe, feeling the woman's incomprehensible resentment. At the corner, she stopped the chair and came around to face Mason, leaving him oriented toward the vast space. Far below, another tramcar was inching up past the giant blue gantry.

"Do you know I can still stand?" he asked conversationally. He didn't look at her, just stared out at the bigness.

"No. I—"

"I could grab the railing and pull myself up right now. Not for long, of course." His voice was flat, almost disinterested, and Cree wondered why he was telling her this. "I could even throw myself over. In fact, I come here whenever I'm in Albuquerque just to savor that knowledge."

She gave him an exasperated smile. "Mason, how about skipping the high drama? Just tell me why we're here."

"Do you know why I might want to do that?"

"I can think of a lot of reasons why someone might—"

"No—why would I, Mason Ambrose, choose to fling myself over and stain the rocks down there with my brain matter?" Now his eyes were on her, and they seemed very deep, like holes to some subterranean pit. Whatever he wanted from her, his intensity was disturbing. Forty feet away, Lupe stood at the rail, watching them from the side of her eyes. Beyond her, the tramcar slid silently up the cable.

"You're trying to upset me. But it won't happen. Sorry."

He shook his head. "Come along, Lucretia! You're the most talented empath I've ever encountered. You know emotions and longings. You *see* them. What do you see in your old mentor?"

She appraised him. There were so many possibilities: that living as a toad in a wheelchair had become intolerable, or that by throwing himself over the edge he'd have some control over himself, otherwise denied him in so many ways. That his noble and good parts wanted to be free of the awful things in him. That his disease was progressing and promised a life of unbearable pain.

Possible, she decided, but too obvious, not what he wanted from her now.

"I don't know," she said finally. "Maybe that you want to know what happens *after*—what's on the other side. That your curiosity is that strong."

Mason looked flattered and proud of her in a proprietary way, the folds around his mouth puckering. "Oh, you unabashed romantic. You poor naïve idealist." He turned his head to frown across the deck at his assistant, and his voice turned into a snarl: "What makes you think I wouldn't do it just to get away from Lupe? Or to punish her? Look at her! My grandfather's old cowhide razor strop had more *give* than that woman!"

Cree knew she couldn't hope to fathom the awful twists and coils of their relationship. She'd always suspected they were lovers, and Mason's treatment of Lupe was among the things that offended her the most about him. And he knew it.

She let her voice get hard: "Okay, now we've done the courtesies, let's cut to the chase. What do you want?"

"There's a situation that will interest you, here in New Mexico. One that I believe requires your talents."

"Mason, I'm due to fly back to Seattle tomorrow. I can't just—"

"Of course you can."

"Sure. And you can cancel your flight to Switzerland and attend to it yourself."

"It's not a matter of travel itinerary, it's a matter of expertise. I was consulted as a neuropsychiatrist. In that capacity, I have determined that there is no neurological or immediately evident psychological cause for the patient's extreme behavioral aberrations. This is a matter for a different set of talents."

"Mason—"

"And it involves a *child,* Lucretia. Obviously, I am not the best confidant for a child already suffering from a surfeit of terror." His hand made a disgusted gesture at his sagging face and squat body.

"Look, I appreciate your thinking of me. But I . . . I got very stressed out this spring. I've had some difficult cases recently, and I made a pact with myself to take some personal time."

"You?" He puffed air out of his lips skeptically. "What could Cree Black do for 'personal time'?"

She stared at him. "Maybe I was wrong about you not being a monster."

But he wasn't baiting her this time, she saw. His voice was sepulchral and his stare without pretense. "How would you ever grant yourself a respite? There is no respite. Not for people like you and me."

She almost argued that, no thanks, she was not like him. But his gaze permitted no escape or deflection. And she knew what he meant.

He looked away to look up at the tram station, where a new flock of visitors was disembarking and fanning out at the railings. "I had another reason for bringing you up here this evening, beyond showing you a majestic view. I wanted to tell you that I've already arranged a meeting between you and the client." Cree started to protest, but he overrode her: "Her name is Julieta McCarty, and she's the founder, president of the board, and principal of a little boarding school for Navajo kids. You'll like her—a woman on a mission, just like you. No, don't bristle at me! All you have to do is talk with her, Lucretia. Afterward, you can tell *her* why your taking some personal time is more important than her whole life and the futures of sixty-odd bright and talented teenagers and the survival of one very special boy in particular."

Cree crossed her arms against the chill wind and looked away from him. "You're laying it on pretty thick here, Mason. The Dickensian sentimentality."

He dropped his voice to an urgent whisper: "You were right that I'd die to know. Just as you would. This situation at the school—it could be the breakthrough we both want, the one that brings us as close to the other side as we can get without dying ourselves. I'd love nothing more than to take it on. But I am simply not the right one for the job! It requires your talents. Beyond the empathic elements needed, this will take someone physically robust and mobile. Don't pass this up, Lucretia! Don't."

His intensity gave her pause. If Mason Ambrose said it might be a breakthrough case, he had good reason. She felt the familiar kindling of her senses, the awakening of that ravening curiosity.

But there was no way to communicate how important it was to take the time she needed. Time for *life*. How last spring in New Orleans she'd realized the full extent to which she'd slipped into obsession, into an emotional world so narrow that she'd become little more than a ghost herself. Preoccupied with death and haunts, with the past. Always looking through but never *at* the sunlit world of daily, physical life, always straining to see into the twilight that lay beyond. How she was, as Mason said, married to a dead man, unable to live as a flesh-and-blood woman. That she'd been turning into a kind of ghost herself.

It had nearly killed her, but out of the Beauforte House investigation and her unexpected attraction to Paul Fitzpatrick had come a hard-won determination to *live*. For the first time in the nine years since Mike's death, she had admitted to herself the need to get over him. To shed the confusion and guilt she felt whenever she felt drawn to another, living, man. Taking this case now would mean that once again she was putting life on hold in favor of the afterlife.

"I can't, Mason," she said finally. "I'm not going to do this one. I'm truly sorry."

Mason gave his head a skeptical toss. "Fine. As I say, you can tell it to Julieta McCarty. That's her now. And she's got the school physician with her—Dr. Tsosie. Excellent!" And he waved to a woman and a man who were descending the ramps toward them wearing expressions Cree knew only too well: the look of people coping, poorly, with the inexplicable.

4

A FTER OUTRAGE at Mason's presumption, Cree's first response was surprise at the woman's appearance. Julieta McCarty was tall, narrow waisted, dressed in snug jeans, cowboy boots, a man's blue work shirt, and a denim jacket with cuffs rolled one turn to reveal silver and turquoise bracelets. She had enviably big black hair that tossed freely in the wind, flashing almond-shaped blue eyes, and a tan augmented by a touch of bronze coloring that suggested Native American or Hispanic blood. Cree's first thought was, *stunning*. Movie star stunning. Definitely not anyone's idea of a typical high school principal. Too curvaceous, too young—no older than her midtwenties.

Seeing her at close range changed Cree's first impression somewhat. Nearer, her real age was evident in her face: closer to forty than thirty. The skin around her eyes and mouth was etched with a skein of fine creases that told of a life in the dry high-desert air and hard sun. Her eyes held a searching look full of wariness, worry, fatigue, doubt, determination.

It was a look Cree had seen in other people trying to deal with an incomprehensible experience, to live when their every belief and expectation had been called into question. It was also a look she saw far too often in the mirror.

The eyes made a twang in Cree's chest, a feeling of such poignancy that she forgot her anger at Mason. In one glance the connection was made, so real Cree could almost *see* it, a shimmering golden cord arcing between them and binding them together.

Remaining a pace behind Julieta, Dr. Tsosie was a Native American man in his midforties. He wore khakis, jogging shoes, a blue nylon windbreaker parted to reveal a white shirt and a belt cinched by an ornate silver buckle. A beeper and cell phone clipped on the belt marked him as a physician. The brown eyes that shone from under the brim of his cowboy hat were somber and appraising, and though he maintained an impassive face Cree sensed that the root of his current caution was a protective urge: He was looking out for Julieta, determined to help her through whatever crisis she was enduring.

Meeting them, especially Julieta, had a fated, inevitable feel. As they shook hands, Cree inwardly cursed Mason, hating that he could tell exactly how she'd react. That he'd known her for the soft touch she was, that her immediate and overpowering empathy for Julieta would compel her to take the woman's problems as her own.

Mason made only a halfhearted effort to keep the pleasure off his face. Cree wanted to kick him.

"Thank you for coming, Julieta. Joseph, it's a pleasure to see you again." Mason had conjured his public persona of charm and authority. He pushed back his cuff to glance at his watch and then smiled up at them. "Shall we stay outside and catch the sunset, or would you like to confer over dinner? I took the liberty of making reservations at the High Finance here—their strip sirloin is quite splendid. In either case, I know Lucretia is eager to hear the specifics of your situation."

Julieta McCarty admitted that she was too tense too eat, so they opted against dinner. Instead, Cree rolled Mason's chair down another series of ramps to the ridge trail below the restaurant, where they strolled slowly as they talked. The wind had died, but the air was turning chilly; Mason took a blanket from a pouch and arranged it over his legs. Back on the deck, Lupe found a position that allowed her to keep an eye on them, opened a paperback, and pretended to read.

The sun was swelling as it descended, a bloated red balloon just above the horizon. On Sandia crest, the light that saturated every west-facing feature had turned a succulent orange-pink, startling in its contrast with the blues of evening infiltrating from the east. The light had named the mountain, Mason explained: *sandia* was the Spanish word for watermelon.

Mason lectured them as if they were a postgrad psych class and he was putting forward a case study for them to solve: "A fifteen-year-old boy, presenting intermittent but extreme symptoms. Two rounds of exhaustive testing show no cranial abnormalities and no seizure activity. Blood chemistry good, no indication of chronic disease or drug abuse. Good general health history. Psychological tests show a fairly normal adolescent male profile: issues with status and self-esteem, resistance to authority—the usual. Appears to be an active, healthy young man with a higher-than-average IQ and a notable talent at visual art, which brought him to the attention of Oak Springs School. Like many kids his age, he has a minor history of trouble—graffiti, a little vandalism, one arrest for underage driving and one for possession of marijuana at the age of thirteen. But he has no drugs in his system now and he claims he hasn't taken anything for two years. The hospital's initial diagnosis is dehydration and stress. After the second and third episodes and the diagnostic batteries that followed, their psych staff conclude he's faking it—this is a desperate bid for attention by a child deeply troubled for reasons not yet understood. They prescribe Prozac and talk therapy on an outpatient basis—"

"Diagnosis completely unsatisfactory to school administrators," Julieta interrupted. "This infuriates me—nobody could fake what he was doing! He—"

She cut herself off as Dr. Tsosie lightly touched her elbow. They exchanged a short glance and Julieta calmed herself with an effort.

"Diagnosis fails," Mason went on, unperturbed, "to consider the severity of symptoms or reliable observations of their anomalous nature by the residential staff, the school nurse, and the school physician. At which point Dr. Tsosie sought me out. I then spent two days at the school, during which I reviewed the patient's medical records, observed him while full symptoms were presenting, and conducted interviews. After which I decided that a further referral was necessary. By serendipitous good fortune, my first choice for that referral was soon to be in the area for a speaking engagement at UNM." Mason shut his eyes, tipped his head, and for a long moment let the rich light play on his skin. "Which brings us to Sandia Ridge for a sumptuous sunset and the joint contemplation of a most unusual and dire neuropsychological phenomenon."

They had stopped at the end of the ridge path. Beyond stood a forest of ponderosa pines, now a shadowy cathedral shot through with shafts of light that cut the tree canopy into an intricate lattice. A few sightseers clung to the rail far behind them, snapping photos. On the lower path, just back of the crest, other visitors had begun returning to the tram station, chattering, clutching sweaters and windbreakers tightly around them.

"I still don't know anything about the boy's condition," Cree said. "From what you've told me so far, I can't see why you think I might be of any help. What—he claims he's seeing ghosts?"

"I think we're getting ahead of ourselves here," Dr. Tsosie interposed. He'd stayed quiet throughout their conversation, maintaining a reserve that he seemed to overcome only with difficulty. "Dr. Ambrose, you have an impressive reputation. But I'm here because I need some reassurance that we're doing the right thing. I don't know anything about Ms. Black and I'm skeptical of supernatural explanations. That we're up here talking to a . . . I don't even know what you call Ms. Black . . . a medium?"

"A parapsychologist," Mason said contentedly. "With a Ph.D. in clinical psychology."

"That we're talking about a supernatural origin for Tommy Keeday's problems, and consulting with a *ghost buster*—my God, Julieta, if the board hears about this—"

"I think the way to address both issues," Mason cut in, "is to begin with Cree telling you something about her theories and her process. That will allow me to explain precisely why I sought her out and will perhaps allay some of your concerns as well, Joseph."

Arms folded against the chill, Julieta nodded. Frustrated, Dr. Tsosie stooped to pick up several stones from the edge of the path. He pitched one hard at the low red sun and watched it disappear into the abyss before he grudgingly dipped his head. "Okay."

"Your skepticism is justified," Cree began. "Movies, horror novels, and urban legends usually portray paranormal events in ways that are sensational and wildly inaccurate. My colleagues and I take a scientific approach. We don't claim anything like an objective understanding of what consciousness is, or the spirit or the soul, or what happens after death. But we do apply a range of investigative techniques that include seeking physical evidence by technological means, historical research, medical testing of witnesses, and psychological analysis. I don't like the word 'supernatural,' because what we study is entirely natural—it's just a domain of complex phenomena that few people have made systematic attempts to explore. We founded Psi Research Associates in 1997 with the goal of researching paranormal phenomena, but people usually come to us only when they have a problem with something inexplicable and troubling, and want to get rid of it. So in that sense, the term 'ghost buster' is not inaccurate. We prefer to say we 'alleviate' or 'remediate' hauntings.''

Tsosie grunted as he winged another stone far out into the air. The sun was setting fast now, flattening on the bottom as if beginning to liquefy. "If there's any real science to parapsychology, why hasn't it become accepted in the mainstream? We know the inner workings of the atom, we've mapped the human genome. Why don't we have reliable information about ghosts?''

"Why?'' Cree snapped. "How about asking why belief in ghosts has existed in remarkably consistent form in every culture throughout the world and throughout history? And why people keep reporting encounters with them today, more than ever, despite skepticism and ridicule from family, community, scientists, religious authorities, news media—''

She stopped, regretting her tone. These people were coping with something deeply upsetting, she reminded herself, something that had challenged their beliefs and made them desperate enough to come here for this meeting. Her heart moved in her chest, and she reached out to touch Julieta's arm before going on.

"There are many reasons why the phenomena I study aren't well understood. Not the least of them is that there's a powerful stigma attached to reporting them. A moment ago, when you mentioned your concern about how your board would react? That's a good example of how information about paranormal events gets repressed. People keep a lid on what they experience. As a result, we don't communicate data, we don't collect and correlate it. We tend to ignore what we see because it doesn't fit in with expectations, or will cause us problems. Scientists dealing with inexplicable anomalies fear for their reputations if they talk about them. In the old days, religious orthodoxy repressed data. You could be burned at the stake if you showed interest in whatever was deemed 'supernatural' at the time—much of which, I should point out, we now call 'science.' Nowadays, scientific orthodoxy just kills careers, but it's a powerful disincentive. So witnesses of ghosts often do a lot of self-censoring.''

Of course, that was just the tip of the iceberg. But a full explanation of her theories of psychology and the ways of the universe wasn't something you could unload on people you'd just met.

Frustrated, Cree found her anger at Mason's manipulations growing. "Look, I'd be happy to skip all the explanations and justifications. Just tell me how any of this relates to your Tommy Whatshisname. I can't see that—"

"What is a ghost?" Julieta McCarty asked. Though she tried hard to control it, her jaw was trembling, teeth beginning to chatter from the cold. Her question seemed as much a challenge as an inquiry.

Cree took a breath to reclaim her patience. " 'Ghost' is a lousy word for a whole set of phenomena we don't understand. There are many kinds of noncorporeal entities. Most of the ones I deal with are fragments of a once-living human personality that somehow keep manifesting in the absence of a physical body. We have several theories as to how this can occur. The most common ghosts or revenants are what we call 'perseverating frag-mentaries'—not so much whole beings as disconnected mental and emotional matrixes that replay independently of a corporeal self. Usually, ghosts are compulsively reliving important experiences, often the moment of their deaths—the perimortem experience—or crucial memories of their lives." She paused to gauge their reactions. "Look, I know this sounds like gobbledygook to you. It's impossible to—"

"How do you 'alleviate' ghosts?" Julieta asked.

Cree was getting increasingly impatient with the whole exercise, with Julieta's probing, Tsosie's skepticism, Mason's veiled amusement. *Might as well give them the whole banana,* she thought. *And if they don't buy it, maybe I can get my butt off this freezing mountain and go home.* "It goes back to theory," she said. "Ghosts don't appear to just anyone. There's always a link of some kind between the ghost and those who experience it. It might be a direct link—a relationship from the past, say—or a purely psychological one, a state of emotional vulnerability that primes the witness's mind for perceiv-ing the ghost. Edgar Mayfield, my partner, thinks the link sensitizes the witness's central nervous system to the electromagnetic emanations of the ghost. I have a somewhat different theory, but in any case, that link is the reason most ghosts are perceived by only one or at best a very few people. Ghosts can be manifestations of any strong emotion or yearning, positive or negative, but they're almost always feelings that are *unresolved.* What I do is try to find that connection between ghost and witness, try to understand the issues that they have in common, what's unresolved for both of them.

One of my clients called me a psychotherapist for ghosts, and that's not far wrong—except that I do it for the witnesses as well because ghost and witnesses need to progress in parallel toward resolution. Dr. Mayfield looks for physical evidence of ghosts and uses various technologies to try to identify the mechanisms of their manifestation. Our assistant, Joyce Wu, supports our work with historical research and forensic investigation. I use psychology and a special set of . . . sensitivities that Mason calls a variant of projective identification. I just call it *empathy*. All it means is that I intuitively mesh with people's feelings. I take on their states of mind, which helps me to see and understand the ghost they've seen. And helps me find the link between them."

To Cree's surprise, the whole banana didn't prompt another skeptical comment or semirhetorical question. On the contrary: Tsosie turned back from the cliff, his eyes seeking Julieta's, and Julieta faced him with a guarded expression that seemed to caution him to silence.

Half the sun's disk was below the distant mountains now, and the lovely light on the near rocks and trees dimmed as if absorbing darkness from the growing shadows. Far below, another tramcar was sliding up its invisible wire.

"Look, I can't package the whole thing in twenty-five words or less," Cree said, "any more than you could explain education or medicine. If you're not going to believe me, and you're not going to tell me anything about this boy, we should get back to the station. Is that the last car for the night? It's getting cold."

"Just one more question, Lucretia, please," Mason said. "*Where* do ghosts occur? Why do they appear in a given place?"

Cree glared at him but went along with it one last time. "We're not entirely sure. They often appear in the place where they died, or in a place that figured importantly in their lives. Some are very limited, able to manifest only in a single house or even just a single room or patch of ground. My partner believes they manifest where local electromagnetic or gravitational conditions are favorable. He has shown a correlation between cycles of manifestation and fluctuations in geomagnetic fields, such as those caused by tidal forces. The living human brain and nervous system is an electrically mediated organ and creates electromagnetic fields—that's what we measure when we take an electroencephalogram. I have a more complex view of it, but Ed believes that the strong emotions of the dying create fields that imprint on local geomagnetic fields, like tape recordings that play back when conditions are right."

"So these favorable conditions," Mason said, "according to Dr. Mayfield, they're electromagnetic fields that support or reinforce the energies of the ghost? Functionally, ghosts come into being when conditions exist that amplify or . . . *host* the ghost's feeble or latent fields?"

"Exactly."

Mason's face, bilious orange in the dying light, smiled hugely. "And, of course, it makes sense that another human brain and nervous system—a living one—would create just the right fields, correct? Would make the perfect amplifier? The perfect host? Isn't that concept entirely congruent with Edgar's thinking? Doesn't it jibe also with your own belief that ghosts manifest when they encounter a supportive neuropsychological or psychosocial environment?"

Oh my, Cree thought, seeing it at last.

They all watched her expectantly as she sorted through it. *Of course.* The history of it went back forever and ever, through every tradition of psychology and spirituality and medicine from the dawn of time. It was just too horrible to contemplate.

She was speechless for a moment before she tried the word. "You mean . . . *possession.* You think this boy is—"

Mason nodded minutely. Julieta and Dr. Tsosie, their faces in shadow now, just watched her.

Possession: The word seemed to linger in the air, a pollutant that hung like smoke between them. Whatever skepticism they'd felt had given way to ambivalence, and in only a few moments the dynamic had changed. It struck Cree that they were sincerely looking to her for answers, for help. Now she understood what their terse questioning really was. The effect of an intense paranormal experience was much like dealing with the death of a loved one: Witnesses went through a predictable sequence of denial, negotiation, anger, and resignation. People who came to a parapsychologist demanding "Prove it!" were actually people who'd already had a deeply convincing experience and were seeking assurance that there was some rational foundation for what they'd already been forced to deal with at an emotional level. That these two were already in the negotiating phase meant they'd had a tough time of it.

The sun had dwindled to a blob of molten magma at the horizon. Nearer now, the tramcar turned on its interior lights, and in the twilight the row of disembodied bright windows flew upward toward the station. Cree was freezing.

Possession: a being that lived inside you, laid its energies along your nerves, invaded the circuits of your brain, and took up residence in your thoughts. Reports of such occurrences stretched from oral traditions come down from prehistory to the Bible to well-documented cases in the present day. Of course, she and Ed had talked about it, but in ten years of paranormal research, Cree had avoided the concept, hoping it was just another example of sensational folklore or Hollywood horror hoopla, like zombies, werewolves, and witches on broomsticks.

But Mason was right, the local field of a human nervous system would create the perfect home for an errant, bodiless being. As would the proximity of a human personality going through parallel psychological processes. Possession was the ultimate affirmation of what Cree had always believed: that it was *people* who were haunted as much as places.

"Yes, that's what I was thinking, Cree," Mason said gleefully. "This boy is, in conventional parlance, possessed. And if I were you, I'd call your colleagues tonight. Tell them you've got what you've always wanted—a paranormal entity in a bottle, just waiting to be studied."

5

CREE PACED the carpet of her hotel room, waiting for the phone to be picked up in New Orleans. From her fifth-floor window, she looked down at the lights of the cars oozing along Central Avenue, the downtown artery better known to visitors as Route 66. Resonances of James Dean and Bob Dylan were few and far between now, but Cree had found them—not so much in the restored Historic 66 sections with their retro restaurants and clubs, but the dingy strip of older motels and greasy spoon diners. Somehow she felt more comfortable there; the restaurant where she'd grabbed a burger on the way back from the mountain was just the kind of place Pop used to like. *Once a daughter of a working stiff,* she thought, *always.*

Paul Fitzpatrick didn't pick up, but she got his answering machine. "Hi, it's me," she said, feeling awkward about the message she needed to leave. "I'm in Albuquerque. At the Hotel Blue—I don't know why it's named that. My talk went really well. I ran into my old mentor, Mason Ambrose." Pause. "Well, I didn't run into him, he showed up and kidnapped me. He sandbagged me completely. Brought a woman to meet me? A client? I kind of agreed to look into a problem at this school she runs over near the Navajo reservation." *Kind of* was inaccurate: She'd already canceled her flight back to Seattle and arranged to ride with Julieta McCarty to the school tomorrow. "She was desperate, and it looks like it could be a really important case. There's this kid who . . . Well, I shouldn't really talk about it. But I won't be showing up this week after all. I'm hoping we can reschedule my visit, maybe put it off . . . oh, three weeks? Can you get some time free then?" With all her hesitations, this was becoming a lengthy message, and it was all wrong anyway, no emotional weight. Hurrying, she tried again: "I'm really disappointed.

I was really looking forward to seeing you sooner. I miss you. I hope you've had a fabulous day. Call me, okay?"

Bleep.

Relationships in the technological era! she cursed.

She put down the phone and got a can of Coors from the minibar. Back at the window, she popped it and took a cold swig. If only she'd taken an immediate dislike to Julieta McCarty. If only Mason hadn't piqued her curiosity despite her fury at him. If only it didn't involve a kid whose life really did seem to be on the line.

Down on Central, a police car sparked as it swerved through slower traffic, turned onto a side street, and finally disappeared into the maze of neighborhood streets. A moment later, an ambulance sped from the other direction and turned onto the same street. Some desperate human situation out there in the sprawling city. It was a lonesome view.

She put down the beer to dial Deirdre's number. Nine o'clock on a Thursday night—no, eight in Seattle—they wouldn't be in bed yet at her sister's house.

One of the twins answered. Hard to tell which on the basis of one word.

"Hi," Cree said tentatively.

"No, this is Zoe."

"I didn't mean 'Hy' as in Hyacinth, I meant 'Hi' as in 'hello.' " This was ritual vaudeville they went through whenever Cree got Zoe. When she got Hyacinth, the stock response was, "How did you know it was me?"

In the background, Cree heard the cacophony of some TV show. She could picture Deirdre and Don and the two girls, sitting in their snug Craftsman home, the lights warm on the nice fabrics Dee had done their living room in. A low-key Thursday night, some family time. Probably watching the Discovery Channel—it was something about crocodiles— and munching microwave popcorn. The image offered an unsettling contrast to the blank, black hotel room window and the naked urban sky.

"Are you still in New Mexico?" Zoe asked.

"Yeah. Actually, the reason I called was to tell you guys I won't be able to make your birthday party on Tuesday."

"Just a minute," Zoe ordered. "Can you guys turn it *down?*" Back to Cree: "What did you say?"

"I said I've got to stay on here for a few days, maybe longer. Kind of an emergency. I won't be able to get there for your birthday party."

"Oh, man. Mom's going to be p— . . . um, peeved." Zoe muffled the receiver, but Cree could still hear the scowl in her voice as she called out to her family, "Great! Aunt Cree isn't coming to the party!"

"I'm really sorry, Zoe. I've got some presents for you girls, though. I miss you like crazy. Hey, you should have seen where I went today—this tram ride that went up the mountain here? Like being in an airplane. Zoe, seriously, you'd have loved it."

Zoe didn't answer. Cree heard the noise of the receiver being handled and then Hyacinth was there. "Hi, Aunt Cree. Why can't you come?"

"Oh, there are some people who need my help here. It's an emergency."

"A ghost emergency?"

"Yeah," Cree said, wondering if that was quite the way to describe it.

"Well, I hope it turns out all right for them. Do you think it's significant?"

The two girls were identical twins, yet they were as different as the Fourth of July and Easter. As always, Hy had gone to the heart of the issue, instantly feeling concern for the client. Just going on eleven years old but so adult. "Significant": She'd heard Cree use the word before.

"Could be, yes. I should talk to your mom now, Hy. Sorry I can't make it Tuesday. Have a great party. I love you girls like a pile of elephants, okay? Big love, right? Tell Zoe for me."

When Deirdre came on, she wasn't peeved but concerned. Cree would have preferred peeved. Dee was two years younger than Cree and, Cree had always thought, much prettier and more grounded, in enviable control of her life. Her voice was smoothly modulated, the tone of a mother and middle-school teacher habituated to setting a good example.

"Everything all right?"

"Sure. Just a case coming up suddenly. You know."

"An important one, I take it."

"It involves a student at a school for Navajo kids. It's urgent or I wouldn't bag out on the party. I know you could have used my help."

"We could have used your *company*. We'll miss you." Dee hesitated. "But what about New Orleans? Weren't you going to go see Paul?"

35

"Yeah. Well. I'll probably go in a couple of weeks." Deirdre had kept the question casual, but Cree knew the concern was there and it pissed her off that everything she did scared people. That any change of plan might signal a problem in her relationship with Paul. Her relationship with the world of the living.

She injected some briskness into her tone: "Anyway, I'm here looking out over the infamous Route 66, and I've been having a great time. The food here is terrific—I could get addicted to the green chili. Everybody you meet is really nice. And the landscape is truly majestic. I don't mind the idea of spending more time here."

"Sounds great," Dee said, a little distantly.

They were quiet for a moment as Cree figured out what she'd wanted to ask. "Dee, I have a question for you. About kids. I feel like I'm kind of out of my league with them, the only ones I hang out with are yours? So I was thinking about this boy I'll be dealing with, what my underlying priority should be. I thought you'd be a good person to ask. As a mom."

"I can't claim to be any expert at that. But give me a try."

Cree thought about how to phrase it. "What's the main thing you do for your kids?"

"I don't understand."

"Well—what do they need most? What's the most important thing you do for them? Not to feed or clothe them, but emotionally. Developmentally. To, I don't know, prepare them for life."

"Oh, *that*. And here I thought you were asking me something weighty and complex!" Dee joked. She thought about it for a long moment, and Cree could hear the TV in the background again: *The female crocodile will guard her nest fiercely, but once her eggs are hatched these baby crocs are on their own in a hostile world.* "Well, when I have a moment to even think about this without noise and distraction and pressing needs, I guess I think of my main job as helping the girls know who they are."

"Explain."

"Maybe I emphasize that because I've got twins, and I don't ever want to treat them as interchangeable personalities? But any mother will agree. A child should know who she is. What she wants, what she *doesn't* want. What she believes in, what her values are."

"Mmmm," Cree agreed.

"She should know the difference between what comes from inside herself, what she gets from her family, and what she absorbs from popular culture. If a kid doesn't know that, she can't make good choices. Right now, for my girls, it's differentiating between personal values and peer pressure—like, oh, whether to try smoking or not, even if friends are. Soon it'll be how far to go with a boyfriend. Then it'll be what career she wants to devote her life to, or what man. Or what values to fight for. So I see my job as laying that foundation of self-knowledge. I'm always kind of asking them to look at who they are, to make decisions based on what they see in themselves." Dee cleared her throat. "That is, if I'm doing my job right. Which I manage, oh, about ten percent of the time."

"Uh-huh," Cree said skeptically. Dee was a terrific mother. In her mind she tried on the question for size: *Who are you, Tommy Keeday?*

"I don't know if any of this applies to your kid out there," Dee went on. "But you need it all your life, right? How can you do *anything* if you don't know who you are?"

So very true, Cree was thinking after they'd said good-bye. Life was indeed an ongoing quest to discover who you were. Or maybe that was just the perspective of the metaphysically inclined, widowed sister, an inadvertent empath who was constantly exploring the nebulous interface between self and others and almost always discovering only uncertainties.

The night scene out the window was bothering Cree, but still she didn't draw the drapes. She looked down at her address book, the list of names and numbers. Why was it that the first thing she did when she took on a big investigation was *this*—this ritual of cutting off contact? Every significant case seemed to demand that she cancel something, put family and friends on hold, postpone things. Make excuses for why she wasn't a normal human being. Say good-bye as if she might not be coming back. Give hollow assurances she was being smart and taking care of herself. It was a rite of making ready. Like an ocean-voyaging ship, casting off the ropes as it got ready to leave shore, she had to sever her ties with the normal world. A way of isolating herself. Of becoming a woman alone.

On one level, that sounded scary, but in fact she liked the feeling. She couldn't deny that it gave her a sense of strength and self-sufficiency. It was like the feeling she used to savor on stormy days when she was a little girl:

putting on her big yellow raincoat and rain hat, borrowing Mom's umbrella, and going out to sit in the pouring rain. That feeling of solitude and tidy self-containment. Everything sopping and wild around you, but you were dry and safe in your glistening yellow armor. Everything you really needed, right there.

She dialed Edgar's home number, and he picked up after two rings. She was glad to hear his voice.

"It's me."

"Hey, Cree. How'd it go?"

"The talk? Really well. The other presenters were great, too."

"But—?"

She'd said, what, a dozen words to him, and he already could tell she was off balance. Suddenly Cree missed him painfully, missed his lanky body and wry grin and the way it felt to be around a man who knew her so well. She wished she could tell him that, but it was best to keep away from the complex of feelings there. Since last spring, when she'd begun an unexpected and still largely undeveloped romance with Paul Fitzpatrick in New Orleans, Ed had pulled away considerably. It was his way of giving her room to explore it without pressure from him. But though she had accepted the necessity of distance, she hated it, and in the last few months she'd learned just how deep her ambivalences ran. Maybe it wasn't just Ed who felt more than friendship. If Ed were here tonight, they'd go out and explore Albuquerque and have a good time. They'd drink and dance—he was a knockout dancer—and confide and tell bad-taste jokes as they walked the night streets together. The thought confused her and she put it away.

"A case dropped into my lap," she explained. "No, it was *thrown* there very deliberately. By Mason Ambrose."

"Ambrose! That old bastard. No kidding."

"Yeah, and it's a doozy. There's a boy with . . . well, with something wrong with him. Mason calls it 'a ghost in a bottle' for us to study."

Ed paused, and she could imagine his long face frowning. "Like what—the kid's *possessed?*"

"Something like that, yeah. So I agreed to go look into it, starting tomorrow. I was thinking you and Joyce should get down here."

"Jesus, Cree—"

"I know."

"Do you really?" The condescension, she knew, was just the sound of Ed's protective reflexes kicking in. "Hey, Cree, let me spell something out for you. You're the most vulnerable person I've ever known. You almost *died* in New Orleans last spring. You're like a psychic petri dish, okay? An entity that can move right in on a normal person's nervous system is going to find *you* a pretty tempting little—"

"Not necessarily."

"Oh, come on! Even a *nice* ghost puts your sanity at risk. You get 'possessed' by our goddamned *clients!*"

Of course, he was right. But, as always, she felt an unreasoning flash of resentment at him for pointing it out.

"This isn't *The Exorcist,* Ed," she said witheringly.

"How do you know? You haven't been there yet. You have no idea what you're dealing with."

Cree would have retorted sharply, but a shiver took her, as if her body recognized the danger her mind refused to accept. She opened her mouth and shut it again and listened to the hiss of the telephone line for several moments.

"Cree," Ed said into the silence. His voice had changed, and now he just sounded concerned. Dear Ed: He'd never shown much stomach for fighting with her. "Listen to me. Let me say one thing. Take a step back, okay? Third person. I'm just a guy in Seattle whose . . . friend, Cree, does risky things. Okay. But ever since he's known her, she's been very absorbed in her husband's death, right? Her husband, who appeared to her exactly once for about thirty seconds ten years ago, practically lives in her. I mean, possession, obsession, where's the line?"

Cree shut her eyes, not wanting to hear this.

He went on, still more quietly: "In any case, we *know* you're vulnerable. You're temperamentally predisposed to this kind of thing. Okay, suppose it's not a monster out of *Damian III* or whatever, fine, maybe it's just a lost personality who's so afraid to die it lives parasitically on any nervous system it can cling to. So what? You let it into you, you're still *possessed.* And who do Joyce and I and your family go to for help? There's no Cree Black to help us out." He paused and then finished deliberately: "Cree. If there is one parapsychological phenomenon you personally should absolutely stay away from, it's possession."

He was right, and there was no logical rebuttal because this wasn't a logical thing. There wasn't really anything she could say. "Ed," she said fondly.

"What?"

"Nothing. Just *Ed*."

She listened to his breathing. After a moment she heard a rustling at the other end, Edgar moving papers around on his desk, then the faint pecking that she knew was him pulling up the calendar on his digital assistant.

"Sunday," he said resignedly. "Couldn't possibly get there before Sunday night."

When the phone rang at ten, she knew who it was before she snatched it off the hook. Her heart was suddenly pounding. "Hello, you."

Paul chuckled. "Sorry I missed your call. I was up on the roof. Hurricane Isidore's arriving, first big blow of the year. I had to get the furniture down or it'd end up in Baton Rouge. Luckily it's more rain than wind." His voice was warm with just a faint luster of sunny Southern vowels, and the sound of it transported her back there, to his rooftop deck where they'd drunk wine and talked and kissed. The big umbrella and teak table and chairs, the nighttime views of the French Quarter, narrow streets lined by lovely decrepit buildings and secret courtyards. The lush vegetation of New Orleans and the humid air with its sleepy, sexual charge.

"How are you?" she asked.

"Well, I was pretty good until I got your message. I had big plans for when you got here."

"Think you can rearrange things so you can take some time in another few weeks?"

"I'll try." His tone suggested he was put out, as he had every right to be. For a clinical psychologist with a highly successful private practice, it was not easy to carve time away.

"The situation here is a crisis, or I'd never—"

"Somebody else's crisis. Isn't that the key to surviving the psychotherapy business, Cree? Getting some distance on it? I get people in crisis every week. You learn to put up a little wall that keeps your own life intact, or else—"

"I'm not good with walls."

He made a frustrated sound. "Okay, a levee then. A dike. Just high enough to keep floodwaters out, right? Look, I don't want to argue about the right metaphor. I miss you. I want to see you. I've been checking the days off my calendar!"

She accepted his chastening, letting a silence give them some distance from their dissonance. "What kind of big plans?" she asked at last.

"Frankly, very sexy plans that involved superb wine, candlelight, and good music on the stereo. As well as tickets to a couple of jazz concerts." There was still some reproach in his voice. "Jogging together up at the lake in the morning. Dinner at Antoine's. Then some more of the wine and candlelight thing."

She thought of his bed in the tall room with its lazy ceiling fan; the fascinating scent of his pillows, his smell overlaid on clean linen. He had a wonderful body and a sweet physicality, and the urgency was there for both of them. But it hadn't been easy, either the first time she'd returned or her second visit in midsummer. She'd felt so inexperienced, so confused by her memories of Mike's body and the lovemaking they'd shared so long ago—a sense of betrayal that she had to fight off. And Paul had been a man in disarray after his shocking experience in Lafayette Cemetery; she suspected part of him feared her, as the agent of his shattering transformation—maybe something of what she felt around Mason Ambrose.

And still it had been sweet. Enough to make her ache, thinking about him now.

"That sounds splendid," she said shyly. "I had the same general plan."

He sighed. "So it's a crisis. And it's a case that promises to be instructive?"

"Yes."

"You want to tell me about it?"

"I can't. I don't know enough yet, and if I did it'd be confidential. I'll tell you when I can, I promise."

"Just tell me which way we're going here, Cree. Forward or backward?"

"Forward," she said immediately. "Of course, Paul!" But who really knew where it would go? It was so new. Untested, uncertain. They were not at the stage where either could say with absolute conviction, with the sweet release that came of confession, "I love you." And while distance could obstruct the path of love, raising doubts that were unwarranted, it could also nurture false hopes and illusions that more sustained contact might set straight.

"Forward!" he cried. A cavalry charge.

She laughed with him, and her doubts receded a bit. They talked about other things. Paul said he'd work on his calendar and let her know when to make reservations. She told him about the conference, about Albuquerque. After a while the sense of intimacy grew, and the plastic phone became more and more a frustrating impediment. Phones required talk, and talk required thought, and there were times when rationality was simply not the right process. Reason was based on inquiry, and inquiry was based on doubt, and doubt was not good for building something between a man and a woman. Your body was often so much wiser.

"What are you thinking?" he asked.

"Long-distance relationships," Cree said. "Miserable, huh?"

"All relationships are long-distance," he told her.

She was still awake when the front desk called to tell her that a package had arrived for her. When they sent it up, she found it was an overstuffed manila envelope from Mason, with a terse note scrawled on the front: *Some materials you might find useful.*

She opened it to find a two-inch stack of photocopied articles about possession. The top page featured a medieval woodcut of some saint exorcising a naked victim who lay on the ground with a snake or worm coiling endlessly out of his mouth.

She read through the first few pages, a historical survey of possession compiled by somebody or other. Typically, symptoms came in cycles, periods of normalcy giving way to "fits" in which the victim fell down, went into convulsions, made contorted movements, screamed and shrieked, "displayed a frightening and horrible countenance" that often included an alarmingly extended tongue. Other classical symptoms: vomiting up strange objects such as toads, stones, broken glass, pins, worms. Breathing problems such as choking, coughing, wheezing. Foaming at the mouth, foul body smell, speaking in tongues, speaking in an altered voice. Blasphemy, hypersexuality.

She turned hurriedly past that section to the summary of purported causes. Historically, the victim was thought to be inhabited by a demon or "unclean spirit," a Satanic entity conjured or inflicted by someone nearby, usually an old woman or man who was thought to be a witch. Such accusations often resulted in the torture and execution of the accused, usually by burning or crushing. In later centuries, medical explanations came into favor, with the torture reserved for the victim: physical "purging" treatments such as whipping, immersion in ice water, lifelong incarceration in madhouses, exotic drug therapies. Toward the end of this list were the modern interpretations: epilepsy, hysteria, schizophrenia, multiple personality disorder. Though the recent perspective was more enlightened, contemporary cures didn't strike Cree as all that improved: electroshock therapy, lobotomy, mind-altering pharmaceuticals.

Feeling shaky, she put the stack on the desk. The woodcut bothered her: its dark, blocky rendering, the agonized victim, the serpent demon's nasty face. She knew she should read more tonight, but she didn't feel up for it. Instead, she put the whole pile back in its envelope as if that would contain the superstition and terror, keep it from getting loose in the room.

Thanks loads, Mason, she thought.

Her beer had gone flat and metallic-tasting from sitting so long in its can, but she finished it, welcoming the soothing effect of the alcohol. The numbing effect, whatever.

She dialed Joyce's number, got her answering machine, left a message asking her to coordinate with Ed and fly down as soon as she could. Then she turned out the lights and got into bed. Sleep didn't come for a long time. The fat envelope waiting on the desk bothered her. She thought about Paul and about the odd oscillations between doubt and warmth they'd just been through. Then she wondered about what Ed had said, about just where the line between preoccupation and obsession was, and, further up the spectrum, the line between obsession and possession. There wasn't any easy answer.

Later, closer to the void, she wondered where Joyce was. Where Tommy Keeday was. Where Cree Black was.

6

JULIETA DROVE like a bat out of hell. But everyone drove fast out here, Cree noticed. The distances were long, the horizons endlessly unfolding in low swells of bare, rocky earth, largely unchanging. If you didn't put the pedal down, you might think you weren't moving at all.

They'd left the university at one o'clock, after Cree's obligatory participation in a morning panel session and a speakers' luncheon with the UNM psych faculty. The way Julieta drove the Oak Springs School pickup, they covered the distance from Albuquerque to Gallup in under two hours. In Gallup, they stopped at a restaurant supply wholesaler to load the bed of the truck with paper towels and cafeteria napkins, six big bales wrapped in plastic that now nattered and flapped in the wind. They cut north on Route 666 and turned west on Route 264 toward Window Rock for the last hour of the drive.

After spending a week on the Hopi reservation, four years ago, Cree knew that the Big Rez of the Navajo was a separate world in more ways than one. The formal treaty borders enclosed an area as big as New England, but even that was little more than an island on the Colorado Plateau, isolated from more populated regions by a million square miles of deserts and mountains that stretched from central Mexico up the backbone of the continent. It was big enough to resist not only physical but also social change, and the Native American reservation lands were the home of cultures in many ways thousands of years as well as thousands of miles removed from the rest of the country.

Dr. Tsosie had driven ahead in his own truck earlier, and Cree had looked forward to her three hours alone with Julieta as a chance to talk.

Cree gave her a general idea of how PRA conducted an investigation: Ed and his high tech, Joyce and her historical and forensic detective work,

Cree's own brand of psychological analysis and empathic communion. She did her best to make it sound routine, avoiding the scary stuff.

"Each line of inquiry supports the others. Often, when I'm . . . making contact, my impressions are ambiguous. Most locations are layered with lingering human experiences from different periods, so it can be hard for me to pin down what's relevant and what isn't. And it can take me a while to progress from feeling vague moods and auras and sensations to actually seeing a ghost or *living* its thoughts and feelings. My goal is to know what motivates the entity, figure out why it's there, what remains unresolved for it. But sometimes my intuitive experience of its world is not enough. That's where Ed and Joyce's work, and my own interviewing, comes into play. Having some hard information helps me identify the ghost. Once I know who it is, how it died, and so on, it's easier for me to determine why it's here—what motivates it and which living person figures in its compulsions. There's almost invariably a connection of some kind between the ghost and the witnesses or other people in the vicinity of a haunting. Once we know what that link is, we have a better chance of setting the ghost free."

To her surprise, Julieta didn't voice skepticism about these far-fetched points. But none of it seemed to soothe her, either. A strange reserve and tension remained between them, and the closer they got to Oak Springs School, the more she seemed to close off.

Still, when Cree prompted her with questions, Julieta was generally forthcoming.

She'd been born and raised in Santa Fe, an only child. Her mother was of Mexican descent, mostly, while her father's ancestors were black Irish; both families had been in the area for a long time. Her father had owned a heavy-equipment supply company that involved big money but always seemed to be overextended and in trouble. They were proud and respected but still very much striving, proving themselves, and therefore very—overly, Julieta admitted—conscious of symbols of wealth and status.

"I only mention that as an explanation for the stupid things I did when I was younger," Julieta said.

"More stupid than the things everybody does when they're young?"

"Probably."

Julieta explained: When she was fifteen, she began trying out for modeling jobs. She had always been told she was gorgeous, and ever since she was thirteen, seeing herself mirrored in the eyes of men, she could almost believe it. From modeling, it was a short step to beauty contests. Her parents were as suckered as she was by the incentives the pageants offered: prizes, scholarships, a chance to meet the rich and famous, a line in your résumé that would help nail lucrative modeling work. At first it was easy. She won some of the local pageants, did modeling for more prestigious agencies, and then felt confident enough to compete for the title of Miss New Mexico in 1982. She spent all the money she'd saved on the tailored evening gown and bathing suit and the deportment coaching everybody said she'd need. Preparing for the contest took almost a year, during which every hour outside of school was occupied with exercising, fitting clothes, going to the orthodontist, practicing her smile and posture, pursuing the community service that would perk up her citizenship score. When at last the competition began, it was a whirlwind that completely carried her away. She entered the last stages utterly self-brainwashed into believing that this was her destiny, the absolute best and only course for her life. That winning really, really mattered. That win it she certainly would.

She made it only to third runner-up.

She tried to smile for the cameras while her heart crash-landed and the tears exploded behind her eyes. The spotlight lingered on her briefly, impatiently, and for the last time, before it moved on to the more beautiful, talented young women.

"Barely twenty years old," Julieta said. "I felt like the ugly duckling. The instant my name was announced, I had this epiphany that I'd completely wasted five years of my life, posing with a fake smile and sticking my chest out. By that time I had no friends. I'd never had *time* for friends, and anyway the kids at high school and UNM all thought I was hopelessly stuck-up. And I realized suddenly just how completely I'd learned to quantify every aspect of myself. I didn't even know what I really liked to *do* or was good at! My only reason for doing anything had always been, 'Gee, I'd better take up ballet or . . . or chess so I'm more competitive in the talent judging.'"

Maybe that painful epiphany would have driven her to redirect her life, but the pageant of 1982 had yet one more damaging and lasting effect. At some point, she'd been introduced to Garrett McCarty, one of several corporate bigwigs who'd helped sponsor the proceedings. He was CEO and sole owner of McCarty Energy, a big thing in western New Mexico, coal and uranium mining. And Garrett, forty-nine-year-old millionaire, famously eligible twice-divorced bachelor, took an interest in one of the good-looking pieces of prime stock at the pageant: a dark-haired, blue-eyed Hispanic-Irish girl from suburban Santa Fe.

"Long and short of it, he bowled me over. I was bruised and demoralized after the contest, but when he contacted me I was handed an instant remedy. He courted me for six months and it was heady—power, money, important people, nice clothes, expensive cars, good food. I thought, 'Hell, maybe I won the damned thing after all!' When he proposed to me, my father and mother were ecstatic. Garrett had gotten chummy with Dad, talked about buying tons of equipment from his firm. Marrying him would mean a guaranteed living for me, grandkids for them, and best of all a way to meet the *real* people, to hobnob with the movers and shakers. Which would prove we were taking our rightful place in the world. And all I had to do was look nice, keep the smile in place!" Julieta made a face as if she wanted to spit. "I hate talking about it. It's a tawdry, pathetic soap opera."

"But did you love him? Were you attracted to him? Apart from his money, I mean."

"I don't know. I couldn't tell him apart from his money—hell, I couldn't tell him apart from his Corvette! He was very handsome, didn't look his age at all. I think I told myself I was in love with him. But it's a long time ago now. The girl who married Garrett McCarty was a different person. I could just as easily recite the facts of the life of Helen Keller or . . . Mary, Queen of Scots, and it would feel neither more nor less 'me'!" Julieta looked over at Cree as if checking her response. "I know I should be able to toss off a wry grin and chuckle at it, but I can't."

"Would it help if I told you about my own youthful follies? I've got plenty—we could probably manage a yuck or two about 'em. My mother says if you haven't got regrets you haven't lived right."

Julieta brought her attention back to driving. "I've got regrets," she said.

Ones you can laugh about later, Cree had meant to add. She bit her tongue.

★   ★   ★

They drove without talking for a while, a vertical crease deepening between Julieta's eyebrows. Ten minutes out of Gallup, she announced that she had another stop to make.

"I don't mean to take up your time with these errands," she apologized. "With drive times the way they are out here, the rule of thumb is to get several things done on any long trip. This one'll only take a minute."

She turned onto a side road that ran through a spread-out scattering of tiny houses and mobile homes. No trees relieved the bare-dirt desert; the land stretched in every direction without any notable features. The laundry on the clotheslines, the satellite dishes on the parched yards, the pairs and trios of playing kids and their tagalong dogs: on one level, not so different from any neighborhood. But set in this arid moonscape, blasted by the westering sun, the little human outpost struck Cree as marvelously foreign.

Julieta drove slowly along the hard-packed dirt street. "One of my maintenance staff had to have a hip replacement. Earl Craig. It's his second. He's been out for three weeks and he's had some complications. He'll need to miss another month or more, so I had to hire someone to cover. I know he's secretly worried about whether he'll be able to keep his job—employment is hard to come by out here. So whenever I pass by, I try to stop in to kind of reassure him."

She pulled the truck into a short driveway to a tiny shoe box house. A thickset, midfifties Navajo man sat in a wheelchair not far from the front door, face tipped to the late-afternoon sun. When he heard the truck, he rotated his chair and a small dog jumped off his lap and began yapping. Julieta shut off the engine, rummaged behind the seat, and came out with a rumpled grocery bag full of something heavy.

"You should probably just wait here," Julieta told Cree. "I'll only be a minute."

Earl's face relaxed into a smile as Julieta got out. The little dog sped toward Julieta and without pausing hurtled itself through the air at her. She clearly wasn't ready for the greeting, but she managed to stoop and catch the dog with one hand. She winced into a vigorous face licking, then slid the animal down onto one hip and awkwardly carried it back to its master.

Cree couldn't hear what they were saying, but Earl laughed and appeared to be apologizing for his pet. When Julieta set the bag at his feet, he bent to pull out several paperback books and exclaimed gratefully.

Then they talked seriously for a moment, Earl shifting in his chair to point to parts of his hip and thigh, Julieta still holding the wriggling dog and nodding.

It was only two or three minutes until she handed back the dog, touched Earl's shoulder in farewell, and returned to the truck. Earl waved good-bye with his free hand and then bent to dig more books out of the bag.

When Julieta climbed back into the truck, she explained quietly to Cree, "Mysteries, thrillers, that's all he'll read. I get them by the pound from a used paperback place in Albuquerque. Last time I slipped in *Memoirs of a Geisha,* but that didn't go over too well." Remembering that mischief made her grin. "Arthritis. He had a healing Way sung, too. The Hand-Trembler—that's the medicine man who diagnoses illness—blamed it on Earl's walking on the grave of an ancestor. Earl sincerely and completely believes that, but it didn't stop him from getting high-tech molybdenum joints put in. And if you asked him whether it was the Way or the surgery that fixed him, he'd credit both. That's pretty typical."

Looking back now, Cree saw Earl differently: to outward appearances, an ordinary middle-aged man in jeans and T-shirt; in fact, a person who lived in the knowledge he was poised on the brink of infinite mystery. Another reminder that in coming here she was entering a different world, where nothing was quite what it seemed.

Julieta's expression of contentment remained as she backed the truck out of the driveway. Such a lovely woman, Cree thought. Such a lovely smile, all the more beautiful for its rarity. She covertly watched Julieta during the quarter-mile drive back to the highway. By the time they'd turned onto the asphalt again, the lines of worry had returned.

They drove on in silence. Still the land had not changed: As far as the eye could see were low hills of bone-dry brown earth, low-growing brush, scattered scrubby piñon trees. The only indication of human presence was an occasional trailer or prefab house at the end of a dirt driveway, a defunct pickup truck, maybe a corral occupied by a gaunt, drowsing horse.

Closer to Window Rock, they passed an area where the ridges visible from the road struck Cree as too uniform to be natural mesas; it wasn't until she saw the sign for the P & M Coal Company that she realized they must be recovered strip-mine tailing mounds. Sure enough, beyond the farther hills she saw a gargantuan derrick rotating slowly against the sky. Near the highway, several preposterously outsized yellow dump trucks and front loaders moved around piles of dirt, putting up clouds of dust.

Julieta's frown deepened as they passed the operation. She squinted into the lowering sun, gripped the wheel, and drove as if eager to get past.

"So you married Garrett McCarty—" Cree prompted.

"The long and short of it is, we were married for five years," Julieta said curtly. "It was not so good. The details are irrelevant. Divorced in eighty-seven. I did all right in the settlement—ended up with our residence here, the land around it, and some money. Somewhere in there I decided I needed to do something with my life. Went to UNM and got a master's in education administration. Spent every cent of the divorce money to build Oak Springs School."

"How do you get along with your ex now?"

"Garrett? He died three years ago. He was sixty-six. Now his son from his first marriage owns McCarty Energy. Donny McCarty—my former stepson, can you believe it?—is four years older than I am. We have a mutual-loathing arrangement. He resented me from the start, and his feelings didn't sweeten when I walked away with some of his father's holdings. The bad part is that the court partitioned off my land from a much larger chunk Garrett owned, so the company is our neighbor. Donny likes to make our lives miserable with right-of-way problems or whatever he can dream up."

The question seemed to drive Julieta back inside herself, and they were quiet again as they approached Window Rock. Julieta's anxiety was rising as they got closer to the school and what awaited them there. It occurred to Cree that for all she'd learned about Julieta's past, she'd hardly gotten to know the woman at all. She realized she was rather dazzled by her beauty, her vividness, and that for all the immediate empathy she'd felt, her dazzlement distanced her. Except for that glimpse of a grin at Earl Craig's house, she knew next to nothing about Julieta's emotional life.

"I can't help wondering . . ." Cree began. "You had what sounds like a crappy marriage. Why did you keep McCarty's name?"

Julieta made a face of distaste. "Sheer pragmatism. The name carries clout around here. To make the school happen, I needed all the weight I could sling. Having the name, even as an ex-wife, helps me get access and ask for favors in the right places. Make contacts in the legislature, raise money from other rich mining families."

"So you've never remarried? Never had children?"

"I've had relationships. None of them ever quite made it to the marrying stage," Julieta said distantly. Abruptly she seemed to catch herself, and she turned to Cree with an angry face. "But I don't see what my past has to do with Tommy Keeday and his *terrible* problem. Why aren't we talking about that? Joseph and I came to Dr. Ambrose as a last resort when nobody else was giving us satisfactory answers. We wouldn't buy into this at all if we hadn't seen what we'd seen and spent the last few weeks trying every other imaginable solution. I could really use some reassurance that there's substance to his conclusions or your methods. This isn't about *me*. It's about Tommy. And, frankly, if you're going to work with him, it's about *you*."

Cree couldn't help feeling personally rebuffed. But she made a mental note of Julieta's sudden defensiveness and decided to press on with a less intrusive line of inquiry.

"I wish I could offer more reassurance, but I can't. I've never dealt with a situation like this. But what you've told me so far is very helpful. It's especially useful for me to know about the school and the history of the immediate area, because often a . . . an unknown entity is anchored in a place and connected to past events there. But as I said, every environment is deeply layered with human experience—it can be hard for me to pin down whether a given entity is from a year ago or a thousand years ago or anywhere in between. So the more I know, the better. Can you tell me anything about the school or the land it's on?"

Julieta nodded and continued in a subdued tone that suggested she regretted her outburst.

The school buildings were new, she said, built five years ago. All but her own house—that was something of a historic building, a former trading post built around 1890 on what was then a trail from Oak Springs to Black Hat. The McCartys bought the land in 1922 and began using the building as their site office. Over the years, mining operations drifted several miles to the north, following the coal, and in 1950 Garrett McCarty's father converted it to a residence. Garrett renovated and modernized it once again before Julieta married him, and that's where she

51

had lived, mostly, for the five years of their marriage. The old road ended at the house now; the mine's access and rail spur now came down from Route 264, about twenty miles to the north. Both Julieta's twelve hundred acres and the mine's much larger holding, over forty square miles, were situated in New Mexico, just over the Arizona border from the Big Rez.

As for the history of the school land, she said, there wasn't any. It was just a little patch of ground in a desert that stretched to the horizon in every direction. The region was first populated by the early Pueblo ancestors, popularly called by the Navajo term, Anasazi, who had first started arriving around two thousand years ago, followed a thousand years later by the Navajos and Apaches. The first European explorers were the Spanish, who came in 1540, looking for gold and converts to Catholicism, but a few hundred years of Indian resistance and the Mexican revolution destroyed their dreams of empire. When Mexico ceded the region to the United States in 1848, Yankees began pouring in the region, suppressing the Indians in wars and pogroms. The government created the Navajo reservation in 1868 during a flash of contrition for atrocities perpetrated upon the Diné.

Julieta didn't think Spanish explorers had ever made it to the Black Creek area, but the American entrepreneurs certainly had. From the middle of the nineteenth century on, they'd set up trading, lumbering, mining, and cattle ranching operations, along with the military posts needed to protect them and the railroads needed to move goods. Her Irish ancestors, like Garrett McCarty's, had arrived in a wave of migration in the 1870s.

But as far as she knew, the area of the school itself didn't figure in any of this. A few Navajos had no doubt lived there once, but if so they'd left no traces. Possibly some Anasazis had lived there a thousand years ago, but she had ridden her horses over every inch of the land nearby and had never seen any ruins or petroglyphs. Her house might have had some colorful early history in its years as a trading post, but if so she'd never heard a word of it.

The whole place was so obscure that the little mesa just east of the school didn't even warrant a name on the maps. She'd once heard an old Navajo ranch hand call it Lost Goats Mesa, but that generation had died off and now it was nameless again—none of her staff or faculty had ever mentioned any history of the place.

Cree got the picture. The land was big and enduring; people were small and transient, and the details of their little lives got lost in the sweep of things.

Another few minutes of silence. Julieta put on a pair of sunglasses to help ward the sun that now drilled straight into their eyes, and the reflective plastic seemed to make her very remote.

Soon a big mesa rose and cut off the northwestern horizon, presenting a line of sandstone bluffs that broke into freestanding pillars and buttes at the edges, carved by time into marvelous shapes. They struck Cree as gorgeous, and despite her growing trepidation she felt a shiver of excitement when she saw the sign at the edge of Window Rock: WELCOME TO THE NAVAJO NATION. The highway led into a typical strip of shopping centers, fast-food restaurants, and gas stations, but it felt to her like a gateway to something far larger and older. Behind every plastic sign and faux-adobe façade loomed the ancient rock faces, stark yet sensuous, patient yet playful. The lowering sun filled the red stone with light, softening and smoothing it; she wanted to reach out and stroke the wind-sculpted forms.

"So lovely!" Cree exclaimed.

Julieta glanced over as if startled to find someone in the truck with her. She followed Cree's gaze. "Yes," she admitted. "I guess it is, isn't it. I kind of forget."

7

HORSES. THEY turned onto the school's access road through a little band of horses that milled across the gravel and onto the verge, engaged in some minor scuffle and unconcerned by the approaching pickup. Other than to slow down, Julieta ignored them, but they struck Cree as beautiful, a poem of motion—big, rangy animals with ropy veins in their legs, running free beneath the open sky. They were all pale dapple grays and caramel-and-white palominos, their mottled hides vivid in the lowering sun, long shadows behind.

"The Navajos tend to let their stock roam loose," Julieta explained. "These guys are from Shurley's place, on the rez just the other side of Black Creek—the stallion comes to check out my mares. I should call him to let him know they've come over this way again."

As the truck came among them, the stallion wheeled, showed a wide eye and yellow teeth to one of his harem, then harried her. The whole group turned irritable and skittish, ears back, as they trotted away.

The sign at the turnoff had said the school was nine miles away, and they drove it in what was becoming for Cree a loaded silence. Julieta's tension was palpable, a dark, heavy mass. The sun was directly behind the truck now, painting the stark landscape with a lush glow, but Cree couldn't savor its beauty anymore. Ahead lay something she'd never encountered, a brooding thing burgeoning like the line of blue dark that rimmed the eastern horizon. Already, she was unsure whether her sense of it was her own or something acquired from Julieta. For the thousandth time, she cursed her proclivity—her talent, her disability—for resonating so strongly with her clients, taking on their states of mind until the borders of identity blurred. If ever there was a time to remain objective, this was it. And she was off to a lousy start.

The horses veered away from the road and descended out of view into a dip of land to the north. Julieta's knuckles had gone white on the steering wheel, her pretty hands turned to naked bone, pressure rising until after another five minutes she slowed and stopped the truck. The plume of dust that had been following them blew past on a light breeze. Once it was gone, she shut off the motor and rolled down her window.

"You can see pretty much the whole thing from here," Julieta said hollowly, as if it were something lost to her.

They had stopped on a little rise. About a mile away, the school lay at the base of some low cliffs, a cluster of new-looking sandstone and steel buildings surfaced in pastel beiges and pinks that complemented the desert palette. The road curved due north through a parking lot and then through the center of the little campus. Julieta pointed out each building. "Just this side of the water tower, that's the garage and utility shed. The next building on that side of the road is our main classroom and cafeteria, and the steel building beyond that is the gym. On this side, the first one's our administration and faculty housing building, and the two beyond that are the dorms. That little log house in the middle there is our hogan. At the far end, that little bell tower is left over from the old days—the trading post would ring it to announce that they were open for business. We think of it as a school bell now, but we only bang on it once a year, at graduation. Past that, where the road ends, that's my house."

The last was a low, sandstone block building at the north end, well removed from the main cluster. A pair of huge cottonwood trees bracketed the front porch; a swimming pool made a startling turquoise oval on one side, and behind the house stood a barn, a few sheds, and a corral surrounded by a wooden rail fence.

"My once and future house," Julieta corrected herself. "Now I keep quarters in the faculty housing unit. Until we can add a wing to the admin building, we're using my home as the infirmary and nurse's residence. That's where Tommy's been staying."

They spent a moment looking over the scene and listening to the tick of the cooling truck motor. A breeze came lightly through the open windows, carrying the dry, clean scent of the desert.

There was nothing overtly menacing about the sight, Cree thought, but its isolation was extreme. Not a human being was visible, and aside from the hard red glare of reflected sun in the west-facing windows, no lights shone. The parking lots were mostly empty of cars, and the shadows of the buildings stretched long over the bare ground. All the distances seemed very great.

Lonesome, Cree thought.

"Friday night is always quiet," Julieta explained. "Most of the kids go home for the weekends. A handful stay on campus, but under the circumstances I figured this would be a good time for a field trip. They're off to Taos to visit artists' studios. So Tommy's the only student here for the next couple of days, and we've got just a skeleton staff for the weekend. I thought it would be the best conditions for . . . whatever it is you're going to do."

"Excellent."

Still Julieta made no move to start the truck. She sat looking at the scene with eyes full of desperation. "There's something we should talk about before we get there," she said at last.

"Sure."

"What you tell me about your . . . theory of ghosts—it makes intuitive sense to me. I've always been pretty agnostic about such things, but after what we've been through during the last few weeks, I'm willing to . . . reconsider my views. But I still have serious doubts about bringing you here. You should know that what's happening to Tommy could kill this school in any number of ways."

"How so?"

"All but three of the faculty and staff are Navajo, and if they start to think there's a supernatural aspect to this, they'll leave and we'll never find anyone to fill their positions. If the parents hear there's something super-natural going on here, they'll pull their kids out, word will spread, and we'll never get another student. If the school authorities hear about my bringing in a . . . ghost buster to cope with a student health problem, they'll yank our accreditation. If any of my board or my private funders hear about it, I'll lose my financial support. If the state social services people think we haven't handled Tommy the right way, they'll close us down."

Cree nodded, accepting also the unspoken message behind Julieta's words: *This place means everything to me.*

Several miles to the west, the horses came into view again and continued their long arc toward the corral behind Julieta's house. Avoiding Cree's eyes, Julieta watched them with a desperate intensity.

"Julieta, you do have an awful lot at risk. Have you thought about ways you might dodge the problem? Couldn't you just, I don't know, find another place for the boy? I don't want to sound callous, but his condition shouldn't jeopardize the whole school. Couldn't you get him referred to a facility that's better set up for kids with medical or behavioral problems?"

"For now, this *is* where he's been referred! Putting him into long-term care somewhere is one of the options we've discussed. But Tommy hates the idea, and so do his grandparents—they're his legal guardians, his parents are dead. And so do I. As Dr. Ambrose said, the doctors have decided it's a behavioral issue—a . . . hoax, a gambit for attention by a troubled boy. Personally, I think that's a load of manure, but for now that's what we're going on—formally, anyway. I argued that in that case, it's best to keep him among his peers, have him keep up with school and other normalizing activities."

"What about sending him home? Could he take a leave of absence, or—"

Julieta shook her head decisively. "We discussed that, too. That was his family's preference, and that may be where he ends up. But his grandparents are getting frail, and they'd never be able to cope with a problem like this. His extended family, aunts and uncles and so on, is very dispersed. Their outfit's in a remote area where getting supervision and regular treatment would be difficult. It's also an area without the social and learning resources to stimulate a boy with so much potential."

As always, Julieta had a logical answer, but Cree couldn't escape the feeling that the mere thought of Tommy going elsewhere had terrified her. So much urgency and vehemence there. Through the administrator's reasoning answer had come one of the most personal communications Julieta had yet offered, even if its subtext wasn't yet clear.

Julieta was looking intently at her as if to make sure she got the message. "My point is, the buck stops here," she said, turning hard again.

"You're saying this is Tommy's last resort. That you're taking a big chance on me, and I'd better not let you down."

"Something like that," Julieta said. "Yes."

57

8

THEY PULLED into the parking area in front of Julieta's once and future house, next to Dr. Tsosie's dusty blue Ford pickup. It was Cree's turn to be silent as she got out of the truck, hoisted her suitcase from the bed, and started inside. She was instinctively listening, wrapping her thoughts around the faint impressions that seemed to swirl in the sunset light.

The hair on the back of her neck lifted.

The feeling was very, very faint, but it told her there was definitely something nearby. Maybe it was just the land, vast and naked and hard, and there was truth to the idea of earth spirits—looking around her now, Cree could easily believe that the shadowed rocks were inhabited.

At this early stage it was vague, a subliminal sensation like the tingling of the skin that signaled an approaching electrical storm or the feeling of being watched when there was no one nearby. She wondered if this was what livestock felt when they sensed an impending earthquake, hours before seismic sensors did. *Have to talk to Ed about that,* she thought, *the earthquake thing. Another geomagnetic connection with psi phenomena.* She pictured Ed's long, agreeable face, and suddenly she missed him terribly, missed Seattle and the clean light over the Sound and the hubbub of First Avenue and Joyce's no-nonsense, upbeat attitude.

"Are you okay?" Julieta watched askance as she hesitated on the walkway.

"Fine," Cree said. "Sorry. Just . . . thinking of something."

They didn't find anyone inside the infirmary building, but Julieta said she knew where Dr. Tsosie and Tommy must be. "We've been trying to keep him busy. He enjoys taking care of my horses, so Joseph is probably helping him do the night feeding out at the corral. Our nurse, Lynn Pierce, is probably using the time to get some dinner for herself at the cafeteria. You'll meet her later."

Julieta led Cree down a hall to a six-bed ward room on the right side of the building. They switched on some lights and dropped Cree's gear next to one of the beds, then went out through a rear door to a pleasant backyard, where the L of the house, a trellis, another couple of cotton-wood trees, and a small, separate barn created a sense of enclosure. The flagstone walk split around a well-maintained circular garden centered on a group of sandstone benches; to the left, beyond the trellis, a bathhouse stood over the turquoise-painted swimming pool, drained now. To the right, extending beyond the barn, a rail fence wrapped about four acres. A few hundred yards east, the near cliffs of the mesa glowed orange as if lit from inside. In every other direction, the land stretched empty to the horizon.

"Do you ride?" Julieta asked.

"Not for quite a few years. Took lessons at camp for a couple of summers, once in a blue moon since, that's about it."

"You're welcome to come with me sometime, if you're here for a while. They need the exercise, and I've been too busy recently."

Standing together at the far end, the three horses turned their heads as Julieta opened the gate. At first there was no sign of Dr. Tsosie or Tommy, but after a moment Cree spotted two figures approaching from the northern curve of the mesa, half a mile off in the watery red light.

The horses crossed the corral, two fine chestnut mares and a black gelding with a distinctive yin-yang blaze on his forehead. They nuzzled Cree's hands with soft noses, gave her mild glances with their long-lashed eyes, and turned their attention to Julieta. They looked expectant.

"Looks like they haven't been fed," Julieta explained. "Maybe you could help me. We should do it while there's still light."

They walked between the high round rumps to the barn, where Julieta opened the door to the feed room.

"If you could keep them out of my hair—" Julieta said.

Leaving Cree at the door, she went into the room, hit a light switch, and began rummaging among feed bins. Cree stood with the horses, feeling a little overwhelmed by their size and warmth. They crowded toward the door, pushing their long heads past her to look inside. When she put her hands against the great slabs of their necks and pushed back, she was amazed at how hard the muscles were beneath their coats. They smelled like sun-dried grass, good leather, and sweet honeycomb.

"Hang on, kids," Julieta called as she scooped grain into three dented aluminum pans. "It's coming. Hang on."

A moment later she came out with the grain pans and pushed through the horses. They clumped after her into the middle of the corral and began munching as soon as she put the pans down. Dr. Tsosie and Tommy were closer now; the boy had his hands in his pockets and he scuffed at the ground as he walked. Instinctively, Cree's every nerve awoke and craned toward him, her senses alert for the buzz and tremble, the hidden turbulence, of a paranormal presence. She found only ambiguity. Or maybe it was "interference," as Ed liked to call it: Every space was loaded with divergent energies, multiply haunted by the residual echoes of human experience accumulating through time. Perhaps it was just the welter of ambient impressions, a spray of vague auras and sparks, that obscured her sense of whatever lived in Tommy. Or maybe when his symptoms were in remission it literally wasn't there.

Julieta broke into her thoughts. "Would you mind helping me with the hay?"

"Love to."

Occupied with their grain, the horses stayed put as Cree and Julieta went back to the barn. The bales were stacked to the ceiling along one side of the feed room, and Cree helped muscle one of them down. She sneezed in the dust as Julieta cut the twine and pulled it away.

Very quietly, Julieta said, "The idea of possession terrifies me."

"No kidding."

"Does that mean you and Dr. Ambrose believe in . . . demons? Evil beings who want to . . . whatever they want to do—corrupt and hurt the innocent, conquer the world for Satan?"

Julieta began pulling at the bale, separating it into smaller blocks of hay. She worked efficiently, but her hands were shaking as they clawed at the brittle strands.

"I haven't seen Tommy yet, but if there's one thing we need to get past at the outset it's images and ideas from pop culture or folklore. I don't believe there's an evil mastermind behind supernatural phenomena. I don't believe in purely evil beings of any kind, for that matter. 'Satan' is a concept people created to make it easier to rationalize the difficult or painful things that happen. The demonic thing is strictly a European, Christian outlook. I tend to go with Freud, who said we should treat ghosts with respect and neutrality, help patients come to terms with them and make them benign. Whatever this entity is, I wouldn't assume it's evil."

"Then what *is* this goddamned thing? Why does it want to hurt Tommy?" Julieta's voice cracked, and she glanced back at the door as if afraid the boy would overhear.

Cree felt her breath flutter shallowly at the base of her throat as Julieta's fear leaped into her. "It may not 'want' anything. Ghosts are usually caught up in compulsions—they're seldom conscious of the existence of the current world, let alone the ways their actions affect the living."

Julieta looked dubious as she finished separating the hay, setting out two flakes for each horse. When she'd made three piles, she gathered up an armful and headed for the door. Cree took the rest and followed her past the munching animals to set out the hay near a water tank at the middle of the enclosure. As Julieta bent to fluff the packed flakes, she frowned up at the approaching figures of Dr. Tsosie and Tommy.

"I should tell you that even though he's the one who recommended we go to Dr. Ambrose, Joseph is having a hard time with this."

" 'This' meaning *me*."

"It's not personal. Joseph is Navajo. He was born on the rez and has lived here all his life except when he went to college. He's an excellent doctor, went to Johns Hopkins. He chose to come back to a job as an underpaid rural GP because he felt his skills were needed here. He wanted to help his people."

A man on a mission, Cree was thinking. *Not unlike Julieta. So the three of us have something in common.*

The black gelding had finished his grain and was coming toward them for the hay. A hundred yards away, Dr. Tsosie raised an arm to block the sunset light, watching them as he and the boy walked.

Julieta rubbed the glossy neck as the horse bent to pull at the hay with his soft lips. "It's a cultural issue. Joseph often has to deal with problems created by the old ways of treating sickness. He isn't opposed to a patient having a Way sung, or taking traditional herbs, as long as people also come to him early on. But too often he gets patients who've spent months doing ceremonials and other cures and have come to Joseph too late—after their cancer has spread too far, or they're dying of pneumonia or bubonic plague. Or they've got pregnancy complications that could have been avoided if they'd been caught early. The Navajo curing Ways usually blame sickness on ghosts or witches, or the victim's failure to observe some ritual or taboo. Joseph would rather his patients blamed poor nutrition or inadequate sanitation or alcoholism or neglect." She toed a mound of hay closer to the horse's tugging lips. "My point is, he's learned to be skeptical. And he's pretty hard-nosed about it."

"I can understand that," Cree acknowledged. "Are you telling me this so my feelings won't be hurt, or so I'll be nicer to him when he challenges me?"

Julieta leaned her head back, her face hardening. "You're very observant. But I sure hope you have something more to offer than hypersensitive psychoanalysis. Because I'm not the one on the couch here, and you're going to need something better, trust me." Immediately, she looked surprised at her own words. She looked as if she were about to apologize but apparently changed her mind. "Here come Breeze and Madie," she said instead. "I'm going to get their curry brush."

Cree waited with the horses as Julieta disappeared into the barn and Tommy and the doctor ducked through the fence at the far end. Tommy didn't look like a monster. In fact, he looked like a typical kid from Cree's neighborhood in Seattle: slim, bronze skinned, a round face that made him look younger than his fifteen years, big T-shirt embossed with images of the Wu-Tang Clan rap group, baggy jeans draped over basketball shoes. When he got closer, she saw that his buzz-cut hair had some kind of design shaved into the bristle.

"Hey," Julieta called from the feed room door. "Hey, Tommy. Hey, Joseph. We're just feeding the critters. Tommy, there's someone I'd like to introduce you to."

The forced lightness of her tone broke Cree's heart. Julieta had shaken the loose hay from her beautiful hair and dusted it from her shirt, and she wore a smile that would have done Miss New Mexico proud.

Doubleness, Cree was thinking. She stood with Dr. Tsosie, watching Julieta and Tommy curry the horses, trying to put a name to the feeling of this place, this moment, these strangers she found herself among. It was like swimming in deep water with your eyes just at the surface, she decided, one moment getting a view of the sky and sun and boats and people, then submerging only a fraction of an inch and seeing the blue depths and the vague shapes moving in them. Two planes of existence, hidden from one other yet moving restlessly against each other and separated by only the thinnest membrane.

When he'd first joined them, Dr. Tsosie presented a piece of rock to Julieta, and for a moment they bent their heads together to look at it. They argued briefly, and then Julieta broke away, laughing and shaking her head.

"It *is*," he insisted. "I've brought you a valuable historical relic!"

"It's gravel," she countered. "And you know it. But thank you so much for thinking of me."

Joseph turned to Tommy. "What's your vote? Anasazi arrowhead or random chip of useless rock?"

Tommy just made a *go away* gesture with his hand, grinning shyly.

Joseph mimed dismay and betrayal, then smiled and tossed the rock over his shoulder. He joined Cree to watch as the others cared for the horses.

"So—are you an equestrian fan, too?" Cree asked him.

"Me? I've always hated them," Tsosie said. "They've got the brains and temperament of chickens. For pets, I like dogs and cats. As for vehicles, I prefer the ones with steering wheels and brakes."

"Don't go saying bad things about my kids," Julieta called. "Joseph's just down on them because he's a lousy rider and whenever he takes them out they sense his inexperience. So they never do what he tells them. They're sweeties and he knows it."

Tommy said nothing, just rubbed the big muscles in the gelding's shoulders.

The interplay among the three of them was deeply double and deeply touching. Julieta and Joseph were obviously good friends of long standing, and though both were very tense they were making an effort to create a simulacrum of a family for this boy. Tommy, at least the part of him above the waves, was reluctantly appreciative, willing to play along with it as much for their sake as his own. It was so compassionate and respectful, so fragile and artificial. A lance pierced Cree's heart.

On the individual level, each of the players was double, too. Beneath Julieta's roles as officious administrator and chipper surrogate mom was some other act, some part of her life hidden yet running parallel to the actions and emotions she expressed outwardly. The doctor, too.

And of course Tommy was double most of all. When he'd first been introduced to her, he'd shaken her hand, said a quiet hello, asked if she were another doctor, and gone with Julieta to tend the animals. Quite reasonably, he was a little dubious about meeting yet another stranger wanting to probe and scrutinize him. A pretty regular kid. But there was a parallel Tommy, a hidden unease and pressure below the surface. There was the Tommy you could see, the one who stuck his head above the waves, and there was the rest of him moving in a different and darker medium.

Julieta went back to the barn and returned with another handful of grain. She put it into one of the pans and held it out to the horses, rattling it temptingly. "Come on, kids," she called. "Let's take our evening constitutional. C'mon, Breeze. Spence! Shake a leg!"

The horses sashayed toward her. As Julieta coaxed them into a walk around the fence line, the sun drifted below the shoulder of a rise to the west. Only a dwindling strip of orange lingered at the top of the mesa, and a mercury vapor light came on at the corner of the house, gilding the near wall of the barn with a silver tinge. Julieta strode in front of the ambling horses, Tommy among them with an arm thrown over one or another. As they headed along the far fence, he slipped onto the back of one of the mares and lay comfortably along her spine. The horse ignored him. After a few paces, he slid off the mare and up onto the gelding, where he sat with one leg down the horse's belly and the other crossed over its shoulder, hands relaxed on his thighs.

Cree was struck by the pleasure on Julieta's face, how lovely and rare. Despite his tension, Dr. Tsosie made a soft noise of satisfaction as he watched them.

And Tommy: Tommy looked almost happy. Maybe Mason Ambrose was wrong about this whole thing, Cree thought. Maybe the hospital doctors were right and the nagging buzz she felt was just Tommy Keeday, a relatively typical teenager with some normal-world issues that made him act out in an unusual way.

As if he'd read Cree's thoughts, Dr. Tsosie turned to her. The sunlight was almost gone now, and his face was lit with silver from the searing light on the house as he regarded her thoughtfully.

"Just wait," he told her.

9

Y OU'D NEVER *know there was anything wrong with him,* Lynn Pierce thought, watching Tommy. *Good luck, Dr. Lucretia Black.*

The boy was playing with the little marshmallows that floated on the top of his cup. He dipped his teaspoon and boated the white clots back and forth across the surface of steaming chocolate, then selected one and ate it. Some of it was an act; with the new psychologist there, he was working hard to play normal. Julieta sat at one end of the table, positively dripping martyred noblesse oblige, making quick insincere smiles whenever Tommy or Joseph looked her way and losing them just as fast when either male focused on anything else. The psychologist, who introduced herself as Cree, had alert hazel eyes and a neutral expression as she watched Tommy. Lynn wondered if she was perceptive enough to see just how bogus Queen Julieta was, how many secrets lurked below the surface here.

The five of them had settled in the infirmary's dayroom to drink hot chocolate and play cards, an exercise transparently thought up by Julieta to allow the psychologist to observe Tommy at close range. The wide, beam-ceilinged chamber was furnished with more institutional furniture than it no doubt had been when the queen was in her heyday here, but more than any other room in the building it retained reminders that this had once been a rich person's home: creamy stucco walls, huge fireplace with a step-shouldered mantel, brilliantly varnished old-board floors, built-in book-shelves, fancy light switches—something of a Santa Fe ambience. Right now the windows were hard black rectangles of night, and outside the temperature had dropped, but Lynn had lit a fire in the grate. It crackled behind its screen and made the place feel snug and pleasant despite Julieta's preening and that god-awful sense of latent menace in Tommy.

Joseph was shuffling the cards, not saying anything. He looked tired.

"So," Cree Black said, "your grandparents must be very proud of you. I haven't seen your work, but everyone tells me you're a talented artist."

Tommy looked embarrassed by the prompt and busied himself with stirring his chocolate. "I guess."

"*Very* talented," Julieta affirmed proudly, as if she were personally responsible for his abilities. "So much so that he won a complete private scholarship, just for visual artists, to come here. Tomorrow, you'll have to show Cree your work, Tommy."

Tommy looked into his cup and blew across the top.

"How did you start?" Cree asked. "Are there artists in your family?"

"Yeah. My dad was a potter and sculptor. In summer, he'd sell stuff to the tourists in Window Rock. He kind of got me going." Tommy didn't look up as he answered. Under the edge of the table, his right knee started to bob, and the taut, unconscious motion, so at odds with the false calm of his face and the controlled movements of his hands, frightened Lynn. Was that a sign of it? Kids bobbed their knees, but with Tommy you couldn't be sure. Was it an ordinary nervous knee, or the . . . the seizure, starting to kindle again?

"Okay," Joseph said at last. "Julieta, your turn to start."

They were playing rummy. Everyone took up the cards Joseph had dealt and looked them over. Cree's eyes moved to Tommy, who was scrupulously intent on his fan of cards, to Julieta to Joseph.

Julieta drew a card, slipped it into her hand, discarded.

"I was watching you with the horses," Cree went on. "Another talent, looks like. You must have spent a lot of time with them when you were growing up."

"Yeah. My dad liked them. He taught me to ride when I was a baby." The subject seemed to embarrass Tommy, and silence followed hard on his words.

"Well, my dad was no artist. He was a plumber," Cree said, as if she hadn't noticed the conversational stall. She took her card and considered it. "He was from Brooklyn. I loved him to pieces, but I sure wasn't going to follow in his footsteps and set toilet bowls for a living. You're lucky you got the artistic influence. But Pop did have one thing in common with your father—he liked horses, too." She chuckled as if at some fond memory, discarded, and went on, "Probably in a different way, though.

He liked to bet on the races. You have to understand, my father was the kind of Brooklyn guy you see in the movies who talks like this: 'So dis guy sez to me, he sez, "I got a sure t'ing for ya, put yaself a sawbuck on a win for Sugar Baby inna eight'."' Even I could hardly understand him half the time!"

Tommy flicked his gaze at her, a glimmer of appreciation there.

"You're up, Lynn," Joseph said, startling her.

She had a bad hand, of course, all low numbers and nothing to match. *Like life,* she thought savagely. She picked up and discarded.

"He died," Tommy said. "Killed himself." This time he raised his eyes to look challengingly at Cree. The words froze Julieta and Joseph.

"Who did?" the psychologist asked blandly.

"He drunk himself and my mother to death. Got into a car crash because he was so loaded he couldn't see cows on the road."

The psychologist didn't blink. "I'm sorry, Tommy," she said, with sincere but not excessive sympathy. "You must miss him terribly. I know I miss my pop every day."

Tommy looked to his cards again and shrugged his shoulders, *doesn't matter* or *not really*. He seemed puzzled and maybe put out by her response—clearly he'd been fishing for something more dramatic. He picked up a card, laid out three twos, discarded a six of spades. Meanwhile, Julieta was making heartbroken moon eyes and trying to hide the expression from Tommy. Joseph gave her a supportive, steadying gaze. It made Lynn sick. The craving for nicotine was beginning to gnaw at her in a way that couldn't be ignored, and she tried to remember which one she was on—number four? Or five? Whichever, she needed a cigarette.

"Alcoholism is one of our leading health problems," Joseph told Cree. "It's the root cause of most crimes and accidents here. Native Americans carry a genetic predisposition for it, a difference in the way carbohydrates are metabolized. That's one reason liquor's illegal on the rez."

Cree nodded as she took her turn, keeping whatever it was she picked up, discarding but not laying out any cards. They went around again in silence, as if nobody was sure what to say.

The psychologist broke the quiet. "This is such a gorgeous room. I love the fireplace!"

"This was the main store of the trading post, and then it was my living room," Julieta said, deliberating theatrically over her hand. "I told you this was my house before we converted it, didn't I?"

"Yes. You must miss having it all to yourself."

Julieta shook her head. "Nope. Never once. Haven't had time to miss it since we got the school going. Anyway, I get so many rewards from my job, especially when I work with the kids and their parents. And I gave myself one indulgence, teaching one of the drawing classes. Beyond that, I don't feel any need for the luxury. Really, I wouldn't know what to do with this much space all to myself now."

How touching, Lynn thought. *How very admirable of you.*

It would be bad enough to have to listen to this crap, but it broke her heart to watch Joseph falling for it. He was a brilliant man in every other respect, but when it came to Julieta he seemed to have no brains at all. He took her posing at face value. Like just now, that decisive little shake of her head: the way her lustrous big black hair swung so alluringly, half covered one eye, got swept casually aside—she learned that one in beauty queen school for sure. Over the last three years, Lynn had seen her too many times around other men to believe it was unconscious. Board members, prospective donors, maintenance contractors, whoever—they all went knock-kneed around her. And she didn't hesitate to exploit the effect to get what she wanted.

The tragic part was that in Joseph's case the feelings so obviously went much deeper. Of course they did: He was too sincere and decent for his affection to be anything but genuine, even if it was deluded. The deceptions those two pulled were obviously not *his* choice! The thing that really made Lynn sick was that Julieta was too self-preoccupied or stupid or whatever to treat him with the respect he deserved, and to—

"Lynn?"

She startled at Joseph's voice and looked up from the fan of cards she'd been staring sightlessly at. She realized it was the second time he'd said her name.

"Your turn," he said, smiling. He chuckled and explained to the psychologist, "We're all a little tired, I think."

"Sorry!" Lynn forced a laugh as she picked up another useless card, the seven of hearts, and threw it down again.

Tommy's turn. He picked up her seven from the discard pile.

"How about you, Tommy? How do you feel?" Cree asked. "Tired?"

"Not so much. Pretty boring to sit around."

"Think you'll be up for spending time with me tomorrow?"

He made a frown. "They already talked to me. The headshrinkers at the hospital."

"You must be sick of it, huh?"

He smiled weakly, unsure how to answer, courtesy at odds with candor.

"It's okay. You won't insult me if you say yes—"

He shrugged, looking at his cards. "They didn't know anything."

Cree nodded.

Sitting at Tommy's side, Lynn noticed that his leg had stopped bobbing. But down on the floor, his feet writhed in his socks. She tried not to make her reaction obvious as she darted her eyes down. It almost didn't look like human feet—the bumps that came and went as the bones flexed, the arching and tensing and twisting! And still the rest of him, everything above the tabletop, kept an artificial calm.

Lynn felt sick at the sight. It reminded her of just how bizarre this whole situation was. Between crises, it was so tempting to doubt the strangeness of what she'd seen. But she'd never forget that time she'd seen his arm moving, on its own, when he was dead asleep—the queer *awareness* it moved with. And she could still feel the marks of his teeth on her forearm, three double arcs of scab now set in purple-green bruises, that she'd kept hidden since last week. Julieta had been out of the room when he'd attacked her, and during a lull she'd managed to bandage her wounds and change into a long-sleeved blouse. The queen had been so distraught during that whole episode, on the verge of panic, that Lynn had hidden the biting in an effort to keep her boss from going to pieces utterly. The sight of the feet and their almost inhuman contortions brought back the horror of the other nights, and she wondered again just what Julieta hoped to gain from having this oddly blue-collar psychologist here.

"You believe in ghosts, Tommy?" Cree asked suddenly.

Joseph and Julieta froze again. The question caught Tommy off guard. His carefully maintained expression of mild boredom dropped away for an instant.

Tommy didn't answer. His eyes flicked to Julieta and Joseph.

"I guess your talking about your dad got me thinking about my father,"

Cree explained. "He died, oh, twelve years ago. I've never seen his ghost, but when I miss him a lot I sometimes wish I could. I wondered if you've ever felt that way."

"That's a Navajo superstition, ghosts." Tommy frowned. "Everything bad happens to you is ghosts. Bunch of crap."

"I'm not familiar with Navajo beliefs. Is that what people generally think?" The psychologist made a small, expectant smile. Julieta was looking at her with that stricken intensity again.

"I think if people look for supernatural explanations of their problems, they ignore the social and political stuff that really matters," Tommy went on. "Especially a disadvantaged socioeconomic group like the Diné."

A couple of points to Cree Black, Lynn decided. She'd finally provoked him into saying more than three words in a row, into showing that he had a brain. Even if his answer was probably quoted verbatim from Mr. Clah, his opinionated social studies teacher.

"That's a very mature perspective!" Cree sounded genuinely impressed. "From that, I can guess that art and horses aren't your only interests. Also that you're far too smart for the headshrinkers at the hospital. No wonder they didn't do anything for you!"

Tommy closed up again and shrugged off the praise.

But the psychologist was not going to be deflected. "Tell you what. I'll make a deal with you. I'll trade you. You let go of your fear and distrust of me because I'm a white stranger, and I'll let go of my condescension of you because you're only fifteen and have never been off the rez."

Tommy hunched his shoulders, a little shocked, resenting her.

"Look, Tommy, I could beat around the bush forever, and you'd know I was just trying to figure out what makes you tick. It's better if we just get there straightaway and treat each other as equals. We've got to get you feeling better. That's all I'm here for."

Her tone had been hard and the whole thing was confrontational. But it was honest, Lynn thought, impressed again. The woman was frank that she was here to work with him, not pretending this was just some social call out on the desert.

Tommy still didn't answer, but Cree didn't let up. She bored at him with her eyes.

"So is it a deal? The trade?"

71

"I guess," Tommy mumbled at last. Beneath the table, his feet continued writhing.

"I'm out," Joseph announced suddenly. He looked relieved to break the tension as he slapped down three queens, flipped an ace onto the discard pile, and mimed raking in a pot of money. "Read 'em and weep, ladies and gents. Another hand, or should we call it quits?"

The way he said it was so . . . sorrowful, somehow, and with the glow of firelight on his face he looked so resigned and handsome that Lynn almost reached out a hand to console him.

"Joseph is the rummy king," Julieta told Cree. "He murders us every time." She threw back her shoulders, stretching her elbows wide and arching her perfect breasts forward as she pulled her hair away from her face with both hands.

Lynn noticed the way Joseph's eyes lingered briefly on her body, a steady soft heat like coals. The sight made her stomach hurt.

—*And too self-preoccupied to show him the respect he deserves, to honor their past together by reciprocating his feelings,* Lynn finished, hating her. *The way any woman with anything like a human heart in her body would.*

She begged off the next hand, claiming she had work to do. The others played another round in the dayroom while she went back to the office and began filling out a pharmaceutical requisition form. She heard their voices faintly through the half-closed door. Were they more talkative now that she was gone, more cheerful? The nicotine craving had intensified and was screaming in her veins now. Outside, the wind had picked up a little, whispering around the building.

Her face seemed to burn, scalded by her own acid thoughts and searing feelings. After a while she realized she couldn't concentrate on her paperwork. She fled to the bathroom, where the ventilator fan made a welcome white noise, a camouflage as well as a safe haven from the faint sounds from the dayroom. She locked the door and stood facing the brightly lit, merciless mirror above the sink.

Envious, she said to the face in the mirror. *Jealous. All sick inside. Nasty. Hateful, spiteful creature. You're full of everything little and nasty. You're ugly and you have a crazy speck in your eye. You're festering with jealousy and resentment and you're all twisted up and repressed. Hateful, hateful, bad, bad.*

She wanted to smack the cheeks of the awful, fleck-eyed face, slap at all the nasties there, so obvious.

At the same time, she felt like going out to the dayroom and telling the psychologist, *Don't let her fool you! She claims to work so damn hard for the kids and for the school, and yet every other time you look for her she's out riding her horse at the foot of the mesa, ever so gay and devil-may-care, big hair blowing free on the wind. You'll fall for it just as I did when I first met her, but soon you'll come to look back on that feeling with disgust. She pretends she loves Navajos all to pieces, yet she won't acknowledge Joseph's love and give hers in return, even with everything that happened all those years ago. Because at bottom she's a spoiled rich white princess who thinks she's too good even for such a fine man. She treats him like he's a servant, has him come here for pro bono care with her students after his long workdays, even has him help shovel the horse manure like some stable hand! She acts so upright and forthcoming, and everyone believes her, but trust me, she's got dirty secrets in her past and it makes for very strange relationships with some of the kids. Especially Tommy. And that's not right.*

That thought brought her back a little. She looked at the blotched, scalded-looking face in the mirror and recoiled. She turned on the tap and began to splash cold water against her burning cheeks. She loosened the elastic at the back of her head, straightened her braid, tucked in loose strands of hair. She fumbled in her pockets for her cigarettes, lit up, and stood gratefully taking the fix and blowing smoke up into the exhaust fan. When she was done, she flushed the butt down the toilet.

The face in the mirror looked much better. This wasn't a personal issue, it was an issue of professional responsibility. That was the only way to see it. The well-being of the children was her only real concern, and if she observed misbehavior on the school administration's part, she had a duty to respond. This thing with Tommy was only one example.

The problem was that so far there was nothing overt, nothing provable that she could put before someone with the authority to do anything. And Julieta was so good at charming people into seeing things her way, it probably wouldn't matter anyway.

But. Fortunately, there were a few people who saw Julieta for what she was. There were others who would be very glad to know about the situation with Tommy, who would probably know what to make of it, what to do about it, even if there was nothing that could be done through formal channels.

She waited another couple of minutes to make sure the smoke was fully exhausted, checked the mirror one last time, then turned toward the door.

That's what it's about, she told herself. *The children. Professional responsibility.*

10

CREE BURST gasping out of a chaotic dream into the darkness of the ward room. Something was screaming in her mind.

It took her a moment to remember where she was. She had chosen a bed against the wall farthest from the inner door, near the window that looked out toward the mesa. A pair of night-lights plugged into wall sockets shed enough light to see the other five beds, green-white rectangles in the gloom. The windows were black, the silence so absolute it hissed in her ears.

In the dream, the night-dark rocks of Lost Goats Mesa had twisted and swarmed and metamorphosed into faces, grotesque brows and cheeks and gaping mouths of beings crying from the depths of the earth. There were crowds of them pushing at the cliffs, and there were air creatures, too, sharp electric things in the sky, flying with cruel stabbing motions. The landscape was alive: things pressing against its inner surfaces, straining against each other, contending with each other.

Dream, she told herself. *Just a dream. Get a grip.* She sat up and took deep, steady breaths to dispel the feeling.

But it didn't go away. Abruptly, she knew with certainty there was something happening nearby, telegraphing itself directly to her central nervous system.

The part of her mind that didn't recoil in fear registered that the night-lights were throbbing gently, erratically. *The flicker phenomenon,* she and Edgar called it: the tendency for light sources to become unsteady when paranormal phenomena manifested.

A noise came from the window. A muffled stamp or thump, then a . . . what? A breath, a deep exhalation. The horses? She listened and heard nothing.

She got quietly out of bed. In her stockinged feet, wearing the sweat pants and T-shirt she'd used as pajamas, she crept to the door of the room. She looked into the hallway and entry area and listened. The dim corridor, lit by several softly pulsing night-lights, stretched away to the bend that led to the dayroom, the nurse's bedroom, and the ward room where Tommy slept.

Ringing silence, charged with a sense of invisible motion.

She walked stealthily down the hall, through the entry, and into the hall on the other side, thinking to check on Lynn Pierce. The silver-haired nurse with the astonishing fleck in her eye had played hostess to the four of them after they'd come in from the horses, starting a fire in the dayroom hearth, making hot chocolate in the kitchen. They had played cards until Tommy's bedtime. It was like no other card game Cree had ever played: five people trying to chat and act relaxed when all felt a rising dread of anticipation. With the night pressed around the building, she had been acutely aware of how isolated they were, not just physically but socially. For the five of them there was no other recourse, no aid or comfort from the larger world of humankind. They were on an island.

She had pushed Tommy pretty hard, confronting him as candidly as she dared, and by and large was not unhappy with his response. He'd been defiant, embarrassed, shy, reluctant. But every patient of every age resisted probing, quite justifiably. She got a sense of an intelligent, complex person, decent and very much wanting to please, but confused by typical adolescent identity issues and troubled by ambivalent feelings toward his dead parents.

And though he tried hard to hide it, he was also terrified by the inexplicable things happening to him.

If only she'd gotten as good a sense of the supposed entity. The dissonance she sensed was so subdued that she doubted her own perceptions. Was the entity in him at all times but languishing in some kind of latency between crises? Or was it simply not there now—did it come out of the desert night each time, settling into him for a while and then leaving again? Or was there nothing there but a troubled teenage boy?

When it had gotten late, Joseph had driven off to Fort Defiance for his rotation at the hospital, and Julieta had gone to her room in the faculty housing building. Cree and Lynn had promised they'd wake her "if anything happened." Hoping nothing would.

Cree continued down the hall past the nurse's office, turned right, passed the dayroom, and paused at the door to Lynn Pierce's bedroom. It was pitch-dark inside, but her eyes had adapted enough to see the mounded blankets and the long braid trailing over the side of the bed. Tense as a wound spring, she warily approached the door to the smaller ward room. It struck her that the night-lights in this hall were throbbing faster.

Tommy's bed was empty.

Cree backed out of the doorway, followed the hall as it doglegged, and found the rear exit door. It was slightly ajar, rocking softly. When she opened it, the chill wind hit her, straight from the north, and she quickly realized that sweat pants, T-shirt, and socks weren't good enough for the high desert in late September. But a sense of imminence propelled her, and she didn't want to take the time to go back for shoes and sweater. She stepped out into the night and shut the door softly behind her.

The exterior light was on, glazing the yard between infirmary and barn with a hard bright silver. Beyond, the corral fence stood like a construction of bones against the darkness. At the far end of the enclosure, just at the edge of the circle of light, Julieta's three horses were vague forms against deep black night.

No sign of Tommy. No motion or sound at all but the wind.

The blue-white area light blinded her. Beyond its sphere of chemical illumination, the night wrapped a curtain of black felt around the infirmary, the barn, the corral.

Instinctively, she went toward the horses. They were facing away from her, heads up, legs braced, alert but absolutely motionless. She opened the corral gate and went inside, feeling blind and very exposed as she crossed the bare, silver-gilded ground. Sharp stones stabbed up through her socks. Her breath came out in wraiths of steam that fled away instantly; her shadow preceded her, looking like a deformed thing. Beyond the curtain of darkness, she could feel the cliffs of the mesa, in her imagination still moving like flesh. As she got farther away from the buildings, the light on the side of the infirmary shrank to a distant sharp point.

She forgot the discomfort of her feet as she got closer to the horses. There was something wrong with them.

Their breath steamed and their tails rippled in the icy wind, but they didn't turn as she approached, didn't whicker or snort. Hadn't they heard her? She stopped ten feet away, suddenly afraid of being among such big animals, aware that for all their docility earlier they didn't know her well. "Hey, Breeze," she whispered. "Madie. Spence." But they didn't move. They just stood with their necks arched erect. Their chins were raised in an attitude of listening, but their ears were pressed flat against their heads.

It took her a moment to realize that they were making a sound after all. It was a dry, fast rustling noise that didn't make sense until she got closer and saw that they were shivering, all three of them, their bulging haunches and shoulders and great neck tendons standing out, hard with tension. The noise she was hearing was the vibrating contraction of the surface muscles of their great bodies, the quick shifting of their hides. A sound like a tree of dry leaves rattling softly in a winter wind, or the palms of two dry hands rubbing rapidly.

It appalled and transfixed her. *Not right,* her mind was screaming, *wrong wrong wrong—*

She had been standing there in the dim light for several moments, terrified and perplexed, when abruptly she realized there were other shapes in the night. The darkness beyond the fence was suddenly full of faint, uprearing gray-silver shapes where there should have been only empty desert. Nightmare forms just visible against the black. She felt her stomach drop.

She stared into the gloom and suddenly knew the monstrous night beings as horses—six or eight pale horses with heads stiffly erect, ears back, glazed eyes. Motionless. Cree caught one jagged breath as she recognized them: the little band of free-roaming grays and palominos she and Julieta had seen on the way in.

Like Julieta's horses, they stood locked into shivering, stiff stances. After a moment she saw a shadow slide in among them, eclipsing their phantom glow.

It was Tommy Keeday.

What was he doing? Dancing? He ducked under one horse's belly, disappearing and then emerging again to slide his body among the rigid animals. Even in this faint light, Cree could see that he was wearing only pajama pants, no top, no shoes, and that his movements were oddly stylized. He took queer, uneven steps, a crablike sideways shuffle with one arm upraised to stroke a shivering flank and the other pressed down at his side. Several times he seemed to be stepping over invisible objects on the ground, trying to stride over them, checking himself, trying and checking again with rhythmic, repetitive motions. His head remained cocked to the right.

The gray stallion stood closest to the fence, and as Cree's night vision improved she caught the glint of one round eye.

Tommy turned and began his complicated dance toward the corral, facing Cree directly but giving no indication he'd seen her. When he came near the fence, his left arm groped forward, his right leg took a half step and held his weight as his left leg bent sharply at the knee and drew up several times before setting itself tentatively down. By the time he reached the rails and inserted himself through them, his body had contorted in a sideways bend and his limbs weren't cooperating with each other at all. Erratic puffs of steam came from his open mouth and vanished with the wind. She heard the faint, uneven rasp of breath.

Pawing at the air, his left arm reached for something that didn't exist. His right leg stepped through while his left leg stood and then went down on one knee, tangling him on the lowest rail.

It struck Cree that there were two people coming through the fence.

When he'd managed to get most of his body through, he fell forward onto the ground, directly onto his chest and chin. Only after he'd lain facedown for a moment did his limbs start moving again, the agonized effort of an overturned turtle or beetle, trying to right itself. After he'd flopped onto his back, he lay facing the cloak of sky with one arm pushing up and out and snapping back and one leg scraping the soil in slow, deliberate motions.

Thirty feet away, Cree stood unable to move, sick with horror.

After a moment his arm dropped and he just lay there. Only his bare chest was moving, a lateral ripple, lifting on one side and falling on the other with the sinuous flexibility of a belly dancer. His mouth was stretched wide, a black round hole in his face, but no steam came from it. No breath came from his open throat.

Cree's hypnotic terror shattered as she realized she was watching a boy suffocating. "Tommy!" she shouted. She lunged forward to help him just as the world exploded.

As if their invisible bonds had snapped, the three horses in the corral burst to life, pivoting away from Tommy. The gelding's wheeling shoulder struck Cree and sent her flying backward. She landed on her back, bounced hard, sat up immediately into a storm of flailing knobby legs as the mares hurtled past her, over her, shrieking. Something hard hit her head and knocked her flat, a string of firecrackers went off between her ears. The impact stunned her, but she jerked herself upright again and stared around her through the bloody yellow explosions in her head. Julieta's horses were back near the barn, wheeling and snorting as they raced up and down the far fence line. The phantom horses on the far side of the fence were gone. She heard their fading hoofbeats and their dwindling screams, so like the screams of women.

A yellow beam lit the ground as she struggled to her feet and lurched toward Tommy. Julieta's voice called from the infirmary door. Cree fell before she got to the boy, but she managed to crawl the rest of the way on her hands and knees. Tommy's chest continued its writhing, his mouth gaped for air but none came. When she dared to touch his skin, it was ice-cold.

Not knowing what else to do, she put her mouth over his and blew into it. The convulsing chest changed its rhythm but didn't seem to receive any air. She took her mouth away, shoved hard on his breastbone with both hands, put her lips over his and exhaled again.

The flashlight beam panned wildly, and she heard Lynn Pierce's voice as well and knew that the nurse and Julieta were running toward them, that's why the light gyred and came and went so jaggedly. She felt herself go distant and confused, but pulled her mouth away from Tommy again. This time she saw blood on Tommy's cheeks and realized it was her own, she was bleeding from her forehead and raining drops of red onto him. And it didn't matter, what mattered was getting air into the fish-gaping black mouth. She put her hands against his chest and brought her weight down hard once more. Before she could lean to his face, a wave of dizziness broke over her, rocked her back so that she lost her balance. But as she fell away, she heard a gasp at the back of Tommy's throat, and immediately another. And then Julieta was there, and light, and Lynn's hands holding her shoulders so she wouldn't topple.

11

" A SYNCHRONOUS BREATHING," Cree said. "One lung is inhaling while the other is exhaling."

"That's not possible," the nurse said. "It's not anatomically possible!"

But of course it was, because they were looking at it. Tommy lay on the table beneath the bright, faltering lights of the examining room, eyes closed, arms at his sides. Once you understood what was going on, it was easy to see: The left side of his ribs rose and fell rapidly, while the right side drew slower, deeper breaths.

Ashen faced, speechless, Julieta stroked his forehead and gazed at him intensely, as if passion alone would allow her to see inside his skull.

Cree shut her eyes against the pounding pain and held the ice pack back against her forehead. "As long as the two sides don't get into regular opposition, he draws in enough air. But if one side inhales at the same time the other exhales, if they get into rhythm that way, the air just passes from lung to lung. That's what was happening when he came through the fence. He blacked out because he was suffocating. He was just rebreathing his own used-up air."

It was hard to think straight, but Cree realized they were talking about him as if he wasn't there. He acted like he was asleep, but she wasn't so sure. Through the pulsing haze in her head, she thought she felt him in there, disoriented but conscious.

Felt *them* in there.

"Tommy," she said softly. "Hey, Tommy."

Tommy stirred, hitching one shoulder. Julieta's eyes caught Cree's, terrified.

"You awake?" Cree persisted.

Tommy's eyes opened, rolled, stabilized. "Yeah."

"What's going on with you? What do you feel?"

"Nothing. I don't know." His speech was punctuated with wheezes, one lung laboring out of sync.

Cree gave him a moment to elaborate, but he didn't. "Up for Mrs. Pierce poking at you? We want to make sure you're not hurt."

He didn't answer but acquiesced by sitting up awkwardly, pushing himself up off the table with his left arm. He looked around him, blinking in the light, waiting. His breath steadied.

Lynn Pierce took over. "I need to ask you things, and I want you to answer even if they seem stupid to you. Is that okay?"

"Like we did the other times?"

"Yep, same thing." Lynn tried to smile. "You're a great patient, Tommy."

She looked into his eyes and ears, checked his reflexes with a rubber mallet, listened to his chest, and tried to conceal the alarm she obviously felt. "What's your name?" she asked. "I told you this would be stupid."

"Tom Keeday."

A tiny expression of relief on Lynn's face. "Where are you from?"

"East of Sheep Springs."

"What day is this?"

"Friday. September twenty-seventh."

"Who's the president?"

"Begaye. But there's an election coming up, he'll probably lose."

"Tribal president," Lynn explained to Cree. "Very good, Tommy. Can you stand up for me, good and straight?"

Tommy pushed aside the blankets and stepped off the table. His left leg wrongly anticipated the ground and he lurched, but after his right had tried twice to gauge the distance to the tile floor he managed to steady himself.

"Are you as straight as you can be?"

"Yeah."

Arms at his sides, he was bent sideways, the middle of his spine bowed noticeably to the left, his head cocked to the right. Cree shot a glance at Julieta, standing behind Tommy, and found that her eyes had filled and overflowed.

"Tommy, I want you to shut your eyes now. I'm going to touch you, and I want you to tell me where I'm touching you. Just like before."

He nodded and shut his eyes. When she gently prodded his left arm, he said, "Arm."

"You have to say left or right."

"Left."

"Great! Now this. And this." She touched his left pectoral muscle, his forehead, his left thigh, his stomach, and he named them all correctly.

Lynn prodded him on his spine in the middle of his back.

"Arm," he said. "Right arm."

Julieta's face folded in agony.

"This?" Another touch, this time on his neck, just below his buzz-cut hairline.

"Right shoulder."

The nurse bit her lips so hard Cree could have sworn her teeth would come through, but she went on. "Tommy, open your eyes now. What's this?" She had lifted his limp right arm, bending it at the elbow and so she could hold the limb right in front of him.

He opened his eyes and looked at it as if surprised and dismayed by the object's sudden appearance. "I don't know."

Holding the arm out in her right hand, Lynn used her left to stroke the bare skin, elbow to shoulder. "Keep your eyes open. What's this I'm touching?"

"I don't like it!"

"Don't like what?"

"That thing. The thing you're holding." He craned away, afraid of it.

"Where's your right arm?"

"I already told you!"

Lynn put the arm down and ran her fingers over the knobs of his side-bowed spine again. "Here?"

"Yes! I told you!"

"I'm sorry to keep at you. You're doing great. One more thing, and then we'll move on. We're almost done. Okay?"

"Yeah." He was getting sullen now. He mumbled something in what Cree assumed was Navajo.

"Shut your eyes again, please. I want you to tell me when you feel something."

When Tommy had winced his eyes shut, she placed his right hand, palm up, on the tabletop. Lynn dabbed alcohol on his fingertips, opened a sterilized lancet, and held his hand against the table as she isolated his ring finger. With one sharp stab, she drove the lancet into the pad of the immobilized finger.

Tommy didn't say anything. Didn't move, didn't even flinch. A fat bead of blood appeared when Lynn pulled the needle away.

She gripped his middle finger and stabbed deep again. "Feel anything?"

"No."

Lynn Pierce's chin was quivering as she tossed away the lancet and bandaged the fingers. Tommy stood obediently, shoulders squared but spine as bent as a hitchhiker's thumb. Julieta looked at him with heartbreak in her eyes.

Cree's head was throbbing so hard she couldn't make sense of the shrill alarms going off throughout her body and brain. All she could think was *doubleness*. Too much at once. The three women looked at each other and at the bent, bare-chested boy, and the only thing Cree could feel clearly was horror at the freakish phenomenon she was witnessing. She could almost see the shape of the compound being that stood before her, a doubled thing like some monstrous, unviable conjoined twins with half-merged bodies, arms and legs misplaced and deformed. The outlandish, pretzeling interpenetration, so unbearably wrong.

Again Cree was conscious of their isolation. Two o'clock in the morning, and beyond this tiny island of unsteady light everything was dark for miles in every direction. Three scared women and one lost boy stood in an abandoned school in the desert. There was something invisible among them. And there was no explanation and no succor anywhere.

The room seemed to waver, and Cree had to sit down. She had no idea what to do. There was a powerful paranormal entity three feet from her, and she couldn't begin to approach it. Whenever she tried, she found the pain in her head in the way, obstructing every sense. Everything else was a blur full of shifting impressions. Doubleness, yes, and that stark sense of isolation. Besides that, all she knew was an almost overpowering need to take Tommy to her, hold him against herself, enfold him, protect him. Her heart, her womb ached with the need. But her enclosing arms wouldn't help. The danger, the enemy, was already inside.

★   ★   ★

"I'd say a mild concussion," Lynn told her. "Lot of blood, but that's typical of a scalp wound. The cut is superficial, you don't even need stitches. You really should go to the hospital for X-rays—we can get one of the maintenance staff to drive you, but I think it can wait until morning if you'd prefer."

The two of them were sitting in the examination room. The nurse had cleaned and bandaged the wound above Cree's eyebrow and then had carefully checked her eyes and reflexes and balance. Julieta had called Joseph Tsosie at the hospital and was told he'd be paged and would return the call. Through the slats of the blinds over the window into the ward room, they could see Tommy sitting on his bed. Eyes mostly closed, his chest moved in a slight lateral ripple, the left and right almost in sync now, and he kept bending his back to the right and tipping his head, almost as if trying to shake water out of his ear. Julieta sat in a chair against the wall, watching him but clearly fighting sleep.

"How long does it last?"

The nurse followed her gaze. "Getting longer. The first time, maybe half an hour. Last time, closer to two hours. He's never made it to the hospital when the full symptoms are presenting."

"Same thing every time?"

"The problem placing his limbs is much worse this time. And the breathing problem—that's new. First time I've observed it, anyway."

"So it's . . . progressing."

The silver head made a small, reluctant nod.

"Did Dr. Ambrose see him when he was like this?"

"Some of it. He saw the spinal curvature and the confusion about his arm and spine. The lack of sensation in his right arm."

Cree thought about that. It was always hard to tell what Mason perceived and what conclusions he'd drawn, but usually he knew more than he let on and had devious reasons for doing what he did. Mason's Machiavellian approach to manipulating people infuriated her—it was his way of viewing every living person as a test subject, a lab rat. If she found out he was keeping some insight to himself in this case, Cree decided, she'd shove him off Sandia Peak herself.

The phone rang and startled them both. Lynn snatched it up.

"Hi, Joseph! Yes. Yes. No, worse. Can you? Good." Lynn glanced up at the slatted window, and the corners of her mouth tightened with disapproval. "Well, she's upset, but she's doing all right so far—she's in there with him now. Dr. Black sustained a head injury. No, one of the horses. Not too bad, mainly a scalp cut. We're holding the fort. Just get here soon, please?"

She put the receiver down. "Joseph's on his way. He'll be here in about an hour." Relief was evident on her face—obviously, both women put a great deal of trust in Dr. Tsosie.

They waited. Two-fifteen. Tommy was fast asleep and Julieta had dropped off at last, head tipped back against the wall, mouth open; her light snores came through the monitor. Lynn Pierce was at her desk, wearily occupied with some paperwork. Cree was bleary and numb and was fighting off sleep herself when a movement from the ward room startled her.

Tommy's right hand had begun to move. First it swung slowly side to side on the wrist, like the head of a snake. The fingers played lightly on the blanket at Tommy's thigh, as if feeling the texture of the fabric. Then the arm bent, drawing the hand up along Tommy's side. When it encountered the edge of the folded-back sheet, it paused as the fingers deftly explored. In another instant, the hand was at Tommy's head. When it touched his hair, it pulled back suddenly as if the feel of his bristles startled it. It came back again tentatively, found his ear, traced the curve of it.

Cree watched, spellbound, horrified. The arm and hand clearly belonged to someone other than Tommy. Some blind being, trying to make sense of invisible surroundings.

Tommy groaned in his sleep and moved his head away from the probing fingers, but in another moment his whole body arched and suddenly he sat up and swung his feet off the bed. His eyes opened, rolled wildly, and then found Julieta. They burned at her from beneath his dark brows.

He began to lean forward, the feral gaze intensifying. Cree felt a sudden sense of alarm as the ceiling lights, relatively stable for some time, began to strobe and stutter, and then she watched in stunned horror as Tommy seemed to brace himself. Before she could move, he had propelled himself off the bed toward Julieta with a deep, guttural grunt.

Lynn Pierce's chair skated away as she jumped up. Tommy fell halfway across the room but continued writhing toward Julieta, his gaze still fixed on her. She had awakened and now sat in her chair, her expression a mix of shock and concern as the lights blinked on and off, steadied, fluttered again. The doubled Tommy clawed his way toward her in a series of aborted lunges, face contorted, and still Julieta didn't move.

By the time Cree and Lynn made it into the ward room, Julieta had broken from her paralysis and was crouching at Tommy's side. As she leaned toward him, he rolled and raked at her face with one hand. And then his body went into convulsions again, everything flailing and battering. Lynn and Cree threw themselves on him, holding back the savage clawing and the pumping legs. Julieta fell back, two streaks of red across her cheek near her eye. Lynn's face was held hard as a skull as she subdued the bucking body.

What are you? Cree's thoughts screamed. *Who are you?* But the effort to hold Tommy down brought back the pain, blinding big mallet blows to her forehead. She couldn't think, could hardly see.

Looking down into his face as she held the twisting shoulders, Cree saw a difference in his eyes. One pupil was a great, dilated black hole, the other much smaller. As she looked down his right eye fixed her, held steady despite the tossing of his head. And with what looked like great effort, the eye winced itself shut. It opened again, still staring straight at her, and did it once more.

Maybe it was purely accidental, some fluke of his chaotic movements, but she couldn't escape the feeling it had been a *wink*. Had to be. Was it lascivious, taunting, pleading, threatening? She couldn't guess. But she could swear it had been a kind of communication—a signal from something living inside Tommy's skull.

12

JULIETA TIGHTENED her legs around the big barrel of Spence's body as she urged him into a full gallop. The ground jolted and rolled away, and the cold rush of early-morning air gave her the feeling of being airborne. The black gelding was a powerful horse, smart with his feet, and now she goaded him to his utmost. His rhythmic lunging and the pumping bellows of his breathing soothed the painful nerve deep inside her. A welcome narcotic.

"Take me away, Spence," she called to him. "Fly me away."

The sun hadn't yet broken the top of the mesa and the world was raw and fresh as she bucketed west from the rear corral gate. A wide track of disturbed ground showed that horses had been this way not long ago—Shurley's bunch, no doubt. The gray stallion and his mares must have visited Spence and the girls last night. From the deep bite of hoofs and wide scatter of soil, she could tell they'd left in a hurry. `

Tommy's breathing had returned to normal by the time Joseph had arrived and inspected him. There'd been nothing for him to see but a very sleepy fifteen-year-old, understandably surly at being poked and prodded in the middle of the night. Once he was certain Tommy was stable, Joseph had checked Cree Black, looking for signs of concussion. Finally, he had come to Julieta to lightly touch the scrapes on her cheek, his eyes making it clear he was ministering not to the physical injury but to the deeper hurt she'd suffered from the assault. Julieta had left the infirmary at around four, leaving Joseph to spend what remained of the night in the bed next to Tommy's, and had gone back to her quarters.

Where of course sleep had been impossible. She was as tense as a bowstring, charged with hysterical energy and fear and need. When Joseph had walked her out to the infirmary's porch and the night had wrapped around them, she'd experienced an almost overwhelming urge to grab him, envelop his mouth with hers, tell him to take her back to her room and make love to her until the world got real again and there was warmth and safety somewhere and some things were certain and it was okay.

But of course she didn't. She went alone to the dark of her room, where the nightmare of Tommy kept at her. After an hour or so she gave up and sought the only little remedy she could think of. She dressed again, went out to the corral. The wind had died and the night was full of a waiting feeling, the stillness before dawn. Spence had been skittish at first, but she'd tempted him with an apple and spent a long time gently stroking him, and eventually he'd calmed down enough to accept the saddle. The sky had paled to slate gray by the time she swung herself onto him. She didn't look back once as the school dwindled and disappeared from view.

A mile out, the track of Shurley's horses veered to the southwest, but she reined Spence to the right, heading north along a little ridge in the undulating plain. She let him open up, find his own speed. He responded as if he needed this, too, this wild flight away from what had happened.

The image of Tommy came back to her: the impossible breathing, the independent movement of his anguished eyes, the horrible strength of his convulsions. Trying to restrain him, she'd felt an eerie fibrillation in his chest and shoulders as if individual strands of muscle were separately alive, steel wires trying to animate him against the resistance of the rest of his flesh. Then, later, awakening to the awful predatory fixity of his gaze and his sudden lunging, clawing attack. Beyond scaring her, it had felt like . . . what? A betrayal. Love rebuffed. The whole thing had been so wrenching she'd feared her mind, her whole world, would deform with the twisted force of it.

She'd never been a determined skeptic like Joseph; she'd been raised listening to Grandma Sandoval's tales of family ghosts, which as a child she'd believed as fact and as an adult had accepted as licensed but not utterly implausible. And you couldn't live out here without hearing rumors of mysterious and inexplicable events, wondering about the livestock mutilations, or sensing other presences in the rocks and shadows—it was one of the things she loved about this country. And yet, though she'd always been fairly open-minded about supernatural things, she would have described herself as a rationalist. Even two days ago, when she and Joseph had gone to meet Cree Black on Sandia Peak, she would have claimed a fairly secure belief in science and conventional medicine and the whole trend of rational, empirical Western thought since Aristotle.

But the events of the last few hours had busted all that up pretty good.

It was almost funny. Really, all she'd been doing for the last three weeks was continuing to live her mental habits, operating from her old paradigms. She was like that cartoon coyote, hurtling off a cliff and running in midair before he realizes he's suspended over a mile-deep canyon. As if the momentum of belief or habit or ignorance could defy the law of gravity!

"I don't believe in anything!" she called to Spence. His hide hitched at the sound of her voice, and he quickened his stride. She laughed bitterly at the realization and yelled to the empty land, "I don't know what to believe! I have no idea what's *real!*" She wanted to laugh and cry and scream. She wanted to hit something, strike something and punish the world for its fickleness. For its unfairness in visiting this catastrophe on her. On Tommy Keeday, of all people.

The thought of Tommy brought her thoughts back a little. This wasn't about Julieta McCarty, she reminded herself, this was about Tommy. A beautiful child, a talented artist, a boy with a lot of potential that would surely be destroyed if they couldn't cure him. A boy who knew nothing about the psychodrama he'd walked into at Oak Springs School, the role he played in the principal's secret fantasies and neuroses. Who was not to blame and who must never know of any of it.

Spence was laboring now, still willing but getting tired. She spoke to him softly and brought him down to a trot. The big horse huffed and snorted, glad for a chance to get his wind back. Already they were three miles beyond school property and well onto McCarty Energy's Hunters Point coalfield. The land immediately around her looked the same, but a mile to the west a series of low, flat-topped ridges appeared, the spoil mounds from mining operations of thirty years ago. Even now, the desert vegetation had not returned to those dry slopes. She hated the sight of them—why had she come this way? She nudged Spence a little more toward the northeast.

She marshaled her thoughts. The gallop had tired her as well as Spence, burnt off the worst of the crazy energy. *Principal,* she reminded herself. *Administrator. Head honcha. It's executive decision time: Where do we go from here?*

Was there really any point in allowing Cree Black to work with Tommy? She'd been all but useless last night.

On the other hand, Julieta couldn't really blame her, given that she'd just about gotten her skull fractured as she'd rushed to help him. And no, actually, she hadn't been useless. Quite the opposite. If her psychic radar or whatever it was hadn't prompted her to go out to the corral, Tommy might have died, suffocating as his lungs labored to rebreathe each other's air. So they already owed her a great deal.

And Julieta had to admit there was something about Cree, some inner determination that she'd noticed at their very first meeting. She was a woman of about her own age and height, with medium-length brown hair full of chestnut-red highlights. A pageant coach would have appraised her as pretty, but not glamorous enough to be competitive. What made her looks compelling was the keen alertness and candor in her eyes, the expressiveness of her mouth. You got the feeling she was a person who *cared*. She was also someone who told it like it was, had no stake in misrepresenting anything. Whatever Cree Black's personal history, she had obviously faced some tough things, maybe something like the crisis of belief Julieta felt in herself now. Somehow she'd seen it through, had come to some faith or truth despite the maelstrom of uncertainties.

Which was kind of reassuring.

And right now, Cree Black's explanations seemed as apt as anything Julieta had heard from the doctors they'd consulted.

But there were other issues to consider. The symptoms were more extreme and lasted longer every time. The breathing problem demonstrated clearly that Tommy's physical survival, not just his mental well-being, was at risk, and that the school was not well prepared to assure his safety. From the standpoint of the school, the issue was clear: If Tommy died or got badly injured at Oak Springs, especially if any education or health authority heard she'd dealt with it as a supernatural issue, she could face criminal charges. Last night, citing both Tommy's needs and the school's, Joseph had been explicit that he couldn't let this go on: One more crisis and he'd insist on Tommy's being hospitalized again.

And he was right. Clearly, the safest and easiest route would be to remand him to the care of some public authority, or to his grandparents, and wash her hands of the problem. And try to forget him and the world of fantasies she'd constructed around him.

She felt her lips curl in a hard smile. *Fat fucking chance.*

The scary part of Joseph's dictum was that the next hospital visit would change Tommy's life. From there, the road took a crucial fork. Certainly, in long-term care, some anonymous clinic or institution, his acute needs would be better met. But no doctor was likely to believe—or risk a career by admitting—that some unknown entity was occupying his body and mind. And therefore he wouldn't get the real help he needed. The Indian Health Services would soon find they didn't have the resources for him, and they'd send him on to the state. A bunch of well-meaning, over-worked doctors would drug him and talk at him, and if it didn't go away, they'd wedge him deeper and deeper into the system, until he was warehoused in some institution and forgotten. Or they might go for more drastic treatments; she'd read recently that electroshock therapy and lobotomy were coming back into fashion.

She shuddered and shook off the thought.

The other most likely option would be to send him home. That was the choice his grandparents had endorsed—the Navajo way, removing him from whatever bad influences had triggered his problem, wrapping him close against the bosom of family, performing some archaic healing Way for him. But, again, he would probably not get cured. And even with in-home support from the state or tribe, he'd be far away from appropriate medical help, from educational resources, from—

From Julieta McCarty.

A shiver of panic rattled her. The scariest aspect of those options was that they took him away. She couldn't even tell how much that thought was biasing what should be objective analysis of Tommy's needs.

The third possibility was that she could again persuade his grandparents to keep him here. She'd met them twice, and they seemed to trust her judgment. Here at the school, he'd have decent, if not optimum, medical care; he'd have social contacts and educational options and all those lovely "normalizing" things. Plus there was the possibility, one she found increasingly credible, that Cree Black could do something for him. The problem there would be Joseph. And the liability issues, of course.

What was the right thing? What did he really need? You couldn't decide that without deciding whether he was suffering from a neurological dysfunction, a psychological problem—or, as Dr. Ambrose and Cree Black insisted and his impossible symptoms seemed to prove, the literal invasion of his central nervous system by some foreign entity.

"It comes down to what we believe, doesn't it?" she asked Spence. Then she corrected herself: "What *I* believe." This time he whickered in agreement, and she stroked his shoulder, whispering gratefully, "You're my man, Spence. My debonair gent."

Sometimes you had to make decisions entirely on your own. It was hard, it was scary, it was lonely, but it was what you did if you had any guts. You did what you believed was right and necessary. No, she resolved, letting go of Tommy was out of the question. She'd fight to keep him at the school. She'd play whatever hand she had, legal or financial or personal, to retain a say in what happened to him.

"Screw *safe!*" she shouted. "Huh, Spence? Screw *easy!*"

He picked up his trot as if he agreed. She felt a little better. An angry inner fire warmed her against the chill. When had she ever done anything easy?

The full disk of the sun had nudged above the horizon by the time she came within sight of McCarty Energy's current operations. She reined Spence to a stop and then sat there, looking north to a ruined ridge and the gigantic rearing boom of a dragline just visible a couple of miles away. Again she wondered why she'd come this way. She hated the sight of it. She'd been there often enough to fight with Garrett and Donny to visualize what lay beyond the screen of hills.

There was a wasteland of dug-up soil and rock heaped in man-made mountains, meandering dirt roads and ramps for the big machines, and gaping trenches blasted and scraped into the ground. There was the crusher and the huge mounds of coal waiting to be loaded onto trains. There were the walking draglines, whole movable buildings that supported the colossal girdered booms and buckets, one of which was the same dragline Garrett had led her through when he was in his phase of impressing her with the many large, expensive things he owned. With the boom from which sixty-six-year-old Garrett had fallen and died while showing off for his latest tramp girlfriend.

There were yellow dump trucks and front loaders the size of houses. There was the office and repair complex and a parking lot full of pickup trucks. And sometimes there was Donny's Lincoln Navigator or Porsche in the lot, and Donny, along with a gaggle of rapacious bean counters, going over the operation's records and being an officious pain in the ass and thinking up clever ways to make more money. And as a sideline, kind of a hobby, thinking up ways to make Julieta's life miserable.

Just like his father.

"One mistake," she told Spence. "That's all it takes. One. Then your whole life is spent living it down or trying to compensate."

Spence swiveled one ear as if to hear her better but didn't answer. And of course it wasn't that simple. Which was the one mistake? Being suckered into that first teen modeling job? Sticking to the competitions despite growing misgivings? Going out for lunch that first time with a man old enough to be her father?

Or maybe the mistake was one of the avalanche of decisions that had come later and that had haunted her, every day, ever since.

It was hard to think of the creature inside Tommy as anything but a demon, a supernatural monster existing only to cause anguish—some horrible being from Navajo mythology, or a violent spirit of the ancient rocks, a distillation of sheer malevolence from old, angry gods. But maybe Cree Black was right about everything. Maybe she was right to look at Julieta, to put her on the couch along with Tommy. Maybe she was right in her theory that the psychological situations of people in proximity to the haunting created the conditions needed to support a ghost's manifestation. That what had invaded Tommy was a part of a once-human consciousness, taking someone else's flesh in an attempt to fulfill its deepest compulsions.

If that was true, there was only one person Julieta could imagine having the malice to do what it was doing. One person who'd have the fiendish insight and the motivation to destroy a child, *this* child, in an effort to strike at Julieta herself.

That's why she'd come here today, she realized. To remind herself.

She stood up on the stirrups and beamed hatred at the rearing boom where Garrett McCarty had gotten himself killed, as if she might see his vicious ghost and by sheer force of will send it screaming back to hell.

13

ANOTHER PICKUP truck ride. Every bump in the gravel banged up through the suspension of Dr. Tsosie's Ford and up Cree's spine to be delivered like a hammer blow on the inside of her forehead. She had gone to bed determined not to take the time for a visit to the hospital, but this morning as she'd bent to look for her shoes a sick red-purple haze of pain suddenly filled the room, and she'd changed her mind. She had agreed readily when Dr. Tsosie insisted she accompany him to the hospital in Fort Defiance.

Joseph's first act upon arising had been to inspect Tommy, and when he'd assured himself that the boy was stable he'd looked Cree over with the same thoroughness. Then he'd taken her to the school cafeteria, where along with a handful of weekend staff they'd grabbed a breakfast of scrambled eggs, bacon, and toast. Julieta didn't join them; Joseph said she was probably out riding—it was what she did when she needed to think.

Now the two of them drove in silence as an ebullient sun bounded up from the mesa, promising a brilliant day as open and guileless as the night had been cloaked and full of dire things. Joseph seemed content to ride next to this stranger without making small talk, and Cree didn't mind. There was a lot to think about.

The problem was that any impressions she might have received had been muddled by the pain, which had obstructed any empathic resonance with Tommy and whatever had invaded him.

Inspecting her memory of the movements of his hand and that awful wink, she'd decided that the being now resident in Tommy was not some unknown category of entity—some relief there, maybe—but had once been human. She couldn't say why she thought that, except that she'd felt *seen* by it, felt its rude self-awareness glimmering there, enough to feel its similarity to her own. The eerie movements of the hand and arm suggested intentionality, some level of awareness of itself and its circumstances. But she'd garnered nothing of its character, identity, origin—or, crucially, its motivations.

No, the few insights she'd come away with had little to do with the boy.

One observation had to do with the way Joseph had dealt with Julieta when he'd arrived last night. The moment he was confident Tommy was resting safely and that Cree's injury wasn't serious, he'd gone to Julieta. He took her by the shoulders and with one hand swept the loose hair away from her face so he could study her. She looked like hell, exhausted, eyes puffy from crying, but as she gazed into his face her unguarded expression revealed how relieved and grateful she was to have him there. Joseph had first lightly touched her scraped cheek, and then his hand had turned and he'd delicately brushed the back of his fingers along her jawline before he turned away. It lasted only an instant, but even through her pain Cree could see that though the first touch had been a physician's, the second had been much more.

These two people knew each other well and cared deeply about each other.

Another was, irrelevantly, about Lynn Pierce. She was pleasant and certainly competent, but she radiated a sense of tension, a hypervigilance and -sensitivity. Some internal warring was going on, and though it made sense that the nurse would be keyed up with a patient like Tommy in her care, Cree felt intuitively there was more to it. For reasons Cree couldn't guess, a good measure of that odd, sideways hyperalertness seemed directed toward Julieta and Joseph.

One final insight concerned Julieta—Julieta and Tommy. Unquestionably, Julieta was a dedicated educator, deeply committed to the well-being of her students. But there was also some special connection between the two, much more than the concern called for by professional obligations or general altruism. It was something Cree felt achingly in her own belly whenever she saw them together, heard in Julieta's voice as she tried to comfort him. It awakened her own yearnings, the feeling she felt around Hyacinth and Zoe: the DNA-deep calling to have a child, to love and nurture. Julieta's concern grew out of instincts and longings that deep and irresistible.

That thought suggested another set of questions. If Julieta wanted children, why didn't she have them? It couldn't be for want of willing males. If Cree knew one thing about men and women, it was that nature abhorred a vacuum, and that a woman so beautiful and vivid would attract the attentions of any man who saw her. Julieta had spoken in passing about other relationships, but there had to be a reason why she'd never remarried in the many years since her divorce from Garrett McCarty.

The sudden smooth hum of the truck tires on pavement brought Cree out of her musings. They had made it to Indian Route 12, and now Joseph turned north, leaving behind the dust plume that had trailed them since they'd left the school. He maintained an impassive face as he drove. The hands that gripped the steering wheel were long fingered and neatly manicured, the competent hands of a physician. Cree wished with sudden intensity she could break through to him, enlist him as an ally.

"Dr. Tsosie—can we talk?"

"If you like."

"My process is difficult to accept at first. But it's worked for me and for the benefit of many others. If you and I can cooperate, it'll really help. If we can't, it'll really get in the way."

"It may become moot. Another night like last night and he can't stay at the school anymore."

"I understand. But the pattern so far is that there's an interval between crises, right? If I can have even a few days with him, I can make progress. With your help."

He stayed quiet for a long moment. "A month ago, if somebody like you came here, I'd have advised Julieta to throw him off the grounds."

"If one of the kids got sick and asked for a Hand-Trembler or a Singer, would you throw him off, too?"

He looked at her more closely. It wasn't a long and confrontational gaze, but a short, lateral look of appraisal. Tsosie was a handsome man, with deep brown eyes that seemed to take in the sunlight and give it back, warm and clear. The reserve she sensed in him was not one of arrogance or uptightness, not even a product of his skepticism; it struck her as a habit born of a desire to deliberate, to show respect, to assert mutuality.

"Depends," Tsosie said at last. "On whether I thought he'd do some good or not."

"Can you give me the same benefit of the doubt?"

"You're here, aren't you?"

She felt like thanking him but didn't yet know what he was giving his highly conditional approval to. "The problem is," she said reluctantly, "I'm going to ask all kinds of questions that seem irrelevant and intrusive and impolite."

He chuckled with resigned amusement. "I'm a physician. I ask people about how they're peeing and pooping. I ask women what their period's like and men how their sexual functions are working. And Tommy—in the last three weeks, I'm sure he's heard it all. After last night, he'll be willing to answer you."

"I wasn't thinking only of Tommy."

He waited for her explanation, but she wasn't ready to articulate it. There was too much to explain: That every human experience, normal or paranormal, took place in a larger context. That to understand Tommy she had to know the situation here—all the layers, the reasons for the doubleness she'd felt ever since she'd arrived. That there had to be a reason why he started experiencing the possession only since he'd arrived at Oak Springs School, not at his prior school or his home, and that maybe one of the reasons the hospital doctors had never witnessed his symptoms was that the entity was spatially anchored in this anonymous patch of desert. Or limited to manifestation within the constellation of personalities, the interpersonal dynamics, surrounding Tommy at the school.

As she hesitated, trying to find the right starting place, Joseph slowed the truck and swerved to the side of the road. They were approaching a trio of people standing on the shoulder, a young Navajo couple and a little girl of about four. All three wore jeans and quilted nylon jackets of different colors; the man stood with one hand up and displaying something green, while the woman sat on a pair of large, narrow plywood boxes, clasping the little girl on her lap. When Joseph stopped the truck, the man came around to the driver's window. They exchanged a few words in what Cree assumed was Navajo—clearly a tone language like Chinese but with odd glottal stops and an underlying warm buzz like a hive of honeybees. The man put his hand through the window and Cree saw he held a one-dollar bill, which Joseph waved away with a smile. In another moment, the little family had loaded the boxes and had climbed into the bed of the truck beside them. When they were settled, the man knocked on the window and Joseph started off. The woman smiled as the wind came around her and lifted her thick ponytail.

"On their way to the Chihootsoo market in Window Rock," Joseph explained. "Going to sell their jewelry to tourists. Truck wouldn't start today."

In the side mirror, Cree could see the little girl, sticking her hands out to play with the wind. The mother's face was bright with cold as she held her daughter against her body. Her husband lit a cigarette with difficulty, put his lighter away, and slouched down with his cowboy boots up on the boxes.

"What can you tell me about Tommy? Not medically—his family history?"

Joseph's brow rippled as he deliberated. "He comes from a rural area north of here. He's always lived way out in the sticks. His family still lives partly by herding, so he grew up with sheep, goats, horses. His parents died about six years ago—as he said, a car crash while his father was drunk. So he's been living with his grandparents. He's always been in boarding schools because busing him every day would be impossible for the public schools—his home's too far out and the roads are too bad. It's not unusual on the rez. I went to boarding school—when I was his age, most kids did. Nowadays the roads are better, more people live in towns, so most kids go to public schools."

"How did he happen to come to Oak Springs?"

"Julieta has a recruiter who goes to the other schools and asks about kids with special talents and needy circumstances. Julieta's a good fund-raiser, so she's got scholarships to offer. The recruiter talked to him and his grandparents and they put together a deal with the state."

"You've known her for a long time, haven't you?"

"Yes," he answered. It was clear Cree's change of tack had caught him by surprise.

"From before she started the school?"

"Does it matter?"

"I wondered if you knew her well enough to tell me why Tommy is so important to her."

Joseph's face remained impassive, but Cree got the sense she'd offended him. Behind them, the little girl was laughing as she found wisps of straw in the truck bed and let them go into the slipstream. One arm around the girl's waist, the mother used her other hand to rummage for something in her shoulder bag. The father looked asleep, battened down against the wind.

After a time, Joseph said, "Ask Julieta about Julieta."

His answer was not a dodge but a correct and courteous response, Cree realized. He was telling her that it was Julieta's decision how much to tell Cree, not his. And at least he didn't try to hide behind the "good educator" excuse. Cree was tempted to inquire if he'd answer questions about Joseph Tsosie but decided not to push her luck.

"So, based on your contact with him, can you tell me what kind of person Tommy is? I mean . . . what does he want? What does he like? What does he want to be when he grows up?"

"If I'd seen Tommy outside of the current situation, I'd describe him as a pretty normal Navajo kid from the rez in 2002. Aside from his high IQ—emotionally, I mean."

"Which means—?"

"Which means he's not sure who he is or what he really wants. All these kids, they watch TV and go to the movies, they walk around with their headsets on, listening to CDs. They think they want to be 'normal' Americans. Which means white. They don't know what it means to be Diné."

"So . . . what *does* it mean to be Diné?"

Joseph grunted softly. "To a lot of them, it means being a loser. Being a drunk. Being a hick with sheep shit on his boots and no future. If they hear any history at all, it sounds like a lot of superstition and whining and a bunch of illogical prohibitions and taboos."

He seemed to reconsider as he slowed the truck for a little flock of sheep that milled across the road ahead. Once the stragglers had made it safely onto the shoulder, he frowned and shook his head. "No, I take it back, Tommy's not typical. The typical kid comes from a government housing complex in a town and goes to public school—starts closer to the middle, the place where Navajo and white America are already mixing. Tommy comes from the extremes. He's gone to modern boarding schools, but he was raised in a traditional home. He's helped take care of his family's sheep, listened to his grandfather tell the old stories, lived without electricity or running water when he was little. So he knows more about the old way of life than the typical kid. Which is probably why he's trying so hard to get away from all that, dissociate himself from it."

"Most kids go through identity confusions at his age," Cree suggested.

"For Tommy it's worse. His parents are dead. He's got an exceptionally hungry mind. Look at his artwork and you can tell he needs to know where he comes from, how life works, what really matters. He can't get answers from his parents, and he resents them as much as he loves them. Same as with his Navajo heritage."

Cree thought back to the rap T-shirt, the close-shaved head. The pain behind her eyes was mounting, but even through the red throb she sensed from Joseph's intensity that she had touched upon something huge and troubling. Tommy wasn't the only one with a dissonant sense of his heritage; Joseph, for all his accomplishment and self-possession, was divided, too. Big forces came together here. What she felt was a tiny part of the great historical collision between Native American and European culture. Clearly that crash, though four hundred years old, was reverberating still in Dr. Joseph Tsosie. And in Tommy Keeday.

The thought sobered her, and she was suddenly aware of how little knowledge she brought to any aspect of this problem. She felt like asking what being Diné meant to Joseph Tsosie. Then, humbled, realized she lacked the insight to probe him any further.

They drove into the strip in Window Rock and dropped off their passengers at the parking lot where dozens of people had set up booths and racks to sell their wares. Continuing north on 12, they passed more of the lovely stone forms Cree had admired on her way in, and then veered away into open land again. They passed a cemetery with American flags flying on almost every grave—the Navajo Veterans Cemetery, according to a flaking sign. The graves were knee-high mounds of rock rubble, topped by festoons of plastic flowers, colorful trinkets, flags, and the standard government-issue white tab of a vet's headstone. Beyond the barbed-wire fence that marked the cemetery's formal confines, a bulldozer had pushed aside the brush, cutting a narrow red-dirt slash that was entirely filled by a single long row of graves, bright and forlorn as an abandoned circus.

As if the cemetery reminded him of something he'd been wanting to say, Joseph cleared his throat deliberately. "I want to be very clear about Tommy's status. I've generally agreed with Julieta that the IHS or state mental health systems may not know what to do with him, so I've been willing to take some risk and let him come back to the school. But I'm not as pessimistic about the system as Julieta is, and as his primary physician, I have to see he receives appropriate care. Which means one more crisis and he's got to go back to the hospital. I gave instructions to Lynn Pierce to that effect. She doesn't call me first. She calls an ambulance."

"And what happens to him then?"

"It's up to his grandparents. Personally, I'd recommend long-term treatment somewhere." He paused, then articulated his point: "You may or may not have access to him. The hospital probably won't let you treat him in any way. The grandparents, it's hard to say, but I'd guess not."

Cree thought about it, feeling headachy and overwhelmed. She agreed with Joseph, but she was also sure that no conventional methods would remove the invader from Tommy. If she and Edgar couldn't have access to him, he might never be freed of the thing. The whole situation put even more pressure on her investigation.

"Thank you for being candid with me, Joseph," she said at last.

He nodded, and they didn't say any more as he drove into Fort Defiance and pulled up in a new-looking hospital complex. There were trees here, Cree saw, and beyond the hospital grounds residential streets with actual green lawns and paved sidewalks. Joseph shut off the truck, and before Cree could gather her bag he'd come around to open her door. She let him help her down.

"We'll get you to the ER. I'll leave you there, but I'll check in later to make sure you're okay. Ask for Dr. Bannock, he should be on today. If you're released, you can rest up here until I can drive you back tonight. Or Julieta can come up and get you." He looked at her for her response, steady brown eyes, and she nodded.

Joseph had slept for at most three hours, and he was about to begin a long day of caring for others. Yet he looked fit for it, weary but capable and in command of himself.

Abruptly she knew why Lynn Pierce and Julieta took such comfort from him. She felt an almost overpowering desire to tell him how much she appreciated his help, his innate courtesy and restraint, his calm, his concern for Julieta and Tommy. But she didn't know him well enough to tell him. It would only embarrass him and possibly offend him.

Instead, she raised one hand and lightly took his arm. If he sensed any intent besides an unsteady woman's need for assistance, he didn't show it. They went up the sidewalk like that, and Cree saw their reflections in the hospital's big glass doors: one beat-up-looking Anglo parapsychologist looking very much out of her depth, shyly holding the arm of a tired but trim Navajo doctor who wore a bemused expression as he thought ahead to his day's rounds.

14

CREE MADE it back to Oak Springs at one o'clock, getting a ride with a grocery supplier who was bringing a load of mutton and eggs to the school's kitchen. Expecting the delivery, Julieta had called the company and arranged for her to be picked up, apparently a fairly common ride-sharing procedure. The Navajo man who drove the refrigerated box truck was plump and talkative and a big baseball fan who probed Cree for everything she knew about the Seattle Mariners. She was surprised at how much she did know and began to suspect she'd inherited Pop's baseball gene after all. They parted as good friends at the cafeteria building's service entrance.

Cree cut over to the central drive, the pain in her head a fading memory. X-rays had shown no skull fracture, and Dr. Bannock had concluded that it was safe to take painkillers. It felt good to move, to be outside. The air was dry and comfortably warm, just right. In the bright daylight, the school had a different aspect: isolated, but very much full of the fizz of bright energy Cree associated with young people. Like batteries, these buildings had been daily charged with their chatter, earnest effort, laughter, flirtation, passing hurts and worries, frustration, homesickness, and discovery. A rainbow mix.

Just east of the athletic field, the mesa presented a palisade of cliffs and fallen rock rubble. In the bright sun, it looked merely melancholy and anonymous, not threatening. None of the formations resembled faces in the slightest; the nightmare she'd had last night receded, and the pall of menace dissipated. In fact, the endless rolling desert all around seemed to invite her, to encourage big physical gestures, and she wished she could go running. A long one, out and out until she was alone in the circle of horizon.

Maybe tomorrow, she decided, when her bruised braincase had regrouped.

Where to start? She needed to call Edgar and Joyce, get Joyce going on some research before she came, suggest some ideas about diagnostic technology to Ed. And she should call Paul, too, just to check in. But most important, she needed to spend time with Tommy, feel him out when her head wasn't killing her. She should see his living space, too, look at his drawings or notebooks, his school essays, the things he'd brought from home, whatever he surrounded himself with. Somehow begin to answer the question, *Who is Tommy Keeday?*

She came around the corner of the gym building to see Tommy and several others taking turns batting a softball on the baseball diamond. Lynn Pierce sat on a bench to the left of home plate, watching. Cree assessed the state of her skull and decided that opportunity took precedence over discomfort.

Play stopped when she ambled over to the batter's cage, the weekend staffers and Tommy looking at her in perplexity. *"Yá'át'ééh!"* she called. The truck driver had coached her on how to pronounce the Navajo hello, and it seemed to melt the ice. "Can I join you? Looks like you need a catcher."

In the role of pitcher now, Tommy looked dubious, but he said some few words of introduction in Navajo that made the others smile and relax. Cree took it as a welcome. She dropped her purse on the bench, rummaged in the equipment bag there, and came up with a glove that would do. Lynn caught her eye with a bronze-flecked glance.

The rules were like pickup goofing anywhere, she quickly determined, just like the neighborhood "games" she sometimes joined with Zoe and Hy and friends. Not enough people to have a real game, so you took turns batting and enduring the insults of the others until general consensus determined you'd embarrassed yourself enough and it was someone else's turn. Scattered rather randomly on the bare-dirt diamond, the fielders tossed each hit around before bouncing the ball back to the pitcher.

Besides Tommy, the other players were three men and one woman, and a pair of young teenagers, a boy and a girl. From behind the fence, Lynn explained that they were all staff; the teenagers were children of one of the men, visiting for the weekend.

"What did Tommy say when I came?" Cree asked quietly.

"He introduced you as a friend of mine and Julieta's. Very politely, I might add."

The batter who had just come up was a short, muscular man in his early thirties, dressed in the school's kitchen uniform of blue slacks and smock. He was wearing Nike running shoes, but he took up the aluminum bat and tapped the edges of his soles meaningfully, as if clearing his cleats. The fielders laughed, pretended to be fearful, and began yammering about long-ball hitters. That quickly evolved into suggestive puns about long balls and long bats until the teenage girl, scandalized, laughed and shushed them.

"It's better to have a catcher," the batter said over his shoulder. "Otherwise the batter chases it every time, you fall asleep out there, waiting. What happened to your head?"

Cree touched the butterfly bandage above her right eyebrow, grimaced, and told him, "A stupid accident with Ms. McCarty's horses."

He relayed the news to the others in Navajo, and they nodded commiseratingly.

Standing behind the plate, she savored the feel of the group. They had folded around her quickly, perfectly content to have this stranger among them as long as she was willing to play. Aside from the thump inside her head, it was very pleasant: the sun warm on her cheek, the air clean and sweet-spicy, the sky a vast dome of blue that set off the rust hues of the mesa.

Even Tommy looked okay. She watched him as he caught the ball and briefly inspected it. He appeared to have a problem with a muscle cramp in his left calf, and he looked less than pleased to have her butting in, but otherwise, outwardly, he seemed like a pretty normal kid, playing some softball.

Tight-lipped, Tommy pitched, the batter swung and missed; Cree nailed it in her glove and flipped it back to Tommy as the fielders jeered the batter. As if to set them straight, he knocked the next pitch over their heads. It landed with a puff of dust well out in the desert, where the lonesome-looking outfielders had to chase it.

"Not too bad," Tommy called. "For an old man."

The batter watched with satisfaction as they retrieved the ball and tossed it around. "What's your name?" he asked over his shoulder.

"Cree."

He grinned back at her. "You don't look Indian."

"It's not after the tribe. Just a nickname."

He nodded and turned back to the field, then freed a hand from the bat to mime shaking hands in the air. "Ben," he told her.

He hit another two dozen balls and then it was Tommy's turn at bat. Coming in from the mound, the boy seemed to approach Cree warily. He traded his glove for Ben's bat and scowled as he took a practice swing off to one side.

"Don't worry," Cree told him quietly. "I won't hassle you. I'm off duty."

He made a small, tight smile. "Like I believe you."

"I never mix business with pleasure, trust me." It was a lie, actually. She wouldn't outwardly probe him, but with him standing only five feet away she found herself extending her senses toward him, straining to feel the thing that must be lurking in him. The best she could do was to note a tiny, ambiguous buzz of dissonance.

"I'm serious," she went on. "I can use some exercise. Outside, sunshine, some air in my lungs—it feels good. Being here is very exciting for me. It's so different where I come from. You're probably used to it, but for me it's beautiful and new."

He nodded as he set his stance, then swung at the first pitch and missed. Ben pitched hard, letting the ball go in a shallow arc after a fast bolo windup. Cree caught it with a smack, looked wide-eyed at her hands and yelled at him as she tossed it back, "Hey, take it easy! Wanna burn a hole in my glove?"

Ben grinned and underhanded another fast one, which Tommy slapped on the ground toward the left. The woman at third base fielded it badly, then made a wild throw to first, laughing at herself and earning the scorn of everyone. As Tommy watched them toss it around he rotated his left ankle, pointed his toe, leaned on it to stretch out the muscle cramp. Cree waited, hands on knees behind him.

Who are you? she asked in her thoughts. *What do you want?*

"Why did you ask me about ghosts last night?" Tommy whispered over his shoulder. "Is that what you do? Something with ghosts?"

He must have been thinking about that comment ever since last night, Cree knew suddenly, and she chided herself for her carelessness—for tossing that provocation at him, failing to realize how closely a very smart boy would inspect what had been said. How much it would frighten a confused kid, no matter how skeptical he claimed to be.

She shook her head. "I'm off duty, remember? I really don't have you under a microscope. We should both just play and relax now. I think we both could use it."

"Is that what you're thinking is the matter with me?" Tommy persisted.

Ben caught the ball again and made an elaborate show of preparing to pitch. Tommy got set and when the ball came he whapped it over the first baseman's head, foul.

"The answer I have is complicated," she told him quietly. "Because I don't think of these things the way other people do. If you want, I'll be happy to explain later, when we have more time."

Tommy turned his back on the chattering fielders as they flipped the ball around. "Does that mean Mrs. McCarty and Dr. Tsosie think it, too?"

"The more important question is, What do *you* think?"

Tommy eyes were wide and desperate. He seemed to struggle with how to answer, and at last whispered hoarsely, "I have to fight it. All the time."

Appalled, Cree realized for the first time the terror that Tommy must be living with, and how bravely he concealed it. Take the fear anyone felt when struck by a severe illness, and compound it a hundred times with the fear of the unknown—the awful, sick sense of strangeness that so often accompanied the paranormal. That metaphysical terror. The fact that he was talking to her now showed how desperate this boy was. She felt her heart leap out toward him, an unbearable desire to comfort and protect.

"You can feel it? Now?" Cree was aware that Lynn Pierce was watching them closely. She wondered how much the nurse could hear.

In a tiny voice, he said, "In my calf. It's like a charley horse. This little ball that tightens up. Like it's trying to make my leg move by itself."

Ben pitched and Tommy swung and missed. Cree returned it and put her hands on her knees to wait for the next pitch. Ben wound up, slung it, Tommy fouled it far away east of first base, toward the mesa.

"What about when it gets bad? Times like last night?"

Tommy's leg was really bothering him now. He laid the bat down so he could use both hands to rub the calf fiercely. Cree caught only the briefest of glimpses when his pants leg hitched, but she was shocked at the striating bands and mounds moving under his smooth skin. He kept his face half turned to the field, barely moved his lips as if to conceal his urgency from the others: "I can't remember."

"Is it always the same?"

The bent head gave a shake. "Sometimes it's different. Sometimes it's fast, it just *snaps,* it catches you off guard. But the way it was last night, when it's coming it's like . . . when you're going to throw up. You try not to think about it, try not to let it get worse, but it keeps coming and coming until you can't help it."

"Oh, man, Tommy. That must be so hard!" Cree said. Tommy's brown eyes reconnoitered hers and seemed relieved not to find condescension there. Still, craning her senses toward him she felt nothing but that queer sizzle that could be a foreign presence or, she had to admit, the mind of a troubled teen with a psychological problem—some unconscious need so desperate that it had to seek this drastic, exotic form of expression. Her spine tingled at the thought: That was terrifying, too. She had to quell the urge to go to him, hold him, stroke away the tension in his face.

"Hey, batter!" Ben yelled. "Incoming!"

Tommy picked up the bat. He took a pitch, waited for the next, swung and missed. Ben kept at him until he swatted one into the outfield. They didn't talk for a time as he hit a few more. Each metallic *pank!* of the aluminum bat rang painfully in Cree's head.

"So what do you think is the best thing to do for it?" she whispered. "What would be the best thing for you?"

"Just to die. Not to feel that ever again."

"No! Not a good solution. Let's work on a better one, huh?"

He shook his head as he turned mostly toward her. "You don't get it. You don't know."

"I know I don't! That's why I need you to tell me!"

His eyes flicked at her, glistening with an animal quality. "One time our sheep had this thing. There'd been a big hatch of this kind of fly . . . You couldn't see it until after shearing, but then you could see these . . . lumps.

On their backs, their stomachs? The lumps moved by themselves. Kind of . . . pulsing. It was the worms, the maggots, under the skin. Eating the sheep alive."

The image stunned and sickened Cree: the parasite inside, remorseless, growing, consuming its living host. Tommy's alert eyes reacted to her inability to respond, and she felt she'd failed him.

"Okay, Tommy," Ben called. His voice startled them both. For the last few moments, a suffocating, fearful intimacy had wrapped around them, isolating the two of them, closing them off from the big sky and brisk air and the warm camaraderie of the other players. "A few more and it's Judy's turn. Stop flirting with the cute *bilagáana* and let's go. She's too old for you, yeah?"

The others laughed shyly, watching to see how Cree took it. She made a smile that she knew looked forced. But Tommy managed some comeback in Navajo that got them all laughing again. On the next pitch, he connected hard and sent a level drive straight back at the pitcher's mound. Ben ducked under the ball as it hummed low up the middle and over second base. The fielders whistled appreciatively and then berated Ben for his arrogance and cowardice and general lifestyle: "Duck and cover, huh, Ben?" " 'Stop, drop, and roll,' man!" "Hey, no—for Ben, more like 'sex, drugs, and rock and roll.' "

Tommy put down the bat as the woman at third base began to come in. He jogged out into the field with only a slight hitch in his leg.

"What does *bilagáana* mean?" Cree called back to Lynn Pierce.

"White person."

"So what was that Tommy said to them?"

Lynn was looking after him with a proprietary pride. "He said something like, 'Yeah, I'm too young and you're too ugly.' And then a pun that doesn't translate perfectly—it's better in Navajo. Ben was making an indirect pass at you and Tommy was telling him to mind his manners." She turned to Cree with a prim, apologetic smile. "Make any progress, Doctor? I was . . . kind of listening."

"I don't know," Cree told her. "I really don't know."

15

"CREE!"

She was walking back toward the infirmary, determined to lie down, when the voice startled her out of her thoughts. She looked back to see Julieta, striding toward her from the administration building. She walked quickly and wore a frown full of the angry determination of a prize-fighter coming out of his corner. "How's your head?"

Cree put her hand to her bandaged forehead. "I'm fine. Going to be headachy for a few days, that's all. What's going on?"

"I know who the ghost is."

Cree's jaw dropped: This was quite a shift for a woman who'd expressed so many reservations not so long ago. "Um, that's terrific. Who?"

Julieta hesitated, making some decision as she looked at Cree through narrowed eyes. "Are you up for riding? I'll show you."

Cree assessed her weariness, measured the gas in the tank and found maybe just enough. "Sure," she said.

They saddled the two mares. Cree found she remembered most of the ritual of blanket and saddle, bridle and bit and stirrups; Julieta checked her work and needed only to draw Breeze's belly cinch tighter. The black gelding looked on curiously as they led the mares out the rear corral gate and mounted.

Astride her horse, Julieta looked ravishing. Her black hair floated around her head and over her shoulders as she sat straight and proud. Once they were on their way, she pulled back the thick mane and put on a cowboy hat that held it behind her, then slipped on a pair of sunglasses. In the shades and hat, leather jacket and snug jeans, she looked gorgeous and dangerous, a woman warrior.

Julieta said nothing as she led them straight north at a trot. Cree posted adequately, rediscovering more of her rusty riding skills by the minute. It helped that Breeze was a gentle horse and seemed to want to go today. The rhythm of the trot echoed in Cree's sore head, but the pain was manageable. Especially with her curiosity piqued. She wished Julieta would slow down and explain what this was all about.

And the land was beautiful. Here was the big gesture she'd hungered for since coming to this place, a way of taking in the landscape. Sky. Earth. Rocks. Distance. The wordless company of the willing animal between her knees. Cree savored the air, clean but faintly spiced with a perfume that the grocery truck driver had told her was piñon-wood smoke. The only sound was the drum of hoofs, the creak of leather, the *whuff* of Breeze's breathing.

They put a couple of miles behind them before Julieta slowed and allowed Cree to fall into a walk beside her.

The iridescent green sunglasses turned toward her. Beneath the glistening ovals, Julieta's mouth was a thin, straight line. "It's Garrett McCarty. My ex. He was always a complete and total bastard and I guess he still is." The sunglasses turned back to the north without waiting for a response.

Cree felt a sudden trepidation. Old animosities could cloud a witness's perspective on a haunting, and she had learned to be wary of making assumptions based on them. Especially if it involved an ex-husband or -wife or -lover. Yes, there was always a lot left unresolved between people who had once been deeply intimate and then had broken away, and of course a revenant often *did* prove to be an ex, driven to settle the accounts of love or hate. But just as often the kind of dead-certain identification she saw in Julieta now was merely the product of lingering hostility and paranoia in the living person.

"Why do you say that?"

"Because he died not far from here. I told you about that, didn't I?"

"Up at the mine area?"

Julieta nodded.

"That's, what, fifteen miles or so from the school?"

"As the crow flies, more like ten. Why? Is that too far for a ghost to come?"

A memory flashed in front of Cree's eyes, real enough to touch: Mike, standing there in downtown Philadelphia at the moment of his death in Los Angeles. "No," she said sadly. "Not necessarily. But why—"

"Why would Garrett come back? To hurt me."

"But—"

"He hated me because I divorced him and because I came out better in the settlement terms and because I won a couple of fights with McCarty Energy over the years. Maybe because I had the gall to have a couple of relationships over the years, didn't live like a *nun* after divorcing the great man. I think he also suspected I had a lover while we were still married, or at least before the divorce was final."

"Did you?"

Julieta's jaw dropped at Cree's presumption and she appeared to catch herself on the edge of an indignant denial. She took a deep breath and then her shoulders slumped. "Yes," she said quietly. But then the resistance flared again: "Yes! I had a lover, okay? I was twenty-four and I was married to an old man who I never saw and who was screwing every secretary in his employ and every female social climber in New Mexico! I had a lover. But Garrett never knew about it. I made damn sure he never knew, because I wasn't going to let him use it against me in the divorce. It was perfectly all right for him to chase tail, but for *me* to actually *love* somebody for the first and only time in my life, that would have been unforgivable!"

It was so clearly a defensive outpouring, and for Cree a little piece of the puzzle fell into place: Julieta's hard side, this angry warrior woman and the efficient administrator who explained her every action so logically and dispassionately—it was just the armor over the vulnerable person who lived inside. The woman who had invited her to go for a ride within moments of Cree's arriving yesterday and then concealed the gesture by explaining that the horses needed exercise. The woman who'd so badly needed Joseph Tsosie's brief touch last night.

Julieta clucked to Madie, slapped the reins, and began to canter ahead as if fleeing her own words. Cree touched her heels to Breeze's flanks, urging her to follow, and soon they were pummeling full tilt over the rolling land. The canter was less jolting than the trot, the air seemed to flow through Cree's head and wash away the pain. The bare ground and low sagebrush rolled away beneath the lunging horse, unchanging.

When Julieta finally slowed again, Cree caught up and they walked again as the horses blew. *So many questions,* Cree was thinking. *Where to even start?*

"But, Julieta—why would he come into one of your students as a way to punish *you?*"

"Because it's a great way to bring the school down. He knew it was the one thing I loved, the one thing I believed in doing on my own. Trust me, Garrett was very smart, very insightful when it came to figuring out somebody's weaknesses. He built an empire on knowing the best way to hurt somebody."

Cree wanted to point out that ghosts were seldom so intentional and devious. Usually their motives, if you could call so elemental an urge a motive, were more like compulsions, just reflexes of their psyches. But there were more pressing issues to get out of the way.

"Why would it settle in Tommy Keeday? Instead any of the other kids?"

"I don't know!" Even behind the camouflage of the sunglasses, Julieta's face looked agonized. "How could I possibly know?"

"Does Tommy have any characteristics that would make him particularly vulnerable? Joseph describes him as a boy with a lot of internal conflicts—"

"Look, before all this, I'd spent maybe four hours with him. Once for his admission interview. A couple of chance encounters around school. He was in the drawing class I teach, along with six other kids, but we had only two classes before all this came up! Beyond that, I don't know anything about him but what I've read in his records."

"Then why do you care so deeply about him?"

"I care about all of my students! Every one of them! He's a very sick and troubled boy! I'd be the same with—"

"Why didn't you ever have children? You want children."

"Why didn't *you?*" Julieta shot back. "We're about the same age."

Cree bobbed her head: Clearly, Julieta would demand reciprocation for everything she revealed. "My husband died unexpectedly before we had kids. We were going to. I'd like to, but I've never . . . I've never found the right man. Sometimes it makes me feel very sad, very incomplete. No—it just about kills me, Julieta. I'm thirty-nine and probably I'll never have a child. But I'm lucky to have two beautiful nieces who I'm very close to. Kind of their half-mom."

"So I'm half mom to my students." Julieta tipped her hat brim lower over her face.

The horses huffed and shied. As they craned their heads, Cree saw the object of their concern: a dead coyote, fifty feet ahead, stretched along the ground as if it had died running. Its gray fur was matted, and something had been nibbling it, leaving the eye sockets round black pits on its narrow skull. The belly had been eaten away, too, leaving a dark cavity and baring a length of dirty white spine. She caught the smell as they let the horses find a wide route around it. The sight struck Cree as sorrowful, a dark omen.

She waited until they were well past before continuing what increasingly felt like an interrogation: "Is that why you started the school? To be near children—to be half mom?"

Julieta had found her armor in the interim. "What does my past have to do with Tommy? Look, I came to you with my best guess as to who this 'entity' is. I've come a long way, haven't I? Aren't I doing a good job of embracing your worldview? Why don't you go do whatever it is you do to find out if it's the rotten awful ghost of Garrett and then . . . exorcise it or kill it or whatever's supposed to happen?"

"If it *is* Garrett's ghost, I need you to help me figure Garrett out. Tell me why his compulsion to hurt you would be so strong. That it would manifest as an urge to vengeance so enduring it would continue even in the absence of his body, so deliberate it could do anything as complex and devious as this."

Julieta's face was set as if indicating that she'd said as much as she'd intended to.

Frustrated, Cree briefly let go the reins, threw her shoulders back, and brushed her hair away from her face with both hands. The bandage above her brow pinched.

They rode on at a walk for another ten minutes in silence. Julieta showed no indication she was going to say any more.

"Whatever it is," Cree said at last, "if it's the ghost of Garrett or someone else, I don't kill it. I wouldn't know how to do that."

"Then what do you do?" Julieta said numbly.

"I figure out a way for it to come to terms with why it's there. And if you have any role in why it's there, I can only do that if you do the same—come to terms with why it's there. If you're part of its world or play a role in its compulsions, you're the one who has to let it free."

"If it's Garrett, I'd rather kill it."

Cree shook her head. "Can't. It's already dead. You've got to integrate it in some constructive way. Release it by somehow dealing with its impulse."

Julieta brought Madie's head up and angled her path toward the left, up a low rise. Ahead, Cree saw the tip of a huge derrick like the one she'd seen from the highway.

"I'd rather kill it," Julieta repeated quietly to herself.

16

THEY DISMOUNTED on a hilltop a hundred yards back from the edge of a cliff that marked a natural fold in the land. The broad, shallow valley ran several miles to the east and west and was full of activity: swirling dust, vehicles, and, tiny as ants next to the equipment, men. Mounds of mineral stuff lay heaped randomly, roads winding between them. Broad ramps led out of coal trenches and up both sides of the valley, giant trucks inching up or down. About a mile to their left, Cree saw a colossal orange cube surmounted by a towering crane like the one she'd seen from the highway, rotating as it dragged soil and rock in a bucket the size of a house. Closer, along the near side of the valley, a complex of yellow steel buildings stood surrounded by parking lots full of cars and pickup trucks. A rumble of engines filled the air, and diesel exhaust smothered the sweet scent of the desert.

Julieta took off her sunglasses, squinting against the glare and the distance. She pointed to a little sports car, incongruous among the pickups. "Proof positive our industrious Donny is on the job today."

"He won't mind you being here? If you're such enemies—"

"I called him earlier. He gave me permission to trespass. We occasionally trade such little courtesies as part of our arbitrated right-of-way settlement. Not that I don't ride on McCarty property all the time anyway—this isn't their only mine site, Donny's here only on Saturdays. And nobody else would give a damn."

"Why did we come here today, Julieta? I don't need to see this. I need to hear your story."

"You want to see where Garrett died, don't you? The dragline—that's the huge derrick thing—has moved since then. I wanted to show you where it was when he died, so if the ghost had, whatever you call it,

117

perimortem memories, you'd know where the accident happened. I don't know how this works—would its memories kind of cling to the dragline, or to the place where the dragline was? He fell off it when it was over there"—she gestured with her sunglasses to the east—"about where that spit of land sticks out above the valley. You can't see it from here, but there's a used-up pit there. The whole operation was—"

"Julieta. I've done the math, okay?"

"What math?" Julieta started to replace her sunglasses, but Cree caught her arm and held her gaze. Beautiful astonishing dark blue eyes, suddenly frightened.

"Tommy's age, your divorce. He's your child, isn't he? That's where we should begin."

Julieta's expression changed suddenly. It was the face of a person receiving an arrow—one that had been expected. Feeling it pierce deep, painful yet familiar from years of anticipating and imagining its stab. She dropped her sunglasses and shook Cree's hand away as she stepped clumsily back to sit on a slab of sandstone.

Cree took Madie's reins and tied both horses to a piñon tree before retrieving the glasses and sitting next to Julieta. Below, the mine ground away at its business. A solitary crow, flying above them out over the rim, seemed to change its mind when it saw the operation and veered away to the east.

"Is this how it's supposed to be?" Julieta said quietly. "The way you . . . do what you do?"

Cree was anything but certain, but some reassurance was called for. She arched her shoulders, took a deep breath, and swept her hair back with both hands. "There are a lot of aspects to it. But right now, yes, this is what we should do."

"Why do you do that?"

"Do—?"

"You're talking like me. You're acting like me. That gesture." Julieta took off her hat, shook her hair free, and then repeated Cree's movements. Only then did Cree realize she'd been doing it.

"I'm sorry. It's . . . unconscious." Cree nodded and tried to smile.

"It's what I do when I'm frustrated," Julieta went on. "Or getting down to business. To something that's hard but that has to be done."

"This is definitely one of those."

Julieta looked out over the mine. "I'm not the confiding type. I'm not the confessing type. I've never been to a priest or a psychoanalyst in my life, and I have no desire to."

"I'm not your psychoanalyst."

"What are you, then?"

Cree didn't know the name for it. *Think of me as your mirror. Your echo.* No, too solitary. *Your sister. Your friend.* Too presumptuous.

"I'm someone kind of like you," she said at last. "Different enough from other people that I don't often trust them to understand me. And not the confessing type."

Maybe that helped a little. Julieta nodded. Still, it took her a long time to begin.

She married Garrett in 1982, full of optimism. Twenty years old. She dropped out of the university to devote herself to her exciting new life. Oh, she had doubts—it had all happened so fast. Sometimes she wondered if what she felt was love; more often she wondered if he really loved her, if there was anything in it for him besides her looks and sex and having a young thing on his arm to impress his fellow rich codgers. For a while the answer she gave herself was that, if that were all he'd wanted, he could have had it with lots of women without bothering to marry. There were moments when he seemed to show real tenderness and appreciation. And she wasn't just some young thing, she reminded herself, she was the smart, presentable, well-mannered daughter of a good family.

Anyway, she swore, if she wasn't good enough, she'd work twice as hard to become good enough.

She got part of the answer within the first year. Patrick Kelly sold his new son-in-law his struggling heavy-equipment business, handing over several lots full of earth-moving machinery at fire sale prices. Julieta never knew exactly what the arrangement was, but it involved keeping the name Kelly Equipment and retaining her father as its boss. The deal was a rescue from likely bankruptcy, and anyway, as Garrett reminded them, it was all in the family now.

Within six months of their wedding, pressing duties obligated Garrett to spend most of his time at their house in Albuquerque, leaving Julieta alone at the Oak Springs house. Occasionally they did things together, but always in public settings—corporate events, charity balls, or political fund-raisers where Garrett needed a well-mannered beauty on his arm and where there was no chance to talk about their relationship.

At first, it really wasn't too bad. True, she was often lonely; her main company consisted of the servants and groundskeepers who maintained what was then a handsome ranch estate. But living mostly apart, that was only temporary, Julieta told herself. She loved the house and the land. She'd always wanted horses, and now she had four of them; she rode every day. She kept busy, volunteering at the Gallup hospital where she first met Joseph Tsosie. Garrett was kind, in his way, and she wanted to be a good wife; she was willing to wait for this period of preoccupation with business to end so they could talk about their marriage, their plans, the prospect of having kids.

Anyway, she told herself, this was probably the way love worked, especially if you were married to such an important, busy man. Her parents were certainly no kind of example to follow.

Somewhere in that first year, though, a number of troubling things happened. Coal prices were depressed, and in a cost-saving move McCarty Energy consolidated management; Kelly Equipment got swallowed whole by the bigger company. When the dust settled, the result of the deal was that Garrett had made off with Kelly's equipment inventory and accounts receivable, netting about ten million dollars, and Kelly had ceased to exist.

But it was still all in the family, Julieta assured herself. It wasn't Garrett's fault; Kelly had been floundering for years. And Daddy still had a terrific job. Sure, he had less authority, but frankly he was probably in a niche better suited to his talents.

It was about then that she began noticing the amused or averted eyes of some of their acquaintances in Albuquerque. One of them, an older woman Julieta thought she knew well enough to confide in, took her aside at some function. She was an energy exec's wife, too, a slim, hard, fifty-year-old with a high silicone chest and a taut-skinned face that had been maintained with ruthless discipline, and she explained that this was how it worked. They like us younger, she said, because it makes them feel more virile around their buddies and competitors. But they're busy. They can't drag us along everywhere. They like having company where they are, but they don't need to be held down by their wives, even much younger ones. And we don't really want to do everything with them, all those boring meetings and golf and the backroom deal making and all, do we? We don't really want to know everything. Give it a few years. You get used to it.

Used to it, Julieta mumbled. To what?

Honey baby, this is not some kind of a secret, is it? You were a beauty queen, weren't you? That means you're a practical girl. You figured out what counts, and you did *very* well for yourself. All you have to do is keep being practical.

What isn't a secret?

You're his *wife,* the older woman reminded her reassuringly. But then her kindness took on a cruel, satisfied edge as she swigged some more scotch and went on: Really, none of us ever thought Garrett would marry again, not with his tastes. So you did very well. The others don't matter. They appear for a few weeks or months, they get a sports car or a diamond bracelet, and they go away. Trust me. I've been married to Elliot for twenty-six years. Now he's a doddering old fart, too old to get up to much mischief, and I'm the one who gets to have the fun. But if I'd raised a fuss about it back whenever, it wouldn't have lasted this long. I wouldn't be where I am now. But I was like you. Smart. Practical.

It turned out that Garrett's affairs were no big secret or even much of a scandal. In his social circle, it was something of a gentleman's hobby. One of the things they acquired and compared notes on. Almost a little competition, like their golf.

It devastated Julieta. For the first time, she realized that this was not and never would be the true love she yearned for. Garrett had shrewdly folded together several objectives by marrying her: He'd attained both a presentable trophy wife, naïve and isolated enough to be conveniently set aside when not needed, and, as a little sweetener, the easy conquest of Kelly Equipment. But the things she wanted—a relationship and a family—weren't part of anybody's plans.

She was afraid to do anything about it. She couldn't bring it up with Garrett: She knew that the older woman was right, he'd shed her completely if she made it an issue. And she couldn't admit to her parents that there was a problem. They'd only blame *her.* Now she saw, too, that her father's job depended on her staying married to Garrett. Dad had ended up losing money on the deal with McCarty Energy; her parents needed his salary.

She spent a year or so trying to think it through. When she was with Garrett, she tried hard to be a better companion and wife, beautiful and spirited and devoted, hoping to win his full attention; but she began to feel increasingly used and soiled after his rare visits to the house. She made excuses to stop going to those excruciating social events. She rode her horses hard, every day. She volunteered at the Indian Hospital. Without any real friends from high school or UNM, unable to talk to her parents about her situation, she remained a virtual exile at the house.

Julieta had taken off her hat and was sitting cross-legged on the slab of sandstone, elbows on knees, shoulders slumped. Staring at the ground, hair veiling her face, she looked like a teenager, angry at herself but abject and so much softer now.

Given what Julieta was revealing, Cree thought, and the intensity of the feelings involved, the idea of Garrett McCarty's perseverating after death was well worth exploring. She stared speculatively at the mammoth dragline as Julieta continued.

"I was too young to know what to do. I really didn't have enough perspective to decide if this whole arrangement was maybe sort of okay or completely wrong and horrible. And I didn't have anyone to talk to about it. Well, except Joseph . . . we got together once in a while, and I felt safe confiding in him."

"What was his take on your situation?"

"He very tactfully always told me the same thing—I should think better of myself, I should follow my heart and not let anyone treat me like that. But he never forced his opinion on me." The memory brought a wan smile to her lips, and the glance she gave Cree was quick and shy. "His response was very 'Navajo'—restrained and patient. Our conversations always included a lot of silence. He was my first Navajo friend." The smile widened, then suddenly faltered and faded as some other memory intruded.

When she went on, she seemed to hurry, as if telling it before she could change her mind: "So this had been going on for two years and I was pretty much a wreck. And then one day I rode out to the foot of the mesa and was sitting on a boulder staring back at the house when I saw another rider coming. He was riding like a crazy person, hell-bent for leather, but he wasn't actually *going* anywhere, he was just . . . it's hard to describe . . . *riding. Playing.* He went back and forth, around in circles, the way the swallows fly at sunset, just . . . swooping and spiraling for the fun of it."

The rider was a young man, dressed in denim work clothes with his shirt unbuttoned and flapping behind him, hair long, chest bare and belly tucked lean below the chiseled lines of his ribs. He'd ride with his hands up above him, he'd get up on his knees with arms spread wide, staying on the wiry palomino by meshing perfectly with the horse's movements. He'd lie down with his feet over the rump and arms around the lunging neck, he'd jump over brush and boulders. All this was bareback. He was laughing for the sheer pleasure it gave him.

As he circled closer to Julieta, she recognized him: He was one of the estate's grounds crew, a Navajo named Peter Yellowhorse who came three days a week to tend to the gardens and pool and fix things around the house and barns. Back among the boulders, she watched him for about fifteen minutes. He didn't see her until he was about a hundred feet away, and when he did, he just about fell off.

He drew up and stood, both horse and rider breathing hard. Peter's eyes were wide and wary, and Julieta understood: He was afraid he'd get in trouble for goofing around when he was supposed to be at work.

This is my pony, he told her lamely. She ranges pretty far. I saw her out here, so I figured I'd . . .

Julieta knew that the rest of what he'd wanted to say wouldn't make sense: catch her, then ride her like crazy because if she'd wandered here from wherever he lived, it had to be sort of fated. Something that the beautiful day intended.

Julieta played the role of the indulgent boss lady, smiling in a condescending way, riding back to the house with him, letting him feel a bit awkward but also letting him off the hook. She asked him his horse's name and he told her it was Bird, and that seemed just right: a horse that could fly. The whole time, all she wanted to do was say, *Show me how to do that.*

Not the horsemanship, the attitude. The outlook. The freedom.

★   ★   ★

Julieta stopped and turned her head quickly toward the office building half a mile away. A flash of light came and went, sunlight reflected off glass. Cree shielded her eyes and squinted to see a man standing near the Porsche, binoculars trained on them.

"Crap!" Julieta exploded. "That's Donny. I didn't want him to see you here." She looked back at the tiny figure, made a big insincere grin, and waved condescendingly. Donny McCarty watched them for a few seconds longer, then lowered the binocs and headed back inside the building.

"Why?"

"If you need to talk to him, or look at the dragline or whatever, he'll be less inclined to play along if he knows you're associated with me. God damn it!"

"Julieta, please keep going. This is important. You fell in love with Peter Yellowhorse. You had his child. How did it all happen? Did Garrett find out?"

But Donny had come out of the trailer again and this time went toward a green and white company Jeep. He got in, started it with a roar they could hear even this far away, and pulled out quickly. The Jeep headed west, away from them, trailing dust behind it.

"He's headed for one of the ramps on this side," Julieta said. All the hardness had returned. "Brace yourself. We're about to have company. And it's lousy company, let me tell you."

17

THEY'D REMOUNTED the horses by the time the McCarty Energy Jeep nosed its way out of a shallow draw to the west. Julieta had put on her hat and sunglasses again and waited in perfect composure with her hands folded on her saddle horn. She was gorgeous, armored with unapproachable beauty. The horses stamped nervously as the Jeep approached.

When Donny McCarty got out, Cree was surprised at his appearance. Somehow she'd expected a businessman cowboy aristocrat out of a *Dynasty* rerun: sharp suit, bolo tie, cowboy hat and boots, contemptuous sneer. But he was tall, with narrow shoulders and thinning red-blond hair, dressed in pleated khakis, a nylon jacket parted to reveal a polo shirt, lightweight leather hiking shoes. Something about his face reminded her of William Hurt—pale, troubled, the touch of injured sensitivity.

He stood next to the Jeep's open door. "Spying, Julieta? I hope everything meets with your approval." A soft voice with only a hint of the laconic cowboy twang.

"Looks like business as usual, Donny," Julieta said, gazing out over the mine. Then she looked down at him and Cree was startled at the intensity of the antagonism that leaped between them. "Nice of you to come up here to say hello, though."

Donny's eyes glinted at the acid in her tone, but his face remained resigned, almost bored or sad. He stared back at Julieta for a moment and then swiveled his gaze to Cree. "How about you? You're trespassing, you know. Which one are you from? I'll file a complaint after I throw you off my property."

"I—I'm sorry," Cree stuttered. "Which—?"

"He thinks you're from an environmental watchdog group," Julieta explained. "Donny doesn't like scrutiny. He likes to break the law and just gets all bent out of shape when anybody finds out and takes exception to it."

Donny's eyes glittered again, but his face remained controlled. He took out a cell phone, thumbed a button, and put it to his head. He turned to look down at the headquarters building. "Nick? Yeah. Listen, send Buck and Marty and a couple boys up here. We've got some trespassers, I think we'll need to hold them while we wait for the sheriff to come. South rim, just step out and turn around, you'll see me." He snapped the phone shut and put it away.

"Legal nuance, Donny," Julieta said scornfully. "You gave me permission, you didn't specify where, nobody's spying on you. You touch either of us, I'll have you for assault or kidnapping or something problematic for you. And you're always such a loser in court, aren't you."

Donny just made a small, unhappy smile.

"This is a misunderstanding, Mr. McCarty," Cree said. "And it's my doing—I asked Julieta to bring me here today. I was hoping to meet you. I'm sorry I didn't call you myself, but I thought Julieta would have explained everything when she talked to you. I had no idea it would be a problem. I didn't know you two were—"

"Such good friends?" Donny finished. "Well. That does take some getting used to, doesn't it." He checked his watch and glanced down at the parking lot. "And you wanted to meet me because—?"

"I'm not from an environmental organization. This'll sound weird, but I'm a parapsychologist. I study paranormal events. I was in the area to give a lecture at UNM, and I was doing some research out this way when I heard there were some . . . interesting things taking place on McCarty property. I'd hoped—"

"The mutilations? They were nowhere near here. You're about five miles off target, Ms.—?"

"Black. Lucretia Black. Actually—"

"Bunch of bullshit anyway. I've looked at half a dozen mutes over the years, and I can guarantee you it's just scavenger activity. That, or some druggie Navajo trying to play Skinwalker and scare people. Nowadays, every time somebody's cow dies and the critters get at it, it's space aliens. Simple fact is, scavengers go for the easy parts first—eyes, lips, tongue, the organs."

Cree was scrambling to adapt. When Donny had first pulled up, she'd had no idea how to explain her presence in a way that wouldn't imperil future contact. Now this unexpected tangent had provided the way, and she seized it gratefully: "You're probably right. Still, I've never personally seen one, and I'd very much like more information from people who *have*. When I heard there'd been some on your property, too, I asked Julieta to introduce us. I was hoping you and I could schedule a meeting to talk about it."

A couple of men had arrived at the front of the office complex and stood waiting, occasionally looking up toward the rim. Donny watched them thoughtfully for a moment.

"So when I call the university and ask if anyone's ever heard of you—"

"Call Dr. William Zentcy, head of the Psychology Department at the Albuquerque campus." Remembering suddenly, Cree groped in the pockets of her windbreaker and found that, yes, there was a crumpled Psi Research Associates card among the tissues and miscellany there. She fished it out, blew the lint off, and held it out to him. "Here's my business card. You're welcome to visit our Web site, too."

Donny walked over, took it from her, looked at it with minimal interest. From above him, she could see the pink scalp through his sparse, pale hair. Down at the parking lot, another company Jeep pulled in and its driver began conferring with the men who were waiting. Binoculars flashed from the passenger-side window, and Cree caught another glint from something held by one of the standing men. A rifle?

"Seattle? You're a long way from home, Dr. Black." Donny pocketed the card and looked up at Julieta. "So I take it you've found mutes on school property, too?" The thought seemed to give him some wan satisfaction.

"We've had some disturbing activity, yes," Julieta said flatly.

"If I can call you sometime soon," Cree told him, "I'd be very grateful . . ."

Another man joined the group, and the three of them got into the back of the Jeep, which pulled out and headed toward the south rim ramp Donny had used. Outwardly, Julieta maintained her scornful calm, but Cree felt her tension rising.

Donny turned to watch the truck's dust, then gave a resigned sigh and took out his cell phone again.

"Nick? Forget it. I can handle it . . . No, more of a bullshit exercise in community relations. Yeah. I'll see 'em off the property myself. Send the boys back to work. Yeah." He snapped the phone shut. Ignoring Julieta, he took the bridle of Cree's horse and turned her around, facing away from the valley. "We can't have people coming this close to mine operations, Dr. Black. It's not safe—you could take a fall. Might be weeks before anyone found you, and you'd end up looking like one of those mutes. Now it's time for you to leave."

"Is there any chance we can meet? At your convenience—"

He regarded Cree briefly, and she sensed an analytic mind at work behind the weary gray eyes, some calculation of value or opportunity. "We'll see. Possible. Call my secretary." He appeared to give Breeze a shrewd once-over, stroking her cheek and neck and haunches. Then he spat and thrust the horse's head away from him. He started back to the Jeep. "Your horses, Julieta—not the quality you were once used to, are they?"

Julieta's eyes shot daggers. "Screw you, Donny! How dare you!"

He ignored her but paused at the Jeep's door to look at Cree again. "Another piece of advice—don't associate with the wrong people. Get off on the wrong foot around here, people don't forget. Bad reputations kind of rub off on you."

Julieta wheeled Madie around and led the way back toward the open desert, deliberately holding the horse to a slow walk. Cree rode next to her. Donny McCarty trailed a hundred yards behind for several miles, making a point, before finally pulling the Jeep around and speeding away.

18

"'MUTES'?" Cree asked. "I had no idea livestock mutilations were so common they'd earned a vernacular term."

Julieta's jaw had been clenched for the first ten minutes or so, but her rage had gradually given way to exhausted despondency. Now she shrugged. "There's more of it up in the northern part of the state, southern Colorado. We get a little wave of them, every few years. Makes the papers." She looked numbed and dispirited, back slumped, a negligent hand on the reins.

"People take it seriously?"

Another listless shrug. "Some do. He could be right about scavengers. I've never thought about it much. But I found a mutilated calf once. The face had been . . . well." She frowned over at Cree. "I thought you'd be an expert at that kind of thing."

"No. I'm a psychologist, Julieta. I may have a unique theory of psychology, but it all pertains to the human mind. They didn't teach us a thing about extraterrestrial intelligences at Harvard or Duke."

Julieta bobbed her head, unable to share the joke.

"Think Donny will agree to meet me?" Cree asked.

"Depends. I'd give it even odds. He will if he thinks he might get some useful information out of you—dirt about me or the school. Or if he thinks he can use you to get some publicity that makes McCarty look nice. He'll do anything—last month, they did a local TV special about handicapped grade-school kids taking a field trip to the mine. So very heartwarming. He calls it 'image management.'"

They rode on in silence for a time. It was only three o'clock, but the day had dimmed as a thin film of clouds formed high in the atmosphere and diffused the sun's glow. Though the light was still bright, it had begun to take on a milky quality that muted the landscape, softened the shadows, blurred the distances. The celebratory crispness was gone from the land, leaving it forlorn.

"We got interrupted," Cree ventured. "You were telling me some really important things. I'd love to hear the rest."

Julieta turned quickly, and even behind the mask of the sunglasses her face looked stricken. She whipped her head to the front again and looked as if she were about to flee once more, to gallop away from her own past.

"Julieta!" Cree barked. "You can do this, damn it! You're an administrator and you know how to do hard things! Tell me!"

Julieta caught herself as she raised the reins. She slumped again, took off her sunglasses, and looked at Cree with glittering eyes.

"You're being me again," she said. "The boss me." She grunted with bitter amusement.

"Whatever it takes," Cree told her curtly.

Peter Yellowhorse was about her age, twenty-four, twenty-five. He was from Teec Nos Pos, up near Shiprock, but he'd moved south a year earlier to take a job doing grounds work for the tribal facilities in Window Rock. Always late, he'd gotten fired pretty quickly, but then he'd been lucky enough to get work with the little company that took care of the McCartys' estate. He lived in a wreck of a house just over the rez line, about eight miles away. He was dirt-poor, by white standards, anyway, lucky to have a job. He owned exactly three things of any value whatsoever: his horse, a beat-up Chevy truck, and a belt with a fancy silver and turquoise buckle that had been made by some uncle who was a well-known silversmith. He loved to ride and occasionally did bronc riding at local rodeos, but mainly what he wanted was to get into radio, become a DJ. He did janitorial work three nights a week at a Gallup station in exchange for the studio time and training that would earn him his FCC license.

Easy to be DJ on a Navajo station, he joked. All those long moments of respectful silence, yeah?

At first she found excuses to chat with him during the day about repairs or landscaping she wanted done. Then she started talking to him about her horses; she asked him to help train them and, eventually, to ride with her.

Peter was the restless type, she could see why he didn't hold a job. But he was very smart, with a relentless sense of humor and a gift for turns of phrase that always surprised her. He was innately courteous and, compared to Garrett's social set, surprisingly *proper*, traditional. She liked that. Also unlike them, he was honest, never tried to hide what he was, couldn't have if he'd tried. And oh God, he was handsome—whipcord thin, smooth bronze skin, a fast smile and quick flashing eyes. He wore his hair long because there'd been an American Indian Movement protest nearby a while ago, and though he'd considered them just a bunch of troublemaking Sioux coming down from the Midwest to get their pictures in the papers, he'd liked their rebellious look and style.

One day she was bold enough to ask him to do some work, just him, during off hours. After a while, when he came, all they did was talk or ride together. The desire she felt was as bright and hot as lightning, except it didn't flicker, didn't come and go. It was a remorseless current that flowed continuously, almost painfully. Yet despite its power, they were just friends for almost a year. Julieta was still waiting for Garrett.

Peter felt it, too, but even with his reckless attitude, he would never have broached it. He was too decent, too respectful. And he was no doubt more aware than she was of the risks that would come with having an affair with the wife of Garrett McCarty. A poor Navajo kid getting on the bad side of an old rich white coal exec wasn't likely to do too well in any arena of life.

Julieta was the one who led the way. Something had sprung loose inside her the first time she'd seen him riding Bird so joyously. She'd determined she would taste that freedom. She'd been a physical virgin when she'd married Garrett; as she and Peter began to make love, that first time, she realized that in every way that mattered she still was one. It happened in a worn sandstone gully far around the south end of the mesa, among smooth, sensuous rock curves that invited their bodies to collide and entwine.

"He touched my face. He caressed my face for a long time, like he wanted to know my *bones*. My expressions, the feelings I'd had? It was slow, but it was . . . urgent the whole time." Julieta's eyes went wide as if she'd just heard herself, the degree of confidence she'd indulged.

Cree held her breath, unwilling even to mutter encouragement, afraid it would break the flow. Or that Julieta would notice her reaction: The image of Mike had materialized and she could feel the shape of his body against hers. In the vaulted architecture of her heart, some supporting pillar or buttress bent and faltered agonizingly. Blind, she let Breeze find her own way. The sky had taken on the same feeling, turning gradually an opaque, cataracted white; the sun was the color of a blood orange, dimming, and in the odd light the landscape felt artificial—some stark, digital, virtual place. The school was still several miles away.

They were lovers for a year. They were very careful to keep it secret. Julieta confided only in Joseph, whom she trusted absolutely. She introduced Peter to Joseph, they liked each other. She grew stronger. She realized she'd have to divorce Garrett, even if her father lost his job as a result. Now when she took her husband's arm for the occasional function they attended together, she felt dirty not because of his infidelities but because of hers: She was betraying Peter. When Garrett came home, she made excuses to avoid sleeping with him.

At first, she did a good job of planning the divorce. She hired a private detective to take photos of Garrett entering motel rooms with different women. She made copies of his credit card bills showing incriminating purchases, travel, and hotel stays, which she kept in a secret file. When they went to court, she'd have him by the balls.

But just about the time she was ready to file and move out of the house, two things happened to blow the whole thing apart.

She discovered she was pregnant. She knew it was Peter's child because she hadn't slept with Garrett for months and because, yes, she had been less than cautious with Peter. When she told Peter about it, he was shocked and, understandably, perturbed. As she was: Being visibly pregnant or having a baby that was obviously not red-blond Garrett's child would reveal her infidelity and put the impending divorce process at risk.

At the same time, she never once considered having an abortion. She wanted that child. Really, it was no accident that she'd gotten pregnant. She'd let that last, most intimate barrier fall, she'd needed it to. She'd wanted her life to begin at last.

When she told Joseph, he helped her make a plan: keep the pregnancy secret, file for divorce immediately—before she started to show—and move to her own place.

But before she got that far, Peter left her.

The first time he didn't show up to visit her, she was upset, but she didn't worry until the next day, when she called his house and got no answer. The following day, she drove past his place and found it abandoned: The truck was gone, Bird wasn't in the corral.

He's young, Joseph told her. You know how he is, Julieta, he's a free spirit. That's one of the things you love about him. He got scared. If not of Garrett, then of being a father, making a commitment. But he's a good guy. He'll think about it for a while and he'll call you. He'll realize pretty quick he can't live without you. Don't worry.

And it was true that Peter was intimidated at the prospect of being a father, a husband, a full-time companion. The ardor and excitement in his eyes had been mixed with doubt ever since she'd told him.

But he didn't come back. Weeks went by and he didn't reappear.

Julieta went through with her plan. One horrible afternoon she told Garrett she was divorcing him, then moved out of the house and set up in a cramped third-floor apartment in Gallup.

For a while she tried to make excuses for Peter: Maybe Garrett had found out about him, had threatened him or had him beat up and scared him away. But then she thought, no, there was no way Garrett could have found out, they had been too careful. The proof was that if he had, he'd be using her infidelity against her in the divorce; he certainly fought her proposed settlement terms tooth and nail, and he followed through on his threat to fire her father, but he never brought Peter into it.

Still, she couldn't bear to believe Peter had left of his own accord. But when she finally mustered the courage to call Peter's mother, up near Shiprock, she said yes, he'd brought Bird to stay at her house and had left the rez. He'd said he was going to California, but she hadn't heard from him. Julieta begged her to have him contact her if he came back or called.

Heartbroken, she lived on in her little apartment. Every day brought a dozen changes of heart toward Peter: hope and fear, strength and devastation, anger and forgiveness. Her confusion wasn't just about men, or even love, it was about *life*. The sense of betrayal that all the good things you believed should be so untrue.

She started to show, a little. The divorce process dragged on. She received no visitors. She saw Joseph often, always at the hospital or at restaurants. The longer she stayed in her tiny apartment, the more anger she felt toward Peter. But she still wanted to have the baby. It was the child of those beautiful moments, when the world opened up and it seemed there was love in it after all. And maybe Peter would come back. Maybe he just needed more time.

"In retrospect, I wish I didn't do it the way I did. But you have to understand how angry I was. How terrified I was of what Garrett would do if he found out."

"That he'd hurt you? Physically, I mean?"

The muscles on Julieta jaws rippled. "Remember Donny's remark about the quality of my horses? It goes back to the day I told Garrett I was divorcing him. He didn't love me, but he liked sex with me and he *owned* me—plus he knew the divorce would cost him some money and property. And by God one thing Garrett did was, he fought for what he *owned!* The day I handed him the papers he argued and threatened me and his eyes literally turned this horrible bloody color. He . . . he did something very terrible."

"What?"

"I had gone to my bedroom and locked the door, I was that afraid of him. So Garrett went out to the barn. He shot my horses. All four. I listened to the shots and screams. One after the other."

Sickened, Cree couldn't imagine a response.

It took her a while, but after a few minutes Julieta managed to grind out the rest of the story: "I was scared to death. What he'd do if he found out about the baby. About Peter and me. Especially that I'd slept with a *Navajo,* was carrying a Navajo child. That would be a blow to his ego he'd never forgive."

The searing fear and horror of that day fired her determination to get away from Garrett, cemented her sense that he really *owed* her. He had betrayed her, turned her into a paid courtesan, not a wife; he'd made her practically a prisoner for four years, he'd ruined her father, he'd murdered her horses. Even now, he ruled her life through fear and intimidation. Turning over a new leaf meant not accepting that crap from him, or anyone, ever again. Despite Joseph's tactful recommendation that she divorce quietly and amicably, even if it meant a less lucrative settlement, she continued to press ahead with the very hard terms her attorney said she would certainly get. All she had to do was keep her pregnancy secret and get the divorce over with quickly.

But the final court date ended up being set for late winter. Showing up in court eight months pregnant was out of the question. She had to change plans.

Again, Joseph helped her think it through. The solution they came up with was to have the baby in secret. Postpone the court date until spring, a month or so after she'd given birth. In the meantime, live a covert life in Gallup, withdraw from public contact, do all her business by phone, let her lawyer handle everything. It was only a few more months, and over the last five years she'd gotten good at waiting, at living alone. At having a secret life, a secret self.

By the time she was six months pregnant, she was in bad shape. She'd been cooped up forever and ever. She'd received every heartbreak imaginable. She felt burdened and heavy and tired all the time. The hope that Peter would return had worn thin. She was so lonely she wanted to die; she probably would have if Joseph hadn't been there.

Then one day she found a letter from Peter in her mailbox. It had been mailed from California to the old address and had been forwarded by the post office. At the sight of his scrawl on the envelope, familiar from the occasional love letters he'd written, the hope and fear exploded in her. She practically fell down in the stairwell as she ripped it open and read it.

He was in California. He'd tried to start up in LA but had drifted down to San Diego. Things were going pretty well. He'd found a job maintaining vending machines at the naval base. He had gotten some regular air-time at a community radio station; he had also registered with a film agency up in Hollywood and was excited at the prospect of maybe some work as an extra, there were a couple of films coming up that needed Indian types. He loved her, he would never forget a single moment with her. But he couldn't be with her. He was a poor backcountry Navajo, she was a rich Santa Fe white girl. They should have known better than to try, with the deck stacked so badly against them. He was seeing somebody else now, a Jicarilla Apache woman who was escaping reservation life just as he was. Julieta should move on with her life. He was very, very sorry.

A few days later, while she was still reeling from that, she saw a car slide past the building, its driver looking up at the windows. She realized she'd seen the same car on several occasions. And this time, she recognized the driver's face: one of Garrett's assistants, a thug named Nick Stephanovic. Garrett was having her watched!

Suddenly the whole absurdity of her plan struck her. A naïve twenty-five-year-old idiot and a thirty-year-old idealistic Navajo doctor were no strategists for the kind of war she was fighting or the kind of enemy she had. She'd never keep her secrets. Even if the divorce went through without a hitch, Garrett could keep watching. If she suddenly appeared with a baby in her arms, a Navajo baby, he'd know everything. She didn't dare ask her lawyer, but she suspected that proof of her infidelity would be cause to retroactively overturn a settlement. Far more frightening, the extent of her deception would conjure in Garrett the rage she'd glimpsed when he'd killed her horses. At that point it would've had nothing to do with love anymore, or even ownership: He'd get back at her because his pride demanded it. She'd seen his vengeful side in business dealings—cross him, and he never forgot. She'd never be safe. Her nightmare would go on and on with no reprieve, ever.

The whole thing had been a mistake, she saw, error upon error, stupidity upon stupidity. If she really wanted to start a new life, she realized, she had to let go not just of Garrett and of Peter, but of the baby, too.

Yes, she'd have to give up the baby.

It wasn't just her anger at Peter or her fear of Garrett that resolved her. She saw with frightening clarity that she was in no shape to be anybody's mother. She was too confused, impulsive, damaged; she had too much angry pride and had made too many mistakes because of it. The baby should have stable, sane, capable parents—two of them. The baby should be removed as far as possible from the wrath of Garrett McCarty and the emptiness left by an abandoning father and the mess of Julieta's life.

She talked it over with Joseph. Again, he served as her sounding board, didn't suggest or force her decisions in any way. The only time he put his foot down was after she'd told him her decision. He would help her, he said, if she was absolutely sure, if she'd considered every option and felt there was truly only that one. But it has to be forever, he warned her. You have to let go completely. You can't change your mind in a month or a year or five years. You can't rip a family's life apart by coming in later and claiming the child they've raised as their own. You can't do that to a child who loves the people it knows as its parents.

I know, she told him. That's right. I know.

There's another reason, Joseph went on. You can't second-guess yourself, either—can't hold your future hostage to the bad things that have happened. Your heart has to have freedom to grow and move on. If you emotionally cling to this child after it's gone, it'll be like having an open wound that can never heal. If you ever change your mind, you'll only hurt yourself and other innocent people. It's a one-way street, Julieta. It's got to be.

Off-record, at-home births were common on the rez—as a rural GP, Joseph had delivered his share. He said he knew of an infertile couple in a remote area of the eastern rez, good people who dearly wanted a child. When Julieta's time came, Joseph delivered the baby and brought the boy to them.

Julieta saw her son for only those minutes after his birth: Joseph laid him on her chest while he did some repairs on her. She looked at the wrinkled little face, saw those tiny lips working, and at that moment felt a force in her that she never imagined existed. It changed her inside. It was as if her whole body and mind became one big magnet, as if she existed only as that pull toward the baby. Her breasts ached and tingled with the desire to nurture him, but he wasn't ready to suckle. She looked at him for a long time. Marveling at him. But labor had exhausted her, and after a while she closed her eyes and forgot everything but the glow of that warm little weight against her skin, the minute movements. She drowsed. When she awoke the baby was gone. As they'd agreed.

Joseph never told her the details of where the boy went. There was never any question of finding him again. The new parents would report the arrival as a home birth and fill out the papers in their names. With a Navajo father and a black Irish–Hispanic mother, he'd have the right coloring to blend in. He'd grow up as a Navajo, share the good and bad of a Navajo's fate in twentieth-century America.

For once, their plans went off without a hitch. With all the heartbreak and tension, Julieta had gained barely any weight during the pregnancy. She was far too thin, but the bright side was that nobody would suspect she'd recently given birth. The divorce took place in April, and it went as her lawyer predicted. She ended up with the Oak Springs house and twelve hundred acres and three million dollars, plus an uneasy proximity to

McCarty Energy's Hunters Point field and the enduring hostility of Garrett and his nasty son.

She never saw her baby again. She never heard from Peter Yellowhorse again. She was twenty-five when she began her new life.

Julieta reined Madie to a stop. A mile away, the school was just visible over a swell in the land, the buildings new and clean but sad-looking in the wan, milky light. Julieta just sat in the saddle and looked at the lonely little cluster. The sun was not far from the horizon, so dulled by the uniform overcast its glow didn't impart any warmth to the buildings or the walls of the mesa.

Cree stopped Breeze beside her. She was astonished at how differently she saw the scene now. It was rooted in all the reasons Julieta had done this monumental thing. The buildings were not just objects of stone and steel but manifestations of feeling and purpose. They were built not just on the bare red desert earth but on a foundation of one person's past pain and error and the profound drive to turn it all around, to remedy wrongs and atone for them, to act for the good rather than react to the bad.

Julieta's accomplishment awed her.

Of course, it was also built on a subconscious desire to find the lost child again. Or to sublimate and channel the mothering urge, frustrated then, in the act of nurturing and guiding many children.

Screw Sigmund, Cree thought, impatient with her Freudian reflexes. That urban, neurotic, fin-de-siècle sensibility stripped things of scope and nobility and poetry. This woman faced herself. She acknowledged her failings and turned every one of them around. She did a marvelously good thing. Turned a disaster into a brilliant achievement.

Of course, there were so many questions left unanswered. One of them was *not* whether, or why, Julieta would seek her lost baby in every child she encountered: Joseph's advice had been both wise and kind, but of course that wound in her heart would never close.

But why Tommy? Cree wanted to ask. How did she know he was her long-lost child? His records? Some resemblance to Peter Yellowhorse? Maybe Joseph told her. But why would he identify the boy to Julieta after making sure the cord was so completely severed?

But Julieta had pulled into herself, and she deserved a break from the relentless probing and prodding Cree had subjected her to.

Julieta put her hand to her face and seemed startled to find her sunglasses still there. She took them off, folded them away, wiped her cheeks with the balls of both hands.

"Going to get cold tonight," she said. "Sunset's coming. Better get to the chores." She glanced at the chilly horizon and urged Madie toward the school.

19

THE SIGHT OF Ben's body disappearing into the Hobart made Tommy break out into a sweat.

The big dishwasher was on the blink, but Ben said he knew how to fix it, no need to call in the maintenance guys. Tommy had gladly volunteered to help and Ben had let him tag along when the softball game broke up.

The Hobart was seven feet long and had doors on both ends, just like a casket-sized car wash. The dishes went in dirty at one end and came out the other clean and so hot they steamed dry in seconds. Ben lay on his back on the counter, arranged a flashlight and some tools on his chest, and then shoved himself into the open maw until only his bottom half emerged from between the strips of the spray curtain.

It reminded Tommy of the times he'd been fed into the MRI machine during the last couple of weeks: the claustrophobic panic of being strapped to the plastic shelf and sliding inch by inch into the huge, roaring white doughnut.

Ben grunted and made clanking noises inside the housing. His legs bent and scissored, as if he were struggling to get out, and Tommy had to look away. Still, he'd rather be here in the kitchen instead of walking around with the nurse. She creeped him out, always hovering near him, prying at him. Even now, she was just the other side of the swinging doors, waiting at one of the cafeteria tables.

"Just don't turn it on while I'm in here, huh?" Ben joked. From inside the stainless steel housing, his voice had a metallic ring.

"Why not? You look like you could use it."

"Hey, I took a shower just last month!" Ben chuckled. "Wouldn't help, anyway. Even this thing won't clean a dirty mind."

Tommy couldn't laugh. That hit too close to the mark: The worst part of the MRI had been the fear of what it might see in his head.

"So, what's the matter with you, anyway? Not going on the field trip. Sick last week, too, right?"

"Cooties. Bad case of cooties."

Ben chuckled again. His legs braced and pushed, as if he were being eaten by the machine and was fighting it. In another moment, his hand emerged with some kind of a valve. Tommy took it and set it on the counter.

"So," Ben said, "the good-looking *bilagáana*—what, she's a doctor or something?"

Tommy didn't want to answer, couldn't stand to turn their talk serious. This was good—just hanging with someone, like he was a regular person and not some kind of specimen or freak. And if Ben knew the truth, he wouldn't let Tommy anywhere near him. Ignoring the question, Tommy quickly inspected the industrial meat grinder bolted to the opposite counter and turned back to slap the housing of the Hobart.

"What's this red button for?" he asked innocently.

"Don't touch that!"

Tommy reached over and flipped the toggle on the grinder, and he could see from the sudden tensing of Ben's legs that the loud, grating whine had caught him off guard. He let it run for a few seconds, then hit the switch and let the motor wind down.

Ben's legs were shaking as he laughed. "Just about peed myself! Gonna feed you into that thing when I get out of here! Hey, see my toolbox? Want to hand me the half-inch box wrench?"

Tommy found the wrench, but before he could give it to Ben it slipped from his fingers and bounced under the counter. His right hand wasn't working. He felt a growing confusion about it: The waistband of his jeans pressed against him in back, and if he shut his eyes he could swear it was something tightening on his *wrist*.

The feeling was coming on him again, slowly but remorselessly.

He was on his knees, reaching under the counter for the wrench, when a long, thin, jointed thing darted in toward it from the right side. He reared away so hard he smashed his head on the counter supports. His own right hand! It had come so quickly and purposefully, like some awful animal that lived under the counter. He felt, he *knew,* his real arm was back behind him, stretched along his spine. It took him a moment to catch his breath and stop shaking. He got the wrench with his left hand, extricated himself from under the counter, and put it into Ben's waiting palm.

"Butterfingers," Ben complained good-naturedly. "You think I want to be in here all day?"

Tommy felt tears in his eyes. He moved away from the feed opening to make sure Ben couldn't see his face. "What'd you say this red button was for?" he asked.

"Couldn't we skip it? Please? I'm fine now." He couldn't stand the thought of another examination, Mrs. Pierce's flecked eyes narrowing as they inspected him.

"Sorry, Tommy. Doctor's orders. I'm supposed to track your vital signs."

She shut the examining room door. As if there was anyone going to come in. He wished she'd leave it open.

"You'll have to take off your shirt," Mrs. Pierce said.

Tommy wasn't sure he could. He was too twisted. He knew the thing at his side had to be his arm, but it felt like he was standing in a packed crowd so that someone else's arm was pressed against his body. No, it was worse: It was as if there was someone invisible *overlapping* him on the right side. He couldn't even *think* about the arm completely. When he lifted his T-shirt with his left hand, the right arm thing just hung there. He got stuck with the shirt over his head, tangled and disoriented. Mrs. Pierce had to help him. When they got it off, he felt uncomfortable, standing half naked in the room with her looking at him.

She put on her stethoscope and listened to his chest and back, cold rings against his skin. Her eyes had an excited, curious look, like on some level she enjoyed this. When she was done, she guided him by his shoulders to sit on the crinkly paper of the examining table, then wrapped the blood pressure cuff around his left arm. She pumped it up and let the air out slowly, listening with the stethoscope, watching the gauge. She jotted something on her clipboard, but she didn't remove the cuff. Instead, she lifted the strange thing to his right.

"Tommy, what's this I'm holding?"

"My arm," he muttered. He didn't look at it. If he looked at it, he knew it would seem like a huge thing emerging inexplicably from the side of his face, near the hinge of his jaw.

"Is it? So, tell me about your arm."

"What do you mean?"

"Tell me more about it. How it feels. What it does."

"You've already asked me so many times!"

"I mean, what it does when nobody's looking."

He felt nausea surge in his stomach. He refused to answer or to look at the awful thing she held.

"I guess you don't know," she whispered. "And of course you don't know what it does when you're asleep."

At that, he couldn't help but look at her, horrified.

A little smile stayed glued to her mouth as she made a gesture with her own hand, as if she was rubbing something small between finger and thumb. Then more gestures, her hand gripping, then beckoning. When the miming hand touched his face, he jerked away.

Once when he'd been almost drowsing he'd looked over to see something groping stealthily around the edge of the bedside table. It was like suddenly finding a tarantula right next to his head. The scariest part was that it had stopped immediately, as if it didn't want him to see.

So it did things while he was asleep, too.

He slid off the examining table, wanting to run out of the room. But he was still hooked up to the blood pressure machine. Without two hands there was no way to take it off himself.

"We're *not* done with our examination, Tommy!" the nurse said commandingly.

He stopped tugging at the tubes, frightened by her tone, and stood as she released the rest of the pressure and ripped the Velcro loose. Once she'd put it away, she clamped his wrist in her hard fingers and timed his pulse. Her eyebrows rose as if his racing heart alarmed her.

She gazed at him for a long moment, then checked her clipboard. "Okay. So, let's weigh you. Then let's go for a nice, long walk. Exercise will help you get your appetite back, we can't have you losing so much weight. Would you like that?"

"Yes," he said readily. She'd probably ask him weird questions about his parents or about what supernatural stuff the other kids talked about, like last time, almost as if she *wanted* to scare him. But being outside would be better than being in here alone with her.

They walked along the edge of the athletic fields, not far from the foot of the mesa. The sky had turned dull white and featureless, dimming the sun. Tommy struggled to coordinate his legs and arms. He had a rising feeling of expectancy, as if there was another person coming, or maybe was already silently walking with them and was about to do something. A third person, listening, even more sneaky than the nurse.

"You know," Mrs. Pierce said, "sometimes it helps to talk about what frightens you. It can be therapeutic. Even if you have angry feelings, talking about them can be what we call *cathartic*."

"I know what 'cathartic' means!"

"Of course you do," she said soothingly. "You're a highly intelligent young man. You're smart enough to be nervous about all this medical business, aren't you? The technology can be intimidating. But everyone feels the same way, believe me."

He nodded. There was some small relief in hearing that.

"Like what?" she persisted. "What's the worst? The MRI?" She glanced over at him expectantly.

He still didn't want to answer. But her question had made him think of the magazine in the cranial diagnostics waiting room. He'd sat there in his hospital gown while they prepared the MRI and he'd picked it up, some kind of doctor's magazine, not anything they should've let a patient see. He'd opened it to find an article about lobotomies.

The first photo showed a woman with her head in a clamp, a doctor putting a long, thin blade into her nose. Other pictures illustrated how to hit the tool with a special hammer that drove the blade through the thin bones behind your sinus cavity, right into your brain. It cut the connections, so the sick part just sat there, probably still doing its crazy thing but not screwing up the rest of your mind. The article said the procedure had been mostly abandoned for twenty years but was now making a big comeback. Sometimes people couldn't walk or talk or recognize their family afterward, but it was worth it if their brain problems were really severe.

Whatever was the matter with him, he knew it was severe. So maybe that's what they'd end up doing to him.

Tommy felt panic coming and tried desperately to think of something reassuring. He told himself Dr. Tsosie and Mrs. McCarty would help, they were very smart, they acted like they really did care about him. And maybe that new psychologist could do something, she seemed like she understood things. But he hardly knew any of them, it was hard to trust them.

His back twisted, and though he willed himself straight it was like big invisible hands were wringing him, so hard he heard his own backbone crackle. From the way she looked over at him, the nurse must have heard it, too.

He knew what it meant: The other person, the controlling stranger, was getting closer.

He had to unkink and calm himself. Find some safe place in his mind. His thoughts kept fleeing back to the family homesite, the smell of the sheep pens, the familiar shape of the land, and most of all his grandparents.

Grandfather, particularly—he could do anything with his hands, he could make anything, he totally knew sheep and horses and cars, he remembered everything from long ago, he could tell stories really well. What Tommy admired most was how deeply he believed in helping people—he'd do anything for someone in need, give anything he owned. He'd never in his life complained about his responsibilities. But he was old-fashioned and stuck in his habits and getting tired and weak. He was negative about every change, even things like when they graded the county road, and was paranoid about white people, technology, the government. He and Grandmother believed the old myths about First Man and First Woman, the Hero Twins, and Spider Woman, they saw the world as full of mysterious things that required all this respect and doing things in very particular, pointless ways every time. They were down on Tommy's choice of music and clothes and friends, frowned whenever he talked about his career ambitions, asked suspiciously about the clan of any girl he mentioned. He loved them so much it hurt inside, and he knew how much he owed them. But they couldn't offer any safety or reassurance now. And they shouldn't have to, he was fifteen, he should be taking care of *them*.

Sometimes he thought maybe he should confide in Mr. Clah, his social studies teacher, he was smart and seemed to know how things worked. He wore khakis and carried a laptop computer, he did mountain biking and had a white lawyer girlfriend. He treated Tommy like an equal. But though Tommy mostly agreed with his opinions, too often they sounded like complaining, making excuses, and accusing. He wasn't strong the way Grandfather was. He'd never worked as hard as Grandfather, had never gotten his hands dirty, didn't know what it meant to sacrifice for anybody. In any case, he didn't care enough about Tommy to help him now.

As always, his thoughts spiraled back to his parents. If they were alive, maybe they'd know how to help. Maybe they'd figured something out about how to live. They put up with Grandfather's Diné heritage stuff but weren't particularly into it. Some nights Tommy missed them, crying secretly into his pillow, but the more he missed them, the more he hated them for getting themselves killed. They had no right to do that to him and the family! Once when he was obsessing about it last year, he'd gone to the library and looked at some psychology books. He'd discovered that his attitude was typical: adolescent kid loving but resenting dead parents, searching around for role models. Cliché or not, it was true: You had to know something about your people or you couldn't know who you were. Especially right now, knowing who they were would help him sort out what he was going through. But all he had was a collection of mental snapshots: rolling on the ground and wrestling with Father when he was five or six, feeling safe against his strong chest, laughing at the silly way he pretended to fight. Mother teaching him how to fry an egg when he was maybe four, proudly showing Aunt Ellen and everybody how incredibly big a mess he made of the stove. Beyond that, all he knew was they liked country-and-western music, they fought a lot and drank too much. What he remembered wasn't enough to help him figure out anything.

Tommy heard his backbone crackle again, and he steered his thoughts away from the fading images of those faces. There wasn't any refuge there.

So then at some point he'd decided, *Okay, I'll define myself.* From his reading about great artists and from his own drawing, he'd figured that you were defined by your passions, by what you loved and believed in.

Sometimes he thought that might mean "doing something for the tribe." But what? The People didn't know what they wanted. If you believed the *Navajo Times,* every little businessman who opened up a

Laundromat was "doing something for the tribe" by contributing to Navajo-owned enterprise and economic growth. When what it looked like to Tommy was just more greedy self-interest, like Mr. Clah said, just another form of colonialism, co-opting real Navajo culture with white American consumerism.

His art was the one thing. He loved looking at something until its hidden meaning came clear and then distilling the image and the meaning into something powerful. He could experiment with different ways of seeing the same thing, trying on definitions of himself, his parents, his friends, his surroundings, life, the past, until one seemed to capture something unarguably *true*. Just the physical act was almost ecstatic— moving the pencil on the page, not so much drawing as *carving* the blank white into three dimensions. There were moments when he could believe that in the way he saw things and drew things he was giving something back to the world. It had always been good, but it wasn't until he'd come to Oak Springs that he'd learned how much he could do, how much it could mean. It was so much better than the other schools. He'd learned so much in the few classes he'd had, Miss Chee and Mrs. McCarty had shown him how to put the way he saw and thought into his pictures. Made him feel that his work was important, that it was a way to figure things out, a way to a halfway decent future.

The thing at his side moved suddenly, the fingers clenching and then clawing the air like someone scratching a bug bite. Tommy grabbed it with his left hand and squeezed it hard, digging his nails into it, wanting to hurt it, feeling nothing.

His heart plummeted. It reminded him of another heartbreaking fact of where he was at. Without a right arm he couldn't draw. If he didn't get better, he'd have to leave Oak Springs School. The one way through would be lost.

"You okay?" the nurse asked.

"Yeah." He realized he hadn't answered her earlier question.

"You want to tell me what you're feeling?"

He couldn't. Because as bad as the things with his body were, the *feelings* were worse—harder to describe and more frightening. Suddenly, he'd notice he'd been having something like a daydream, but the instant he'd realize it, it would go away, he couldn't remember what it was about. It was like the one time he'd gone to the multiplex theater in Gallup, watching one movie but hearing sounds and music from a different movie through the wall. It didn't make sense, a mood that had nothing to do with what he was doing. A feeling or an urge would come out of nowhere. He'd feel the need to *hurry,* like he had to go somewhere or do something very important. A couple of times he'd gotten sexually aroused, once even in the examining room when Mrs. McCarty was there and might have noticed. Or he'd feel this horrible fear and then fill with hate and want to hurt someone so much he could hardly hold himself back. Sometimes he wondered if it could be a witch or a ghost trying to kill him, maybe all the things the kids talked about in the dorm at night were true: the black humping shapes coming out of the desert at night, the strange noises in the wind, the unusual behavior of a crow on the roof. A shadow moving on the rocks with nothing making it. Maybe he had a chindi in him. Or maybe it was coming from his subconscious, wasn't this how schizophrenia worked? Maybe he was really a person full of fear and hate and violence.

Whichever, it was happening right now.

Mrs. Pierce was watching him and he realized that once more he hadn't answered her question, he'd been lost in the feeling and the effort to fight it. He quickly let go of the arm thing and hoped she didn't notice the blood where he'd dug in his nails. He looked over at her, and abruptly he wanted to spring at her, tear her to pieces. Afraid he couldn't stop it this time, he picked up his speed so he got ahead of her, got her out of his sight.

From behind, Mrs. Pierce called in her phony cheerful voice, "Never mind. I'm sure you'd rather talk about something else. Of course you would. We'll just walk along and just be good buddies for a while. Just good buds out for a walk."

20

B Y THE TIME they'd made it back to the corral and cared for the horses, it was nearing sunset. Cree's head was throbbing, and she knew she was too exhausted to try another session with Tommy right away. She absolutely had to be clearheaded and strong enough to take a peek inside his skull. Anyway, Lynn had left a note, letting her know that she'd taken him for a walk and then planned to go to the cafeteria for some dinner.

Cree seized the moment of comparative calm. She felt herself spiraling in on her bed, drawn irresistibly into its field of gravity, but first there was some business to attend to. Ten minutes on the phone, then a nap. She'd spend time with Tommy later in the evening.

It was late Saturday afternoon in Seattle, a good time to catch Joyce and Edgar before the evening's entertainments took them out for the night. She commandeered the phone in Lynn's office to make the calls.

When Ed answered, she could barely hear his hello over the stereo blasting in the background: the Gypsy Kings, belting out songs of unrequited passion.

Ed quickly brought the volume down. "Hey, Cree. Good timing. I was about to go out."

"I can call back later if—"

"No, this is fine. I won't be home later—going out to dinner. Now I'm just going to run some errands. What's up?"

"What're you going to bring, Ed?"

"Hm. Sounds like you have some recommendations."

"The lights flickered last time. Did I tell you? Very pronounced flicker phenomenon."

"So we'll need to rule out electrical system problems. I'll bring the kit for that, no problem there. But—"

"Yeah. We're getting into some EVP possibilities. Then there's the DNS issue."

It felt good to speak in the private vernacular they shared, to talk with someone who didn't need explanations or justifications. Nice to pretend there was any kind of conceptual map to this territory. But the idea brought them both up short as they thought it through.

EVP stood for electronic voice phenomena, a paranormal manifestation that had become evident only in the age of electronic media. In some cases, voices or sounds not audible to the human ear could be picked up by electronic recording equipment placed in haunted environments. Rarer still, telephones or radios sometimes produced sounds without a discernible signal source. The implication was that some unknown energies or entities were directly affecting the wires and chips and magnetic media of electronic equipment, creating patterns of electricity that ultimately emerged as audible noises or voices. Because it was an easily faked medium, Ed had been highly skeptical of EVP evidence until, despite every safeguard against hoax or error, he'd recorded a voice in an abandoned house in Gloucester, Massachusetts.

EVP was all the more complex because it tied in with a whole body of paranormal theory called DNS, direct neural stimulus. The idea here was that the energies of paranormal entities might create only the *experience* of images, sounds, or sensations: They didn't actually create light, vibrations in the air, or tangible bodily contact but directly activated the human brain and nervous system. Someone witnessing a phantom figure might not actually be *seeing*—receiving light through her eyes, which a camera would also record—at all. Rather, she might be having her optic nerve or visual cortex directly stimulated by some other form of energy.

The DNS concept helped explain the difficulty of providing a physical record of a ghost's presence. It particularly appealed to Cree because it supported her conviction that ghosts were linked to witnesses and manifested only within particular psychosocial environments: People experienced ghosts when their mental and emotional states created neurological conditions that sensitized them to the emanations of noncorporeal entities.

In the case of the flicker phenomenon, the well-documented pulsing of lights in the vicinity of paranormal events could be related to either EVP or DNS. Some form of energy could be affecting the wiring of a house or the filaments of a lightbulb and cause currents to fluctuate. Or it could affect the soft, wet wiring of the brain, causing the visual sensing circuits to misbehave. Subjectively, the end result would be indistinguishable to a witness.

"So, for the DNS, you're thinking functional microelectroencephalogram?" Ed suggested.

FMEEG was a medical technology that monitored tiny variations in the brain's electrical activity. Beyond its use in detecting brain impairment or seizure activity, FMEEG could be used to map normal brain function, allowing researchers to watch which areas lit up when the subject felt a particular emotion or responded to a particular stimulus. It had several advantages over functional MRI, one of them being that the scalp-wiring harness was light and minimally intrusive, and could easily be employed at the sites of hauntings.

"Think you can get the stuff?"

"On a Saturday afternoon or Sunday morning? What're the odds, Cree? Shit."

"Call Frank. Tell him we need the gear for a week, we'll Air Express it back if we have to."

"Yeah." Ed paused, no doubt jotting a note to call their skeptical but helpful friend Frank Markowitz. Frank worked at Cascades Neurological Research Institute, coordinating multisite research initiatives with other labs and clinics. He was occasionally willing to bend the definition of "lab" enough to rent equipment to PRA.

"Okay," Ed said. "So. Otherwise. How's it going? You sound, um, good—decisive. In charge, um—"

"Bossy?"

"Well, I wasn't going to—"

"Julieta McCarty has an assertive side, okay? It's her get-things-done mode."

"So, what's the other side?"

"I'm *okay,* Ed," she said defensively. *The other side is grief and sorrow,* she thought, *fear and self-doubt. Spinning out of control into anger and regret and making huge mistakes by acting upon those feelings.* If only it were possible to screen out which aspects of a personality you absorbed. But of course it wasn't.

She repressed the urge to ask him where he was going tonight, wondering inappropriately if he was dating someone, at last moving past his attachment to Cree Black and her indecisions and complications. But she just thanked him. He urged her to take good care of herself, and they said good-bye.

After she hung up, Cree was left recalling the first time she'd heard the EVP recording Ed had made in Gloucester. They'd listened to it together in his tech studio in Seattle, and it had left them both badly shaken. Emerging from a mist of electronic noise, barely more coherent than static and hum, a plaintive human voice: *Jenny? Jen? Where are you? I'm so sorry. You must believe me. Where are you, Jenny?*

Some person or fragment of a person, lost in a timeless electronic ether, searching for a companion and a world it once knew, unaware that neither existed anymore.

She would never forget the anguish of fear and sympathy she'd felt as she listened to it. In a way, it was far more frightening than the direct encounters she'd had. The fear was not one of danger in any ordinary sense—that the ghost could hurt you. It came from understanding with stark clarity how lost and alone that being was, and wondering, *Is that what will happen to me?*

She quickly packed the thought away, picked up the phone again, and pecked in Joyce's number. Busy.

Thinking to kill a few minutes and try again, she went back to the ward room to finally begin reading the materials Mason had provided her. This time she went straight to some of the older source material. She read it in fascinated horror.

She was struck by how many of Tommy's symptoms resembled the typical case: the intensifying cycles followed by relative normalcy, the convulsions and contortions. The often-reported breathing problems, she saw now, could easily result from the asynchronous breathing they'd observed in Tommy—obviously, the intruder and the host vying for control of basic bodily functions. A chilling idea.

On the bright side, she consoled herself, *at least he ain't vomiting up toads and broken glass.*

But reading on, she discovered another typical aspect of possession that struck her as particularly relevant and disturbing. Even discounting most incidents as cases of what was now called hysteria, epilepsy, or schizophrenia, this was a well-documented phenomenon that had been observed well into the age of rational medicine, right into present-day cases of dissociative identity disorder.

Possession could *spread*. It was catching.

In fact, most historical incidents of possession weren't confined to single individuals; the records showed dozens of "epidemics" of possession. In 1656, almost the whole community of Paderborn was "taken," but more often the contagion spread in contained populations like hospitals, orphanages, schools, and convents. Groups of nuns seemed particularly susceptible: 1491 in Cambrai, 1526 in Lyons, 1554 in Rome, on and on, with the 1634 episode in Loudon being perhaps the most famous.

After nuns, children were the most likely to get possessed in large numbers. Rome, 1555, eighty children at an orphanage; Amsterdam, 1566, thirty boys in a hospital; 1744, a group of young girls in Landes. In a famous American incident, the Goodwin children, the problem began with the eldest daughter and spread to the other three siblings: They went into fits, had convulsions, and contorted their bodies so that their spines, shoulder blades, elbows, wrists, and other joints appeared impossibly deformed.

The mechanisms of "contagion" might be responsible for the apparent paralysis of the other boys in Tommy's dorm, and the limb-locked, shivering horses. Cree had felt it herself: that stunning, numbing force around Tommy during his extreme moments.

Then there were the reports of the victim hurting himself, or attempting suicide. Was that something they had to worry about with Tommy?

Feeling overwhelmed, she pulled out of a particularly grisly case history and leafed through the remainder of the stack. There was a lot more here deserving close review; of particular interest were Mason's own studies and others that drew parallels between possession and multiple personality disorder, now called dissociative identity disorder. She really should read these, and the sooner the better.

But not now, she decided. She glanced at her watch and was startled to see the time: She'd planned to give Joyce a few minutes to get off the line, and here it had been over half an hour. She put the papers aside, went back to the nurse's office, and dialed. This time it rang.

"Cree! Thank Gawd you called!"

"Oh?"

"I have no idea what you're supposed to *wear* down there. I mean, what? Cowboy outfits? I haven't got a thing."

Cree chuckled. It was nice to hear Joyce's Long Island accent and improbable husky contralto, and her spirit rallied considerably. "No cowboy outfits. Your usual will do. If you want to walk around or ride the horses, you'll need jeans, a sweater, and hiking boots. And a good coat—it's freezing at night. But definitely no cowboy outfits. Please!"

"Too bad." Joyce laughed. "So what's up?"

"Any chance you can do some preliminary research tomorrow, before your flight?"

"Not tonight? How very considerate of you."

"I assumed you were going out."

Joyce sighed with patient exasperation. "You have this impression of me as such a swinger. What, I was going down to Linda's Bar and boogie? For your information, I was planning on calling my mom back east and then watching a video."

"Oh, yeah? What kind of video? With whom?"

"Tell me about the research, Cree. I've already worked up a brief on recent cases of possession for you. There's no shortage—you'll see, there was a real wild one in New Jersey just last year. What else you need?"

Cree enumerated the avenues that had suggested themselves: "McCarty Energy, a coal-mining company that's big in the region. Especially Garrett McCarty, the former owner, who died in 1999 at their Hunters Point mine."

"Aha. Think he's our entity?"

"Could be. Too soon, though, I'm just curious. While you're at it, I wouldn't mind some material on his son, Donny McCarty, current CEO. Education, marital status, legal stuff, whatever's come up in the newspapers. Then, let's see . . . bring me that Wilkins study on multiple personality disorder and anything else you can grab on the subject. You'll need to search for dissociative identity disorder, that's the current DSM classification. Mason gave me some materials, but I want to know more about the neurological mechanisms of identity disorders, see if there're any parallels, anything we can apply to possession."

"Smart cookie!"

"Also, some regional history, especially about Navajo culture. History, mysticism, contemporary social issues. I'm especially interested in Navajo witches—the Skinwalkers, the Navajo Wolves."

"Right out of Tony Hillerman, huh? This is a pretty rich mix, Cree. I'm leavin' on a jet plane, right, in twenty-one hours—"

"Oh, and one more—livestock mutilations."

Joyce made a shuddering noise. "Now *that* stuff completely and totally grosses me out. Seriously. So, what—they've been having them? At the school?"

"I don't think there's any connection. Actually, I don't know what I think about mutes, I just—"

" *'Mutes'?*"

"Local term. Listen, there's likely to be a ton on the Web, gotta really weed out the idiots on this one."

" 'Mutes'!" Joyce said again. "Isn't it supposed to be a UFO thing? Little green men I'm fine with, but little green vivisectionists? Brrrrr! You know?" While she paused to make notes, Cree distinctly heard the sound of the doorbell ringing in her Seattle apartment, and Joyce said quickly, "Well, okay. That's it, then, right? Gotta go. Gotta call Mom and get to work on this. See you tomorrow night, yeah? Take care. Bye-byee."

One last call, she told herself—this one for pleasure, not for business. It would be good to talk to Paul, to remind herself that life wasn't exclusively about lost love, ancient regrets, paranormal beings, grotesque syndromes, and existential mysteries. Talking to a living and romantically attractive man would help her get her feet on the ground. Remind herself that she had her own life, she wasn't just an extension of Julieta McCarty's troubled psyche.

"Hello?" Paul answered. In the background, Cree heard a din of conversation and music.

"It's me—Annie Oakley," she told him. *Actually,* she thought, *at the moment it's more like Calamity Jane.* "What's going on?"

"Hey, Cree!" he said warmly. "Oh, the racket? My annual shrink shindig. Didn't I tell you about this? I've got two dozen esteemed members of the greater New Orleans mental health establishment here, supposedly networking but really just wining and dining and telling war stories. We're just getting to the fast-and-loose stage. Hang on, Cree, just a second." She heard him turn away and call out, "Elaine, not that one, please. No, the other. The bigger one. Yes." Then back to Cree: "Hi. Sorry. Why Annie Oakley?"

"Well, it's this Western ambience out here. Also, I just went for a long horseback ride. Out on the desert."

"Oh, yeah? How was it?"

Cree surprised herself by blurting, "Paul, does anybody find love and keep it? Is it ever easy? Or is that just romance novels and fairy tales?"

"Whoa! That was quite a horseback ride. What happened?"

Before she could answer, a burst of laughter came through the phone, and the music in Paul's apartment swelled: zydeco. "I should call back later," she said.

"I could switch phones—"

"No. No, I just called to . . . I don't know, hear your voice, let you know I was okay. You go back to your guests. I'll call back later, okay?"

He paused. "Yeah, I guess that would be better." Another hesitation. "Cree, listen. I don't know about love—how it turns out, whether it's ever easy. Probably it's not. But I have to believe it's worth the effort. If it's . . . real, it'll survive anything. Sometimes you just have to . . . stick with it."

Cree went to her bed and lay down in her clothes. Just a nap. The windows were going dark already, but it was still early enough. She could nap for an hour, then get up and meet with Tommy.

The fat envelope of possession materials troubled her, and to get it out of her thoughts she put it into the side-table drawer. Better. She needed to keep her vision clear, unbiased by either ancient or modern preconceptions. But still her thoughts pestered her.

She didn't understand why her call to Paul should bother her so much. Of course he'd be distracted, with a crowd of guests there. Maybe it was that she didn't even know he held that gathering, which reminded her that there was a lot they didn't know about each other. Or maybe it was that the situation here, Julieta's past and Tommy's entity and the lonely, mystic desert all around, was pulling her away from her own life. As she'd feared it would. She was being tugged out of the warm orbit of love and life and away into the colder reaches. Her efforts to nudge herself back were so easily frustrated. Paul seemed very far away. The way her question had unsettled him showed how uncertain things still were with them.

On the other hand, she agreed with his comment about love: never easy, but always deserving persistence. Love had enduring powers, too, despite all the obstacles. Good to remember.

And it would be good to see Joyce and Edgar. She'd feel more confident of handling this with the two of them around. Joyce was a crackerjack forensic and historical investigator, relentless, adaptive, good at spotting the possibilities in seemingly unlikely links. And Ed: Surprisingly, though his ostensible specialty was physics and though he primarily saw to the technological side of investigations, the most useful, crucial thing he did was talk to Cree. *Be there* for her. His insight into her emotional processes was deep and subtle. He steadied her and gently guided her through the labyrinth of her own knots, often providing her with the solutions to intractable problems.

As Joseph Tsosie seems to do for Julieta, it occurred to her. Which invited the question whether their motivations sprang from the same source— whether Joseph felt about Julieta the way Edgar felt about Cree.

It wasn't even a question. Joseph Tsosie was in love with Julieta. It was evident in every word and gesture. After listening to Julieta tell her story, Cree suspected he'd been in love with her for a long, long time.

But how did Julieta feel about Joseph? There was a lot of tenderness there, certainly, a lot of trust and reliance. But love? Desire? Need? If not, why not? The questions buzzed in Cree's thoughts as if there was a lot more to consider there.

She drew herself into lotus position, her hands seeking the dhyana mudra, slowing her breath and letting every last thought drain out of her.

A moment later, she caught herself as her head bobbed: She'd almost fallen asleep sitting up. Groggily, she laid her aching head on the pillow and pulled the spread over herself. Already the inside of her thighs had begun to stiffen from the unaccustomed exertion of riding. She liked the feeling. Sleep came in a series of big smooth sweeps, a great hand moving across a blackboard and erasing her entirely.

When she awoke, the room was dark. She pushed the glow button on her travel alarm to find that it was almost eight o'clock. She'd slept for three hours! Sensing that something was wrong, she scanned the dimly lit room and realized that the darkness was flickering. Adrenaline spiked in her fingertips before she noticed that the strobing effect wasn't coming from the night-lights or the ceiling light in the hall. It came from outside. Again and again, the windows flashed and darkened, a racing heartbeat of light.

She stumbled to one of the south-facing windows, which gave a view down the center of campus, the road and buildings lit at intervals by mercury vapor lamps. A quarter of a mile away, in front of the cafeteria, a different kind of light sparkled: the strobe panel on an ambulance van. As she clutched the windowsill, the boxy truck pulled out and turned away toward the main entrance. Its flasher lit the angles of the administration and classroom buildings in fitful red and white lightning, and then darkness steadied around the school as it accelerated out of the main entrance.

Cree could make out several figures, left behind in a cone of streetlight glow. They stood in a clump, looking after the ambulance: Lynn, no doubt, and a couple of other staff members. Standing apart from them, a motionless figure that could only be Julieta.

Cree felt a lurch in her chest, a twang of alarm and devastation and longing, and couldn't tell if it was her own feeling or something sprung from Julieta, the anguish of a mother seeing her child borne away and gone from the insufficient shelter of her love.

21

JULIETA'S OFFICE in the admin building was big enough to include a large desk, a low Mission-style coffee table surrounded by four leather chairs, a side table with a chrome coffeemaker on it, a floor-to-ceiling bookcase, a pair of splendid jade plants. Julieta sat behind her desk, her chair swiveled toward one of the west-facing windows. Ghosted in the rectangle of black glass, her features looked painfully lovely, perfect, ruined. When Cree walked in, her face tipped to regard Cree's reflection, but she didn't turn.

"Why didn't you call me?" Cree demanded.

Julieta shook her head. "You needed to rest. I doubt there was anything you could have done."

"What happened?"

"He was eating dinner. He . . . started stabbing himself in the hand and arm with his knife. *It* did, I mean. God knows what would have happened if the staff hadn't stopped it."

Another classic symptom, Cree thought with dismay, remembering the awful illustrations among Mason's materials.

Julieta stared out at the night for a long moment. "So soon. I thought we'd have some time. A few days, anyway."

"They're bringing him to the Indian Hospital again?"

"No. This time he's going straight to Ketteridge. It's a private hospital in Gallup, highly regarded for neurological diagnostics and psychiatric treatment."

"Think that's where he'll stay?"

The chair pivoted as Julieta came around, her face hardening. "Not if I have anything to do with it."

"What options are there?"

"I'm not sure. I've got a call in to our attorneys. Technically, he's still enrolled here as a resident student, which could mean I have some limited rights and responsibilities. There are probably some legal gray areas I could exploit. I might preserve access to him during litigation, anyway, or retain some say in medical decision making."

"What do the grandparents want to do?"

Julieta shook her head. "Can't get through—they don't have a regular phone, and cell reception's no good up there. But my guess is they'll want him to come home. I might be able to persuade them to send him back here one more time, but if I can't, I could probably delay his going home by legal means. Give you some time with him."

Cree digested that as she turned to look at Julieta's photo gallery, which covered half of one wall. Nicely framed, most were of class groups, rows of smiling faces of teenagers posing with their teachers. There were four whole-school photos, too, sixty-odd kids and twenty or more faculty and staff, sitting and standing in front of the log hogan at the center of campus. In each of them, Julieta looked radiant with pleasure and pride. Cree spotted Joseph in one group photo, standing next to Julieta, both smiling as if they'd just shared a joke. Nearer the desk was another of Joseph, caught off guard as he turned to look out the side window of his truck: a disturbingly straight-on gaze from a very handsome man.

Over closer to the door, in a separate cluster were half a dozen smaller pictures of horses. Cree recognized Spence from the yin-yang blaze.

"Spence," she said. "Huh. Why'd you name him that?"

The question clearly caught Julieta by surprise, slipping past her defenses. "After Spencer Tracy. I just . . . I've liked those movies ever since I was a little girl. That whole . . . style." A choked voice, someone fighting tears.

Another angle of view on Julieta: the little girl, spellbound by the debonair, dashing men and beautiful, clever women and their droll yet passionate romances where everything was fated to work out just right in the end. Cree spent another minute looking at the photos before she turned to face Julieta again. "You think the family would let me near him?"

"Possibly," Julieta said tightly. The angry resolve had taken over again.

"He's a terrific person, isn't he? I really saw that today. He tries to play resentful and rebellious, but he can't hide what he really is. He's decent and respectful. Very smart, yet at the same time so . . . innocent."

"Yes, he's a very special young man. Which is exactly why I'll fight to make sure he has the opportunities he needs and deserves."

Cree nodded, trying to muster the courage to say what she knew had to be said. "Can I make a suggestion? A frank one?"

"Like—?"

"Like, Julieta—every time you've screwed up in your life, it's been when you've gotten angry and confrontational and self-righteous and proud. When you've held on to what you felt you were owed." Julieta frowned and she tucked her chin, beginning to bristle. Cree's heart was thudding hard in her chest, but she made herself go on: "Don't do it this time, Julieta! Don't get your back up. And don't put Tommy in a tug-of-war over who's in charge of him. He's already torn about five ways. He doesn't need it. Sometimes you have to let go a little."

Outraged, Julieta said through her teeth, "I *have* 'let go,' Dr. Black. Of all too much."

Her fierceness was intimidating, but Cree pushed back: "Have you really?" She made a gesture toward her, *Look at yourself. Where you're at right now.*

"What would you suggest?" Julieta said icily. But Cree sensed that behind the hardness was a measure of grudging agreement.

"See what the grandparents say. Roll with it. Encourage them to let me spend time with him, wherever he ends up."

"And if they don't agree?"

"Don't assume that yet. Cross that bridge when we come to it. In the meantime, there's work I can do here."

"Like what?" Julieta's anger was veering toward despondency.

"I can explore your idea that the entity is a revenant of Garrett McCarty. Or that it's some formerly place-anchored entity connected with this location. I can get my colleagues out here and do some physical and historical research."

Julieta spun back to the window. Not that there was anything to see, Cree thought, but the same unwelcome reflections, hovering in their black frame. She stared stonily at nothing for a long time. The armored face broke Cree's heart as much as any outright sorrow would have.

"Nobody knows how you feel about him," Cree said gently. "Nobody will understand why you fight so hard to stay near him. They don't know the story. You'll seem pushy and grasping and arrogant. You'll get their backs up. Right?"

Julieta gave it another full minute before she came around again. "Fine," she snapped. She was trying mightily to stay hard, Cree saw, but it wasn't working. "You're right. That's how I screw up. Joseph has also been kind enough to bestow that little piece of wisdom upon me. You're right. Okay? I'll talk to the grandparents. I'll be conciliatory and sweet and charming as all get-out. And now I want to be left alone. I have a whole school to take care of. I've got work backed up to the rafters."

Cree overcame the urge to touch her, to smooth the lines in that lovely face. She turned toward the door to leave, but then paused. "Can I ask one more thing? Something that will help me think about this?"

"What?"

"How did you determine that Tommy is your child? I want to understand your . . . recognition of him. When you first knew, how you knew. Was it from his records, or—"

"It's complicated," Julieta said. She paused, and when she spoke again her voice was soft and husky as regret and doubt overcame the iron. "And it'll just have to wait for tomorrow. Because I don't have anything left today. I haven't got what it takes. It's too much. Too complex. Just like every other goddamned thing in the world."

Cree nodded and went into the hallway.

"Cree."

Surprised, Cree turned back. Julieta sat facing her raptly, but kept her eyes on her desk. "I just wanted to say . . . I think I understand what you're trying to do. And I know I'm not making it easier. I can't believe what a total bitch I've been. I've just . . . it's just . . . *hard* right now. I hope sometime we can get to know each other under . . . other circumstances."

"I'd like that, too. Very much." Cree shot her a smile and shut the door.

22

CREE AWOKE with a shriek, sitting up convulsively and knocking her clock and notebook off the bedside table. The faces in the rocks! They had been writhing and moaning in her dreams, opening wide, devouring mouths and rolling blind eyes. Anger and fear, awful struggle, transformation. For several minutes she sat breathing hard, trying to master her fright. It seemed she could still feel them out there, only a few hundred yards away, invisible but radiating their torment into the night. A wind had picked up outside, making whispers around the infirmary building, a white noise against which her ears strained.

She lay down again, snugged the blankets close, but found she was too wired to sleep. The images wouldn't leave her. They cried their outrage like a curse or a pledge or a warning. Dreaming the same thing two nights in a row: For any psychologist, it would suggest significant subconscious turmoil. For an empathic parapsychologist, it meant much more. Some echo of human experience lingered out there. Some presence.

She'd have to go to the mesa, and soon.

She sat up against the headboard, very aware of the new stiffness of her thighs and the itching ache in her forehead. Listening to the night, she tried to calm her jumpy nerves and thought about Julieta's heartbreaking confessions and her terrifying desperation. A woman so needing comforting yet so unwilling to accept it.

The thought brought her back to the question of Julieta and Joseph. Joseph would comfort her if she'd let him. Did she not see his affection for her, or did she not reciprocate? Had they tried as lovers at some point and decided against it for some reason?

No, she knew intuitively. The longing between them had not been expressed, wasn't the species of desire that former lovers showed. The real answer was simpler: Peter. Though Julieta denied it, she lived with long-gone Peter Yellowhorse always inside her, a phantom of memory. Julieta was "possessed," too, by a young lover from the distant past, transformed with the passage of years from a flesh-and-blood, humanly flawed reality to an unapproachable ideal of passion and potential that no living man could match. Leaving her incapable of finding it with anyone else. Not with the occasional lovers over the years, not even with a handsome, sexy, intelligent, attentive, and patient man like Joseph Tsosie.

Her restlessness grew as her thoughts of Julieta echoed with uneasy resonances in her own life. Her forehead itched, the jacket bunched around her armpits, one leg was falling asleep. She stood up and paced through the ward room in the dim green light, swinging her arms. One forty-three in the morning. She desperately needed sleep, she'd be a wreck tomorrow, but it was impossible while somewhere in Gallup a boy lay with some being inside him, deforming him, damaging him. She needed to get to work. There was no guarantee she'd ever have access to Tommy again, but if she did, she should be better prepared for the encounter. Sleep obviously wasn't going to come tonight, she might as well get on with what she'd planned to do.

Seize the day, she thought. The thought made her chuckle blackly. *Or, rather, the night.* The ghost hunter's credo.

She put on her jacket, zipped it, and snapped the collar snug around her throat. She found the master key that Julieta had given her earlier, then realized she should probably have a flashlight better than the tiny LED on her key ring. She slipped quietly down the hall and into the nurse's office, where she pulled the rechargeable from the wall and tested it briefly. Not great, but it would do. She left the building by the front door and hurried toward the boys' dorm.

The night was black, an opaque darkness clotted by the haze that had crept in toward sunset, and the sharp light of the security lamps scattered through the campus only served to blind her. The wind blew strongly from the northwest, stirring the dry leaves of the cottonwood trees and drawing a faint, plaintive song from the old bronze bell in its little tower. Not far beyond the mercury-gilt gym building, she knew, the mesa hunkered in the dark. In her mind, its rock faces were alive: She could still feel them there, twisting and swarming, thrusting hopelessly at their mineral barrier.

The lock on the dorm's north door gave her trouble, but she wiggled and jammed the key and at last it turned. She stepped inside and eased the door shut.

A long corridor stretched the length of the building, lit by ankle-high night-lights every fifteen feet. Doorways lined both sides. With the handful of weekenders gone on their field trip, Julieta had let the new residence staffer take a couple of nights off. The building was empty and almost completely dark, just as Cree wanted it.

Julieta had told her that Tommy's room was the second from the north end, on the right. Cree hesitated at the doorway, peering into a darkness lit only by the red eyes of emergency lighting system batteries high on the wall. A long, narrow room the size of a small classroom, six beds and dressers against the west wall, six desks against the inner wall. The scent of pubescent boys—sweat, deodorant, the rubbery perfume of athletic shoes. On the walls, posters, photos, artwork, awards, stolen highway signs, miscellany.

Cree stepped inside, still avoiding using the flashlight, wanting to remain as long as possible in the hyperalert state darkness always induced. Her antennae were buzzing with a nervous electricity that made her jumpy but also seemed to extend the reach of her subtler senses. In the dim red glow, the room had a secret, enclosed feel, like the interior of a photo darkroom. The wind probed at the windows with soft, persistent fingers.

There was no question which bed was Tommy's. No athletic posters here: The wall above was covered with drawings. Reluctantly, she brought out the flashlight and turned it on. When her eyes recovered from the glare, she panned the circle of light from one drawing to the other, increasingly impressed.

There was a portrait of some rap star with a credibly aloof gangsta face, and a savage scene of a group of white policemen shooting an African-American man—the Diallo shooting? There were two interior still lifes: a stove with pots and pans and utensils hung on the wall above it, a stark windowsill with a lonely-looking book open on it. Cree's eyes devoured each one in turn.

Most compelling were the portraits. One was of a very old man with a face deeply cut by seams of worry and determination, rendered with meticulous care that captured the subject's weary dignity and strength. Tommy's grandfather? Cree was no interpretive expert, but this level of attention to detail had to derive from considerable affection for the subject. Another was a series of studies of a Navajo man and woman, side by side, drawn repeatedly on the big page. His parents? Again the level of detail was astonishing. Looking more closely, Cree found that each of the six sketches characterized the subjects differently: In one, their faces looked bland and ordinary; in the next, unmistakably shifty or sleazy; the others portrayed them as rather heroic, cruel, pathetic, kindly. The third portrait featured the same couple, drawn twice—astonishingly, one rendered them as decidedly "Indian," with feathers in their hair and traditional robes, while the other as completely Caucasian, with pale skin and tidy, suburban, casual clothes. When she peeled loose the tape that held it to the wall, she found the date scrawled on the back: July 2002. She lifted corners of the other drawings and found that all were from the spring or summer, just before he'd come to Oak Springs School.

A noise from the hall made her heart leap. She straightened quickly and shut off the flashlight, listening, hands tingling with alarm. The wind buffeted the windows, and as she listened she heard the sound again: a repetitive click and chunk. Relieved, she realized it was just the outer door at the end of the hall, rocking against its latch—she must not have shut it fully behind her.

She turned on the flashlight again and moved to the bedside dresser. Its top was cluttered: a bunch of pencils bound together with a rubber band, a couple of kneaded erasers, a half-consumed package of chewing gum, a pile of photocopied handouts from a math class; coins, CD cases, a calculator. A framed photo showed a man and woman who were clearly the subjects of the portrait studies. As the camera had caught them, they were a thirty-something Navajo couple with the slightly stilted smiles you often saw in studio shots. She scrutinized their faces for the qualities Tommy had emphasized in his studies. On the back, someone had written *Thomas and Bernice Keeday, 1996*. Tommy's adoptive parents.

Comparing the photo to the portraits, Cree had to acknowledge that Tommy was a hugely talented kid. Also, as Joseph said, a kid with deep ambivalence about the people he'd known as his parents. Or maybe simply a kid trying to figure out who they were, experimenting with different conceptions of them. The thought made her heart ache.

She put the photo down and went through the drawers, feeling like a burglar, apologizing to Tommy in her mind. But she found nothing revealing: just baggy jeans, shirts, underpants, sweatshirts. She knelt to look under the bed, where a pair of well-worn cleated athletic shoes kept company with a shabby suitcase and a shoe box full of cassettes and CDs. Tommy's preference in music reinforced her sense of his identification with angry, urban black rebellion. She thought about Tommy's cultural uncertainties and wondered what he'd feel if he knew that eleven-year-old Seattle white girls like Zoe also ate up the gangsta style. What banner of rebellion would remain for him to carry?

The suitcase was empty and told her nothing.

The outside hall door clicked again, loud enough to startle Cree. She panned the light at the door of the room and into the hall, and decided she'd better shut the damned thing, not waste heat. But as she was heading to the hall, her eyes went to the inner wall, and what she saw drew her immediately to Tommy's desk. On the desktop lay a couple of large, spiral-bound artist's sketchbooks. More drawings had been taped to the wall behind it.

The flashlight was dimming, but it cast enough light to tell that these had been drawn since he'd arrived at Oak Springs. In one, Cree recognized the central campus road, looking north with the hogan just to the left, a delivery truck off to the right, Julieta's once and future house distant in the center. Tommy had compressed the buildings at the bottom of the page, a horizontal band of detail beneath a huge, featureless sky. The radical vertical asymmetry struck Cree as a strong compositional experiment, suggesting that Tommy was growing rapidly as an artist. Another drawing showed a group of fellow students seated in the mottled shade of a trellis. Tommy had done a beautiful job of capturing the boys and girls in their various postures, then had heightened the intensity of the scene by exaggerating the shadows. The hard chiaroscuro was fascinating but a little jarring, cutting the space into two very different dimensions.

The third one really grabbed Cree's eye: a self-portrait. The face was well rendered, instantly recognizable as Tommy's despite the powerful artifice he'd chosen to portray himself with. The face was divided by a line down the middle. He'd rendered the left half in the conventional manner with black lines on the white page, the right half in the negative, white lines on black.

It screamed from all of the newer drawings: two dimensions, two layers, two visions. Two Tommys. Pulse racing, she ignored the pestering wind noise and the puffs of chill creeping along the floor from the hall. She moved aside a tin box full of charcoal and pencils to open one of the sketchbooks.

Holding the feeble flashlight close, she opened the book and saw that these drawings continued the theme of division or doubleness. The first few looked like the mesa near the school: the steep sandstone cliffs, the tumbled boulders and dry gullies. In one, he'd included fellow members of his drawing class, sitting on rocks with sketch pads propped against knees. Again, he'd used shadow and composition to divide every scene into different dimensions.

It was a drawing several pages farther that stopped her cold.

Another pencil sketch of weatherworn cliffs, the angle of the shadows suggesting midday. In this one, Tommy had subtly morphed the features of the rocks into human faces. A half dozen huge faces, deftly rendered in the shadows and highlights of rock shapes and fissures. Agonized stone faces pressed against their interface with the air. Pushing, swarming, silently clamoring.

Just like the ones in her dreams.

Cree felt suddenly weak, and her stomach tightened in a deep, sick clench. She flipped the page and found another drawing similar to the first: faces emerging from patterns of light and shadow. On closer inspection, she saw again the deliberate variation of character: One seemed noble, one brutish, others cruel, cowering, pathetic, wise. The only affect that ran through all of them was suffering.

Cree dropped the book, feeling utterly out of her depth. Her head ached with each pounding heartbeat. Everything was going around, dizzying, her thoughts hyperanimated and chaotic. And she'd been so engrossed that she'd ignored something crucial: The noise in the hall wasn't right. There was a shifting sound now, the quiet sound of cloth moving against cloth.

She switched off the flashlight and inched toward the door, afraid to look into the hall, afraid to stay where she was. Afraid to breathe. She forced herself to the doorway, made herself push her face around the edge of the frame.

23

"LYNN! Good Jesus, you startled me!" Cree felt a flood of relief at the sight of the nurse, standing twenty feet away in the dim green light with arm outstretched, hand against the wall. She looked like a person who had been startled while listening or waiting for something. Cree wondered how long she'd been there.

"As you did me. Oh, my!" Lynn blew out a breath and fluttered a hand against her chest. Then she came toward Cree, trailing her fingers against the corridor wall. "I thought you might be here, but I got a little worried when I found the door open. And no lights on."

Cree backed into the dorm room. "I couldn't sleep. So I figured I'd come and look at Tommy's drawings and things. Before the other kids got back."

Lynn Pierce came through the door and switched on the overhead lights. The tubes flickered and hummed and then came on garishly bright. She took in the room before locking her disconcerting eyes on Cree's. "In the dark?" she asked expressionlessly.

"I borrowed your flashlight."

"I know. I heard you go into the office." A clever expression fled quickly across her face and was banished. "So you still hope to be working with him?"

"It'll probably come down to getting his grandparents' permission. If there's any chance I can, I figured I should make use of the time. Get to know him better."

Lynn looked at the open notebook on Tommy's desk, the bureau drawer Cree had neglected to close. "Finding anything interesting?"

"I think so."

"Like—?"

Cree went to the desk, flipped the notebook pages to one of the drawings of faces. "This, for example. Do you know if it's from life—a real place? Or is it a made-up place?"

Lynn Pierce came to her shoulder to consider the drawing. "It looks like the walls of the mesa. Oh, sure—it's that spot about, oh, maybe a mile north of here. It's the deepest gully on this side, the rock formations are pretty distinctive. Picturesque, I guess you'd say. The art teachers often take classes there before the cold weather sets in. What—the faces?"

"Do they mean anything to you?"

Lynn shrugged and shook her silver head once. "A teenage boy with an active imagination."

Unaccountably ill at ease with Lynn so close to her shoulder, Cree left the desk and went to sit on the end of Tommy's bed. "Did you want to talk to me? Is that why you followed me here?"

Smiling minutely, Lynn turned to face Cree and half sat against the edge of the desk. "Mind if I smoke? Strictly speaking, it's not allowed, but with the kids gone . . ." She rummaged in her pocket and brought out a pack of cigarettes, a lighter, and a little foil ashtray folded into a half circle. She opened the ashtray and smoothed out its creases before setting it on the desk. She lit a cigarette and drew on it hungrily. When she exhaled, she carefully blew the smoke away from Cree, toward the hall door.

"My one vice," she apologized. "Down to five a day. And never in the infirmary, God forbid." Another deep suck that made the ember spark, and then her gaze wandered cautiously from the floor to meet Cree's. "I was wondering what kind of psychologist you are."

"I got my Ph.D. in clinical psychology from Duke."

"But you specialize . . ."

"Didn't Julieta tell you my focus?"

"She's the boss. She tells me only what she thinks I need to hear. I guess I didn't need to hear the details this time."

"It's hard to explain, Lynn. There's really no name for my field of specialty."

"Not 'parapsychologist'? On the Internet, that's the term that seems to come up." Lynn blew another gout of smoke toward the door and with an air of apology swished at it with one hand. "I did a search on you this evening."

"Does that bother you?"

"I can't decide. The strictly orthodox professional in me disapproves. But Tommy . . . it's baffling. I can't imagine what's going on with him."

"Any thoughts you want to share?"

She startled Cree with a direct bolt of her blue-bronze gaze, then tapped ash into the foil tray before answering. "Did you know I was married to a Navajo? Sixteen years. My Vern died fifteen years ago." She hesitated, clearly stumbling over that obstinate fact without meaning to.

"I'm sorry, Lynn."

"Yeah. Well," the nurse said reflexively.

"I know that 'yeah, well.'" Cree smiled. "I lost my husband, too."

The look Lynn returned had a surprised, grateful quality to it. But it lasted only an instant before she half shook her head, refusing the sympathy or resisting the impulse to remember. A drag on her cigarette seemed to help her find her train of thought again. "It took a few years for his family to accept me, a white Midwestern girl, but eventually I got to know them pretty well. The older people told stories about this kind of thing . . . Once we went to a Way sung for one of his nephews. The boy had started having what a mainstream doctor would've diagnosed as grand mal seizures. The Hand-Trembler said he had a ghost in him. That he had offended an ancestor. The family hired a Singer to do the Evil Way."

"Do you believe it? About the ghost?"

"It's completely at odds with my medical training . . ."

"But—" Cree prompted.

Lynn smiled crookedly. "But after the Way, his symptoms were much less extreme."

Cree smiled with her. Despite her unease, she found herself intrigued by this odd, tense, smart, apologetic woman whose aura glinted with the sharp silver flashes of well-concealed anger.

"I guess I'm credulous enough to be curious what a parapsychologist would do about Tommy," Lynn continued. "I was also very impressed with the way you handled him when we were playing cards—responsive but not condescendingly sympathetic. I admire that. Refreshingly unlike our beloved but distinctly overindulgent principal. He respects you now, you could tell by the way he opened up to you during softball. That'll help." She took a last, long drag on her cigarette, blew out a blue-gray plume, stabbed out the butt. Obviously a practiced clandestine smoker, she folded the ashtray like a clam around the remains and returned it to her pocket. "That is, if the doctors at Ketteridge or his grandparents let you work with him."

Despite Lynn's efforts to disperse the smoke, the acrid stink rasped in Cree's lungs. She got up to look again at the drawings over the bed. In the brighter light, the skill of the rendering was more apparent: The old man looked alive.

"You've worked here for, what, two years?"

"Three."

"So you must know her pretty well. Julieta." The old man seemed to be looking over Cree's shoulder, as if watching Lynn on the other side of the room.

"In some ways, maybe."

"She's a remarkable person, isn't she?"

A hesitation. "She certainly is."

"I mean, she's dynamic, she's intelligent, she's beautiful enough to turn any woman green, she's passionate—"

"She is all that and much more."

Cree gave it a beat, and then suggested casually, "But—?"

"But nothing. And I'm not that easy, Dr. Black. Please don't be sly with me."

Cree felt caught out. Her head was hurting again, putting her off her stride, and the hovering layer of cigarette smoke was a distracting irritant. "Your tone seemed to qualify your praise, that's all. I was wondering why."

"She's great. She's my boss. No qualification."

Cree let it go, pretending to give the next drawing a close inspection. "So, okay, ghosts of ancestors can cause things like this. What else can? What's the story on Skinwalkers? Are there really such things—evil Navajo magicians, people capable of changing into animals? Do people still believe any of that?"

"Around white people, Vern always said it was nonsense. Superstition."

"And what did he say when he wasn't around white people? What did the old people say?" Cree half turned and jumped to find that Lynn had come silently up close to her again, standing just behind her shoulder. She moved a step away.

"Sideways comments," the nurse said quietly. "Warnings with their eyes not to talk about it. Once Vern bought a wolf skin from a pawnshop in Gallup—kind of a joke, just to show how above it he was, something we'd put in front of our woodstove. But there'd been some Navajos from our town at the pawnshop, and they recognized him. The next day, that's how fast gossip travels on the rez, three of Vern's uncles came to our house. A delegation from the family. Said he should burn it. Said people were talking about him, they'd get the wrong idea. Of course it was crap—a real Navajo Wolf wouldn't buy his skin at a Gallup pawnshop!"

"Did he burn it?" Claustrophobic, Cree sidled another step away.

"Yes, as a matter of fact." Standing where Cree had just been, the nurse pretended to look over Tommy's drawings. "Why? What does a modern parapsychologist think of old superstitions?"

"This one thinks there's usually some wisdom there."

"You're thinking there's a . . . spirit inhabiting Tommy, aren't you? That he's possessed. Is that what you are? An exorcist?"

Cree would have preferred not to discuss it with Lynn, not yet. But there was no denying the obvious. "No, I'm not an exorcist. I don't believe the popular idea of possession, Lynn. I'm skeptical of the idea of purely evil beings. In my experience, paranormal entities are neither more nor less wicked than living humans. I wouldn't assume this thing has malevolent intentions. It may be just lost or scared or desperate. Or lonely."

Lynn Pierce cocked her head, puzzled. "Am I being obtuse in some way? Because you saw him attack Julieta. And he stabbed himself repeatedly tonight." She winced as she rubbed her forearm and went on. "In fact, I have a confession to make. Something I didn't tell anyone, but I'll tell you." She unbuttoned the cuff of her jacket, tugged back the sleeve, then rolled the sleeve of her blouse. Cree gasped at the sight of the half circles of scabs and the surrounding penumbra of marbled green bruising. "From last week. I didn't tell Julieta because she's so . . . *invested* in Tommy. I didn't want her to worry." Lynn held up the arm and rotated it, looking at the wounds with satisfaction, as if admiring a suntan.

"Do you have any idea why she might be so 'invested' in him? Him particularly?"

Again, Lynn cocked her head. "Why do I keep getting the feeling you're trying to tempt me into indiscretions? Or maybe I'm just being paranoid. That must be it. But." She raised the wounded arm again and pinned Cree with her gaze. "You didn't answer me. Still convinced it's harmless?"

The bites were upsetting, and Cree needed a moment to think about what they implied. She moved farther away from Lynn, around Tommy's bed to one of the windows, where she leaned her pounding forehead gingerly against the pane and cupped her hands around her eyes to look outside. All she could see was the rectangle of bare earth lit by the ceiling fluorescents, stark as a patch of moon landscape, with her own humped shadow cut into it. Beyond the light, dead black. The wind whimpered faintly as if it wanted to get inside. The glass was icy against her skin. The nurse was complex and strange, and seemed to be fencing—to be asking or offering something. But Cree couldn't think well enough to respond in the right way. All she knew was that if Lynn came too far into her physical space one more time, she'd confront her on it.

"The entity is not harmless," Cree said at last. "It's hurting Tommy terribly. We just don't know that it's *intentionally* doing so. There's an important difference."

"Good point. Excellent point. Of course." The admiration in Lynn's voice seemed genuine. "You're very smart, Dr. Black. I can't tell you what a pleasure it is talking with you. Such a refreshing change from . . . well, from my usual diet of conversation."

This time Cree heard her moving, and she spun around quickly.

But Lynn had gone to the door and stood half turned as if about to leave. "You've been very kind, Cree Black. Thank you. I know I'm strange. Hard to get used to. My Vern used to say I was an acquired taste." Her downcast eyes darted around the floor as if searching for something; then, as if she'd found it, she brightened a bit and looked at Cree. "What you said about paranormal entities—you apply the same principle to living humans, too, don't you? I like that very much. You won't assume someone has malevolent intentions. They may be just lost or scared or desperate. Or lonely, huh?" She offered a shy, apologetic smile that quickly failed, and with a tired wave left the room.

174

24

JOSEPH TSOSIE bumped his head on the door frame as he bumbled thick headed and banana fingered into his pickup. Morning at last, the prospect of some sleep. End of a long shift.

Julieta had called at around ten P.M. to tell him Tommy's symptoms had peaked again and that he'd been taken by ambulance to Ketteridge Hospital. She was afraid that she'd lost him now. He'd tried to console her but had to cut it short: He'd had patients waiting. Saturday night was drinking time on the rez. Those who needed it drove into Gallup or Farmington, pawned some family jewelry, put down a bellyful of booze, and got into accidents on the long drive back home. Or they opened up the bottle they'd provided themselves with earlier and got into fights or accidents or other mischief that left them in the emergency ward at some dark hour, where Joseph, or whoever was on shift, dutifully sutured their torn flesh or set their shattered bones or prepped them for internal surgery. Even now, eight o'clock Sunday morning, an old man was tottering around the parking lot of the Tribal Social Services building, blown like a tumbleweed on the random winds of ethyl-crazed impulse.

Joseph chided himself for his dark mood and reminded himself of his priorities: *Hot shower. Bed.*

The sun had just come up and was starting to burn its way through a high, thin ice haze. Along Route 12, where the red disk broke above the Manuelito Plateau, the bluffs wore pleated skirts of blue-black shadow. There were no other cars on the road, and the scattered houses were blank windowed and still. He turned on the radio, listened to the yammer of a commercial station, couldn't stand it, switched to a Sunday-morning Evangelical harangue and couldn't stand that either. He turned it off again and was grateful for the silence.

Tired as he always was, he relished these Sunday morning drives, especially in the autumn when dawn came late and he was there to see the rising sun. On a morning like this, it was easy to imagine this landscape as its first explorers had seen it, thousands of years ago: imponderably vast, humblingly ancient and full of mysteries. They'd have probed it cautiously, appraising the land's capacity to sustain life, alert for signs of water and game and enemies and portents, wary of the spirits who had first claim here. And that wasn't exclusively an Anasazi or Navajo perspective, you couldn't ascribe it to some local gene. Every people throughout the world had populated its pinewoods or deserts or ice fields, its rain forests or mountains or seacoasts with invisible beings that commanded that exalted form of fear called reverence. As a kid at St. Bonaventure's boarding school, he'd often asked his teachers why the Old Testament used the word "fear" to describe what you were supposed to feel about God, and he'd never gotten a satisfactory answer. Later, one kindly priest had explained the way perspectives had evolved in the New Testament, Christ's emphasis upon love between the Almighty and his creations. At the time, he'd found reassurance in that view.

But now, with what was happening to Tommy Keeday, he couldn't help thinking maybe the older texts had it right after all.

He wondered how the parapsychologist saw this stuff. She seemed to have sorted out her metaphysics in some way, forged a personal reconciliation between very divergent worldviews. He envied that equilibrium. For all his doubts about her, he also had to admit that she'd dealt very well with Tommy: sympathetic and responsive, yet never indulging in any of the politically correct walking on eggshells that you so often saw among whites pursuing altruistic motives among Navajos. Not even when Tommy had deliberately tried to prevail upon the liberal guilt reflexes he'd learned to expect from social service and medical types. Cree Black obviously had a talent for getting people to show themselves. Already she had induced Julieta to reveal the long-buried saga of Peter Yellowhorse, the divorce, the baby. It made Joseph's cheeks burn to think of anyone else knowing about the mistakes they'd made together sixteen years ago. Still, the parapsychologist's getting Julieta to talk about her past was a testament to her skills.

Not that it mattered, at this point: With Tommy gone from the school, Cree Black's talents or lack thereof might be irrelevant.

Driving on automatic pilot, he realized that he'd passed his turn into Window Rock. Not really an accident, he knew immediately. Thinking about Julieta's pleading last night made him realize that he had pressing business that took precedence over the need for sleep. He needed to find Uncle Joe Billie, ask him some questions. Given that it was a weekend, he knew where to find his mother's brother. Whether the old man would tell him anything, whether he was sober enough to understand the issues or felt like playing games today, was another matter.

He stopped at the Mustang station to gas up the truck and get a cup of coffee to go. Then he headed east on Route 264, the sun searing straight into his eyes as he left the Navajo Nation, entered the United States, and hit the highway for the drive to Gallup.

He shut off the engine in the rutted dirt lot across the highway from the flea market. Nine-thirty, it was too early for the big crowds, and the parking area was less than half full of pickups and station wagons. The hay sellers were doing a brisk business, though, tossing down bales from towering stacks on flatbed semitrailers to family pickups that nosed up against their flanks like foals to a mare.

Joseph crossed the highway to the dirt access road that ran around the market proper. Some of the smaller vendors were still arriving, moving their tables and racks and paraphernalia on dollies or garden carts. Whole families carried things: little girls carrying nested hand-woven baskets, boys wrestling toppling piles of cowboy hats or burlap sacks of potatoes, fathers and mothers struggling with racks of toys or Chinese-made tools or their own handicrafts. Already the air was filled with the smell of fry bread and roasting mutton, reminding Joseph that he hadn't eaten any breakfast.

Uncle Joe often set up in the first row of stalls, among some of the other herb sellers. But as Joseph scanned the row, he didn't see his uncle's weathered face. He stopped at one of the booths to ask a young woman if she'd seen *Hastiin* Joe Billie, and she said she thought maybe he'd come late and was around one of the side lanes. Joseph thanked her and left her table. The Gallup Flea Market covered many acres and included hundreds of vendors who sold everything from used engine blocks to watermelon juice, potatoes to livestock-castrating tools, snow cones to hand-woven blankets, plastic action-figure toys to saddles to computer components.

When he was younger, it had included more local crafts, but now many of the vendors were small-time entrepreneurs who'd gotten a line on off-brand tools or cooking utensils, T-shirts, Chinese-made electronics, Mexican tourist goods, music CDs and cassettes. Still, there were plenty of family-run stands full of pottery and jewelry, piles of root vegetables, bags of herbs, goat-fat soap, wool and sheepskins and leather. From their rough hands and the reserve in their eyes, you could tell some of these people had come in from remote areas where crowds like this were unknown and the nickels and dimes they'd make here were big-time cash. This was how he imagined some bazaar in Cairo or Istanbul might look: tarp-covered stalls, piles of vegetables, stacks of boxes, food concessions with grills roasting meat or boiling vats of corn stew. There were some whites here, as well as Mexicans, Pueblos, Apaches, even a few Japanese guys and Pakistanis, but most of the vendors and clientele were Navajos. He looked at their faces and felt their collective anarchic energy with a familiar mix of pride and sorrow.

He found another herb vendor whose face he thought he recognized. "*Yá'át'ééh*. Do you know where Joe Billie is today?" he asked.

"Maybe around back," the man answered.

Which meant it could take him a long time to find Uncle Joe. If strung end to end, the meandering rows of stalls would stretch a couple of miles. The thought made him feel weary and he decided he'd better still the complaining of his stomach before going any farther. He stopped at a likely-looking concession, an Airstream trailer fronted by a tarp-covered sitting area with four picnic tables. The roast mutton wasn't ready yet, so he ordered a bowl of stew, a couple of fry breads, and a cup of coffee, and when he got the food took it to a table where he could look out on the lane as he ate. Several booths down, one of the music sellers turned on a boom box, playing a CD of some local country-and-western band, amateurish but full of vigor. Joseph ripped a piece from the huge disk of bread, salted it, and wolfed it down. Time to catch his breath and fortify himself.

Anyway, before he talked to Uncle Joe, he needed another few minutes to gather his thoughts.

Besides pleading with him to tell her whether Tommy really was her long-lost baby, Julieta had begged him to help keep the parapsychologist working with the boy, to intercede with the grandparents or the doctors to keep her on as a consulting psychologist.

Which required he make a decision about Cree Black. As Tommy's primary physician, someone the grandparents trusted, a doctor in good standing at Ketteridge, he could play Roman emperor, give Cree a thumbs-up or a thumbs-down. Thumbs-down: He could recommend against her having access to the boy, and there would be little she could do about it. Thumbs-up, and they'd probably assent to her seeing him.

Two days ago, it would have been an easier decision: good-bye, Dr. Black. But the parapsychologist's methods were not at all what he'd expected. Every time they spoke, she articulated her perspective so clearly and compellingly. And yet it was like nothing he'd ever heard of.

Well, not quite, he realized. Surprisingly, some aspects of her approach resembled the traditional Navajo healing process. Her belief in spirits capable of occupying a human being, that was part of it, and the way real reverence merged with superstition in her personal cosmology. It was also her emphasis on the patient's social environment. By probing the interpersonal relationships around the sufferer, Cree Black made the group part of the process—not unlike the complex Ways the old healers performed, where the whole community came to give the ritual and the patient their support. It was one component of the traditions he'd accepted as both defensible and, for some afflictions anyway, effective.

And she had an impressive résumé, too. During a break yesterday morning, he had looked her up on the Internet and found a surprising number of references: advanced degrees, significant publications, lecturing, a prestigious postdoctoral research prize.

Joseph chuckled cynically, surprised at himself. He couldn't decide which factor influenced him most, but on balance, he decided, he was impressed with her and wouldn't mind seeing what she could accomplish with Tommy. At the very least, arranging for Cree Black to keep working with him would soothe Julieta, maybe discourage her from raising legal challenges to the grandparents' custody, or waging a private, hopeless war against the health-care system. Or otherwise staking claims on the boy that she couldn't defend and that would rip Tommy's world, and hers, apart.

But Cree Black's approach also created potential problems.

The first was simply that her methods might not hold any promise for

Tommy. The woman could be chasing vapors. Despite the baffling strangeness of his symptoms, Joseph still had to believe Tommy was suffering from a neurological or psychological problem that would ultimately need a clinical remedy. Cree Black could do worse than nothing; she could delay or misdirect the treatment that Tommy really needed. In that sense, the very persuasiveness that made her such a skilled interviewer and confidante could make her dangerous. Already, Julieta had bought completely into the idea that Tommy was indeed "possessed," and that the culprit was the nasty ghost of a too-familiar enemy, Garrett McCarty.

The other big problem was that Dr. Black's delving into the past could unearth trouble that was best left alone. It could plunge Julieta into self-doubt and self-castigation and the dangerous instability that he'd seen too many times over the years. Worse, Cree might force to the surface secrets that would expose Joseph himself. Things he'd done that he couldn't forgive himself for, let alone ask Julieta to forgive.

Joseph's appetite faltered at the memories, but he made himself eat, scooping bites of stew with a chunk of bread.

He'd done his best to help Julieta, but they'd both been so young, so naïve. It had rapidly gotten so out of control—the progression of mistakes and deceptions that culminated in the decision to give up her baby. How stupid he'd been to think she could get over that! He should have put his foot down: *Julieta, forget about what Garrett has done to you. Forget about fighting for a favorable divorce settlement. Don't accuse and defame him in court, don't try to hold on to any of his property. Don't give him one more reason to hate or resist you, or any more of a grudge to settle. Just get free of him, as fast and easy as possible, even if it means you end up penniless. Keep the baby, let your new life start now.*

There are other alternatives, he should have said.

Like what? What other alternatives had there been? That's what he'd never articulated. That's where he'd really failed her.

But there were three words he'd had no right to say: *You and me.*

What could he have offered? *Be with me. I'll claim I'm the father, I'll take care of you and the baby. I'll take the heat from McCarty and protect you from him with my life if I have to.*

He had come very close, but it hadn't been possible. At first, she had been deeply in love with Peter Yellowhorse, and for all either of them knew Peter might have come back to her. She'd also been afraid, and blinded by anger and fear, and deeply disillusioned; he couldn't have offered himself without seeming to exploit her confusion and desperation. And then she'd been fighting free of two different but equally devastating relationships with men—the last thing she needed was another male making demands or claims on her. What she'd needed was a *friend*. And she'd looked to Joseph to be that.

It had been a simple choice, really. But in trying, he'd made some mistakes of his own. Terrible mistakes.

Anyway, he hadn't been free, either. When he'd first encountered the beautiful young volunteer at the hospital, he'd been still tangled in the emotional and situational coils of his own divorce process. In 1984, he was twenty-eight, married for six years, not long out of medical school and just beginning to come to grips with the way his years at Johns Hopkins had changed him. Wondering why he'd married Edith Blanco. Realizing that while she was a good person, they were too different; he'd married her during his last semester at UNM as much out of insecurity as affection, a young man intimidated by his pending leap into the unknown of the urban East Coast and desperate to anchor himself to his home place and people. When he'd first met Julieta, he'd already spent a year on the uneasy verge of ending it with Edith.

By the time he'd divorced and she'd divorced and they had each regained a vague semblance of emotional equilibrium, the habits of distance had set in. There were things he was afraid to tell her. He got the sense she was afraid, too—of her own mistakes, maybe, afraid to repeat them with him. In the intervening years, the occasional other relationships had come and gone, never feeling right for either of them, confusing and delaying. The timing never right.

He'd let eighteen years pass since he'd first met her. The worst mistake of all.

The boom box down the row went quiet for a moment and then began playing Navajo chants, sung by a ragged chorus of hoarse voices accompanied by a solitary drum. The monotonous wailing irritated Joseph and reminded him why he'd come here. He mopped up the remains of his stew, ate the last bite of bread, and drank off his coffee. He threw away the paper plate and cup and continued on through the market.

★　★　★

Joe Billie was unusually tall for a Navajo, but also unusually thin, as if his extra height had been attained by stretching a shorter man. He wore the standard uniform of men of his generation—jeans, cowboy boots, western shirt, and cowboy hat—and he had the gaunt, seamed face of a man who had spent a lot of time outdoors. He'd gone to college on the GI Bill and had worked as a rural livestock veterinarian until he'd retired at sixty-five, eight or ten years ago. Though he'd served in the marines during the Korean War, had studied modern medical theory, and had married a Catholic, he'd been drifting back toward a redis-covered Navajo traditionalism for as long as Joseph could remember, and after retirement he'd used his extensive contacts to build a part-time profession as an herbalist. There had always been something of the huckster about Uncle Joe, and Joseph was never quite sure how seriously he took his latest vocation.

Joseph found him talking to a short, squat woman who carried a number of plastic shopping bags in one hand and restrained an impatient toddler with the other. When Uncle Joe saw Joseph, he winked through the cigarette smoke snaking up from the butt between his lips, but he didn't interrupt his discussion with his customer. They were talking about how to prepare some poultice or potion.

Waiting, Joseph pretended to look over Uncle Joe's wares, the rows of ziplock baggies full of crushed leaves, dried berries, chips of bark, shreds and chunks of roots, corn pollen, mineral powders. He made a covert assessment of Uncle Joe. Behind the table, Joe Billie kept a couple of aluminum lawn chairs and an upturned plastic milk crate that held a transistor radio, some magazines, a pack of cigarettes, and the telltale brown paper bag molded to the shape of a bottle.

The woman told Uncle Joe good-bye, and the old man waved at the child before turning his yellow eyes to Joseph.

"*Yá'át'ééh,* Nephew." The seams of his face folded to produce a smile.

"*Aoo' yá'át'ééh,* Uncle. A good weekend?"

"Not so good. Tourists are mostly gone. I'm about done for the year." Uncle Joe looked up and down the way, didn't see any imminent customers, and sat down. He twisted to the side to clear a pile of miscellany off the second aluminum chair, then beckoned to Joseph. "I was just going to eat something. You eat yet? There's extra."

"I just had breakfast. You go ahead, I'll watch and comment on your manners. Where's my aunt?"

A shrug. "Off with some friends, looking at potato peelers or something. I wish she'd come back soon, it's her turn to spell me and I have to take a piss." Uncle Joe began his meal with the appetizer of a quick swig from the paper bag. Then he unwrapped a grease-spotted paper towel and began to gnaw on a chunk of mutton folded into fry bread.

Joseph went around the table and sat. They didn't say anything for a few minutes as Uncle Joe chewed his food, took hits from the bottle, and watched the passing crowd. When he was done he lit another cigarette and looked at Joseph from the side of his face.

"Nice warm day today. Good for my old bones. Used to be colder this time of year. Maybe this global warming business is not such a bad thing."

Joseph smiled. "Let's hear you say that in July when it's so hot your earwax melts."

Uncle Joe scanned the sky as if he could see the climate up there. "Yeah, we haven't seen you around here all summer," he said mildly. "Your mother says you don't go see her, either."

"Busy. Too busy. You know how it is. Sometimes it seems you take care of everybody but your own family. I'll go see her next week."

Uncle Joe nodded. "That's a good idea. Hey, I got a new truck. Dodge double cab. In hock up to my ears, but I'll be dead before I finish paying it off, so why not."

"Only way to go, double cab," Joseph said. He looked out at the crowd.

Uncle Joe nodded again and then waited, smoking in silence. By now he'd be aware that Joseph had something on his mind, but he was giving his troubled nephew the time he needed to open the topic.

"Something has come up," Joseph admitted.

The old man bobbed his head.

"Uncle Joe, I need some information that only you know."

The head stopped moving. "Huh. Long time ago. Why is it important now?"

"You know the school where I treat the kids sometimes?"

"Julieta McCarty's school. For smart Navajo kids. Of course I know it."

Joseph shifted uncomfortably between the arms of the lawn chair.

"There's a student there with a bad problem. He's got a . . . a form of seizure activity that's very unusual."

"You want medical advice or spiritual guidance?" Joe Billie said chidingly. "Those, I can give you, sure. But history advice, we made a deal on that. I kept my part of the deal. You still have to keep yours."

"Things change, Uncle! He's fifteen now. Maybe there comes a time when a kid needs to know the truth about where he came from. Who his parents really were."

Uncle Joe made an unconvinced noise.

"He's from up east of Sheep Springs. Where I remember you used to work, back when I was just coming into practice." Joseph turned to observe the old man's reaction, but the maze of seams was utterly unreadable. "I've met the grandparents at the hospital a couple of times. They say they know you."

"Like you say, I used to work up there. Probably anybody with livestock on the eastern rez knows me."

Frustrated, Joseph lowered his voice: "This boy has a severe problem, like nothing I've ever heard of. It's mystified the hospital doctors. We need to know his real medical background. If we're going to look at the possibility of congenital factors or cranial trauma, we need to know his birth history. Right?"

"Julieta thinks it's her boy. She's pressuring you to tell her, and she doesn't know you don't know."

"That too. Look, Uncle, I wouldn't ask if it wasn't important. I'm asking as a physician."

Uncle Joe thought about it, taking a longer swig from the bottle and then making a face at it as if the taste displeased him. The crowd shuffled past, and an old woman stopped to inspect Uncle Joe's wares. Neither of them said anything until she'd moved on.

"Tell me about this boy's problem," Uncle Joe said at last.

Quietly, Joseph detailed Tommy Keeday's symptoms: the convulsions, the confusion of his body parts, the insensitive arm, the asynchronous breathing. He mentioned Sam Yazzie's observation that when it came upon Tommy it seemed to mesmerize or paralyze the other boys, and he immediately regretted it: The last thing he wanted was to suggest anything supernatural, get the old man prattling about superstitions. He finished up quickly, careful to avoid mentioning that they'd brought in a Seattle parapsychologist to look into it.

"Bad," Uncle Joe said. His yellow eyes floated moist in their sockets, still expressionless. "Bad business. Dangerous for you."

"Uncle—"

"I'll tell you something, Joseph," the old man hissed. He looked quickly around to see if anyone was close enough to overhear and then went on almost inaudibly: "One time I met a guy people said was a witch. In your world, you don't know guys like this. And you don't want to. You look in their eyes and you can see one minute they're one thing, next minute they're something different. They're crazy and sick like a dog with rabies. They can make other people crazy, too. I've seen it."

Joseph ignored the narrowing eyes and rasping voice, and persisted, "His name is Tommy Keeday. His parents were killed in a car crash about six years ago. Keeday, Keedah," he repeated, adding the more traditional pronunciation. He watched his uncle's face carefully, hoping to see a reaction to the name. But either it meant nothing to the old man, or he was truly a master of the poker face.

Uncle Joe stared at him for a full minute. "Here comes your aunt," he said finally. "Maybe we should take a walk. If I don't take a piss, I'm going to embarrass my wife in public. I'll show you the new truck."

Joseph greeted Margaret Billie, a hardy, pretty woman in her midsixties with her graying hair knotted behind her head and bound with strips of fabric. She wore a traditional outfit she admitted was intended to help sell herbs, a calf-length dress decorated with an embroidered bodice and set off by a handsome silver crucifix and turquoise necklaces. They exchanged courtesies and news of relatives for only a moment before Uncle Joe started walking off by himself and Joseph apologized and followed. Aunt Margaret took her seat behind the counter, waving understandingly as Joseph looked back.

They walked up the lane for a bit, then cut between concessions, across the next row, and again between booths to the vendor parking lot. Uncle Joe found his way to a massive new Dodge Ram with spotless burgundy and silver paint, looked quickly around, and urinated in its shadow. When he was done he lit another cigarette and turned to Joseph.

"Power windows, power locks, power mirrors," he said. "Power seats that go every which way. You want me to show you?"

"No, Uncle."

"Didn't think so." Uncle Joe chuckled, as if relieving himself had restored his sense of humor. Or maybe it was just the booze starting to hit him, Joseph thought. The old man walked around to the back of the truck and took a seat on the bumper, tipping himself cautiously back against the tailgate. A hundred yards away among the parked vehicles, a group of teenagers had gathered around a jacked-up muscle car and were listening to rock and roll from its speakers.

"I'm an old drunk, idn't it?" Uncle Joe said.

Surprised, Joseph didn't answer.

"Been a drunk most of my life. But I never stole and never got into fights, never had a car accident. Never shamed my family that way. Stayed married, took care of my kids. Old drunk, but could be worse, idn't it? Cancer will kill me before the booze does." He frowned accusingly at his cigarette and kept the scowl as he looked at Joseph. "Your mother is a strong woman, she did a great job with you kids after your father died. Nobody could have done better. But sometimes a young man needs an older man to talk to. About his problems. About his life. Why don't you talk to your uncles, Joseph? Not even your Uncle Joe Billie, whose name your mother honored by giving it to you?"

Joseph felt the skin of his face, not so much hot as exposed, naked. "I don't know, Uncle."

"Sure you do. So do I." The rheumy eyes in their whorls of wrinkles stayed steady on Joseph's. He was talking about his overeducated nephew's ambivalence and shame, and the shame of being ashamed, and the conflict between reason and magic, belief in modern science and respect for tradition, the whole difficult knot for which Joseph knew no solution.

Frustrated, Joseph scuffed the ground, trying to think of a way to explain it in terms Uncle Joe would comprehend. "I don't understand why if somebody comes to you with a sick cow you'd prescribe surgery or an antibiotic and never think twice about it. But for a man you'd prescribe a Sing."

"Wouldn't treat a cow the way I'd treat a horse, either. Different anatomy, different body chemistry, different diseases—need different kinds of treatment, right? Same way, a man's a different thing. A man has special parts that need a special kind of cure." Uncle Joe tapped his head and his heart meaningfully, then laughed at his own lecturing tone. "Besides, I'm a DVM, not an MD. State catches me treating humans, they'd lock me away for sure."

Uncle Joe chuckled at the thought, then the wrinkles swarmed into a frown again. He waved away the argument as a digression and returned to his thread of thought. "So, in your whole life, you came to me one time, fifteen years ago. I helped you. Didn't I earn your respect then?"

"Yes. Very much so. I am indebted to you."

"Okay. So I'm going to call this visit the second time in your whole life. I'm going to tell you what I think you should hear, but maybe not what you want to hear. Because I have to cram a lifetime of being a good uncle into two times. About this boy, I won't warn you again about ghosts or witches, you've heard it all before from old fogeys like me and you don't believe it, what's the use? But I have two secrets for you. From an old man who some people think knows something."

"Okay . . ."

Joe Billie looked a little unsteady on the bumper as he beckoned Joseph toward him with a gesture from his cigarette. There was a glint in his eye, mischief or command. Closer, Joseph could smell both the stale funk of metabolized booze and the sharp tang of fresh whiskey that surrounded him.

"I'm full of shit," Uncle Joe rasped quietly. "I'm completely full up of shit. And Navajos are full of shit. Every one of them, all the things they do and believe, full up to here with it. Disorganized, can't run their own public services. Politicians in Window Rock corrupt and full of themselves. Old people with their crazy superstitions, kids all spoiled, watching too much TV, doing drugs. Idn't it? This I believe, just like you. But now for the big secret, Joseph: *Everybody* is full of shit! Anglos, Mexicans, French, Jews, Chinese, these Arabs—they're *equally* full of it! The way they live. What they think. Their old beliefs. The way they treat each other. No more and no less than the Diné."

The old man leaned back against the tailgate and drew on his cigarette with a hard glint of satisfaction in his eyes, as if having delivered this drunken pearl he'd accomplished a great deal.

Despite his reflex to dismiss it as the sorry rambling of an aged alcoholic, Joseph felt a surprising shiver, as if hidden in the cynical logic of the message, buried in the human mountain of shit, were the seeds of liberation.

"Okay, and I have one more for you. You're worried about something else than the health of this boy. And you should be. You can't just treat the symptom, can you? Won't help. It's about the kid, but it's about you and Julieta McCarty, and you're scared of it."

Joseph reeled back a step, as if his uncle's words were punches. Uncle Joe turned his attention to his cigarette, tapping it with great care against his chrome trailer hitch. It was a respectful gesture, Joseph saw, the uncle prodding his troubled nephew yet giving him the privacy to react without being observed.

"He wasn't your baby?" Uncle Joe asked softly. "Sometimes I wondered."

"No!" Joseph was appalled at his bluntness, no doubt yet another indication of alcohol's erosion of his character. "Definitely not!" he said through his teeth. "This would have all come down differently, you can bet your life on it."

"So why should you care so much? This Tommy, one more sick kid, plenty of those. Why's this one your problem?"

"I made some mistakes, Uncle," Joseph whispered, surprised at himself.

The gray head bobbed, Uncle Joe's yellow eyes still concerned with the cigarette.

"I did some . . . wrong things. I lied to her. And some other things. I don't want her to find out! And I need to fix it somehow."

"Fix the boy? Or fix her? Fix you? Fix you and her?" Now the old man caught his eye, merciless. "You're a doctor. Got to be specific in your diagnosis if you want the right medicine. So, what needs fixing?"

All of it, Joseph thought. *All of us. Everything.*

Uncle Joe gave him a long moment, and when it was clear no answer was forthcoming he stood up creakily, tossed down his cigarette, and ground it out beneath his pointed toe.

"This damn enlarged prostate," he mourned. "Size of a watermelon by now. Have to piss every ten minutes." He made his way unsteadily to the side of the truck, where he turned away and unzipped. Over his shoulder, he called back, "I'll think about old Keedays with a boy, up in that area, see if I even know who you're talking about. Meantime, you think about what I told you, you come back to me when you know what needs fixing. Then maybe I can help you."

The old man's words had the tone of finality. As if to emphasize it, he took Joseph's arm and, walking with the exaggerated care of the aged or just the very inebriated, led him back into the bustle of the market.

25

CREE FELT A surge of relief when Joyce stepped out of her rental car. Some of it, she realized, was that, appearing magically in the dazzle of lights under the portico of the Navajo Nation Inn, her Long Island–born Chinese-Jewish colleague hadn't after all worn some kind of bogus Western outfit. Joyce was reasonably attired in a quilted nylon jacket over a sweater and trim black jeans, and she had already changed into hiking boots. Her jet-black hair was gathered into a simple fall on one down-plumped shoulder, and though she smiled broadly she radiated also a look Cree treasured: Joyce's getting-down-to-business look. A pro, with a pro's crisp readiness and alertness. Cree kissed her fervently.

Ed pulled his van behind Joyce's car, opened the door, and stepped blinking into the lights. He looked tired, but in his rumpled, khaki-clad, thoughtful way, just as much the pro as Joyce: the consulting physicist and engineer on a field research assignment. The two of them had flown from Seattle, rented the vehicles, and for the last three hours had caravanned in the dark from Albuquerque. Cree went to Ed and kissed him, too, a hard, long one despite his initial show of reserve. When his arms went around her, they felt greatly comforting, and Cree let go of him only with reluctance.

"Am I glad to see you guys!" she told them. "Welcome to the Navajo Nation. Long drive, huh? Have a good flight?"

Ignoring the questions, Joyce looked her up and down. "What do you think, Ed? Bandaged brow notwithstanding, she looks okay, doesn't she? Accent, I'd say is, oh, slight to moderate. Posture and body language are more pronounced, though, don't you think?"

Ed squinted appraisingly at Cree, chewing on his lip. "Not too bad, so far."

They were assessing her unconscious adoption of client characteristics. She could sympathize with how they felt—wondering, every time they caught up with her on a case, who she would be—but couldn't help bristling at the implicit condescension. Frustrated, she threw back her shoulders and swept her hair away from her face before she realized she was using Julieta's gesture again.

She caught herself in midsweep. Joyce shook her head in exasperation, and they all laughed.

She helped them unload their luggage, then accompanied them as they registered and went to their rooms. Cree and Joyce chatted as Ed parked the van and ferried in the six bulky equipment cases he'd brought. It was going on eleven by the time he was done and they all met in his room. Joyce and Ed cracked beers from a six-pack Joyce had innocently bought on their way through Gallup, not knowing it was contraband here on the rez, while Cree went to the minibar for a can of soda water to toast their safe arrival.

"You up for a short conference?" she asked. "It's pretty late. If you're too tired, we—"

"It's an hour earlier out there," Ed reminded her. "Anyway, I napped on the plane."

"I'm a little bleary, but I want to get going on the job," Joyce said. Her gaze turned suspicious. "You, you're looking positively hyper, Cree. And why aren't you having a beer?"

Cree explained that after getting almost no sleep for two nights running, she'd napped for much of the day. With Tommy gone, there'd been little to do at the school anyway. At least during daylight hours.

"I have a few things to attend to tonight," she finished. "That's why I don't want to get soused like you guys."

Ed exchanged a quick glance with Joyce, then frowned at his beer and took another swallow. "So the boy's no longer at the school. Will we have access to him?"

"I hope so. Julieta has talked to his grandparents, they sound somewhat flexible. It'll probably be a few days before he's released from the hospital. If indeed he is released."

"And if he isn't?" Ed persisted. He gestured at the row of equipment cases. "I brought the FMEEG gear and the rest of it. I'd like to be able to use it."

"We might be able to swing access to him anyway. I'm hoping Dr. Tsosie asks me in as a consulting psychologist. In any case, there's work to be done while we're waiting."

Joyce sipped her beer and looked around the room, which was done in lovely Southwestern pastels stenciled with Navajo designs. "What're you up to tonight, Cree?"

They would disapprove, Cree knew. "I'll get there," she stalled. "Let me brief you on developments."

They nodded. Ed kicked off his shoes and settled himself on the bed, leaning against the headboard as he swigged beer and flexed his long, narrow feet. Joyce dug a pen and a legal pad out of her bag and sank into the armchair. She took out her hair band and combed the ebony strands free with her fingers.

Cree sat in the desk chair and filled them in, starting with a description of Tommy's symptoms and his explanations of how it felt to him. For context, she elaborated with Joseph's depiction of the boy and the hospital's initial conclusion that his crises were the result of purely psychological, not physical, problems.

"What do you think of that hypothesis?" Ed asked. "What do you sense when you're near him?"

"Oh, they've got a perfectly good psychological theory. Completely right and completely wrong. What do I sense? You know, I've been so off balance—I got clopped on the head before I saw him while . . . when it was fully on him, before I spent any time one-on-one with him. When we were playing softball yesterday, it was in remission and I honestly couldn't tell. But when he's in crisis, you see it so clearly—two beings in the same body, out of sync with each other, experiencing different worlds. Probably not even really aware of each other except that everything's out of whack." She shook her head, realizing how little this gave them to go on. "There are a couple of empirical signs. There's the flicker phenomenon, for one thing, very pronounced when the manifestation is in full swing. And there's this odd . . . I don't know what to call it . . . this *charisma*. When I found him out by the corral Friday night, the horses were paralyzed. Frozen. The night dorm guy said he felt it, and the other boys were mesmerized. I felt it too, this sort of stunned indecision that you can't shake off. There might be something useful for us in it, I don't know."

"Together with the flicker phenomenon, it could suggest a powerful field of some kind," Ed said doubtfully. "Something we might measure."

Joyce nodded and jotted a note to herself.

"There's another thing," Cree continued. "He's an artist, very accomplished, right? Ever since I've been at the school, I've had these dreams of faces, living faces, emerging from the rocks. So last night, after he'd been taken away, I go to look at his drawings? And I find he's drawn two landscapes where rocks are morphing into faces. The school nurse told me the setting is a particular gully in the mesa, not far from the school."

They nodded soberly, and she felt a sudden wave of affection for these two. She didn't have to explain why she attached importance to the fact that she'd dreamed what Tommy had drawn. They'd know it wasn't coincidental, that both dreams and drawings had their source in some echo of human experience in the vicinity of those ancient rocks.

"So today I went back to his room and checked the dates. He drew the faces on September ninth. After that, his drawings began changing—every one of them shows this . . . I don't know, this double vision. It's hard to explain, but you see it right away when you look at his work."

"So," Ed said after a moment, "what're you thinking? He acquired a formerly place-anchored entity that day? September ninth?"

"It's worth looking into."

"And that's where you're going tonight," Joyce said, eyes narrowing. "Out to the rocks he drew."

Cree nodded and tried to keep looking nonchalant. Ed and Joyce exchanged another quick glance, but to her relief they didn't confront her on it.

"So what're we dealing with?" Ed asked. "A strict perseverator? Or something more intentional?"

"I have no idea. The arm sometimes moves by itself when Tommy's asleep, and it seems so . . . self-aware. It's almost as if it's trying to figure out where it is, what's going on. Very creepy. And when I was wrestling with Tommy, he did this thing with his eye. Like a *wink*. As if it was aware of me and trying to communicate. But I really don't know."

They chewed on that. Cree shuddered and wished she could banish the image.

"What about the idea that the entity is Julieta McCarty's ex?" Joyce asked.

Cree looked to Ed. "Did Joyce tell you about all this?"

Ed nodded. "Bad blood between Julieta McCarty and her former husband, now dead. Ex was killed in an accident three years ago, not far from the school."

"Yes. And there's some complicating context there. Julieta told me yesterday that the boy is her son, fathered by a lover long gone to dreams of glory on the West Coast. She kept the pregnancy secret and hardly even saw the baby. He was adopted by a rural family fifteen years ago."

"Oh my," Ed said quietly. "Oh my my." He finished his beer, levered his long frame off the bed, and pulled another from its plastic collar. With an expression of resignation and melancholy, he popped the can, settled himself again, and took a long swallow. "Well, that would lend credibility to the ex-as-entity theory, wouldn't it? Suggests there'd be lots of high emotions and unresolved issues. The boy's genetic relationship to Julieta could possibly explain why the ex's ghost would home in on him, maybe as a surrogate for the mother."

Ed was talking about what they called the "blood is drawn to blood" axiom. Many of their cases over the years had concerned revenants returning to haunt blood kin, a tendency corroborated by statistical surveys of paranormal activity and echoed in supernatural lore throughout the world. Ghosts tended to "home in" on the individuals involved in their deepest compulsions, the powerful emotions felt in life or at the moment of death. Looking for blood relationships, along with emotional connections, was always a wise starting place in the quest to understand witnesses and to identify an unknown entity.

"Very possibly," Cree agreed. "Which is another piece of business we can be working on. I called Donny McCarty today—he's the ex's son— and managed to swing an appointment to meet with him. It's ostensibly to talk about livestock mutilations, don't ask me to explain how we got *there,* but I want to get a look at the site of his father's death. Maybe hear more about what kind of person Garrett was, see if I can learn anything that will help determine if he's Tommy's entity."

"On the McCartys," Joyce put in, "I've got a pile. Prominent name, lots of press—give it to you tomorrow." She scratched her head with her pen, frowning as if something were bothering her. "This'll sound stupid, but—question: *Is* Tommy Julieta's son? Do we know that for certain? Because it seems to me it would make a big difference here."

Cree shot her a grin. "God, you're smart. You could get a job as, like, an investigator or something! I'm assuming she knows from his records, maybe his appearance. Or maybe Dr. Tsosie told her—he's the one who arranged the adoption."

"Is she credible?" Ed asked.

"I think so. I trust her, I like her a great deal. But you have to understand, she's very beautiful and charismatic, she sort of dazzles you? She's intense and sexy and smart, she's appealingly wounded . . . I guess I'm saying she can overwhelm you. It's hard to make an unbiased appraisal."

"I can't wait to meet her," Ed said, deadpan but for an intrigued lift of his eyebrows.

"Hey, me neither," Joyce quipped, looking alarmed. "And I'm about as hetero as it gets."

They chuckled. But the wan, reflective mood was stealing over them, the late-night lonesomes compounded by pondering the complexity of the human condition. They each retreated into private reflections for a moment.

Joyce broke the silence: "It sounds as if *you* have a lot to do while we're waiting for a crack at Tommy. But what about Ed and me? We can't sit here and watch sitcoms all day."

"There's plenty. Ed, we need you to check out the school's electrical system, rule out system weakness for the flicker phenomenon. Joyce, there's a ton of research to do—a lot of running around western New Mexico and eastern Arizona. We need to learn more about Tommy's adoptive parents' car accident—where, when, exactly what happened. Regardless of his biological parentage, their emotional connection marks them as prime candidates here. Also, when I meet with Donny McCarty, it'd be good if one of you came with me—give me more credibility, maybe help me find an excuse to walk around the mine area."

"But what about Tommy?" Ed asked. "He's our main focus. He's the one who's stuck with the critter. How can we get access to him?"

Cree nodded, chewed her lip. "That's the biggest problem. I think

Joseph Tsosie will be the deciding factor. If Tommy stays at the hospital, Joseph's the one who can swing our access to him or cut us out. And if the boy ends up back with his grandparents, Joseph could be a crucial intermediary for us with them. I'm hoping Julieta can persuade him to help us. Beyond that, I don't think there's anything we can do."

Ed nodded, looking far away. Joyce jotted something in her private shorthand.

"So," Cree said, standing up and taking a last sip of water. "I'd love to linger, but I've got to head back. See you both tomorrow."

Again they exchanged a quick glance, nodded, shrugged. Ed sighed as he unfolded from the bed, then jangled the coins in his pocket and fished out a quarter. "Heads," he called, flipping it with his thumb. Joyce waited expectantly as he caught it and slapped it onto the back of his other hand. "Heads it is," he announced.

"What's with the coin?" Cree asked.

"Deciding who goes with you tonight," Joyce told her in a steely voice. "Don't bother arguing, Cree. Don't even try. You don't know the country. You don't know what's out there. You've been injured recently. It's the middle of the night. There could be coyotes, scorpions, rattlesnakes. You need backup nearby." She stood, stretched, and went to the door. "Me, I'm gonna go back to my room and do some light bedtime reading about mutilated animals, murdered cowboys, massacres of and by Indians, violated graves, and stuff like that. Good luck and good night."

Cree stood openmouthed as the door swung shut behind her.

Ed had been putting on his shoes again. When he was done, he straightened and offered his elbow like a young swain at a formal ball.

"Shall we?" he asked with weary dignity.

26

THE NIGHT wasn't as cold as Cree had expected. Currents of warmer air slid through the chill layers, meandering off the desert toward the mesa. She and Ed walked slowly, talking only rarely and in whispers. When they'd first started out, the lights of the school had blinded them, making the night seem impenetrable, but now the campus had disappeared around an arm of the mesa and their eyes had had time to adapt. The night world was blue and transparent, crisply visible in the light of sparking stars and the residual glow of a setting half moon. To their right loomed the cliffs of the mesa, a chiaroscuro of blue and black, rock surfaces riven with the shadows of cracks, folds, gullies. An occasional piñon tree clung to the lower slope, a hunchbacked blob of darkness. Cree didn't know how far they'd come, but they had not yet seen anything like the higher palisades Tommy had portrayed in his drawings. Already, the vanished school seemed distant as a memory.

Night: Shadows became holes through the surface world into a place of immeasurable depth. In the darkness, the five ordinary senses strained and the subtler ones awakened, the spectrum of extrasensory awarenesses used by the parapsychologist and the mystic. Cree shivered with a familiar tremble of fear and exhilaration. It was joyous, reverent, and keenly mortal: the sense of the imminence of the other dimensions of the world, the true scope of the universe; the awareness that the vacuum of space above didn't end where sky met earth but interpenetrated the ground and the things upon it, that even the solidest-seeming matter was after all full of emptiness and energy, and that mind could merge with it and move within it in myriad ways.

The rocks and sky brooded as if waiting: ancient, starkly inhuman, neither cruel nor kind. *The ghost of the land looks just like its body,* it occurred to her. Its essence and its outward stuff were one and the same. Still, it was not simple; within the big encompassing ghost of mineral and atmospheric wilderness swarmed smaller ghosts, distinct as the different layers of air, alive with separate moods as clear as scent or memory. If you believed that the universe was something like a dreaming mind, you had to accept that it was a mosaic made of lesser dreams and thoughts, yearnings, latencies, echoes of events past, immanences of things to come. It thrilled her and frightened her. It was majestic and merciless.

Thinking about it, Cree remembered the question Ed had asked maybe five minutes ago. The prospect of a long nighttime walk in this wild, empty land clearly made him nervous, and he'd brought a handle from one of the infirmary's brooms to serve as walking stick and weapon. She knew exactly what he meant when he asked, "Why do you think it's a human revenant inside Tommy? Why not something else?" He'd gestured at the dark landscape, so full of secrets, meaning, *Why not something from this?*

Out here, close to the brooding rocks, it was easy to doubt her earlier conviction. In the absence of wind, there was no sound but the crunch of their footsteps and the sweeping noises of the fabric of their jackets or jeans. They were very alone. She struggled to banish images from the possession literature, and the thought of animal mutilations nagged at her; being out here, with the interstellar wilderness above and the hard, unforgiving desert all around, you could easily believe in raptors of every sort.

But at last she said quietly, "You know how sometimes, when you're taking the bus across town and you're unconsciously staring at the side of some guy's head? Maybe you're not even thinking about him, and then suddenly he turns toward you and your eyes meet?"

"Yes."

"I mean, you're both startled by the contact. You've never seen him before, but for an instant you sort of recognize each other, there's this shock of communion. You see his eyes so clearly . . . that spark of awareness. It's very intimate—and then of course you both look away. You retreat from it, right?"

"Yeah."

"That first night, when we were back in the infirmary and trying to hold him down? I felt it startle and recoil as *it* sensed *me*. I recoiled, too. It was just like meeting the gaze of a stranger on the bus. Mutual recognition. I just . . . felt sure it was human."

But telling him about it now, Cree felt her conviction ebb. She saw again the exploring fingers of the hand and that awful, labored wink, and then remembered Tommy's description of the parasites in the sheep, the living, pulsating bumps.

Yeah, it reacted to me, she thought. *The maggots would probably squirm if you prodded them, too.*

She shivered and did her best to concentrate on the cliffs.

"So what are we looking for?" Ed asked. "I mean, if there was an entity anchored here, and it's now in Tommy, what's left here for us?"

"Don't know. All I know is those dreams. Maybe the rocks in the dream are part of the thing's memory? Or maybe it's a divided entity, like the one in New Orleans, with a more intentional element in Tommy and a perimortem element that's still out here. Or maybe there's more than one."

The silhouette that was Ed nodded, accepting her impressionistic way of feeling her way through. She felt a surge of affection for him as they walked on in silence. He didn't experience the world the way she did; in fact, his whole training rebelled against her outlook. And yet he *believed*—he so trusted *her,* personally, that he accepted what she saw or felt as real and valid. No one else had ever crossed such a gulf to come to her, she realized. Not even Mike, not Joyce, not Deirdre or Paul Fitzpatrick. The thought astonished her. She silently cherished Edgar as they walked.

The drive from the motel had been largely silent, too. Ed seemed wary. For her part, Cree felt as though she had a lot to say to him. She wanted to be with him more . . . more straight on and not so lateral. It seemed as if they had a lot to catch up on, some important personal developments to discuss, but she didn't know what those might be. Nothing had changed: She had talked to Paul Fitzpatrick earlier tonight, was feeling romantically toward him and planning to go to New Orleans as soon as she could get free; Ed was getting used to that, keeping some distance from her as he figured out his own feelings. They were business partners, collaborators, and good friends. Nothing had changed.

Puzzling over it, she kept coming back to thoughts of Julieta. She sensed a pattern, a sort of mandala of emotion, around Julieta. It had to do with

Peter Yellowhorse and Joseph Tsosie and unexpressed or unrequited feelings, with Julieta's emotional arc through so many years of self-denial and self-restraint. But every time Cree tried to inspect it, her thoughts shied like skittish horses.

Ed's whispered voice brought her out of her thoughts. "Could this be it?"

He was looking up at the deep blue walls of the mesa, higher and steeper here, perhaps eighty feet of sandstone. They had arrived at a place where a ravine divided the rock, angling deep into the body of the hill, its nearly vertical slopes sculpted by the elements and topped at the rim by boulders. From what she could see in the dark, it all looked crumbling and fragile. Farther into the mesa, the sloping cleft narrowed and disappeared in shadow.

"Maybe," she whispered.

It was hard to tell in the dark, and yet as she studied the scene its familiarity grew. At first she couldn't tell if she recognized the place from her dreams or from Tommy's drawings, but in a moment she knew it was neither. There was something like a song echoing in the ravine, inaudible but charged with deep emotion. She realized now it had been growing in her awareness as she'd approached, preoccupied with her thoughts. It drew her into the embrace of the cliffs, and made her suddenly breathless.

"Yes," she said.

Edgar knew to give her space. He sat on a boulder a stone's throw from the mouth of the ravine and hunched motionless in his jacket with his broom handle across his lap. As Cree moved silently into the shadows, his shape blurred until he became indistinguishable.

A hundred feet up, she leaned against a fallen slab and tried to release the tension in her shoulders. She labored to keep her breathing from going shallow and panicky. She struggled to master her fear, which filled every shadow with furtive movement, goosing her heartbeat and making her hands and feet tingle. She released her thoughts, gently willing them to stillness so that their clamor wouldn't obscure the secret confessions of the rocks.

Even if the next stage was a perpetual surprise and mystery, she knew this part well—this first part, the act of stepping to the entrance to the hidden parts of the world. It started with a mounting pressure as of something impending. The sense that an event of importance was about to take place, the feeling of movement just out of view. She had known the feeling before she became a parapsychologist, living in that third-floor Philly apartment and sensing from subliminal sounds or vibrations that the resident of the apartment below had come home. Was maybe even standing directly below, only five vertical feet away: so close, yet so separate and unknowing.

Yeah, she thought, *except that here your body tells you it's dangerous.*

She startled as a pebble tickled down the rock slope from almost directly above. Her heart answered with jarring thuds. She held her breath and waited for more signs that something was moving up there, but no more fell.

Fear was the big impediment. Your body said, *Don't come here.* Its impulse grew remorselessly: *Get ready to run. You should run. Run now! Runrunrun—*

When it peaked, when the instinctive mutters of warning became screams and seemed unendurable, that was the very moment the empathic parapsychologist had to sustain: the intolerable moment of breakthrough. *Slow the breath,* she chanted to herself. *Let go thoughts. Feel the texture of the dark. Hear the hiss in the ears. Don't break the silence. Don't shatter the mood, the moment. The contact.*

Most important: *Remember, it's made of the same stuff you are. The secret life stuff inside, the quickening light—that's all you are, too.*

Sometimes it started with changes in the phosphene patterns, the shimmering retinal star field that was always there behind closed eyelids. In the deep blue dark of the ravine, she didn't need to shut her eyes to observe the phosphene haze. Were there shapes in the swirl? *Maybe.* Her pulse kicked up.

Without thinking about it, she made her way farther into the cleft, another hundred feet to a place where a dam of fallen slabs and boulders blocked it from side to side. At its deepest, the barrier was only shoulder high, easy to climb over. But she lowered herself to the ground, her back against a rock, facing sideways. An *old* smell here: wind-weathered stone. She could see the cliffs opposite, some of the ravine above, the gentle downward slope and the curtain of dark beyond which, only a hundred yards away, invisible, Edgar would be sitting, patient and alert.

Physically, he wasn't far. In other ways, he was very distant. In a different world.

She waited for a long time, enduring the sense of imminence. She felt very alone. She sensed the darkness changing subtly as the big globe rolled its belly to face a different expanse of sky, and the blue air got colder. After a while, she found she could see her breath: faint curls of mist that moved slowly away, sucked into the ravine by some imperceptible updraft. She tried not to feel isolated and exposed, but the feeling grew and grew. Reflexively she hugged her knees, made herself smaller.

She felt like she was hiding. She was hunkered here, curled into deepest shadow, trying to compress herself into invisibility, silent as she could be. She was waiting, paralyzed with fright and indecision.

She was hiding because fear was moving, somewhere in the dark, and growing closer.

She'd made a mistake in coming here, she realized. It was too dangerous. Abruptly she felt the others nearby, now waiting, now coming down the ravine, coming out of the shadows for her. She couldn't let them come nearer. But she couldn't move.

Another pebble made an insect noise as it scuttered down the cliff.

Cree wanted to bolt up, climb, run, but she couldn't, they'd see her. There was another noise now, a dull tumult that she felt more than heard, a low thrum in her belly. It was shot through with sharp, silver noises. And now there were voices from above and below, calling, warding, threatening.

There was something bad happening out where Ed was, she realized distantly. Somebody or something had come in the dark, and he was out there. They had screwed up badly, thinking it could be this simple. She could hear it clearly now, a rushing and rumbling and something metallic. And in the cleft, urgent wailing voices.

She stood, and as she looked up the ravine she saw the shadows moving. Humped, furtive shapes leaping and alighting, side to side, closer and closer. Her heart wanted to burst at the sight. Panicked, she brayed at them like a crazed, wounded animal, warding them back. But they didn't stop. Suddenly she was rushing back toward Edgar, hurtling between the crazy angles of the cliffs, stumbling over rocks, catching herself, tearing her fingers on the stone, blinded by fear.

"Ed!" she called. The rumble was all around him, the evil had swarmed off the desert to the opening of the ravine. Big movements, manifold movements, a huge thing that she knew was the evil that ate people, took them away to nowhere. She couldn't see him, he was already taken by it, he was consumed in its blue mouth. "Edgar!" she shrieked. "Ed, they're coming! Run! Run!"

She tore toward the boulder where he'd been and suddenly it was moving and a shadow reared out of it and it was a man.

"Cree!" the shape shouted. The horizons swallowed its cry.

"Run, Ed!"

"Cree! Are you all right? What is it?" He was coming toward her, holding his staff, a watchful shepherd attending to an alarm.

There was pain in the air. Pain and piercing loss and every regret. She swore a curse upon it with rage torn from her bowels, her bones. It was monstrous and evil beyond reckoning, and the voices and rumble and jingle, the exploding fear and heartsickness and outrage all merged into one thing, a whole world that gathered into the sound of a cymbal clashed and ringing and then damped and fading and silent.

And there was no one there but Ed, alone beneath the sky on the vast empty desert.

She fell between worlds. She tumbled against him and his arms were around her and his body rocked hers as she tried to catch her breath. Her pounding heartbeat shook her. He wasn't very real and then he was.

"It's okay, Cree! You're okay! What happened? What's up there?"

It wasn't up *there,* she wanted to tell him, it was out here, she had rushed to warn him. Save him. But that didn't make sense. What she had wanted so urgently was evaporating from her mind. She grasped at the knowledge of it but it slipped away, mist between her fingers.

All that she could conjure of it was the thing she'd had to tell him, so urgent, but when it came to her lips it had shrunk to a single word that surprised her and was utterly without meaning: "Goats!" she panted. "The goats!"

27

THE CHIEF of psychiatry at Ketteridge Hospital was a dignified-looking, white-haired man, tall but carrying himself with a stoop that brought his face level with Cree's. He met Cree in the visitors' lounge on the juvenile floor, shook her hand, and took a seat in the chair across from her. The little room was empty and quiet but for the burble of an aquarium against one wall, where three dazed-looking goldfish hovered.

"We think the world of Dr. Tsosie here," Dr. Corcoran told her. "A good man—the best. And Joseph tells me wonderful things about you."

Cree tried to mask her surprise. "Thank you. And thank you for letting me see Tommy."

He put his palms up, *the least I could do,* and smiled. "It's a very troubling case. If you've established good rapport with him, as Dr. Tsosie says you have, perhaps you can make some progress. He talks to me only with great reluctance."

"Why, do you suppose?"

"I'm just an old white guy! What the hell do I know?" Dr. Corcoran chuckled indulgently, then made a sterner face. "Poor kid—little does he know that if he keeps this up he's going to be talking to old white geezers like me for a long, long time." He shook his head and sighed. "Seriously, his reticence ties in with the whole complex. Here's a boy who's very stressed by his new school experience and is seeking a way to retreat from that which frightens and overwhelms him. It has opened up his repressed grief at the death of his parents, the sense of rejection and abandonment. As for why he won't talk to me, it's because, first of all, he's at the stage where he resents all Anglos for their historic and continuing sins against the Diné. But, more important, because he doesn't *want* the problem to go away. He *needs* the problem. If I helped solve it, he'd have no excuse! Part of him is also very ashamed of himself too—of how excessive all this is. Of how obvious and, frankly, *thin* it is."

Again, Cree tried to compose her face and voice. "But he's been in boarding schools all his life. Why would he suddenly feel so much stress just now?"

"Ah. Two reasons. First, because he's been at run-of-the-mill schools where it's been easy to stand out, to wow everybody with his talents and intelligence. But at Oak Springs his peers are equally sharp. I think there's an implicit competition there, and Tommy is making it plain he doesn't feel up to it. I also understand he attended his first college-counseling session not long ago." Dr. Corcoran smiled modestly at his own insightfulness. "Suddenly the bigger world impinges. He wants to shine, to stand out, but now he discovers that as bright and talented as he is, he's just one of many. He's told just how competitive college admissions are going to be, how he's got to mind his p's and q's from here on in. Keep his 'cume' up, prepare for the SATs, and so on. The pressure can be especially hard on these rural kids."

"And the other reason?"

"Conditions at home. His grandparents are getting quite old. Tommy may claim he wants *out,* rejects rural life, and so on, but of course he cares for them, and seeing them in decline makes him feel even more insecure. After Oak Springs, on to college, probably moving far away. He knows his grandparents are approaching some major life passages, too—they can't hang on out there forever. The family home will never be the same, he'll never experience those old rhythms of life again. It scares him. He may also feel responsible, that he should be more help to the grandparents. Part of Tommy wants badly to get out of school, go back to the family hogan, be near his grandparents, care for them and be cared for. Postpone the big changes pending."

Cree nodded. It was all quite plausible. "Did you do any tests on him last night or today?"

"No cranial imaging. He's been through all that twice, no need to subject him to it again just yet. But we ran the EEG and another full blood spectrum. Normal in every respect."

"How about his reflexes? His proprioception? Sensation in his limbs?"

"The business with the right arm and spine? I'll admit it troubled me at

205

first. My colleagues at the Indian Hospital say it always 'vanished' by the time they got a gander at him."

"Wouldn't that suggest that it's lasting longer? That the symptoms are progressing?"

"Oh, definitely." Dr. Corcoran smiled. "He's getting better at it. Practice makes perfect."

"And what about the self-injury yesterday?"

"The veritable cherry on top!" Dr. Corcoran said with satisfaction. "Kills two birds with one stone, you see. It fulfills his need to display another extreme and bizarre behavior, to 'prove' to us that something's badly the matter with him. And, symbolically, it's a reflection of his desire to punish himself—for not measuring up, for not taking care of his grandparents, and, paradoxically, for making all this fuss." He frowned, shook his head gravely. "None of which is intended to suggest this isn't very serious. A very serious situation."

Cree looked into his infuriatingly calm, self-possessed eyes. He was, she saw, one of that breed of psychologists who looked for a tidy, encompassing theory that wrapped the human psyche into a neat diagnostic bundle. The trailing ends, the parts that didn't fit, were to be ignored or cut to size. It was the outlook of a man accustomed to dealing with human problems in quantity: to treating an unending flow of short-term patients, managing their acute stages and referring them on, but never having to dig in for the long haul and the messy, irregular, and highly individual process of healing.

Dr. Corcoran coughed delicately into his fist and asked, "Have you, um, dealt with Native American patients before?"

"Rarely," Cree hedged.

He nodded deeply, wisely. "If I may say so, there are also cultural factors to consider."

"Oh?"

"Yes. As you know, Tommy is Navajo. There are certain beliefs—we might call them superstitions—prevalent among the Diné. These ideas inform their way of thinking about illness. It often leads to a . . . how to put this? A *dramatizing* of the problem." He smiled at her and lowered his voice. "A supernatural approach to anything mysterious. Even with the most educated Navajo, it can be a surprisingly hard paradigm to displace."

He raised his eyebrows meaningfully, confidingly: *Just between us white folks.* "I'm speaking of, oh, spirits, witches, curses, ghosts of ancestors—that kind of thing."

Cree managed to avoid taking him by the shoulders and shaking him and instead just nodded thoughtfully. "Actually," she told him, deadpan, "I do have some experience in that area."

Tommy had been installed in a three-bed room with a single window that looked north to a view of Gallup and the vast land beyond. The middle bed was empty, but through a gap in the curtain Cree could see that the bed nearest the door was occupied by a boy of around ten, sleeping now. An older woman sat in a chair nearby, drowsing, a magazine forgotten on her lap.

"Ah, Mr. Keeday," Dr. Corcoran said heartily. "I've brought someone to see you!"

Tommy was sitting on his bed, facing the window. He turned, looking surprised to see Cree, dismayed to see Dr. Corcoran. He wore a thin terry robe over striped pajamas. His right arm lay inert on the bed, hand and wrist bandaged.

"*Yá'át'ééh,*" Cree said. And to her surprise she felt it immediately, now—felt it startle and quickly go quiet in him, as if hiding when it sensed her.

"I'm just dropping Dr. Black off," Dr. Corcoran reassured him. "You two have a good chat, and we'll all touch bases later." He smiled and left the room.

With her experience at the mesa still urgent in her memory, Cree had to resist the impulse to bombard him with questions. Instead, she went to stand at the end of his bed, looking out the window. Below the hospital, the land sloped downward to a residential district that a mile or so away yielded to the two- and three-story buildings of the old downtown. Beyond were the overpass of Interstate 40 and the freight railyard that cut Gallup in two. Somewhere far out in the emptiness on the other side would be the lonely sheep ranch where Tommy had grown up.

She didn't say anything. The thing stayed inert, camouflaging itself in his body's normal energies and auras, a dark chameleon.

"My grandparents and my aunt will be back soon," he said at last. "They went away for lunch."

"You must be glad to see them."

"No."

"Why not?"

Tommy thought about it. "I scare them. I don't like to see them scared."

"I can imagine. But I don't think you should worry about them."

"Why not?"

She had to think about how to say it. "Well, because they're *brave,* too, aren't they? I mean, even though they're scared, they want you to come home so they can take care of you. Fear is what makes us find our courage. If they want you home, it's because they believe courage will win out over fear."

The thought seemed to please him, but he didn't say anything.

Cree kept looking out the window. "That Dr. Corcoran, he's sure got you all figured out, doesn't he? You must be thrilled."

She glanced sideways at him and caught a flicker of a grin. It felt good to have conjured it in him. He was wary as a cornered animal now, but through the fear and the typical tangle of adolescent emotions she sensed the person that was so evident in his drawings: highly observant, burning with a desire to understand the big questions.

"Know what I did last night?" she asked.

"What."

"I went for a long walk. Out to the mesa, to that ravine about a mile north of the school. You know the one? The steepest one?"

He frowned. "At night?"

"Well, darkness helps me think about things. Sometimes when you can't see very well, other parts of your mind get more active, and you can sense things or imagine things more easily. You went out there with your drawing class, right?"

"You were looking at my drawings?" Disapproval: *Spying on me.*

"Well, I'd wanted to talk to you Saturday night, but then you . . . they brought you here. So I figured I'd at least look at your work." She turned to him. "Tommy, I have to say, you absolutely blow me away! Your drawings open my eyes to things I'd never noticed. Even the most ordinary objects or scenes take on a . . . a *magic,* I guess you'd call it. I'm . . . I'm awed. Really."

The flattery pleased him, but his wandering eyes showed he was wary of condescension. She gave him time, but he didn't say anything. She thought the rightward bow of his body increased slightly in the interim.

"Tell me about the faces in the rocks," she said quietly. "The ones you drew."

"It just seemed like an interesting compositional idea. It's called 'personification.' 'Anthropomorphism.'"

"There's more to it than that. There had to be. You had an interpretive theme—you gave them all very different personalities, just like you did with those studies of your parents. Why?"

His expression suggested he resented her probing but that he was also impressed or pleased that she'd noticed. "I was thinking about Navajos in the old days. All you know is what you read or people tell you, you don't ever know what to believe. Sometimes I just want to know, that's all. Who they really were. I was trying to see which seemed right." From the way his eyes fled hers, she sensed he'd inadvertently revealed something very important to him. "And I liked the idea of putting them in stone, kind of a statement, like they're enduring but also frozen in time. Like stuck in their history."

Same as with your parents, Cree thought. "Were you thinking of any ancestor in particular?" She held her breath: The answer could be crucial.

But abruptly the boy in the other bed woke with a cry and a long moan that ended in coughing. The old woman gently shushed him and muttered reassurances in Spanish.

Tommy half turned to look toward the drawn curtain and whispered, "I think he's dying or something. He's been in here a long time, like six weeks, I heard his parents talking about it."

"Tommy, stay with me on this for a moment. Did anything happen when you were out at the cliffs that day? Did you see anything different or unusual? You wrote the date on your drawings—September ninth."

"If they think they can keep me that long, no way. I'd rather be dead. I'll get out somehow."

Cree thought back to Dr. Corcoran's casual comment, *He'll be talking to old white geezers like me for a long, long time,* and felt a terrible resolve blossom in her, just what Julieta must feel. "They won't have to. You're going to be better. But you have to help me now."

Tommy swiveled his head back to look at her, and the way he did it gave her a little shiver. Something robotic about it, too smooth and controlled. "How did you know?" he asked. "Did Mrs. McCarty tell you?"

"Know what? Tell me what?"

"That day. When I went up the ravine. I was sick of drawing the same rocks, I thought there'd be something more dramatic up there."

"How far up did you go?" Cree tried to conceal her excitement.

"Not far. It just goes up and divides into two little washes that dwindle away at the top. I shouldn't have spent so much time in there. I got too hot."

"Oh?"

"Not too bad. I was sitting on some boulders and trying to draw the ravine, but it didn't work out. Too much glare from the rocks. I just got dizzy."

"So what'd you do?"

Shrug. "Went back down. Drank some water. It went away."

"Your drawings have been changing since then."

"Yeah, Mrs. McCarty and Miss Chee, they're great teachers."

A nurse came in, checked on them briefly, then went to confer in hushed tones with the other boy and the old woman. Cree was thinking about the ravine, the shadow beings skipping down, and the awful thing that she'd feared would devour Edgar. And more and more she felt the thing crouching in Tommy: tense, balled up as if hiding or as if gathering itself to spring. But she didn't feel she could ask him more specific questions without risking programming his responses, giving him ideas. Or scaring him to death.

But she had to make progress. She had to jolt Tommy, or his parasite, off the dime. Provoke a response that would give her something to go on.

She took a deep breath and drew as much calm from it as she could. Then she sat at the head of the bed next to Tommy. The arm lay lifeless on the blanket, bandages crossing the upturned palm and disappearing into the sleeve of his robe.

"Tommy, what's this?" She touched the curled fingers gently.

He looked down at it, dismayed. "It's my hand," he said immediately. "My arm." But the question frightened him.

"That's what you've learned to say, isn't it? That's what Dr. Corcoran wants you to say."

"It's my arm! It looks like an arm, what else could it be!" He sidled away from her. Or from *it*—the slack appendage dragged across the blanket after him and for an instant she saw it as he must, a foreign thing pursuing him, a snake in the bed.

"If you drew a picture of yourself right now, your whole body, what would it look like?"

He glanced back at the doorway as if hoping someone would interrupt. But the nurse had withdrawn again, and the curtained third bed was silent. He refused to answer.

"If it's not an arm, what is it?" Cree persisted.

"I don't know!"

"Okay, so it's a thing of some kind," Cree said. "An unknown thing, yeah?" She touched the bandaged palm, and then, overcoming her revulsion of it, picked up the hand and held it in both of her own. The deadweight was surprisingly heavy.

"Hello, thing," she said to it.

Tommy looked at her, wide-eyed and appalled. "You're crazy," he whispered.

"No! I just refuse to be frightened by things I don't understand." She lightly caressed the inert object, then looked directly into Tommy's face and mustered everything she had to break through to him: "Listen to me, Tommy!" she whispered forcefully. "I'm a scientist. One thing I've learned is, this is a strange world. Man, I have had one damned hard time with how strange it is! But you know the way you feel about being here with a sick kid in the next bed, and guys like Dr. Corcoran treating you like you're retarded, and thinking maybe you're going to be here forever? That feeling of being in a box? Well, just like you, I refuse to be in that box. Being afraid of stuff like this is a box. A cage. *I won't stay in it.*"

She looked down at the hand again and said with all the calm and cordiality she could muster, "Hello, unknown thing."

Tommy made an expression of surprise, as if her words had penetrated him deeply and painfully. For an instant, he looked as if he were going to answer, but instead he made a moan, a shockingly deep voice emerging from his round mouth.

He was off balance now, and she sensed the thing in him moving, flushed from its cover. Cree seized the opening: "Who are you?" she hissed. "What do you want?" *Is that you, Garrett McCarty? Or are you the one from the rocks?*

Tommy looked paralyzed with fright. Abruptly, the hand twitched, and it turned to grip her hand, a quick hard clench as sudden and startling as an electric shock. In reflexive horror, she stood up and flung it away from her. The arm flopped limply back onto the bed, but for a few seconds the fingers clenched as if groping for her hand again, then curled and rolled like the legs of a dying spider. Tommy sidled away from it in terror and it dragged after him over the rumpled bedclothes.

Cree cursed herself. She made herself sit again and take the awful thing back, holding the hand gently and cautiously as if it were a wild animal. But Tommy's look of betrayal showed he wasn't buying it. *No wonder!* she thought. She'd shown him her hypocrisy: how close to the surface her fear and revulsion were, how marginal her own control. Worse, she had addressed the thing, he now knew how she was thinking of his problem. She'd confirmed what had to be his worst fears. And she might very well have programmed his future explanations and descriptions.

"That's why," Tommy said tremulously.

"Why what?" Cree managed.

"Why I stabbed it. It did *that*. It's doing it more and more. It scared me."

Oh, man, Cree thought. *It's so obvious.* They'd all assumed that the entity had made Tommy attack himself, and Cree's only concern had been whether the act suggested intentional malevolence. But they all had it backward. *Tommy* had done the stabbing, attacking his persecutor in an effort to hurt it or drive it out. The full complexity of what she was up against struck her for the first time. With the thing progressively taking control, how long could they be sure who was Tommy and who the invader?

"Mrs. Pierce says it does other things. When I'm asleep." Tommy's rasping whisper sounded like the fear-awed voice of a much younger child. "Some of it was these ordinary gestures, things you do with your hands when you're talking to somebody or just sitting around." His voice dropped almost to inaudibility: "But some were like it was trying to figure out where it was. And some were like . . . it wanted to hurt somebody."

Cree met his round eyes and shared his horror. But they were getting close to something important. If she could frame her next questions just right, she might learn a great deal.

"Hel-*lo*, people!" The jovial voice startled them both. Cree turned to see Dr. Corcoran padding toward them, stooped like a white-coated vulture and wearing his biggest smile and best bedside manner. "How's the man of the hour, Mr. Keeday? Making any progress, Dr. Black?"

Cree wanted to kick him. But Tommy reflexively nodded and mustered a miserable grin for Dr. Corcoran. His first instinct was to please the man, treat him with respect. And, she suspected, by now he'd surely have guessed that acting normal was his only ticket out of the hospital.

28

ONNY MCCARTY spun away from his computer, surprised that the supposed parapsychologist's bona fides checked out. He had visited the Web site listed on her business card, and though it struck him as a pile of supernatural manure cloaked in psychobabble, it did at least seem like a genuine snake-oil stand, not a dummy site. To double-check, he'd done a Google search on her name and had come up with several hundred hits, some linking her with paranormal research topics and some with more mainstream, academic psychology. Just out of curiosity, he'd gone to the University of New Mexico site and brought up the events calendar, where, sure enough, she was listed as a speaker at some conference they'd just had. So she was what she claimed to be.

That is, if the woman who had accompanied Julieta was indeed the mysterious Dr. Lucretia Black referred to. There were no photos on her site, so determining that would take a little more digging, something Nick Stephanovic could see to. Maybe he was just being paranoid, but paranoia had its uses. It had certainly saved his ass more than once.

Donny stood up and went to the big window that covered most of the west wall of his office. There had never been much to see—Albuquerque was a flat town, and the nearby buildings of downtown blocked any views of the land beyond—but since they'd built the Maynard monstrosity across the street there was even less, just a bleak façade of blue-green glass and the wavy reflection of his own building. The sight only served to irritate him, as always.

Mondays were straight CEO days, when what he had to do was the big-issue stuff: legal battles, major purchaser relations, regulatory lobbying, strategic planning, new technologies, energy market analysis. He was good at that stuff—better than Dad had been, certainly—but he looked forward to the end of the week when his role changed with his clothes and he conducted his round of site inspections. He agreed with Garrett's idea that for a family-owned company to succeed the boss had to stay in touch with conditions on the ground. It was how you earned the loyalty of the troops, maintained morale and motivation, kept a real sense of the men, machines, and mountains of rock that lay behind the figures. Donny made a point of dragging some of the number crunchers along with him, just to get their scrawny asses off their chairs and remind them what it really meant to dig coal out of the goddamned ground.

And of course there were also the special projects that needed hands-on supervision, where leaving things to middle-management intermediaries would risk inconveniences and indiscretions.

The sight of the Maynard building began to really get on his nerves, and Donny turned away. Checking his watch, he found that he had less than twenty minutes before he had to leave for the lunch meeting with the audit team. A bilious, burning sensation nagged under his breastbone, chronic heartburn or acid reflux or whatever. Stress related, his doctor insisted. To which Donny had replied, "Tell me something I don't know." Hung in gilt frames on the inner wall, the three oil portraits of his forebears stared back at him, and the eyes of his father seemed to meet his with a glint of contempt. "You're a worrier," Dad had always told him. "Can't be a nervous Nellie in this business. Gotta grow a thick skin."

Garrett certainly hadn't been a worrier. He'd been a man of action. Old school: decisive, blunt, charming as hell, bulldog persistent, clever but not given to deliberation or self-criticism. Dad had neither understood nor accepted the growing complexity of the energy industry and the politics that went with it. Back in the 1890s when Great-grandfather McCarty had started out, even in 1964 when Garrett had taken over his father's holdings, the landscape had been pretty wide open. The rules of the Wild West still pertained, strong guys could still make the rules for themselves and their companies as they went along. If you ruffled some feathers, got some people's backs up, so be it and devil take 'em, you slugged it out and the best man won. But it wasn't that way anymore. Energy sources had diversified, coal had lost market share, margins had shrunk. Regulations had proliferated, citizen action groups had weighed in, the Indians had gotten restless, and politics with the big oil and nuke guys had gotten complex and devious: your good buddies one minute, competitors who would stick a knife in your back the next. Plus technology was changing so fast that by the time you finally decided to invest in the latest equipment it had already been replaced on the cutting edge by something even glitzier, more efficient, and more costly.

Donny looked over the audit materials he'd be reviewing today, increasingly distracted by the gnawing under his ribs. He hated the sensation, but he'd learned to make use of it: The heartburn was often an indicator that something was on his mind and needed attention. So what was today's trigger?

Simple: Julieta. That was it. What was she up to? Because, parapsychologist or no parapsychologist, Julieta didn't just visit the mine for the fun of it.

Garrett's portrait caught his eye, and he could almost hear his father's derisive voice: *Worrier!* To which Donny replied, *Yeah, Dad, I'm a worrier. Partly because you left me with so many things to worry about. One of them being your sweet ex-wife and all the crap that came with.*

A knock sounded at the door to the outer office, and after a pause the heavily paneled walnut slab swung open. Nick Stephanovic poked his blunt head in.

"Sahib," Nick said. "Just to let you know I'm ready when you are." He extended a thick wrist and tapped his watch.

"Hey, Nicko," Donny said. "I'm almost there. Come in for a minute. Shut the door."

Nick stepped inside, swung the door shut, and stood waiting with his hands folded in front of him. His ancestors were immigrants who had come to cut timber and lay railroads in the 1880s and had stayed to work in the mines that had flourished throughout the region. His Czech blood notwithstanding, he had the classic pug nose of the shantytown Irish tough, and though when in Albuquerque he wore a suit expensive enough for a CEO, it tended to cling to his broad shoulders and bulky upper arms and did nothing to conceal what he really was: bodyguard, personal assistant, driver, confidential consultant, and odd-job man. Among the rules Garrett had instilled in Donny from childhood was that you had to build a core of absolutely loyal retainers around you. In Donny's experience, there was no such thing as absolute loyalty—human sentiment being almost infinitely malleable, offered the right persuasions—but Nick came close. He was forty-nine, and Donny had inherited him as his right-hand man, along with the rest of the company, when Garrett had died.

Nothing would surprise Nick. After working for two generations of McCartys, he knew just about everything about McCarty family business, and what he didn't know he'd been given to surmise.

Donny rolled down his shirtsleeves, took his jacket from the coatrack behind his desk, slipped it on, shot his cuffs. He went back to sorting papers, taking his time, letting Nick wait as he thought things through.

"Nick," Donny said finally, "remind me when we found those mutes out at Hunters Point—what was it, last year? Year before?"

"What the hell?"

"You remember our unannounced visitors to the site the other day? Mrs. Ex-McCarty and friend?"

"*That's* what that was about? Mutes?" Nick grinned incredulously.

Donny shrugged. "Supposedly. The woman with her claims to be a paranormal researcher. I've checked her out, she seems legit—for a purveyor of bull, anyway. I agreed to meet her tomorrow to talk about mutes. Like I'm some kind of expert."

"Why meet with her?"

Donny put the last of the papers into his briefcase and snapped it shut. He felt a hard smile on his lips. *Because,* he told the portrait of his father, *there's more than one way to skin a cat. Sometimes it's better not to just bulldoze your way through. Sometimes you want subtlety, Dad. Finesse.* "Call it counterintelligence," he told Nick.

Nick nodded, knowing what he meant: trying to figure out what Julieta was up to. "Last year. Spring. Two cut-up horses, over in the eastern end of Area Eighteen."

"Anything strike you as coincidental about that location?"

Nick's face changed, amused contempt for Julieta giving way to a thoughtful look and then a dangerous glower that Donny savored.

"Oh" was all Nick said.

They didn't say any more as they went through the outer offices, tossed a wave to the secretaries, and walked out to the elevator. They waited in silence, but once the doors had shushed shut, Donny turned to Nick. "So what's your day like?"

"I got a couple of items, but they can wait if you've got something more pressing."

"This Dr. Lucretia Black, 'Cree' Black. From Seattle. I need to find a photo of her from somewhere. Make sure we're talking about the same person before I meet her."

"Okay. What else?"

"Supposedly there's something oddball happening at the school. That's what Julieta implied, and I also got one of those tantalizing wee-hours phone calls from our good friend, suggesting she knew of goings on there that might be of interest to us. It'll take the usual teasing out and flattery and playing games. But my thought here is, if Julieta has in mind making problems for us, I'd like to have something we can throw right back at her. Give her grief in return."

"So I should call the nurse."

"Set up a meet with her. Turn on the charm. Remind her how much we loved and relied upon her husband and the rest of it. And give her my fond regards, of course."

Nick nodded. The elevator braked and the doors hissed open to the basement parking garage. They stepped out and walked to the silver Mercedes Donny kept for town use. Nick beeped the doors open, got in on the driver's side, and leaned across the seat to open the door for Donny. When they came up the ramp and into the daylight of downtown Albuquerque, the sun beat down off the Maynard building with the intensity of a green laser. They turned right and Nick accelerated down the street.

Nick, bless his ugly Czech-Irish mug, knew when to keep quiet and let a man think.

Donny was feeling the familiar weariness come over him, the sense that it was all too much or too pointless. That so much of what happened or what he did was unnecessary, that there had to be more to life. After this meeting, he'd return to the office and work until seven, then go home to his suburban mansion in its rectangle of irrigated green lawns so startling against the brown-dirt desert, and to Liz and the marginal sense of human company she provided. She was young and refreshingly crass and inventive in bed—more so than he deserved or needed, actually, given the state of his libido; no, he wasn't like the old bucks of his father's generation. When he'd let her move in, they'd been seeing each other for six months and he'd thought maybe something would grow between them. But all that had grown was habit. A habitual theater of cohabitation, as good as it could be given her indeterminate status and the lack of any deeper heat or sense of future. When he thought of coming in through the chilly, polished-limestone foyer of his house, calling her name, seeing her emerge from the too-large rooms, the routine faux kiss they'd give each other, he felt a pang of loneliness like a blade that went up through his groin right into the heartburn behind his breastbone.

Another reason to hate the Maynard building, he thought blackly. Because if you stared hard enough at its wavery, bottle-green reflection of the windows of the McCarty Energy offices, you could pick out your own window and with effort even the solitary ghost of a figure standing there. Once he'd leaned close to the glass and waved to see his reflection, a barely discernible silhouette in the distorted surface light, wave back.

It could have been different. He hadn't always been this way. In high school, there'd been girls he'd loved with innocent tenderness, the swooning devotion you saw in the movies. Later, there'd been Bernadette, with whom he'd shared a couple of fairly sweet years until his father had brought home with unnecessary forcefulness just how inappropriate it was to consider marrying a half-breed.

And, admit it, for a short time, there'd been Julieta. An instant when he'd been able to see her as something other than his father's hated ex-wife. Her beauty and keen-edged intelligence had always intimidated him, but in the years right after her divorce she'd seemed to become so much more accessible. So skinny, so fragile. She had to be hurting, Donny knew that much for sure. She'd acquired appealing shadows under her eyes that spoke of sleepless nights and loneliness and doubts about life—all things Donny shared. For a short period, he had let himself imagine something about himself and about her. Almost-forgotten longings had blossomed in him and had made him act like a fool.

Julieta had refused to talk to Garrett or allow him on her property, so Donny had served as the company's go-between about the right-of-way crap Garrett had insisted on fighting out with her after the court had partitioned the property. He'd tried to do it righteously, hadn't he? Treating her with respect, showing a willingness to compromise? Asking, not demanding or threatening? She had no idea what it had cost him with Dad, resisting the old man's pressure to up the ante, turn it hostile, even have Nick do some down and dirty.

Yeah, Donny realized with a shock, that was the last time: that period with Julieta. The last time that whole species of feelings had awakened in him. Twelve, thirteen years ago! *Sweet Jesus, what a mess of a life.*

And that one day he'd been desperate or deluded enough to broach it with her. She'd heard his suggestion—that he had feelings for her, that there might be something to explore between them, and most of all that he was *not like Garrett*—and what he'd seen in her face wasn't the contempt he'd feared but something far worse: sympathy. She'd put her hand to his cheek and said, "No, Donny. Look at me—what's left of me. One McCarty was more than enough for this lifetime. Thank you, but no." A wry and sad grin.

Later, her comparative kindness rankled more than anger or contempt would have. But of course, she was right. Right right right. It had been a stupid impulse on his part, given the situation, given all that had gone down. Under the circumstances, getting together with her would have been something out of a Greek tragedy, what, *Oedipus Rex* or something. It went against the moral order of the universe. The gods didn't forgive such things.

The thought brought Donny out of his musings. Funny how the distant past could smack you upside the head, catch you when you least expected it.

But in this case, maybe there was a reason his subconscious had dredged all that up. He turned to Nick, who was driving placidly with one big-knuckled hand relaxed over the top of the steering wheel.

"You probably still know the lay of the land pretty well out there, don't you?" he asked. "Around the school? The mesa there? You could still find your way around if you had to?"

Puzzled, Nick glanced over at him, and then his eyebrows jumped with surprise. "What—you think this goes that far back?"

Donny shrugged, feeling crappy, injured by life's burdens and impositions, pissed at Garrett, at Julieta, at himself, at everybody. If the audit team gave him any grief today, anything at all, he swore to himself he'd tear somebody's head off.

"Just a thought," Donny told him. "I doubt it. But it always pays to be prepared."

29

THEY MET at the school. It was Joyce's first glimpse of the place, and Edgar had seen it only in the dark. When they got out of their vehicles in front of the infirmary, they both looked around with the cautious curiosity of strangers on new turf. The afternoon was comfortably warm and windless, the desert vast and without sound or movement; to the east, the mesa basked in sunshine.

The school itself was very different. With the students back, the place was alive with energy. Classes were done for the day, and most of the kids were outside. Groups sat under the trellises, skateboarders racketed up and down steps and curbs; a basketball game was in full swing on the court behind the gym, voices calling in Navajo and English. Faculty members strode between buildings, and the main parking lot was full of cars.

Cree felt drained after her session with Tommy. She'd left the hospital before his relatives returned, wanting to let him have an uncomplicated visit with them, and had driven straight back. Though the sparkle of adolescent activity and emotion here felt pleasant and warm, it only deepened the gloomy urgency she was feeling. It took her a moment to understand why: *because Tommy should be part of it*. Enjoying a warm afternoon outside with his friends. Instead, he was in a hospital room with nothing to do but feel the invader growing in him, infiltrating him, turning him moment by moment into more of a monster. He was becoming like . . . like one of the twisted, bloated things you used to see suspended in jars of formaldehyde at freak shows. It wasn't fair, it wasn't right. It had to end. The kid deserved a life.

And it didn't help that as she was leaving Dr. Corcoran had sketched out the pharmaceutical protocols he was considering if Tommy didn't shape up soon: Thorazine, haloperidol, Risperdal, maybe clozapine. Try the empirical approach, see if his condition responded. The trial-and-error method that so often became just that—a wrenching trial for the patient, a lot of errors. Dr. Corcoran talked as if he planned to have Tommy with him for a long time.

Tommy Keeday was in deep trouble. And Cree Black, Mrs. Ultrasensitive Ghost Buster Queen, or whatever the hell she was, didn't have a clue how to help.

"We need to have a conference right away," she told them as they came toward her. "Julieta McCarty is on her way over. I've asked the nurse to join us, too. I want everybody on the same page here."

Ed gave her an appraising look. Joyce frowned and chided her, "Well, hello to you, too, Cree. We're glad to see you, too."

Cree just dipped her chin, took their elbows, and led them up the walk to the infirmary porch.

They convened in the dayroom, taking seats on the couch and chairs that surrounded an oval coffee table. Julieta arrived from the administration building, Lynn came in from her office.

Once Cree had introduced everybody all around, she turned to Julieta. "I've asked Lynn to join us because we need to be able to share information about every detail of Tommy's condition and behavior. Lynn has spent more time with him during his crises than anyone, and she may recall details that didn't strike her as significant at the time but might be crucial for our team. But for her to do that, she'll need to know exactly how we're thinking of the problem. Which means, Julieta, that I need your approval to share information with her. Per our confidentiality agreement."

Julieta didn't answer right away, but looked thoughtfully first at Lynn and then at Cree. She looked tired, but the effect seemed to make her all the more lovely. Today she wore a gray wool pantsuit with a Navajo necklace that complemented the color of her skin and hair, and she looked older, her beauty derived from her poise and dignity.

"Of course," Julieta said at last. But she gave a tiny shake of her head, and the message in her eyes was clear: *Everything but my secret. Peter Yellowhorse. My baby.*

Cree nodded. "Lynn, you already know how we're thinking of this. I'm sure it strikes you as bizarre. Do you think you can you ride with it despite your skepticism? Give our perspective a chance?"

The nurse was sitting in a soft chair and seemed huddled in on herself, slumped, holding her knees or toying with the end of her braid. Her eyes rose to meet Cree's and the bronze speck sparkled. "You mean, the idea that Tommy's possessed?"

"As I told you, I don't like the typical assumptions that come with the term, but that's about it, yeah. What do you think of that hypothesis?"

Lynn directed her coy smile at Julieta. "I just work here. I'll do whatever I'm told. Frankly, having seen him when it's . . . on him, I don't find the idea such a stretch. Maybe being married into a Navajo family for sixteen years kind of wore down my skepticism. Possession—that's what a Navajo diagnostician would probably call it." She turned back to Cree. "As for confidentiality—" She made a lip-zipping gesture.

Cree found she couldn't stay seated. She was too energized, impatient, frustrated. She got up to pace the room as she brought them up to date: "I saw Tommy at the hospital today. It's getting worse. Joseph kindly talked to them and they let me in as a consultant, so I have access to him. But I have no authority to treat or prescribe. The doctor in charge of his case has a tight psychological theory, but if Tommy doesn't improve he's also considering treating him for seizures, impulse control disorders, schizophrenia. Which means lots of drugs, lots of side effects, personality alteration, long-term hospitalization. I sure hate to see it go there. And I don't think it will work."

Julieta's lips had narrowed, and though she didn't move, her aura changed, the resigned dignity turning shaky again as desperation rose beneath it. *A mother's reaction,* Cree thought.

Cree continued, telling them about her pending meeting with Donny McCarty to explore the possibility that the entity was indeed the vengeful ex Julieta seemed so certain of. "Julieta, you've given me an impression of who Donny is and who Garrett was. Is there anything you can add that will help me when I talk to Donny?"

Julieta thought about that and finally shook her head. "What you saw when we met Donny was pretty typical. How about you, Lynn? You had contact with the McCartys when your husband worked for them, right?"

Lynn nodded and explained, "My Vernon worked as chief explosives engineer for McCarty for many years. He got to know them pretty well. Not down here, he worked at the Bloomfield mine, up near Farmington. And I ran the Bloomfield medical unit for a few years, so, yes, I saw both McCartys now and again."

"Can you tell me anything about them?"

Lynn shrugged. "I really don't know what might be helpful to you. I wouldn't know where to start."

"How about beliefs? Was Garrett religious? Is Donny? Or superstitious at all?"

"Garrett went to church, but I don't think he was really religious. I think he saw it as a useful way to network. Donny, he doesn't believe in much of anything, I don't think. Neither struck me as superstitious in the slightest. Pragmatists, both of them."

"What would be Donny's reaction if I suggested, for example, that I'd heard his father's ghost haunted the mine?"

Lynn chuckled. "Well, he'd get a kick out of it. He'd think you were a weak-brained female."

Julieta nodded agreement. "And he'd think I had put you up to it to give him grief in some way. Or that you'd heard it from some superstitious Indian."

Cree turned that over in her thoughts, trying to find a way to engage Donny, enlist his help. "So . . . what is his attitude toward Native Americans?"

"Donny always treated Vern with respect," Lynn said immediately.

"Patronizing," Julieta said. "Condescending. Navajos make up ninety percent of his workforce. He talks respectfully only because he doesn't want to alienate his labor pool and sometimes needs to swing favors with the tribal government. As for Garrett, he was pretty much an out-and-out racist."

Lynn looked like she was biting her tongue but kept a little smile at the corners of her lips.

Cree mentally filed it away as Joyce took notes. "Okay. If I can ask a favor, it's that you both ponder the issue. What can you tell me about Donny that will allow me to ask about his father, the circumstances of his father's death? And Lynn, please look back at every contact you've had with Tommy and tell me anything that you think might be helpful."

They nodded.

"Okay. Julieta, I can't work only on the premise that we're dealing with Garrett's ghost. There are other possibilities to consider. His . . . parents should be a high priority." Cree's eyebrows jumped; she had almost said *adoptive parents.* "Joyce, do you have anything on that?"

"Only the basics so far. Car crash, spring of '97. Father was driving drunk. Both died at the scene. The accident was up near Tuba City. I'll keep looking into it, but if we want to consider one of the parents we'd have to ask ourselves, why would the revenant come *here,* two hundred miles away, and why *now,* six years later? I mean, if one of the parents' ghosts homed in on Tommy, why not at the Keedays' place, or his previous school, and much earlier?"

Cree nodded. "Good questions. We'll look for more information in the coming days. In the meantime, there's another possibility you should know about, Julieta. I was very interested in Tommy's drawings of the cliff faces, so last night, Dr. Mayfield and I went out to the mesa to explore. You had a drawing class with him out there, didn't you? Out at the big ravine?"

Julieta looked puzzled. "Yes. Why?"

"And Tommy said he got a touch of sunstroke up there?"

"Right. I'd forgotten. It didn't seem serious at all."

"His drawings changed drastically after those sessions. And I had a powerful contact with an entity or entities there last night. I can't believe it's a coincidence. So I need to know the area's history better. Julieta, are you sure you can't tell me any more about it? Lynn, do you know anything?"

Julieta shook her head. Lynn ventured, "Locally, I think it was once called Lost Goats Mesa. But I don't think it has a name now."

Ed met Cree's eyes, and he smiled minutely: *goats.*

"So—Joyce, I know you've got a lot on your plate, but can you add that in? Dig up some history for this area? Stories associated with the mesa or the old trading post? Who lived here, when, anything."

Joyce had been taking notes on her pad, and looked up quickly. "I am all over it."

"Ed will need to conduct a comprehensive test of the school's electrical system, particularly the boys' dorm and this building. The flickering of the lights might give us some clues. Julieta, can you put him in touch with your maintenance people so they can help? He'll need to look at the whole grid here—transformers, circuit breakers, incoming lines, everything."

"Frank Nez is our chief physical plant man. I'll take you over to his shop when we're done here, but . . ."

"I'll tell him it has something to do with state safety compliance," Ed put in.

"Perfect." Cree had taken some notes on what she needed to accomplish at this meeting, and now she glanced down at her pad. "I've got two more items on my agenda. One, as I said, I had an important session with Tommy today. The good news is that, thanks to Joseph, Dr. Corcoran is letting me meet with the boy. And when I was there, I was increasingly able to feel it—as something distinct or separate from Tommy. Which means I'm on the road to identifying it."

Julieta said haltingly, "And the bad news?"

"I'm sorry, Julieta. The bad news is, this thing is progressing rapidly. It's taking him over, minute by minute. So far, he's been resisting it pretty well, and he can intentionally cooperate with people trying to help him. But I don't know how long that'll be the case. I think it's wearing him out." Julieta's face broke into lines of grief, and Cree went on quickly, "I didn't meet his grandparents, but on the off chance Tommy goes home, I'll need to have their approval to keep seeing him. Julieta, that's an area where you can help. Speak to them, speak to Joseph. It would be good if Ed and I can rig him with the FMEEG, but the technology there can be intimidating—we'll need some persuasion on our side."

Julieta was looking away, out the window at the empty western horizon, but she nodded.

"Finally, I'll need to go out to the mesa again tonight. Ed or Joyce, it would be good to have one of you there with me." Cree faltered as she tried to explain to Julieta: "It . . . I sometimes have a hard time coming back. It helps to have someone remind me who I am. What world I'm in."

Joyce gave her an approving nod.

"So, with that," Cree said, "off we go. Into the fray, swords upraised, right? All for one and one for all."

"And huzzah," Ed muttered. They all stood soberly and adjourned.

30

J OYCE WENT off to Window Rock to get a start with the archives at the Navajo History Museum before it closed for the day. Ed arranged to meet Cree at nine-thirty for a second trip to the ravine, then went with Julieta to meet the maintenance staff and get a tour of the electrical system's components in preparation for the exhaustive analysis he'd conduct tomorrow. Lynn was called to tend to a boy who had badly scraped both elbows playing basketball.

Cree spent the evening resting and reading more of the materials Mason and Joyce had provided. It was disquieting stuff in more ways than one.

From what she'd read so far, it was clear that most cases of "possession" from earlier eras were actually examples of clinically definable maladies. Many were obviously epilepsy or schizophrenia, but some were more likely DID, dissociative identity disorder, previously referred to as multiple personality disorder. The condition was believed to be caused by a combination of neurological predisposition and early childhood trauma so severe that the victim "quarantined" aspects of his or her personality, locking them away to escape the pain of coping with the trauma. Most people lived in some degree of forgetfulness or denial, but with DID victims the sequestered parts began to develop independently, to grow and articulate as complete, separate personalities that could emerge under the right triggering circumstances. The supposed "epidemic" of MPD during the 1980s had been discredited as a phenomenon largely created by unscrupulous therapists, but a number of cases, stretching back centuries, held up under scrutiny and made it clear that though very rare, the disorder was real.

At the same time, the inverse was also true: To Cree's eyes, some of those now labeled as MPD/DID sufferers were clearly victims of invasion by a separate, roving, extracorporeal entity.

Again, she had to admire the insight and courage of Mason's basic dictum: No theory of human psychology could be considered accurate or complete unless it accommodated the principle that mind is to some degree independent of brain or body and that the human personality is shaped by psychological and social influences that extend beyond the physical lifetime.

Included in the papers Joyce had provided was one of Mason Ambrose's most famous monographs, published eighteen years ago as a slap in the face to the psychological status quo. Describing five specific, well-documented MPD case studies, he had challenged anyone to offer a single fact that was demonstrably inconsistent with the idea that the victims were in fact possessed by a distinct, externally originating entity. Despite their scorn, his detractors mustered only feeble efforts to refute the idea. Some psychologists had applauded the paper, assuming that Mason intended it only as an ironic argument against current diagnostic criteria for MPD, a way of saying that criteria that didn't permit ready refutation of such a wild theory had to be inadequate. Subsequent developments in the field had reinforced that view, and multiple personality disorder had been dropped from the *Diagnostic and Statistical Manual*.

Cree, of course, knew that he'd meant it literally.

Mason had relished the ongoing controversy. But now, rereading that first paper in the light of the bedside lamp in the ward room, with desert-dark windows on all three sides, Cree found herself deeply unsettled. Somehow it made the awful stuff more real—the biblical and medieval accounts and the quasi-religious or pseudomedical reports from the last ten centuries. In particular, she couldn't shake that damned woodcut image, the rearing saint above the contorted sufferer, the worm spewing and coiling. Maybe because it echoed too well Tommy's description of the maggots in the sheep.

There was another perspective, Cree knew: the old faiths of the world, the nature religions and shamanic spiritual traditions, like that of the Navajo. For a moment she wished she wasn't so far from a library, then realized she had access to a knowledgeable source. She went to the nurse's office, dialed Paul's home number.

"Hey."

"Hey, yourself," Paul said. "I was hoping it was you."

229

"You busy?"

"Monday night. I'm busy trying to shed the accumulated stresses of a day of dealing with other people's intractable problems. I've got a tall, slim, sensuous companion named Beaujolais Nouveau who is, shall we say, helping me unwind."

Cree heard a clink of glass, the sound of wine pouring. "Trying to make me jealous? It won't work. I'm calling for professional advice."

"Is that so? I'm kissing her ruby lips even as we speak . . . mmmm." Paul was in a good mood; this obviously wasn't the first such kiss of the evening.

"Okay, it's working, I'm jealous," Cree said sincerely. A sip of the good grape *would* be nice, maybe help ease the growing tension she felt. "Listen, I was thinking about a paper you told me you'd written. On the parallels between modern psychotherapy and shamanistic healing practices."

"Aha."

"I'm interested in . . . well, in possession. I've got a bunch of literature on the Christian/Satanic outlook, and some papers on the parallels between DID and possession. But I'd like to get some perspectives from other traditions."

Paul was quiet for a moment. "So that's what you're dealing with there? Jesus. I hated the idea even when I didn't believe in ghosts. Now . . . Jesus. That sounds like a scary proposition for a . . . you know. A person like you, Cree."

"It's a common diagnosis in the Navajo tradition. The entity is often the ghost of a dead ancestor. Is that typical?"

"You know all this better than I do, Cree."

"Indulge me. Refresh my memory."

"It's universal. All over the world, every culture. All the old religions have the same basic idea. In a few traditions, you find some rough equivalent of the demonic entity, but that's rare. I always saw the ancestor thing as a useful metaphor. Struck me as full of resonances with modern psychotherapy—not so different from Freud putting you on the couch and asking about your mother. A way to cope constructively with our unresolved business with our forebears. But it's not always ancestors. The spirit can be any dead person close to the victim. A mother or father can become possessed by the ghost of a dead child. A widow or widower can be possessed by the dead spouse. It's often a blood relative, but not always—a murderer might be possessed by the spirit of his victim."

"Always someone with a connection to the victim, though."

"Yep. Unless it's a deity or nature spirit of some kind."

"What kind of symptoms? Are they consistent in different cultures?"

"Very. But if you want details . . . well, let me think. It's been a while, Cree." He took another sip of wine and breathed deeply once or twice. "Well, in Melanesia, the possessed person typically speaks in a strange voice, shows glaring eyes, twisting limbs, convulsing body, foam in the throat. The *mana*—that's the spirit of the dead person—overpowers the victim in fits or cycles, leaving him exhausted, almost comatose. Among the Alarsk Buryat of Siberia, the ancestral spirits are called *utcha* and manifest first in dreams, getting to the convulsions and strange voices only as they gain greater control. In Nepal, the Tamangs have a term, um . . . God, I used to know all this stuff . . . I'd impress my fellow grad students, those of the female persuasion, with it . . . uh, yeah, *iha khoiba mayba*. The term means, essentially, 'crazy possession.' As opposed to voluntary possession. Symptoms are typical, your basic convulsive shaking, incoherency, chaotic visions or hallucinations."

" '*Voluntary* possession'?" The idea was appalling to Cree.

"Oh, sure. For shamans, it's a sought-after state. The shaman surrenders to the spirit to get guidance from the dead. Sometimes the ghost gives him prophetic information—advice on what's going to happen, what people should or shouldn't do, warnings, and so on. Advice on how to heal people, how to settle their unresolved issues. I thought you'd know all about *that*—isn't that a lot like what *you* do?"

She hadn't quite thought of it in those terms and wished he hadn't pointed it out. "Let's go back to the involuntary variety. What else? Why do the spirits return? The human type?"

"That's variable. They often come back to seek redress or justice for wrongs. Or to punish the living for offenses—the Tibetan Book of the Dead has a ton of stuff on after-death retribution."

"Terrific. Great."

Paul heard the bleakness in her tone, tried to inject something more hopeful: "But, again, the dead may also have important information to convey. They may be trying to help."

"How nice of them," Cree said acidly. Right now, it was hard to think of spirit invasion as anything but a form of rape.

"Among the Tungas, for example—"

"That's okay, Paul. I get the picture."

"Of course, there are also animal spirits, they're often helping spirits, too. It—"

"This one's human."

"Okay." He was quiet for a minute as her mood really registered. "Do you have to get involved?"

"I'm already 'involved.'"

"And you're . . . at risk?"

"No doubt."

"You want to tell me what you're dealing with?"

He sounded frustrated and worried, and she wanted to cheer him up. "I can't, Paul. Just be yourself. Who you are. And what you've told me is very helpful. This member of the female persuasion is very impressed."

"Tell me more about that," he said huskily, vamping. "How impressed?"

He was fishing for intimate talk, but she felt confused, unable to find the mood. As she hesitated, a change in the light made her turn. Lynn Pierce had come to the door of the office. Seeing Cree on the phone, she smiled apologetically and passed by as if heading toward the big ward room. But Cree didn't hear the other door open. She must have paused, out of view in the hall.

"Anyway," Cree said briskly, "I better get going now. We'll talk another time, okay?"

Paul grunted, put out by her sudden change of tone. "Privacy issues?"

Lynn Pierce still hadn't gone into the examining room. "Apparently," Cree said drily.

31

CREE WENT back to her room and made ready for what promised to
be a difficult visit to the ravine later. She spent a half hour doing
yoga, and when her thoughts intruded she steered them toward the many
good things in her life: the twins, Dee, Edgar and Joyce, hiking in the
Cascades range, her friends in the lovely Emerald City. *And Paul,* she
added.

That was the foundation, she reminded herself. The love, the connection. The world was full of dire things, but love managed to endure. That's
what sustained you.

And, in fact, the things Paul had told her were helpful. In the face of what
she'd seen in Tommy, it was good to be reminded that most supernaturalist
spiritual traditions agreed with her outlook: that the entity was not necessarily hostile or malignant. It wasn't just coiling serpents and rearing saints, or
adolescent girls rotating their heads and spewing green bile.

Feeling a little better, she put on thick socks and loaded a fanny pack
with a couple of energy bars, a bottle of water, and one of the good
flashlights Edgar had brought. As an afterthought, she included the small
canister of pepper spray Joyce had insisted she carry. By nine-fifteen, she
felt almost ready for the night's work.

Then Lynn Pierce came into the ward room.

She drifted across the floor from the hall doorway to stand at the end of
Cree's bed, her silver braid thick as a hawser on one shoulder. "Your
partner called from the admin building, said to tell you he'd be here in ten
minutes."

"Great. I'm just about ready." Cree zipped up the fanny pack and set it
on the bed, then began consolidating the possession literature she'd spread
on the neighboring bed and table.

Lynn watched with interest, tipping her head to catch glimpses of titles and illustrations. "I've been thinking about what you asked. You're right, I've been around Tommy more than anyone else. And I think maybe I have noticed something that could be important."

"Oh?"

Lynn darted her eyes at Cree, and a little grin moved her mouth. Then she crossed over to one of the beds against the south wall and began straightening the blankets, slightly rumpled from Edgar's sitting on it earlier.

"You're so close to your associates," Lynn said. "They really trust you, don't they? And you them. Really, you're more like friends than business partners, aren't you? It must be nice."

"It's the line of work we're in. Sometimes it can get pretty hairy, and so you kind of have to deal with things. Interpersonal things, I mean. You get to know each other pretty well."

"Joyce—one very smart gal, isn't she? I asked her how she got to know you, and she said you'd saved her life. What's that all about?" Her back to Cree, Lynn was plumping the pillow carefully.

"It was some years ago. But it's kind of personal, Lynn. If she didn't offer the details, I don't think it's my place to—"

"And Edgar. Dr. Mayfield. I get the sense he's very devoted to you. Are you and he . . . you know . . . ?"

"Ed and I are very good friends and business partners," Cree answered curtly.

"Hm. So the person you talk to on the phone at night—that's your boyfriend?"

Given that Cree was using the phone in her office, it was unavoidable that Lynn would overhear snatches of conversation. But for her to deduce that it was the same person, and what the relationship might be, confirmed Cree's sense that she'd been deliberately eavesdropping.

"Um, listen, Lynn—"

"Oh, I don't mean to pry." Lynn finished with the bed and rounded on Cree. "I'm just curious. You're all such interesting people. You're so close. I'm just wondering how you all got together. But you're right, you hardly know me. It's inappropriate, isn't it."

Lynn was watching Cree's response closely. At the corners of her mouth, her grin seemed to tremble. Cree's heart went out to her: the perpetual outsider, looking in.

"Maybe later," Cree told her. "It's a long story, you know? When we get the time, let's all sit down with some hot chocolate and they can tell the saga from their own points of view. Right now, I'm anxious to hear what you were going to tell me."

Lynn feigned surprise at herself. "Oh! I'm so sorry! Yes, I thought of a detail that might be useful." She hesitated, as if debating whether to tease and stall further, then opted to continue: "It has to do with Julieta and Tommy."

That got Cree's attention. "What about them?"

Lynn lowered her voice and glanced over her shoulder as if to make sure no one was listening. "I think it gets worse when she's around him."

"Tommy gets worse?"

"Oh, yes. Remember the other night, when he was looking at her that way, and then he lunged at her?"

"How could I forget?"

Lynn shivered. "That look! The only time I've seen anything like that was at the zoo. The big cats, when they stare at you through the bars as if they'd like to—"

"He attacked *you*, too. He bit you!"

"That was different! It happened as I was trying to restrain him. With Julieta, he has this . . . *focus*. I first noticed it during his second crisis, a couple of weeks ago, but it was more ambiguous then. But Saturday night, when we were at the cafeteria, he was doing pretty well until Julieta sat down at our table. I could see it change him to have her around. When he lunged across the table, I think he was going for her. I thought you should know."

"Thank you for bringing it to my attention. Why would that be, do you suppose?"

Lynn came toward her, trailing her fingers along the bedcover, then crossed to the foot of Cree's bed where she absently caressed the tube-steel frame. Reflexively, Cree drew away a step and turned to stack the papers. She wished the old woodcuts and engravings weren't so lurid.

"I can't imagine," Lynn said. "Except maybe it has to do with something I noticed in a couple of your articles." She pointed with her chin at the stack of possession materials.

Cree gaped at her, dumbfounded. "You came in here and went through my things?"

"No, no! God, no. I would never do that! I'm sorry! I didn't think they were personal papers, or I would never have presumed, really. They aren't personal, are they? I would never have looked if I thought it would upset you! I was just checking up on the room, and—"

"What, Lynn? Just tell me what you saw that was interesting." Cree felt like throttling her, but the clever, overearnest, speck-eyed face touched a nerve in her chest. "And in the future, just leave my stuff alone, huh? No, they're not personal papers. But it feels invasive."

"Really, I had no idea it would . . . No, you're right, what was I thinking? How rude and intrusive it must—"

"What struck you? I'm tired, Lynn. I need to charge up my batteries here. Just tell me what you were going to."

Lynn came around the foot of Cree's bed to the table, took the papers and leafed through them.

"It was part of a book on the psychology of superstition. Here. This one."

The set of stapled pages she handed to Cree was a photocopy of a chapter analyzing features of the old literature on possession. Cree scanned it quickly to refresh her memory.

"What about it?"

"Who they always blame. For possession."

Right, Cree thought.

The author had pointed out a constant in the European history of possession: The possessed was believed to be the victim of a human persecutor—an enemy, usually a witch, who "called" or "cast" the demon into the victim. Often the supposed perpetrator was someone already unpopular in the community, or old, or living alone. The accused was invariably tortured and killed by religious authorities or by lynch mobs of fearful citizenry.

"I was going to say, it's the same in the Navajo tradition. They often think of illness or spirit possession as being inflicted on the victim by a Skinwalker. Like a curse. And then this part"—Lynn reached across Cree to put a forefinger to the right paragraph—"here. Where he talks about how they knew who the witch was? I was thinking of . . . well, of Tommy's reaction to Julieta."

Cree resisted the urge to sidle away from the silver head leaning so close to her cheek. She read the paragraph again. The basic technique was the supernatural equivalent of the modern police lineup: parade a bunch of likely suspects past the victim. The possessed person would invariably be seized anew, attacking or cowering, when in the proximity of the "real" witch.

If it were true that Tommy's symptoms intensified when Julieta was around him, Cree thought, it affirmed her sense that the problem was related to the connection between them—the instinctive sense of recognition between mother and child. But what did it reveal about the entity? The best she could do was that maybe Julieta was correct, that the entity was Garrett's revenant, driven by a dying urge centered on his ex-wife.

If Lynn was correct, this could be important. Watching Julieta and Tommy together might help her figure out what was going on. In Cree's view, accusations of witchcraft and demon casting were nothing but superstitious scapegoating or deliberate malice that victimized yet another innocent party. But Tommy's possession did fit the classic on-and-off pattern of "fits" and remission; if his crises resulted from any external catalyst, Cree could learn a great deal about the entity from what—or who—awakened or energized it.

On the other hand, Lynn's observation could be just another example of the inexplicable ill will she seemed to harbor against Julieta.

"It's a good point. Thanks for bringing it to my attention." Cree turned to her and locked eyes. "So what's your interpretation? Think Julieta's a witch?"

"Well, we're not exactly the *most* compatible personalities, but I wouldn't go quite *that* far."

"I'm serious, Lynn. You've got something against her. I'd like to know what it is."

Lynn appraised her sourly. "You know, you can be kind of confrontational sometimes."

Cree didn't break eye contact. "I think you keep information to yourself because you like feeling you've got an edge on other people. Because you habitually feel at a disadvantage and think you need something to even things up. But right now there's a boy who desperately needs our help. He doesn't need people playing games, Lynn!"

"How lovely to be so *thoroughly* understood," Lynn said drily.

"What else? What else about Julieta?"

Lynn's face took on its prim, clever look. "There you go again, tempting me into indiscretions!" Then her façade faltered and revealed the anger just behind: "Let's just say I think her obsession with Tommy might be more complicated and less healthy than people like you want to admit. I thought you'd be grateful I'd pointed out his reaction. I thought I was being helpful."

Cree almost stamped her foot in frustration. There seemed no way to break through the nurse's defenses. Part of the problem was that this transaction was just what Lynn wanted, an intense exchange serving as a bitter surrogate for intimacy. She started to plead with her but then heard noises from the front hall: Ed had arrived.

"I'll watch them carefully from here on in. Okay? But if there's something else you think I should know, for God's sake *tell me*. And in the meantime, I still want you to respect my space, my stuff! How would you like it if I went into your room and rummaged around?"

"Well. I'd probably be a little upset. But I might be kind of flattered, too."

"Lynn—it was intended as a rhetorical question."

The nurse's mouth made a surprised O, then smiled. "Yes. Of course it was."

Cree turned half away to stack the papers again and go on packing for the night's work. She hoped Lynn would get the message, but still she hovered there with her purse-lipped smile. And then Ed was bumping through the doorway with a pair of equipment cases, apologizing for being late, and Cree turned to him with relief.

32

Edgar stood at the crumbling edge of the cliff, looking west, enjoying himself immensely and ignoring the rocks his feet sent tumbling into the ravine. His face was vivid from the climb and the crisp air. From here at the top of the mesa, they could see all the way to the higher land of the Defiance Plateau, a glowing pink-purple band along the horizon. The early-morning sun was at their backs, throwing their shadows off the cliff and spreading the mesa's shadow like a dusky lavender cape on the ground below.

"You know what it looks like to me?" Edgar asked.

"What?" Cree followed his gaze.

He gestured at the boulders, the slabs, the endless expanse of bare soil. "It's like . . . after God created the rest of the world, He had a bunch of raw materials left over. And He just sort of dumped them out here. Piles of stuff, just lying there for a few hundred million years, waiting for the next big project."

He was in a good mood. Last night, he had assented readily when she suggested they change plans and nap before visiting the ravine. Cree's confrontation with Lynn Pierce had drained her, and bringing up witches and demons had obliterated the fleeting sense of relief she'd felt after talking to Paul. Ed was tired, too. They had agreed to sleep for a few hours, go out in the early hours of the morning, and end the vigil with this morning trip to the top of the mesa. It was a good way to get a better sense of the lay of the land.

So for a while they'd lounged in the ward room, talking. Just being around Ed had calmed Cree. After a while she had caught some of his mood of curiosity and excitement, the thrill of the investigation. He loved the landscape here; like Cree, he felt exhilarated by it, wanting to embrace it, get out in it, immerse himself in it. Telling her about it, he'd paced around, gesturing expansively, unselfconscious and looking sexy in T-shirt and boxer shorts.

When at last they'd put out the light, the snores from the other bed told Cree that Edgar had fallen asleep immediately. Lying awake, she found herself soothed by the gentle rhythm of his breathing and the sight of his slumbering profile in the faint light.

The alarm clock had awakened them at two A.M. They'd dressed blearily and gone off into the desert night. At the ravine, Ed had taken up his post on the desert floor as Cree moved up the cleft, found what felt like an appropriate spot, wrapped herself with blankets, and waited.

Waited for nothing, as it turned out. For whatever reason, she couldn't get past the ordinary world and her ordinary, if frightened, thoughts. It never failed to astonish her, the way a haunted place could be so dense at one time, so empty at another. Was it the cycle of manifestation—there when it was there, not when it was not? Or was it just cycles of Cree Black's sensitivity? She'd probably never know. But it was an experience familiar to every serious ghost hunter: the long pointless wait, the empty hours. The only startling moment had been awakening from her drowse to see a blanket-wrapped figure standing before her in the predawn light. For a jolting instant she'd thought it was some Navajo or Anasazi from centuries past. Then she recognized it as Edgar, a blanket draped over his shoulders, grinning. Light was creeping into the sky. She'd left her little nest and they'd set stiffly off up the ravine just as streaks of cloud at the zenith burst into peach-pink flame against the depthless baby blue sky.

The rock dam where she'd sat the first night turned out to be a jumble of fallen boulders and slabs four or five feet high and about twenty feet across, tricky footing. Ed had brought a compact trifield meter and a Geiger counter, and as they picked their way he paused to take readings; though there was some rise in EMF activity, it was well within the normal variations he'd expect.

Beyond, the gully tapered as it rose, then split into shallower runs that meandered toward the mesa top. They walked quickly in the cold shadows, trying to work off the chill of sitting so long in the open.

It was wonderful to come to the top. Suddenly the sandstone walls angled away and then they were beneath the clear sky again, with the half-risen sun blasting at them brassy as a trumpet and a coquettish breeze flirting with their hair. The mesa top was an uneven plane of soil and rock with only a thin cover of scrubby sage and rabbitbrush: as Edgar said, a pile of raw planet-building stuff left here for a few hundred million years, detritus left over from a huge construction project. The image made Cree smile.

They explored the edges of the big ravine for a time, moving very cautiously among the boulders: Some of the rocks seemed precariously perched on the crumbling, undercut cliffs, ready to tumble. After a while Ed informed her that, in his infinite wisdom, he had packed some bananas and a small thermos of coffee. They crouched against the sun-facing side of a boulder as he opened the thermos and poured the black liquid steaming into the plastic cup. Cree warmed her hands on it for a moment, took a scalding sip, and handed it back.

"When you were summing up the situation last night," he said, "I notice you omitted the issue of Julieta's being Tommy's mother. Was that because she doesn't trust the nurse? Or *you* don't?" Ed sipped coffee and grimaced at the burn.

"She didn't feel comfortable about it. I can imagine that having one of your employees know that kind of thing about your past . . . well. And Lynn certainly seems to have 'issues' with her boss. What do you think of her—Julieta?"

His eyes caught hers. "I admire what she's done here. Seems like a decent person."

"And gorgeous, sexy, compelling—"

"Not my type." He sipped some more coffee, blew a gout of steam into the sun, and then sat with his eyes closed, face to the light.

"The nurse told me last night she thinks Tommy's symptoms get worse when Julieta is around."

"You agree?"

She shrugged. "I've seen him sort of . . . *fix* on her. But I'm really not sure—I haven't seen much of them together."

Edgar nodded and thought about that as he peeled a banana, bit off half of it in one mouthful, and appeared to swallow it whole. "That would seem to support her idea it's the ex, no? Driven by lingering hatred or hostility?"

"Or the ex driven by regret and a desire to reconcile. I don't know enough about the dynamics there to tell."

"You know, when we were going over to the maintenance building, she told me some interesting things about her relationship with the McCartys. Did she tell you about the lawsuit she's got going against them? The uranium thing?"

"She said she often fought them in court, but nothing specific."

"Well, this one's still pending, some protracted process involving McCarty Energy and local townships and the Navajo tribe. Seems there's uranium here and there throughout the region—huge profit potential? So McCarty Energy wants to do what's called in situ extraction. That's where they pump a chemical solution into the ground that dissolves the uranium ore. They mix the dissolved ore with water, and pump the slurry back up for separation. But water's rare and valuable out here, right? So the problem with the process is, one, it consumes huge amounts of a crucial resource, and two, the liquefied uranium travels in the aquifers. Given that the process uses up or pollutes groundwater far beyond McCarty property, there's a lot of resistance. A number of nearby water users have joined the suits. Julieta got worried about radioactivity in the school's well, and she's been the ringleader among the other parties involved. And so far, they've won—there's an injunction against in situ extraction, pending resolution in the courts. It's been going on for years already, began while Garrett was still alive. In the meantime, needless to say, McCarty harbors no great love for Julieta."

"Jesus! No wonder Donny was so paranoid when we came to the mine! And why he was so convinced I was conspiring with Julieta."

"Yeah. Something to keep in mind when you meet with him today." Edgar poured some more coffee, recapped the thermos, and handed the cup to Cree. "You don't want to get caught in that crossfire."

Cree nodded, still not sure how she would deal with Donny. She finished the banana Ed had given her, then took a long swallow of coffee, hungry for the caffeine burn in her belly. The heat was nice, but her anxiety was rising again. So much to consider. The in situ issue and Donny's rather understandable distrust was yet another complication, another indication this thing was snowballing out of control.

*　　*　　*

They spent another half hour exploring the western side of the mesa. The small tableland sloped gently to the south and east, where a couple of miles away it broke up and descended to the desert floor in rounded hills and gullies, more thickly scattered with piñon and juniper. Faint vehicle tracks in the hard brown soil suggested that humans sometimes drove up from the gentler slopes at the south end. On this side, the cliffs were higher, and the ravine they'd come up provided the only access to the top. But Julieta was right, Lost Goats Mesa wasn't much, and there were no signs of earlier habitation. Just lots of God's raw materials, dumped after the big job.

Walking back, Ed swung himself along with easy strides. He looked around him with avid curiosity, humming quietly. Cree couldn't make out the tune, but it was energetic and upbeat, maybe some Paul Simon song. She couldn't help absorbing his mood, feeling more confident. Drinking black coffee on an almost-empty stomach probably helped: that feeling of being up for almost anything.

"You're in a good mood," she commented.

"Am I? Yeah, I guess I am."

"Any particular reason?"

He shrugged. "Nice day. New scenery. Good company. Belly full of java. Getting an early start."

She chuckled. "I don't usually see you this early in the morning. I swear to God, Ed, your beard has grown a quarter inch since last night. Seriously."

He rubbed his sandpapery chin, then grimaced and shook his hand as if he'd hurt it.

"We gotta go for hikes more often, back home. I mean, it's been so long—" Cree stopped, aware that she'd moved into uncomfortable territory: Yes, it was the first time they'd done anything like this together since she'd gone to New Orleans and met Paul.

He glanced at her quickly but didn't bog down in it. "Yeah. Jane and Bill Terry were telling me about a nice day hike they did, out on the coast trail. We should try it."

"You ought to ride Julieta's horses while you're here. It's a total and complete blast. Like you're flying."

"Huh. I'd break my neck."

"Nah, they're very well behaved. If we get any time, I'll ask her to take us out."

He tossed his head, *whatever,* and Cree puzzled at his reaction.

"What?" she asked. "You dislike her?"

He looked over at her, surprised. "Not at all. She's just as you described. Gorgeous, sexy, smart. Compelling."

"So why isn't she your 'type'?"

Ed's cheerful face had sobered and now drew into a speculative frown. He kicked at a rock and sent it bounding away. "I don't know. Maybe I'm just wary of extremely beautiful women."

"I don't think she *tries* to be beautiful. I think it's been a huge burden for her all her life. Beauty can be a lot of trouble for a woman. Men get their buttons pushed by it and act like idiots. Or they make unflattering judgments about intelligence and character based on it. Women envy it and compete with it. Lynn Pierce's response is probably typical—she's got Julieta pegged as a complete narcissist, which she emphatically is *not.*"

"Huh. I can see why she would want a child so badly. For once to love and be loved without all those complications."

Ed was very wise, Cree was thinking. Very insightful.

"I know what it is," he went on. "Whenever I'm around her, I feel like she's . . . working on some internal process of great importance, and I instinctively want to defer to it. Not look at her too closely or intrude on her thoughts. On her isolation."

"Exactly," Cree asked. "But why has she isolated herself?"

"Love," Ed said immediately. "She doesn't trust love."

"Hm. With good reason. But what can she do about it?"

Ed didn't answer right away, and when he did, it was with another question: "What's going on between her and Joseph Tsosie?"

"Why do you ask?"

"When he came to the school yesterday, you know what he did? He checked the brakes on her truck—brought it over to the maintenance garage while I was there. He and I talked as he jacked up the front end, checked the pads and disks. A very competent guy. I guess she had mentioned there was a shimmy whenever she put the brakes on."

Cree smiled at the image. "Which implies—?"

He shrugged. "It's just a very . . . *guy* thing to do. It had more importance as a gesture than as a necessity, you know what I'm saying? Given that she's got a maintenance staff for that stuff—I mean, they work on the school buses all the time."

The implication was obvious, but that was difficult territory and neither wanted to articulate it: longtime friendship, deep and full, yet never quite matriculating into romantic love. Thinking about it opened up a deep reservoir of feelings too complicated to face.

They came around a curve in the mesa wall and saw the school. The sun was high enough to bathe all but the easternmost edge of the campus in its angled light. Students were spilling from dorm buildings and heading toward the cafeteria. Without saying anything, they both stopped to gaze at the scene.

As always, the sight moved Cree, a pang in her chest and belly. It was a rainbow of feelings, Julieta's and her own, admixed, and somehow central to it was the image of Joseph Tsosie fixing her brakes, making sure she was safe. It all had to do with love—the labyrinth that love of any kind had to pass through. Why did it have to be so complex? Why was it so easy to get lost?

An insight occurred to her, and though she shied away at first she forced herself to spell it out. *One time,* she told herself, *just once.* She'd let herself think it one time and then she had to let it go away for now. Julieta and Joseph: not unlike Cree and Edgar. But was that real, based on her own feelings, or another example of Cree Black's absorption of Julieta's state of mind? It hurt not to know. And the worst of it was, Ed must have noticed and was probably asking himself the same question. He deserved so much better.

"Hey, Ed," she said quietly. "That was nice. Up on the mesa—our breakfast picnic."

"Yeah."

"I've missed hanging out with you. I can't tell you how much."

He turned away as if there was something to look at in the empty land to the west, then checked his watch. "We should get back. Big day for both of us."

"Yeah. Okay." He was right: This was no time for her to be talking to him this way.

He started walking. When he spoke again it was as if she'd been harrying him for further explanation: "Look, Cree, I don't know how to solve Julieta's thing with love, past, present, or future, or where things stand with her and Joseph, or why. But I do know this—love won't leave us alone until we meet its gaze fairly and fully. Okay? That's what I know. That's my pontification for the day, take it for what it's worth. Now I gotta go be an engineer for a while."

33

DONNY GOT to the restaurant just as Nick pulled his black SUV into the parking lot. He checked his watch and found that it was eleven-twenty, just as they'd planned, a few minutes early. Nick would have time to bring him up to date before the nurse arrived.

They went inside together. He had decided to make it a threesome for the lunch with Lynn Pierce, given that Gallup was directly on the way to the mine and his one-thirty meeting with the parapsychologist. Might as well help flatter and cajole the nurse and hear what she had to offer firsthand. It wasn't Tuesday's regular bill of fare, but Donny was glad to have an excuse to get out of Albuquerque. Anyway, there were some scary overtones to this latest thing of Julieta's. The sooner he cleared them up, the better.

Inside, there were no other customers—they were ahead of the lunch rush. They took seats at a booth toward the rear, ordered coffee, and set the menus to one side. Nick seated himself so that he had a clear view of the front door, Donny noted, and would see the nurse when she arrived, give them a few seconds' warning. A competent guy.

Donny grinned and rubbed his palms together expectantly as Nick put a slim leather briefcase onto the table, opened it, and pulled out a few sheets of paper.

"Okay. The photo I got from the university. That your gal?" Nick turned around a brochure and handed it to Donny.

It was a UNM psychology conference schedule with a photo of each of the featured speakers alongside a one-paragraph bio and a summary of their lecture topic. Donny scanned the faces, found Cree Black's earnest face, and nodded as he read her blurb.

"That's her."

"Good." Nick took it back just as the waitress brought their coffees. The big man thanked her pleasantly and gave her a flash of Czech-Irish charm, warming up for the main act. When she left, he carefully stirred three plastic cups of creamer into his coffee and tasted it doubtfully.

"What else you got?" Donny asked, feeling good as a coffee glow replaced the sharper burn of acid reflux in his chest.

"Ran an Internet search. Lot of entries, but I looked at every one of them. Lot of her activities are like this one, kind of on the margins of academic psychology. Couple of more sensational things about her investigating a famous haunting or something. Sometimes she debunks ghost stories, too. Then I found a few of these." Nick frowned meaningfully as he slid a few sheets across the tabletop.

Donny took the papers and felt his good mood vanish. These were copies of newspaper articles from different parts of the country, Sunday features–type pieces of the "Frustrated Police Turn to Psychic" variety. All three were about homicides in which the police had asked or allowed Lucretia Black to assist. All reported that she was making "substantive contributions" to the solution of the cases. Only one of the articles was a follow-up item: " 'I can't explain it,' said a jubilant Detective Howard Lathrop of the Mason County, Michigan, Sheriff's Department. 'I was highly skeptical at first and it was definitely not the kind of consulting we'd usually solicit. But Dr. Black gave us information that we were able to verify and that led directly to the apprehension of the suspect.' "

Donny tossed the papers back at Nick, who slotted them back into his briefcase.

"I wonder how much she paid jubilant Detective Howard Lathrop for that little endorsement? Must have been quite a shot in the arm for her ghost-busting business."

"I got one more," Nick said. "This was deep in the pile. Seems she's a licensed private investigator in the state of Washington. You want to see?"

Donny scowled and waved it away.

Nick shrugged his big shoulders, put the briefcase on the seat beside him, wrapped his meaty hands around his cup. They both drank reflectively for a moment.

"So—" Nick began.

"So nothing. We see what our friend has to say, meet the spook at the mine, and take it from there." Donny finished his coffee and glared around the restaurant for the waitress. "It's probably nothing. And I sincerely fucking hope so, because that's all the time I have for it—none."

He glanced up to see that Nick's expression had suddenly turned boyish and sunny, and then the big man was sidling out of the booth. Donny turned to see the nurse coming through the door.

"It's been too long, Lynnie," Nick told her. "You're looking great. I take it life's treating you good?"

Sitting across from Donny, Lynn Pierce looked tiny next to Nick's bulk. She had ordered coffee, too, and now tasted her cup delicately. She had dressed up a bit for this meeting, Donny saw, wearing a snappy brown blazer with a silk scarf at her throat; her hair shone like a silver dollar. But in fact she didn't look great. Her speck-eyed gaze seemed more lopsided than ever, and her face looked old and a little crazed, kind of the way she'd looked at Vern's funeral.

"Life," Lynn said, "is treating me . . . *interestingly.*"

"You know, Lynn, I can't tell you how much we miss Vern. Miss both of you. Even after all these years. The Bloomfield site went to hell in a handbasket after Vern died and you left. Seriously." Donny shook his head sadly and sipped his coffee with a pious expression. This was a ritual pronouncement and she'd know it was bullshit, but it was obligatory.

"Thank you. That means a great deal to me."

"It was so great to get your call," Donny went on. "An excuse to have a social lunch. Kind of busy these days, but always happy to squeeze in some time with an old friend and colleague. Life's too short, you know?"

The waitress arrived to stare at them expectantly, hovering with her pad poised. "Are you ready to order?"

They hadn't looked at the menus yet.

"Not quite," Nick told her flatly. "We'll need another few minutes." This time he showed her his other side, a look that told her not to come back until they waved semaphore flags and set off flares. Donny smiled to himself as she scuttled away.

They tossed pleasantries back and forth, and a gentle babble of conversation began to fill the place as other customers filtered in and took seats. The nurse was warming up to her pitch, getting a little flirtatious. Nick was a ball of boyish charm and attentiveness, but Donny thought he'd play it differently. Nice but not too nice; you had to keep her in her place, not let her think anything she had to offer was too valuable. After a few more minutes he decided the foreplay had gone on long enough and it was time to get down to business.

"So Lynn," he said, "you'll never guess what happened Saturday up at the mine. I come out of the site office, I'm about to get into my car, when who do I see on the south rim but Julieta and some other woman. Horseback. And when I go up there, I find out the other woman is a, what do they call it—"

"A parapsychologist," Lynn finished. "Yes. That's one of the things I wanted to tell you."

"What, exactly, *is* a parapsychologist?" Nick asked innocently.

"Someone who claims to study the weirder aspects of the mind," Lynn told him. "Things nobody's ever been able to prove—telepathy, clairvoyance, contact with the dead, things like that."

"So which kind is this one?"

"Her main thing is ghosts," Donny answered. "But she obviously generalizes a bit, because she was there to ask me about animal mutilations. Remember, we had that episode a couple of years ago? Some Navajo kids found those two horses? Made the papers?"

Lynn was frowning. "But that's not what they've talked about. Not when I'm around, anyway. Or no—they mentioned it, but just in passing. It's not their main concern."

"Oh?" That was interesting, Donny thought: Either the mute thing was some kind of a ruse, or it was something Cree Black and Julieta weren't sharing with the nurse.

The waitress hove nearby on her way to another table but ricocheted away as Nick gave her a look that would have stopped a runaway bull.

"You know, Donny," Lynn said as if beginning something long and complex, "I'm a health-care professional. You know how committed I am to my work. That's my only concern. My patients."

"We've noticed it and appreciated it, Lynn. And you know how much McCarty Energy has relied on it in the past." This was how she worked, Donny reminded himself: veering off the subject so that she could be flattered and coaxed back. You just had to grit your teeth and bear it.

The nurse smiled that little smile, as if she knew she'd set her hook and could now reel them in at her leisure. "I love my work at the school. I really do. At the same time, there are . . . personality issues that get in the way. You know what I mean."

"Hey, you don't have to tell *us*," Nick put in. "I don't know how you manage. Working with her these last three, four years."

"She shacked up with the Navajo doctor yet?" Donny couldn't help asking.

Lynn gave him a cardsharp's look, appraising his interest while concealing her own. "Not to my knowledge. But now that you mention it, the . . . um, questions there might bear upon the situation. For me, it's come to the point where it's not just about personality. This parapsychologist being there is an example of very troubling behavior on the part of . . . school administration. And I don't know just what to do about it."

"Maybe we can help," Donny told her.

"There's a sick boy, one of the students. With very unusual symptoms. He's in the hospital now, for the third time." Pause, a prompting look.

Nick gave her an indulgent look of puzzlement. "What does that have to do with the parapsychologist being there?"

"Yesterday we had a conference about it, and I was completely shocked at the way they discussed it. Utterly shocked."

" 'We' meaning you and—"

"Julieta and Dr. Black and her two associates." Lynn took a very feminine sip of coffee. "They flew in from Seattle. An engineer and a woman who as far as I can tell does forensic-type research."

Nick flicked a glance at Donny, and Donny knew what he meant. That Julieta had brought in a whole *team* of people couldn't be good. And an *engineer!* Donny felt the churning burn blossom under his breastbone. This was turning into a disaster.

He mastered his face and kept his voice casual as he asked, "So, what did you all talk about?"

"I don't think I'm getting the whole story—they exchanged looks that suggested a lot was going unsaid? But I know something that should interest you. One is, the reason Cree Black wants to talk to you and go to the pit where your father died is because she wants to see if his ghost is there."

"What the . . . ?" Nick bottled up the expletive, choking on incredulity.

"My father? He had a *soul*? A spirit? First I've heard about it!" Donny chuckled. Saying it gave him great pleasure.

Lynn Pierce bobbed her head, round eyed with concern and disapproval, dramatizing as she savored their attention. "No, really. The parapsychologist wants to see if she can 'experience' something there, where he died. She's also been 'experiencing' something near the school. Over near the big ravine in the mesa."

Donny felt his breakfast move queasily in his stomach, and this time when Nick caught his eye he returned a command: *Let me.* He mastered his alarm quickly and said disinterestedly, "Hm. I wonder what to make of that." Then he deliberately checked his watch and let himself look a little concerned at what he saw. "You know, Lynn, I've got this killer day today. For one thing, I'm meeting the parapsychologist, then I've got appointments until all hours back in Albuquerque. What else? What does this have to do with that sick boy of yours?"

Lynn looked at them both and asked innocently, "Aren't we going to order something to eat?" She pulled over one of the menus and began to read it with satisfaction.

Nick shifted impatiently in his seat, as if he were going to do something drastic, and again Donny had to give him a look. No sense in letting her know she'd touched a nerve with any of this.

"Sure," he said. "She's right, we should order, Nicko." Donny turned to the waitress, who hesitated over near the counter. "I think we're ready to order," he called. Then he turned back and muttered, "Christ, service in this place is going to hell. We've been here for half an hour and that gal hasn't been near this table!"

Kind of a running joke. Nick thought it was a scream.

Another ten minutes of banter, and then the food came. Lynn had ordered a BLT, Donny and Nick bowls of red chili. When the waitress set Donny's bowl down, the lumpy mass struck him as gory and nauseating—he should have ordered the green. Or a salad. Nick dumped a cellophane bag of oyster crackers onto his and began spooning bites into his big face in a businesslike manner.

Between nibbles, Lynn Pierce used her sandwich as a prop to make meaningful gestures. "If I tell you about the boy, it has to be in strictest confidence. Because on one level it's something of a violation of the patient's confidentiality. And I would hate this to have a negative impact on the school."

"Absolutely," Donny assured her. "Of course."

"Because if it's dealt with in the wrong way, it would really hurt the school. If word got out, it could close it down. And I would *never* want that to happen. I guess that's why I'm coming to you instead of, you know . . . the education or health authorities."

Holy shit, Donny thought. The look she was giving him told him everything: *This is it. The weapon you've wanted.* His panicky feeling was suddenly replaced by glee.

The nurse knew she had their undivided attention now, and she couldn't help smiling. She set her sandwich down, leaned forward, and lowered her voice. "They believe this boy is *possessed.* I'm serious. By a ghost. They think that's what's the matter with him. It's making him have convulsions and do strange things. And Julieta brought in the parapsychologist to, basically, exorcise it. And, though I hate to admit it, Joseph Tsosie is going along with it."

She leaned back and watched their faces with satisfaction, knowing full well what she'd just delivered into their hands. Donny's mind was spinning with the implications. Julieta had to know that what she was doing would kill her five ways come Sunday. If word got out into the Navajo community about a chindi possessing the boy, haunting the school, her staff would evacuate the place like there was a bomb threat. Two days later, the last of the kids would be yanked by their parents. And bringing in a ghost buster? Doing an exorcism? The education people would crucify her! And the rumors, let alone an article or two in the papers, would kill Julieta's fund-raising dead; she'd lose too much credibility ever to recover financially.

It would be so easy. With several hundred Navajos working for McCarty Energy at different sites, it would be a cinch to get word moving in the general population.

Donny almost laughed out loud: For all his toughness, even big Nick had been sitting openmouthed, and all he could manage when he finally found his voice was, "No shit!"

★   ★   ★

A half hour later, as they caravanned west to the Hunters Point mine, Donny dialed Nick's cell phone number. In his rearview mirror, he watched Nick's broad silhouette put its hand to its ear.

They had milked the nurse for a while more, and she had milked them in return. At last, with Nick flirting and Donny assuring her that she always had a job at McCarty Energy if she needed it, they'd left the restaurant. Donny's mind was in overdrive.

"We have to do lunch more often, huh, Nicko?"

"Oh fuck, Donny. Oh man. I was going to wring her neck if she did any more dancing around, so help me. This close, man. This close." Nick's voice had a broad smile in it. Donny could visualize him holding his thick thumb and forefinger a millimeter apart. "Seriously, I was thinking, too bad her account wasn't closed when good old Vern's was."

"So what are we up against here?"

"Seems like a good-news-bad-news situation," Nick's voice said. Nick would know to keep it reasonably circumspect, given that cell phones were not the most private form of communication.

"Julieta, she's really planning something major. Gotta be, with the engineer, the bogus thing with the mutilations. And the mesa! Jesus Christ!"

"But we've got her by the balls! The ghost buster, the sick kid. If we can keep the nurse's cooperation. We need her to keep us informed. And she'd need to back us up, maybe testify, if it comes out in the open."

"You'll see to that? Keeping her sweet on us?"

Nick groaned at the thought of more sessions with Lynn Pierce. "Yeah. Provided I get a bonus here, Sahib. Call it hazard pay."

They both chuckled and then were silent as they navigated past a slow-moving pickup truck with a goat tethered in the back and about six Navajos crammed into the single-seat cab. Donny frowned, nagged by the sense that something didn't quite compute with this whole thing. If Julieta had brought in the parapsychologist to deal with the kid's problem, why were they talking about the mutes or the mesa? On the other hand, if she'd brought her and her team in to throw a monkey wrench at McCarty Energy, what was the whole business with the kid? But whatever it was, the only workable hypothesis was that it was aimed at his head in some way, and he'd better think about preemption.

When they were past the truck, Nick's voice crackled over the phone again: "So. With the ghost business. We want to start the word circulating among the men right away?"

Donny had made a strategic decision. He hoped it wasn't overly biased by what he had to admit was some trepidation at the thought of an outright war with Julieta. "Nick!" he scolded. "I'm surprised at you!"

"Why not?"

"Think about it. Julieta's planning something—that's the only explanation. It's got to be a major offensive. She's found out something. I don't know what she knows or how she knows it, but there's no other conclusion. If we shoot our ammo now, she'll be even more pissed off and she'll have no reason left not to shoot us down in return. So we hold our fire. We do our homework, we poke around a little more, get our ducks in order. When we know more about what she's trying to do, we go to her and gently suggest she cease and desist because with what we know we can take her down. We preserve what we know as a disincentive for her to give us grief, not use it prematurely to stir up a hornets' nest."

"Right." Nick was silent for a moment, thinking that through, and then chuckled. "You're good with the big picture. I guess that's why you're the boss, huh?"

"It's all just psychology," Donny told him. "Human psychology."

34

B Y THE TIME Cree got to Ketteridge Hospital, she was almost in a state of panic. She'd been running on an adrenaline overdose for over an hour as she drove a borrowed Oak Springs School car to Gallup.

Inside, the front desk receptionist rang Dr. Corcoran's office, told her he'd be down shortly, and invited her to have a seat in the lobby. After ten minutes of pacing and fretting, she wanted to scream. Or to run through the halls to find Tommy.

After she and Ed had gotten back from her early-morning hike, she had showered and dressed and found she still had an hour to kill before she had to leave for her appointments. She'd used the time to read through the last of the materials Mason had given her.

And had gotten badly shocked.

It was one of Mason's own papers that made her break into a sick sweat of anxiety. In arguing that some apparent cases of seizure disorders, schizophrenia, or DID were in fact examples of possession, he had cited six cases in which conventional pharmaceutical treatment had not only failed to help the victim but had been directly counterproductive. The medications had made the sufferer *worse*. The reason was simple: Most antipsychotic medications had a sedative or suppressive effect, which Mason believed weakened the host personality's resistance to the invader. All victims of possession fought the parasitic beings attempting to move in on them, he said; treatments that made the patient lethargic or passive, or otherwise suspended his volition, gave the invading entity free rein. In each of the cases he cited, the damage had proved irreversible. Of the six victims, two had committed suicide and four had gone on to lifetime institutionalization. Of those, one had later been lobotomized and had never come out of a postoperative catatonia.

Cree had dropped the papers as if they'd burned her hands. She'd left a quick message on Dr. Corcoran's voice mail, hurried out to the car, and driven to Gallup like a madwoman, trying to figure out how to forestall any drastic treatment without telling Corcoran the reason why.

When at last Dr. Corcoran arrived, he was accompanied by a short, officious-looking man wearing a three-piece suit and a trim goatee. Dr. Corcoran wasn't wearing his usual benevolent grin, and the other man looked positively dour.

"I've invited Dr. Schaeffer to join us," Dr. Corcoran said curtly. "He's our head of neuropsychiatry, and he's very . . . interested in Tommy's condition. We've been consulting on pharmacological aspects of Tommy's treatment."

Without waiting for a word from her, the two men turned back into the corridor.

She caught up to them at the elevator bank. "Dr. Corcoran," she panted, "I have a rather urgent recommendation for Tommy that we need to—"

"If it's not too much to ask," Dr. Schaeffer chided, glaring at her, "can we at least wait until we have some privacy? We'll discuss this in my office, like professionals." He gestured at a trio of nurses who also waited for the elevator.

They rode up to the third floor in silence. The two men led Cree down a stretch of corridor to an office on the left, where they stopped and gestured her inside. Dr. Schaeffer came in last, shutting the door behind himself.

It was a small room, with one window overlooking the flat roof of a lower wing of the building and the surrounding parking lots. Dr. Schaeffer's desk was piled with folders, and shelves on one wall were stuffed with hundreds more, but otherwise it was a stark room, without the personalizing effect of family photos, art, curios. Cree automatically moved toward a chair to the right of the desk and then stopped as she realized that neither man had sat. Nor invited her to. Schaeffer positioned himself behind his desk, leaning forward and resting his weight on his knuckles; Corcoran stood at the other side of the room in his vulture's hunch, arms folded disapprovingly.

"You were saying? You were going to recommend—?" Dr. Corcoran prompted icily.

"Yes, do proceed," Dr. Schaeffer said. "We're very curious as to why you're here today."

Cree tried to quash her urgency, to sound professional and objective: "I wanted to speak to you about some literature I've encountered that may bear upon Tommy's treatment. In particular, the application of antipsychotic medications."

The two men exchanged glances. This would be Dr. Schaeffer's turf, but he didn't move except to raise an eyebrow. "Oh?"

"It appears that in certain cases the standard treatments can be counterproductive. That they can exacerbate symptoms."

"Cases of *what*, precisely?" Dr. Corcoran asked.

"If you have reasons to believe Tommy Keeday might have such a reaction, I'd like to hear them," Schaeffer said. "Of course, paradoxical responses are not unheard of. But I'd like very much to hear which specific cases you're referring to." He came around his desk, past Cree, and went to the file cabinet next to the door to fuss with some papers on its top. After a moment he spun back to observe her response.

It put Cree in the awkward position of having to turn her head back and forth to try to address both men. "I just wanted to urge you to allow me to conduct less drastic therapies first. Give talk therapy more time."

Dr. Corcoran cleared his throat. "We are very interested in just that, actually. As to just what direction your therapy is taking. As to just what you and the patient discussed yesterday."

"And I am still waiting to hear about those particular case studies," Dr. Schaeffer put in. "Chapter and verse, Dr. Black. That's how we do things here."

Cree started to reply, then stopped. She'd been in too much of a hurry to pay close attention, but now it hit her in the face: This was a hostile inquisition. Something had changed since yesterday.

A siren broke the silence. Outside, an ambulance sped up to the building and disappeared from view beneath the lower wing. Dr. Schaeffer took the moment to move so that he now stood in front of the closed door, leaning against it with his arms crossed.

"What's going on here?" Cree asked indignantly.

"That's precisely what we expect you to tell us," Dr. Schaeffer snapped. "As you explain why you're here today."

"I need to spend time with Tommy. I'm sure you'll both agree his condition is urgent. I was—"

"His condition is indeed urgent," Schaeffer agreed. "As you no doubt know, he had another crisis yesterday, after your session with him."

"No, I didn't know! What—"

"We were able to observe his symptoms quite closely. Clearly, we're witnessing a very unusual and extreme syndrome. Dr. Corcoran and I agreed that drastic pharmacological intervention was required immediately."

Cree caught her breath. Behind Schaeffer's accusing glare, she recognized the excited gleam of the clinician sensing a rare malady to study and experiment upon. The same hankering for the exotic case had fueled the epidemic of multiple personality disorder diagnoses during the 1980s. An opportunist would see Tommy as material for sensational monographs, book deals, TV talk shows. Instant celebrity in the psych world.

"What, exactly, did you two talk about yesterday?" Dr. Corcoran asked. "What did you tell him about our treatment plans?"

"What?"

"What did you tell his relatives?" Schaeffer asked. He seemed to huff himself up, making himself bigger, and Cree realized that he was blocking the door. A gesture of control and coercion.

"I didn't meet his relatives. I left before they got here. And I certainly didn't speak to Tommy about—"

"You have very interesting hobbies, Dr. Black. You see, we took the liberty of looking you up. We were most impressed with your credentials. But we were unpleasantly surprised to learn about your—what's the terminology?—'interest' in the paranormal."

"I am involved with Tommy at the request of the patient and his primary physician, and I solicited as a courtesy this institution's permission to help with his treatment. I have in no way prejudiced the patient against your treatment of him, if that's what you're implying."

"We need to know—"

"I need to talk to Tommy. Now. You have my recommendation about antipsychotics." She hesitated as a terrible thought occurred to her. "Or, what, you've already treated him? Is that what this is about? You've already seen some reaction that—"

"Not just yet. We're—"

"Good! Now, unless you've got something else you want to tell me, I'm going to see him. Immediately." She tossed her head imperiously, vaguely recognizing Julieta in the gesture.

"You settle down, Dr. Black," Dr. Corcoran ordered. "I'll call security if I have to."

Cree glared at him and crossed the room toward the door.

Dr. Schaeffer only braced his legs and made it clear he wasn't going to budge. "What's your prescription, Dr. Black?" he growled. "Take him to a Navajo witch doctor? Is that what you're trying to do here? Or is it just that you want this one all to yourself?"

Cree drew up in front of him, outraged. In her peripheral vision, she saw Dr. Corcoran coming toward her from behind. "What I'm trying to do, Dr. Schaeffer," she hissed, "is leave this room. And if you don't get out of my way, I'm gonna kick your balls right up into your friggin' *lung!*"

His eyes flared in alarm, and as she made a quick move toward him he scuttled aside. Cree yanked open the door and stepped past him into the hallway. She looked left and right and only then realized she didn't know where she was in the labyrinth of the hospital, how to find her way to Tommy's ward. But she strode off toward the elevator bank, wondering how far Schaeffer and Corcoran would go to stop her from seeing him. The need to be with him, to do something to arrest the terrible thing happening to him, was overpowering.

She stopped at the elevators and slapped the down button.

"You won't see him, Dr. Black."

She whirled to see that Dr. Corcoran had followed her. He stopped in the hallway about fifteen feet away, as if afraid to get any closer.

"Yeah? Well, you scurry off and call security, and we'll see how it goes down. And when his condition deteriorates because of your treatments—after you've been warned by a consulting psychologist?—see what kind of malpractice suit comes down on you."

"No. You won't see him because he isn't there. Tommy Keeday is no longer a patient at Ketteridge. For now."

"What! What have you done with him?"

He took a step back and put up his hands, warding her away. "We did nothing with him. His relatives came and took him away. Late last night. Functionally, they abducted him."

Cree gaped as it suddenly came clear to her. They thought she'd colluded with the family to remove Tommy from the hospital. No wonder they'd seemed confused about why she was here today. In fact, his vanishing was the last thing she wanted. How would she find him again? How would she persuade his relatives to let her treat him? Any delay at all could be catastrophic.

"We've informed New Mexico Child Protective Services. They've got an investigator looking for him. They're considering bringing charges. I'm sure they'll want to talk to you, also."

"Charges?"

"This isn't the first time such a thing has happened, Dr. Black. But fortunately the law sides with science, not superstition. In a case as urgent as Tommy's, the law clearly gives presumptive power of attorney to us, not the family. This institution will assert its legal responsibility to care for a dangerously ill child."

The elevator dinged and the doors shushed open, but Cree couldn't move. "What . . . what will happen if they find him?"

" 'If'? Oh, they'll find him," Dr. Corcoran snapped. "He'll be with one or another of his sheepherding relatives. The state will know where they are because all they have to do is go where the welfare checks are delivered. And they'll bring him back. But you'll never see him again, you can trust me on that."

35

THE MINE access road cut straight south from Highway 264 through low, rolling hills. Running parallel to the wide gravel road, the company's rail spur was occupied by a seemingly endless train of open-topped cars heaped with coal. Cree had picked up Joyce at the Navajo Nation Inn, and they were using the time to bring each other up to date.

Cree felt burnt, little more than a husk of ash, consumed by the flame of anger and anxiety she'd felt at the hospital. On her way out of the building, she'd used a pay phone to call Julieta with the news about Tommy, then spent the drive from Gallup to Window Rock trying to think. With a whirlwind of competing worries, it wasn't easy.

"I've been mostly striking out," Joyce told her. "The museum is gorgeous, but the materials there didn't tell me jack about what might have happened at the mesa. There's lots of good stuff on Navajo spirituality and healing traditions, and the museum proper gives a basic history of the People. But your little mesa doesn't show up."

"Crap."

"Sorry. There's tons of historical drama in the region, though. The Navajos and Apaches began migrating in about eight hundred years ago. Of course, they found the Pueblos' ancestors already living here. For a few centuries there was the usual raiding and feuding among Apaches, Utes, Navajos, Hopis, the whole gang, and then the Spanish came and sub-jugated the bejeezus out of whoever they could lay hands on. Then the area was ceded to the United States and the Yankees began to come in, and it all went downhill from there. The Indians resisted, natch, some more than others, some making alliances with the whites. One of the worst problems was the trade in Indian slaves, run by the Mexicans and white Americans. At one point, one fourth of all Navajos were slaves. The U.S.

government wouldn't do anything about it, so the Diné fought back hard. It all came to a head around 1863, when Kit Carson was sent out to kill or round up every last Navajo. When he couldn't just shoot them, he starved them out—burned their crops, destroyed their flocks. Most of the Navajos were brought to Fort Wingate and then were marched three hundred miles to some hellhole on the eastern side of the state called Bosce Redondo. The Navajos call it the Long Walk, it's one of the defining historical moments for the tribe. It was brutal, a lot of them died en route. And Bosce Redondo was basically a concentration camp—forced labor, starvation, disease, humiliation, the whole Nazi shtick. Eventually it begat some appropriate outrage, several federal commissions looked into the situation and found it abhorrent. So the government felt a twinge of remorse, created the rez, and marched the survivors back in 1868."

Cree didn't answer. She just clung to the steering wheel, mourning the endless and unnecessary cruelty that human beings could inflict on each other. The arid desert landscape was a melancholy stage upon which untold sorrows had been enacted. Like everywhere else. All these years of self-deluding idealism, thinking she could do something about it by alleviating one small, lingering hurt at a time. Insane. Trying to bail the ocean with an eyedropper.

Joyce noticed her sudden dive. "I did pull up some newspaper stuff on livestock mutilations, though," she went on brightly, as if that would cheer Cree up. "Most recent local incident was a couple of years ago, that must be what Donny was talking about. Some Navajo teenagers tracked their horses onto McCarty property, over on the far west end of their Hunters Point land? Supposedly found the horses all . . . well, sliced up. In weird ways. Give you something to chat about with Donny M, anyway. An icebreaker."

Cree nodded. Joyce was trying to be amusing.

Joyce bit her lower lip and then said quietly, "I'm sorry, Cree. I don't have anything sweet and nice to tell you." She turned her face to the window and somberly regarded the passing desert. "How'd we get into this business, anyway? You know?"

"What business? The human being business?"

"I know you're worried about the boy. But we'll find him. Joseph or Julieta will have some idea how."

"Yeah." But that hope didn't cheer her. *I still have no idea who or what is in him,* she thought despondently. *I don't know if I can do my work when I'm trying to stay ahead of an entity that's taking more control every day, not to mention child welfare investigators and eager beavers like Schaeffer looking for an unusual specimen to experiment on.*

They were driving between heaps of crushed mineral material. Up ahead, Cree saw the rearing dragline boom she and Julieta had seen from the other side. A mile or so to the east, several giant yellow machines were trundling along, dumping spoil and putting up a drifting cloud of dust.

Joyce followed her gaze and her brow wrinkled. "We should talk about how to handle Donny, Cree. What we're going to tell him, what we're trying to accomplish here. What's your plan?"

"Plan?" Cree snorted. "I'm going to lie through my teeth—what else?"

Two minutes later, they approached a guardhouse with striped barrier gates lowered across the road. Just this side of it, Donny McCarty sat on the hood of a massive black SUV. With him was a large man with a boyish, pug-nosed face and the build of a weight lifter. As they pulled over, the two men left the truck and approached them.

Cree turned off the car, got out, and introduced Joyce as her associate; Donny introduced the big man as Nick Stephanovic, his "aide-de-camp."

"That's 'gofer' in English," Nick said amiably. Closer to him, Cree felt a glow of menace behind the bearish good humor and for an instant wondered irrationally whether they had anything to worry about from Donny or his sidekick today.

"And what's your role in your firm, Ms. Wu?" Donny asked Joyce.

"Business manager," Joyce said. "And historical investigator, medic, um, devil's advocate, and all-round utility drone. That's English for gofer, too."

Donny nodded with a sour expression that made it clear he wasn't planning to share anyone's attempts at conviviality.

"We're very grateful for your meeting us," Cree said. "Not too many CEOs would make time to show a stranger around. Especially such a, well, *strange* stranger."

Nick chuckled and explained cheerfully, "McCarty Energy has a long-standing policy of public accessibility and accountability."

Donny didn't share his assistant's mood. He struck Cree as preoccupied and suspicious, a man just going through the motions. "I have only an hour to spare for this, so I'd like to get started. What's our agenda? Forgive me if I'm unfamiliar with the concerns of a parapsychologist."

"Well, we had talked about the mutilations—"

"We can take you to the area where we found 'em, but I can't promise you'll see anything of interest. I can't even guarantee we'll find the exact spot again. Even the bones are probably long gone. Coyotes drag 'em around."

Nick Stephanovic nodded.

"I have to be frank, Mr. McCarty," Cree began uneasily. "Since we last met, I've heard some interesting supernatural gossip. This will sound strange, but a couple of staffers at the school mentioned a rumor of a ghost here at the mine. I guess they had worked here, or had relatives who had worked here, and—"

"Oh, yeah? And who would that be? I have something of a photographic memory for some things, including my employees' names."

"You know, I can't remember. Sorry, the Navajo names are so unfamiliar to me—"

"Probably a Begay or a Nez," Nick put in helpfully. "Every other Navajo is a Begay."

"I think that was it," Cree said. "Yes."

The two men exchanged glances, and Cree got the feeling she was fooling no one.

"So we've got a ghost here at the mine—" Donny prompted.

"I told you this would sound odd . . . but they say your father died here three years ago, and someone said it was his ghost. I hoped I might visit the site of his death. I wanted to see if I could . . . make contact with him. As long as I was here anyway." She hesitated, trying to gauge his reaction. "Of course, if this is difficult for you, I completely understand. I don't mean to sound insensitive to your loss—"

"My father," Donny said drily, "was not the type to inspire much sentimentality among his survivors."

He said it with such deliberate understatement, such a hard light in his eyes, that Cree couldn't come up with a reply. Even Nick Stephanovic uneasily hitched a shoulder.

"You know," Joyce put in brightly, as if it had just occurred to her, "I was thinking that, given the limits on our time, maybe we should split up. Why don't I go look at the mutilation site, Cree, and you and Mr. McCarty go where . . . wherever you need to? If Mr. Stephanovic would be kind enough to take me." She turned a sweet smile on the big man.

Donny caught Nick's eyes, thought about it, and shrugged. "Why not," he said.

They took Donny's Lincoln Navigator through a maze of wide gravel roads that wound between heaps of soil and rock and past lumbering earthmovers, ending up at the office complex Cree had seen that first day with Julieta. At the main parking lot, Joyce and Nick bailed out and got into one of the rugged company Jeeps. Joyce brought her shoulder pack containing some basic equipment Ed had suggested would be typical for a mutilation site, given the supposed UFO connection: a Geiger counter, latex gloves, a soil scoop and a dozen plastic sample containers, a digital camera—enough for the charade they were putting on, anyway. Cree waved good-bye to her from the window of Donny's Lincoln, feeling a little trepidation at letting her go with the bearish hulk. Then, thinking about it, she decided that Nick Stephanovic might be one tough bastard, but if it came to any rough-and-tumble, she'd put her money on Joyce every time.

Donny drove east along the valley, passing deep trenches with striated cliffs, then up a winding ramp to the higher land on the north side. At one point he stopped and rolled down Cree's window.

"You can get some idea of the scope of operations from here. Quite a sight, isn't it?"

It was. From their position Cree could see a huge expanse of land, scattered with mountains of earth in pastel reds and grays, cut with meandering ramps and roads. A deep gash, half a mile long and several hundred yards wide, was obviously one of the working pits. Visible through the dust haze at its far end, a dragline swung a bucket the size of a house and let go an avalanche. The boom alone, Donny told her, was the length of a football field, the dirty-orange motor house at its base was six stories tall, its vertical mast another eight above that. Other machines came and went like ponderous prehistoric animals, filling the air with the rumble of engines and the stink of dust and diesel.

Cree startled as a broad ridge of ground about a mile away suddenly rose in a hump, as if the land were alive and flexing muscle. In another instant, a line of geysers blew soil and rock skyward in a rolling wave of explosions that swept across an area a quarter mile square. The sound of thunder hit the truck before the last of it had blown. In another moment, the area was hidden in a pall of downward-sifting dust and rubble.

"We call it 'shooting,'" Donny explained. "The shooters—the explosives guys—drill holes down to the first coal seam, fill 'em with TNT. Setting the charges off in sequence that way helps chase the shock wave. Cracks up the overburden so the big Cats can scrape it off, expose the coal." He watched with satisfaction as the dust cloud thinned and drifted away.

"It's very . . . impressive. Must be dangerous."

"That's coal mining," he agreed with some macho pride. But then he said coldly, as if she'd accused him, "McCarty Energy has one of the best safety records in the industry."

Donny rolled up her window and continued driving. In another moment, he steered the Jeep into a descending ramp that led into a long, flat-bottomed trench hacked into the rock.

"Not that I'm buying into any of this," he said, "but how the hell are you supposed to go to the site of an alleged haunting when the site isn't there anymore? I mean, the general area is just up ahead. But the ground he fell on has been stripped away, the pit floor is about thirty feet below that level now. The spoil's been taken away to fill in other mined-out pits. The coal has long since been sent to power plants in Colorado. The dragline he fell off of has moved to a new pit a mile and a half west. So where's the site? Where's your ghost?"

"I don't know," Cree admitted. If there was a ghost here, she was thinking, it would sure put Ed's geomagnetic theory to a stern test. But then it occurred to her that maybe the unusual circumstances here—the literal disappearance of the material place of Garrett's death—could have been the trigger that set his perseverating energies wandering.

"But," she went on, "there's plenty of historical precedent for haunted mines—shaft mines, anyway—that offer some of the same theoretical problems. And quite often when a house that's haunted is torn down, the empty lot or a new building that's put up will inherit the entity."

Donny blew out a skeptical breath and turned his attention to driving. Again she puzzled at her sense that he was indulging her, just playing along, waiting her out.

"Really, I only need a few minutes here, and then we can move on to the dragline. In the meantime, you can help me by telling me about your father. What kind of person he was. How he talked, how—"

"And how's all that supposed to help you?"

"There are many schools of parapsychological research. My approach is more psychological and intuitive than most. Knowing more about his personality will help me recognize him if I encounter him. The idea that ghosts always appear as visible phantoms is completely false. I usually don't really 'see' a ghost so much as 'become' a ghost, so that inner . . . feeling or quality of character is often the only way I can identify a revenant."

Donny grunted and abruptly pulled the Lincoln to a stop. "Well, good luck. Because this is it." He shut the engine down and glared at Cree, a challenge. He seemed to be struggling with a ticlike gulping movement, as if he had something stuck in his throat.

She got out. The ground here was a scraped plane of solid rock littered with mineral debris. The cliff rose in a broken, jagged wall a hundred feet high, striped with dark striations. She stood, walked a slow circle, and stood again with eyes shut. From here, the rumble of the rest of the mine was distant; she could just hear a crow calling from somewhere to the east.

She sensed nothing. It was as close to a complete psychic vacuum as she'd ever experienced.

Donny surprised her by speaking right at her shoulder. "He was being an idiot. He was vain about how fit he was for his age, how he knew his company from the ground up, and he was showing off to his new girlfriend. They'd had a bit to drink. So Dad climbs out on the boom to show her what a girder monkey he is, and he slips. Only fell about forty feet, but it was enough."

"Did he break his neck, or—"

"Hell, no. Landed upright, just like a cat. But the fall ruptured his spleen. Our on-site paramedics were afraid to move him. It took a while for the ambulance to get here. He was dead by the time it arrived. I was up at the Bloomfield mine when I got the call. What a goddamned mess."

"Were you and he close?"

Donny looked at her with his veiled eyes. Through the impatience and weariness, Cree saw a passing flicker of discomfort. "What's it matter?"

"I want to know what kind of person he was," she reminded him. "What kind of relationship he had."

"He had his life, I had mine. He'd divorced my mother by the time I was ten, and she mostly raised me. Dad and I didn't always see eye to eye. It wasn't easy working for him."

"How about Julieta? How did he feel about her?"

Donny walked away and stooped to pick up a rusted piece of iron, some small mechanical part from one of the behemoths that had worked the site. He inspected it momentarily, then tossed it from him. "You really want to know? When he first met her, he was wild about her. The man was over the moon. Told me she was young, not even my age, and then laughed and warned me to keep my hands off, this one he wanted all to himself. This one was a keeper. He brought her flowers, courted her on bended knee, the whole thing."

"So what happened? Why'd it go so wrong?"

"Come on, Dr. Black, don't pretend Julieta hasn't told you the story. With my father and me featured as the men in black hats."

"I'm happy to hear a different perspective."

"He was who he was. He did things the way he thought you were supposed to if you were a rich, powerful, virile but aging man. Oh, there were affairs and the usual stuff. But he'd have stuck with her. On his own terms, to be sure, but I think he was honestly surprised that she had different expectations. When she said she was going to divorce him, he reacted the way he'd learned to act when somebody hurt him, which was to hurt back harder. He got mad and he got even, both. After a while, there was nothing but that for either of them."

Cree nodded. Donny's tone was still angry, but he'd lapsed into a mood of recollection verging on nostalgia. It was something she had been before when even the most alienated survivor visited the place of a loved one's death.

"It wouldn't have gotten so bad if she hadn't insisted on keeping the house and land here. She could have gone for the place in Albuquerque, but no, she had to set herself up right next to the company's land. Which guaranteed he'd have lots of opportunities to make sure her life wasn't too happy. What the hell'd she expect? He was gonna send her a welcome wagon?"

He paced and scuffed, and the way he looked touched Cree: a slim, balding, harried guy with a worried frown permanently etched into his forehead. Clearly he admired his father a great deal, as much as he resented him. Just as clearly, he still dealt with his dead father every day.

"So he was a man who could hold a grudge," she prompted, "who would never forget a hurt or an insult. What else?"

"Why don't you just out with it? What did Julieta send you to find out?"

Cree stared at him, trying to gauge where that was coming from. "Why are you so afraid of her?"

Donny spluttered in outrage for a moment. "Fuck this. I don't have to do this. I've gone along with this bullshit long enough, let's get down to business. Let's get down to—"

"I'm not judging you or your father. Honestly. You're telling me Garrett was a . . . a mixed bag, just like every other human being. So are you. So am I. I'm not buying into Julieta's anger."

He ignored her and started back toward the truck, but Cree grabbed his elbow. The touch startled him and he looked down at her hand, the reaction of a man unaccustomed to physical contact. He shook his arm free, but he did stop walking.

"We *are* getting down to business, Donny. For me, anyway—what you're telling me is very helpful. Please keep going!"

He looked at his watch and let his shoulders slump in acquiescence. "Three more minutes' worth of this crap here. Then the dragline."

"If I'd met your father at . . . I don't know . . . at a cocktail party, say, what would my impression be? Who would I be talking to?"

"A man with a big appetite for life. A man who liked shiny things—a nice car, an impressive piece of equipment, a beautiful woman. He was impulsive, and sometimes that got him into trouble. But his instincts were usually on target, they worked for people and business. He liked taking on challenges, proving he could master things, people, situations. If you met him at a cocktail party, he'd try to impress you. Charm you, win you over." Donny smiled his bitter, private smile and looked Cree up and down. "You personally? He'd want to get you into bed. And he'd probably succeed. Because he'd make you feel you were at the center of the universe. He'd tell you things about yourself that either were insightful and true or that you would suddenly believe were true, and in either case you'd feel deeply flattered and understood."

"That's a very perceptive observation."

"And he'd get what he wanted from you. Whatever it was. Which was what it was all about."

Cree digested that briefly. "Did he ever talk about death? Things like . . . I don't know . . . how he wanted to die when his time came? Even things like burial preferences or services? Or what he believed would happen after death?"

Donny made a face as if he had a bad taste in his mouth, spat, frowned, then checked his watch again. "We're done here. If you want to see the dragline, we'd better get moving."

It was a signal that he'd overcome his reflective mood, Cree thought. But when they got back to the truck, he hesitated before he went around to the driver's side.

"I don't know what my father believed," he said sourly. "But I do know Garrett McCarty had no intention of dying. Never crossed his mind. Wasn't part of the man's plans in any way."

It took five minutes to cover the mile and a half to the pit where the dragline was currently working, Donny driving slowly through his kingdom of raw rock, machines, and dust. He called ahead on his CB to let the dragline crew know they were coming, telling them to shut it down when they arrived for Cree's tour. Afterward, the air of preoccupation claimed him again, and his replies to Cree's questions were mostly monosyllables.

Still, she gleaned some details that would be useful later, if and when she confronted the entity again. Garrett had been right-handed. He spoke Spanish and had picked up enough of the Navajo language to say a few words to his Navajo employees. For amusement, he played golf and poker and went to rodeos, where he bet large sums in a private pool of fellow execs. He knew horses—he'd personally selected the thoroughbreds he'd bought for Julieta—and was a good rider. When Donny was a kid and made his regular weekend visits to Garrett's Albuquerque house, his favorite place had been the solarium cactus garden: Watching his father lovingly tending the spiny knobs and armatures revealed a side of the man he never saw otherwise.

Donny got quiet again after telling her that, and Cree couldn't tell if it was a guarded silence or just a moment of reflection. His throat began making the gulping movement again—a reaction to stress, Cree decided.

"You've described your father as impulsive, charming, yet a man who'd never forgive, never let go of a grudge. I guess what I'm trying to figure out is, if he did live on in some form, what would his psychological engine be— what obsessional feelings or motivations might animate his ghost? Would he be so angry about something, or sad or guilty about something—"

"Like what—Julieta? Is that what you're getting at? Julieta thinks she's haunted by my father's ghost? Jesus Christ, this is turning into science fiction here!"

"Believe it or not, I'm trying to turn it into just plain science."

"Because if she does, tell her to get over it. Tell her that the world doesn't revolve around her ass. He had plenty of younger and better afterward, trust me. If Garrett ever had such a huge grudge against her, he'd long since gotten it out of his system."

That couldn't be true, Cree thought, not if the years of conflict that followed were any indication. She bounced some of his ire back at him: "How'd he do that? Shooting her horses?"

He stared at her, surprised she knew about it, and he seemed about to say something nasty. But he just closed his thin mouth and ignored the question.

"So why do *you* hate her? Why do you want to hurt her?"

He rolled his eyes—a martyred, frustrated expression. "I don't want to hurt her. She's got it all wrong. If I wanted to hurt her, trust me, she'd know it. I'm just trying to run my business without her interference."

"Interference like the in situ uranium suit? Doesn't that make you want to get back at her?"

That got his attention: a flash of pure ire and calculation in the eyes, a radiant chill Cree could feel from four feet away. "That's a matter for the courts to decide. What she doesn't get is, a business this size, I've got two dozen suits, injunctions, regulatory hassles, you name it, pending at any time! She's the one with the 'psychological engine' here. She's the one can't leave well enough alone!"

Donny swerved the truck hard enough to throw Cree against the door, and then they were pulling up near the walking dragline.

They got out and for a moment Cree had to just stand there, looking up at it in awe.

It was one of the biggest man-made objects she had ever seen. A gargantuan rusty orange cube supported a vertical mast about fifteen stories tall, connected by cables to the main boom, which angled up and out over a deep trench. The whole structure pivoted on a steel disk seven feet thick as it dragged its enormous bucket up the slope on its cables. Each of the bucket's steel chisel teeth was as big as Cree's dining-room table. To her surprise, there was no diesel roar; the loudest sound was the massive groaning of metal under stress.

"Electric," Donny explained. "Eight separate motors. Thing cost my father thirty-two million bucks when he bought it in 1979. It's one of three we keep going twenty-four/seven."

From this angle, she could see the operator's cab, a tiny glass box at the base of the boom, and the platform between the boom's huge hinges. The boom itself was a girder of tube steel, massive as a suspension bridge, with welded rungs on the main tubes providing ladders to the upper reaches. Cree could visualize Garrett, clambering drunkenly up this outsize phallic symbol, turning to observe his lady friend's reaction, losing his footing. His grip would've stayed his fall for an instant, but the jerk was too much. He dropped, just missing the superstructure below him. The jolting collision with the ground, the awful pain inside as his organs ruptured. It would have been an agonizing death.

But that was all imagination. She didn't feel an entity here. The only echo of human feeling was a faint swirl of the ever-changing moods of the men who worked here.

They had just started toward the thing when Donny's cell phone rang and he stopped to put it to his ear.

"Hey, Nicko. Yeah, we're there now." He turned his head away from Cree. "Oh, yeah? Okay. Okay. Just hold on. You just get here, let me handle it."

When he flipped the phone shut, his affect had changed utterly. His face hardened into a baleful mask, immobile but for the striating muscles in his jaw.

"Is everything okay?" Cree asked.

Donny flashed her a look of contempt, then gazed past her to the access road they'd come by. A company Jeep was barreling down it, trailing a plume of dust, sliding through the turns. In another moment it had skidded to a stop not far away, and Joyce exploded out of it as if she'd been thrown. She slammed the door and hurried over to Cree, breathing fast, wide eyes signaling alarm.

Nick Stephanovic got out to stand with his legs braced, hands clasped in front like a club bouncer, glaring at them. No trace of the boyish charm remained.

"Wait here," Donny snapped. He went over to Nick, and the two men conferred. Nick lit a cigarette and gestured with it as Donny glanced from Joyce to Cree, nodding. The dragline had gone still and silent.

"What the hell?" Cree whispered. "I didn't think you two would be done for a while."

"I think I screwed up badly, Cree! But I'm not sure how."

"What happened?"

Joyce checked to make sure the men were still out of hearing. "I get into the Jeep, right, and we drive up out of the mine and go east? We're getting along fine, flirting a little, talking about our jobs, he seems like a nice guy. After a few minutes he stops and says okay, this is where the mutilated horses were found. I get out, walk around. No sign of anything, no bones or whatever. So I ask how he even knows we're in the right area, the ground's all the same as far as you can see, not so much as a big cactus or something. So he opens this map of the mine property, right? It's all marked in sections. He shows me where we are—out on the far eastern border, Area Two. So I open the pack, I'm gonna go through the motions. There's nothing to take a sample of, so I figure I'll run the Geiger counter around, then take site photos? And when Nick sees the Geiger counter, everything changes. He asks me what's that for, I tell him it's routine with mutes, looking for trace radioactivity. And by the way, I say—it hasn't totally dawned on me that something's the matter yet, I'm just being conversational, I figure maybe I've got it wrong?—I say I thought the mutes were found at the other end of the property, closer to Highway 12. I point to the map and tell him I thought it was in, like, Area Eighteen on that map. And then the guy goes ballistic! He—"

"They're coming over," Cree interrupted. The men had finished their conference and were striding toward them.

"Okay," Donny said. "This is good. This is very good. We're getting down to brass tacks here, I like that. We could have done this straight off without all the song and dance, Dr. Black. So here's the deal: You two go back like good little gofers and tell Julieta she needs to think twice about making shit for us. Tell her we need a face-to-face. Tell her it's in her best interests."

"What are you talking about?" Cree stammered.

Nick tossed his cigarette and moved laterally around to face them from one side, a man prepared for anything. Joyce dropped her backpack as she turned to track him, not quite taking a martial arts stance but also very much at the ready.

"Be nice, Nicko," she warned him quietly.

"Tell her we know about the boy and the exorcism thing and some other stuff, and that we'll close her down if she gives us any grief. She has my cell number. I'll expect a call today." He turned back toward his truck but paused at Nick's side to jab a thumb over his shoulder at Cree. "See them off the property, huh, Nick? But watch this one. Don't let her play with your mind when you drive them up to their car."

A couple of hard-hatted men had emerged on a catwalk high on the side of the dragline housing, bellying up to the railing, lighting cigarettes, and looking down curiously.

Donny's cool slipped when he noticed them. "What the hell are you looking at!" he roared. "Get back to work!"

They were back inside before their spiraling cigarettes hit the ground.

36

CREE WAITED in the outer office as Julieta finished up with a student-parent conference. Across the room, a secretary pecked at a computer, paused, pecked again. From what Cree could hear through the half-open door, a worried mother had come to talk with Julieta about her daughter, who was very homesick and wanted to leave the school.

When they came to the door, Cree saw that the student was a moon-faced girl who barely looked old enough for high school. The mother was a young Navajo woman, pretty and professional looking, now glowing with relief or gratitude: Julieta must have found a way to set things right. Julieta kissed them both as they left and promised them that things would be okay. She looked much older, Cree thought. Worn.

"Such a sweet girl," Julieta said quietly. "A math prodigy. It's all her teachers can do to keep up with her. She's one of our full-timers, and she misses her baby sister. We just had to figure out a way to get her home on weekends. Look what she gave me—she made it herself. I'm so flattered. I just love it." It was a little garnet and turquoise brooch in the shape of a hummingbird, inexpertly made. Julieta pinned it to her blouse, patted it, then took a deep, resigned breath as if preparing herself for something. "I know we've got a lot to talk about. Would you mind going for a walk? I could really use some fresh air."

"Sure."

Julieta found a windbreaker and pulled it on as they left the building. They walked slowly away from the school to the west, their shadows behind them: Three-thirty, the sun was beginning to roll down the far side of the day. On the hilly land to the west, the scrubby trees seemed larger as their shadows darkened the near slopes.

"After you called, I talked to Joseph," Julieta said. "He's going to help us find Tommy. He's really the only one who can. He'll go talk to the grandparents today."

Cree detailed her concern about the doctors' treatment plans, then described her visit to the mine: Nick's attempt to mislead Joyce about the location of the mutilation site, Donny's anger and his threatening message.

Julieta shook her head, weary and unbelieving. "Everything's a mess, isn't it. Everything's coming apart. It's like a train wreck."

"It's looking dicey, yeah," Cree said. "But as my father used to say, 'It ain't over till it's over, and it's never over.' "

A wan smile.

"It would have to be Lynn, wouldn't it? Who told him about Tommy?"

Julieta bobbed her head sadly. Cree had expected outrage, but to her surprise Julieta just chewed her lip and hunched herself into her windbreaker. "That poor woman. She doesn't have much, does she. She must be so desperate. I should have seen how bad it was with her."

"What does she have against you? She makes these veiled, dark allusions to your relationship with Tommy, your past . . . Could she know the story?"

"I have no idea, Cree. I hardly know her. All I can guess is that she resents my authority here. And I think she . . . she fancies Joseph. Envies my friendship with him."

That struck Cree as right. "So what does Donny think is going on? What's he so afraid of?"

"Donny's paranoid! He thinks I'm out to get him. It must have to do with his in situ uranium project. An unfortunate coincidence—Joyce bringing a Geiger counter and then mentioning Area Eighteen, he thought I sent you to spy on him. Area Eighteen is where they wanted to build the extraction plant. I don't know why he's so hot and bothered, but probably he's doing something illegal. It wouldn't be the first time. McCarty Energy is famous for its lousy record on safety and environmental compliance. Just like Garrett, Donny figures it's cheaper to buy off the inspectors than pay the cost of reclamation. A few years ago, OSHA took them to court for huge safety violations they'd been covering up for years. But I don't know what this one's about."

Clearly, she didn't care much, either. Everything about Julieta, her scuffing walk, the hunched shoulders, the resignation in her voice, radiated an affect Cree had seen only in the briefest of glimpses before. Something was breaking up inside her. She had abandoned hope and resistance. Curiously, Cree thought, she wore the mood beautifully. *Surrender,* that's what it was. Grace came with it. She put her arm through Julieta's and was pleased to feel her draw Cree's elbow against her side.

"Julieta, what can we do about Donny? If anything could ruin the school, this could. And he knows it. He wants to use it to bargain with you."

"For what? I don't have anything to bargain with. Not a thing. I'll call him. I'll do whatever he wants."

They walked on, shoulder to shoulder. They were already a good distance from the school, two women alone in the red-brown landscape of desert, the silvery blue sky. Julieta wasn't dressed for the outdoors. A little wind scurried along the plain, blowing their hair around and entwining Julieta's longer, darker curls with Cree's.

"I learned a lot about Garrett, anyway," Cree said, wanting to give her something, anything. "If I can get near Tommy again, I'll be better able to recognize him. If it is him, I mean."

Julieta nodded dubiously. "We need to talk about that," she said.

"About—?"

"Recognition. You had asked me how I recognized Tommy as my son."

Cree felt a sudden premonitory trepidation. "Right. Yes."

"It's a couple of different things. First, his records show him as a home birth, from the general area where I know my child went, the eastern rez."

"How about his birth date?"

"Well, the papers claim he was born about five months after I gave birth. But the discrepancy doesn't mean anything—the family might have taken their time reporting and filing, or fudging the date might have helped them claim the child was their own in some way. Allowed time for a supposed pregnancy to have occurred, I don't know."

"But it sure doesn't prove he *is* your son."

"No. It just puts him in the ballpark. The way I knew him, Cree, it was intuitive. You of all people can understand that, can't you? I *need* you to understand it. I *felt* it the moment I met him for the admissions interview. I just . . . *felt* it." Julieta pulled away a little and turned so she could look Cree in the eye. The look was pleading.

"What about his appearance? He doesn't seem to resemble you. Does he look like Peter Yellowhorse?"

Julieta's mouth made the saddest of smiles. "I keep telling myself he does, but the truth is, I can't remember. And I never had a photo of Peter, or I'd show it to you. I have memory, that's all. And it changes, it's astonishingly malleable. The best I can do is, he got a part in *Dances with Wolves*—playing a Sioux, of course. This was a few years later. Seeing him again upset me so much I had to leave the theater. But we could rent the video, if you want to get a look at him."

"That might be good—"

"But it has nothing to do with Tommy's appearance. It's just . . . *here*. She spread one hand against her chest and one on her stomach, inhaling and exhaling deeply, once. "It's something I feel here." *Inside.*

Cree nodded, knowing exactly what she meant. It was rationally indefensible, but it was the kind of instinctive *knowing* she trusted completely. She depended on it herself for every investigation. She'd never known it to be without some basis in reality.

They joined arms again and walked on. Their isolation on the bare earth of the undulating plain, under the endless sky, felt very private.

"I don't think of Peter," Julieta said. "This isn't about him, I don't hold anything against him anymore. He was right—we wouldn't have worked out. And I don't live in the past, I really don't, I've had other lovers since then. I live in the here and now and I've got far too much to do to mope around. It's just that when I try to figure out how . . . I got to this place, my life feels all . . . out of kilter. Like all the right pieces are there, but they're stacked wrong? The foundation is out of whack? And when I trace it back to where it went wrong, it's that period. Garrett, Peter. The baby. And I don't know how to stack it up right after that."

"But what's so out of kilter? You're beautiful, you're still young, you've got the school . . . ?"

Julieta just scuffed along, pondering the ground in front of them.

A little while later, Julieta brought them around to face back toward the campus, and they stopped to gaze at it. The sun made the angles of the buildings sharp and their planes brilliant. It all looked bright and little and far away, a thing receding.

"There's just one other thing you should probably know," Julieta said sadly. Her affect was one of utter surrender, yet she spoke with great decision.

Again Cree felt a lurch, as if the ground beneath her feet had shifted. She tried to mask her burgeoning alarm as she searched Julieta's eyes and saw how deep this vulnerability and pain went. The liquid spark in the dark blue eyes was utterly naked.

"Tommy . . . he isn't the only one. He isn't the first."

"What?" Cree panted.

"There was a boy the second year. I wanted him to be my child. So badly. But he wasn't. There was even a girl last year, I thought maybe Joseph had misled me about my baby's gender to put me off the track. So you see, it's very complex. I'm kind of crazy. Joseph knows. He's very kind to me. But it's not fair of me to impose it on you, or the kids, anymore. I thought you should know."

37

JOSEPH BEGGED off his rotation at the hospital, telling the shift supervisor he had emergency family obligations that might require several days.

He called ahead on his cell phone, got Uncle Joe's answering machine, left a message saying only that he was coming to see him, no explanation of why. Uncle Joe and Margaret lived off the rez not far from Crownpoint, about seventy miles from Window Rock. The drive gave him time to try to put his priorities in order.

The Keedays wouldn't have just brought Tommy back to the grandparents' place—too obvious. Which meant he'd need to persuade Uncle Joe to help him locate the boy and to encourage the family to let them see him. To do that, he'd need to overcome his uncle's resistance to talking about the past, his placing the baby. To do that, he'd have to persuade Uncle Joe that it was truly urgent, that there was a compelling reason to reveal the boy's whereabouts. The most compelling reason he could think of was that Julieta was coming apart at the seams, that she needed something drastic to break the chain, set her free from the past. And if Tommy was her son, he could argue that maybe there comes a time when a young man needs to know who his real parents were. That certainly seemed a big part of Tommy's predicament.

But Uncle Joe would demand more than that. He'd given Joseph a charge: to think about what needed fixing, to diagnose the problem so that he could prescribe himself a cure. Joseph could truthfully claim he'd thought about it, long and hard. The hard part was deciding on the cure.

Then he'd have to explain why it was important for Cree Black to be able to see the boy, and that would open up a supernatural, religious, philosophical can of worms. The old man would ask him why he'd trust some white parapsychologist, why he'd buy into weird quasi-medical, quasi-occult beliefs but had such a distrust of traditional Navajo ways of seeing and coping with the same things.

To which Joseph didn't have an answer. It wasn't so much that he'd come to agree with Cree Black's worldview, but that his habitual beliefs had become full of cracks and gaps. He could no longer decide what was science and what was superstition, fact or supposition, personal view or unbiased observation. He couldn't argue with Uncle Joe anymore because he didn't know what to believe.

He cut up 666 and then east on 9, settling into the forty-mile empty stretch between Nakaibito and Crownpoint. He was awed by the vast open sweep of the Chuska Valley, but still the region had always depressed him: its poverty and aridity, its air of desperation. The litter caught in the fences. People living in isolated, shabby hogans and trailers or new, generic, sterile complexes of government housing, without history or beauty or anything particularly Navajo about them. The scenery was bleak, especially after the recent years of drought. In thirty minutes of driving, he encountered only two other vehicles on the road. And this was positively urban compared to where the Keedays lived, somewhere way up above the dirt road between Naschitti and White Rock.

Uncle Joe and Margaret were comparatively well-off and lived in an eighties-era ranch-style house within view of Highway 371, south of Crownpoint. At the end of the quarter-mile driveway, Joseph was relieved to see the new double-cab truck parked near the house, which meant his uncle was at home or nearby. He turned his own truck around in the space between house and corral, turned it off, and sat, giving Uncle Joe time to adapt to his unannounced arrival.

When no one appeared, he got out and went to the door of the house. He knocked and waited again.

"Nobody home," Uncle Joe called from behind him. The old man had come around the corner of the stock shed, accompanied by two mutt puppies that bounced and bit at each other in high good spirits.

"*Yá'át'ééh,* Uncle," Joseph said uneasily.

"I got your message on the machine. You're just in time." Uncle Joe frowned as if Joseph were late for an appointment. "I could use a hand in here. My ram is too tough for me." Without further explanation, he disappeared back into the shed. The little dogs watched Joseph, heads canted expectantly.

Joseph crossed the yard, opened the corral gate, and waded through the frisking puppies around to the other side of the shed. Uncle Joe stood in the open end of the three-sided enclosure, smoking a cigarette and blocking the escape of a burly gray ram that chewed some feed and watched him suspiciously. The rest of Uncle Joe's little flock, six ewes and a handful of this spring's lambs, stood nearby, unconcerned.

When Joseph came in, Uncle Joe tucked his cigarette into the corner of his lips, bent quickly, and grabbed the ram. He expertly tipped the barrel-shaped body onto its side and with his head beckoned Joseph to hold the animal down. Helping, the little dogs darted in to nip out tufts of wool until Uncle Joe kicked at them and they backed away. When Joseph had put a knee on the panting chest and gotten a firm grip on two legs, Uncle Joe took a bolt cutter and clipped back the curled toes on one of the double hoofs. The ram's struggles subsided to a perfunctory kicking as Uncle Joe began paring the glistening flat-cut ends with a jackknife.

"You look like hell," Uncle Joe chided. One eye winced as cigarette smoke trickled up his seamed cheek. "Young man your age shouldn't look so bad."

"Young? I'm forty-six. How old do you have to be before you can use it as an excuse? I get tired like anyone else."

"Good-looking young man. Got the pretty nurses at the hospital all giving you moon eyes, is what I hear. Could have your pick." Uncle Joe scrutinized the neat double points he'd sculpted, then let go and went on to the next foot.

Joseph grinned sadly as he changed his grip. "Who'd you hear that from?"

Uncle Joe just grunted as he levered the bolt cutter. He took up his knife again, gouged muck from between the hooves, wiped the blade on his overalls, and carved away another crescent. Neither man said anything more for a time as they worked, Joseph shifting his grip, Uncle Joe's leathery hands deftly sculpting.

When Uncle Joe had finished the last hoof, they both stood up. The ram rolled quickly onto his feet and trotted out to join the ewes, looking officious to conceal his injured dignity. Uncle Joe wiped his hands on a rag and then used it to slap dust off his overalls. He looked at Joseph critically. It was a sharp look, and long enough for a light plane to drone overhead, drop toward the little airstrip on the other side of Crownpoint, and disappear.

Joseph looked back at him. He still hadn't said anything about why he was here today, and there was a lot to explain. But he didn't have the faintest idea of where to start.

Uncle Joe tossed down his cigarette, ground it out carefully, and walked around Joseph toward the corral gate. He held it open for Joseph, then latched it behind them.

Joseph was surprised when his uncle didn't head for the house door but straight for the big burgundy truck.

"We should take my chitty," Uncle Joe called over his shoulder. "Those roads back in there by Keedays', they'll take the oil pan off yours. Anyway, it'll give me a chance to show off the options."

"They'll have scheduled a Hand-Trembler for the boy," Uncle Joe told him. They were still on the paved road, halfway to Tsaya on 371. Uncle Joe had spent the first ten minutes demonstrating the widgets and gadgets that came with his new truck. Joseph had dutifully tested his own seat adjustments, the interior climate control, and the illuminated vanity mirror in the visor.

"The Hand-Trembler will probably make his diagnosis pretty soon, but it'll take some days for the Singer to get ready, people to be invited, sheep to be butchered, all that. In the meantime, the family will be hiding him from the child services people. I know the Keeday place, it's pretty spread out, they couldn't ever live too close together and now a lot of them have relocated. They've got an old summer sheep camp way up on the plateau, and I guess if they're serious about keeping him out of the state's hands they'll have brought him up there."

"I have *Hastiin* Keeday's cell phone number. Don't you think we should call them before we get there?"

Uncle Joe shook his head. "No. No reception from here. Anyway, it's better to do this the old-fashioned way. Face-to-face. That way we all trust each other."

"Think they'll let us see him?"

"You and me? Sure. But not today. Their house is, oh, fifteen miles off the county road, the camp is maybe five miles beyond that. Gotta take a horse or go on foot unless you've got an ATV. Take too long to get up there today."

"I meant Julieta and me. And the psychologist she brought in."

"Huh. The psychologist, I doubt."

"They will if they meet her. That's one of the things I need your help with. Help me get them to meet her. To let her see Tommy."

"What's so special about this psychologist? They just went to a lot of trouble to take him away from a bunch of *bilagáana* shrinks."

Joseph hesitated at the brink and then told him Tommy's symptoms in detail. That Cree Black believed Tommy was possessed by a ghost, that to help her patients she looked at the whole history of emotional debts and unresolved feelings and motives around her patients, among the living and dead alike. He didn't have to explain to Uncle Joe that that's about what the Keedays would be thinking, too, and what general beliefs lay behind the traditional curing Ways.

Uncle Joe's frown had deepened as Joseph described Tommy's condition. His quick sideways glance showed a canny glint, meaning he saw Joseph's request for what it was: an admission that he had lost his bearings, his certainties.

The old man couldn't resist a prod: "Why are you helping her? I thought you didn't believe in that kind of stuff."

"I thought about what you said. About being full of shit. And you're right. Everybody's full of shit, Navajo or whatever, all the superstition and belief, the habits—none of it's any better. Or any worse. Thanks for screwing up my outlook completely, Uncle. Doesn't leave a guy with much, does it? So now I'm trying to take it as it comes. Best I can do."

Joseph saw Uncle Joe's lips move in a wry smile and felt it mirrored on his own lips. He remembered the bittersweet epiphany he'd felt when he'd been lying awake wrestling with his uncle's drunken riddle. With it, of course, came acceptance and absolution: for being Navajo, for his years of rejection of things Navajo. *The problem isn't being Navajo, it's being human. We're all equally full of shit and we're therefore all equally okay.* The realization had broken a chain that had bound and chafed for decades.

No sense in letting Uncle Joe get too smug, though. He decided to turn it around on the old man. "So why are *you* helping *me?*"

Uncle Joe snorted. "I took one look at you and I knew, here's a guy who needs all the help he can get."

"You know what I mean. Why'd you change your mind about our old agreement?"

A shrug. "I see my nephew all screwed up, wrapped around his own axle. He can't untie his knot until Julieta unties hers, she can't untie hers until she knows about her baby. And I'm seventy-four and a worn-out drunk, who the hell am I to make judgments. Besides, I don't need this hanging over me anymore. The pressure."

"I'm sorry, Uncle. Thank you."

Uncle Joe tugged a cigarette pack out of his shirt pocket, stuck a Marlboro between his lips. He drove with it unlit for a mile or so before saying sadly, "We'll see if you thank me when we're done with this."

Forty minutes later, they were west of White Rock on one of the innumerable side roads that branched off of County 7760. They had left the vast desert plains of the Chuska Valley and had wound north into a maze of low, decaying mesas and crumbling buttes. Eons of wind and water had ground the land into freestanding forms of sandstone topped by a harder mantel of black rock, leaving grim, crumbling pillars, undercut mushrooms, shapes like castles and creatures. It was so dry that in places dunes of blown sand had drifted across the roads. Uncle Joe carefully navigated his truck over the uneven track. He steered with his cigarette between his knuckles, frowning at the occasional faint tire tracks that led away on the right. Many were barely visible in the brown grit, or disappeared as they crossed sandstone shelves higher up. Joseph couldn't imagine how anyone could find the right one.

"I have to piss again," Uncle Joe said abruptly. He stopped the truck in the middle of the track, shut it down, and got out. He walked down the track a way, selected a rock to water, and unzipped. Joseph got out and joined him.

It was completely silent here. The only sound was the tick of the truck's engine and the flow of their urine. They were in a hollow in the land where the surrounding buttes and humps cut off any long views. No wind stirred. After a long moment Uncle Joe finished and zipped himself up.

Joseph was halfway back to the truck before he realized Uncle Joe wasn't with him. He looked back to see the old man still over there, standing with one boot up on the rock, hands on his knee, staring ruminatively toward the northwest.

When Joseph walked back to him, Uncle Joe dug a wrinkled cigarette pack out of his jacket pocket, withdrew a bent Marlboro. He scowled deeply at it before he lit it.

"Just up ahead, you see where that outcrop comes near the road?" Uncle Joe blew smoke to indicate where to look. "Back forty years ago, used to be a little track went up just the other side. Nobody goes there now, can't even see where it was, but I went up there one time. This was about ten years after I got back from the war. I was hawking a new sheep-dip formula to my customers out this way, had a good deal going with the manufacturer. I was driving an old Willys, everybody thought I was rich to have a car, most people still got around on horses. Best little chitty I ever had, but it died on me right about this same spot. Couldn't get it going again. Out here, I knew nobody was going to come by for a long time, so I started walking and when I saw that track, I went up it. I thought I'd ask to borrow somebody's horse, or hitch a ride to where there was a phone. But there was a Wolf lived up there."

Joseph didn't ask what kind of wolf. Looking up at the black-topped, austere outcrop and the invisible country beyond, he felt a little quake inside. The day wasn't hot enough to make an inversion layer, but the air seemed to quiver over the land in that direction.

"He was very old, eighty, ninety, who knows. He probably would have died by himself but later I learned he had a daughter who checked in on him sometimes. Even she was old, even she was afraid of him. Nobody else would come near him. I had heard stories about a Wolf somewhere around here, but I didn't know it was the same guy until I saw him."

Obviously, Joseph realized, Uncle Joe hadn't stopped at this spot by chance. "What did he do?" he asked.

"He was bad. He took other people's animals. Sometimes he'd steal sheep to eat them, but sometimes he'd kill someone's horse or sheep just to do bad for them. Anything anybody did that he didn't like, he'd become their enemy. He dug up dead people from their graves, made poisons of their flesh, and some people said he ate it, too. People said he made their children sick, made them die. Made women have deformed babies."

"How would anyone know it was him who made the kids sick?"

"So this time I went up there, I'm going up the track and about, oh, two miles up I come to a hogan and back behind it a couple of pole sheds and a stock pen up near one of these little buttes, right up against the cliff. It's a real beat-up place—trash, rags caught in the bushes, tools on the ground, roof no good. I call hello and no one answers, but I know someone's there, I can smell smoke. The hogan's door is open, and after I stand there for a few minutes, I go closer to it and look inside. First thing I see is that the north wall is broken down. It's a dead person's hogan. But it looks like somebody lives in there anyway, inside it's a mess of dishes, blankets, food bones, the fire on the floor's smoldering a little."

The cigarette was trembling between Uncle Joe's fingers. He gave Joseph a round-eyed look, and Joseph nodded. Only an extremely antisocial, possibly even sociopathic, person would live in a death hogan. You didn't have to believe the superstitions to be frightened of someone who would commit such a grave offense against social norms.

Uncle Joe fell silent, staring at the sandstone outcrop. From here, its profile resembled a huge dead iguana, angling up from the rocky desert floor.

The old man was shaking his head regretfully. "I should have known better. Because on the way in, before I got to the hogan, I'd seen a couple of dead animals. Dead coyote. Dead crow. Dead rabbit. That's how a Skinwalker moves around. This one was too old to get around in his human body, but he could still use theirs. The Skinwalker projects his chindi into the animal, gets all the animal's powers—see in the dark, walk with no sound, smell people out, fly. When he's done using it, he goes back to his own body and the animal body dies. That's what those animals were. What he'd cast off."

The silence pressed around them again. Joseph felt unaccountably exposed out here, under the naked sky, the truck sitting in the middle of the track in the certain knowledge no one would come by.

"Maybe we should get going, Uncle Joe. What is it, another ten miles or so, right?"

"But at the time I just thought, okay, whoever lives up here was shooting pests or something. Then up at the hogan, I'm thinking, I don't know, maybe somebody died here just yesterday, the family's got another hogan, maybe back beyond the sheds and the little cliff, out of view. I'm still hoping I can borrow a horse. So I head back to the sheds, I'm thinking maybe somebody's working over there and doesn't hear me yet. And when I get over there, I see there's a sort of a cave in the ledge, the opening's about ten feet wide, half hidden behind a shed and a dead piñon tree. I looked into that cave."

Even resting on his knee, Uncle Joe's cigarette hand was shaking so hard the ash scattered. He paused for so long that Joseph thought he wouldn't go on, and he realized suddenly what a huge effort it required for Uncle Joe to tell this.

At last the rasping voice continued, quavering yet determined: "I ducked my head to look inside. Wasn't really a cave, more of an under-cut—maybe only ten feet deep. The back wall sloped up to meet the ceiling, real rough, just broken rock. It took my eyes a second to adapt to the darkness under there, but the first thing I see is clumps of dark shapes up where the wall meets the ceiling. Took me a second to see it's bats, maybe fifty, a hundred of them. Then I see that part of the rock wall isn't a rock wall, it's a naked dead man, hanging upside down like the bats. He's as dried up as a mummy, just skin over bones, he's the same color as the rocks, he's streaked with guano same as the wall. He's got his ankles hooked into a loop of rope pegged in up near the ceiling, hands folded across his chest."

"What the hell—"

"And just when I realize what I'm looking at, the fingers of his hands start to spread! Then his eyes open, he looks straight at me and bends at the waist so he sits partway up, sticking out from the wall. He spreads his arms wide, he's still being a *bat*. All this took maybe three seconds total elapsed time since I first looked in there. My heart stopped dead. I had actual, medical cardiac arrest. And then I went running down that track. I ran all the way back to where we are now and maybe two miles back toward White Rock."

Joseph felt sick. From Uncle Joe's trembling voice, the quiver of his jaw, it was clear that the old man was telling it factually. Some senile old hermit, gone crazy, maybe nearing death, morbid with Alzheimer's, lost in sick fantasies, violating taboos. No one to supervise him, bring him back home to his humanity.

"I wish I'd never looked into that cave," Uncle Joe said, voice hollow with regret. "I wish I'd never seen that. It was bad enough when I thought he was a dead man, a mummy like over in Canyon del Muerte. But what I felt when those fingers began to spread . . . I don't like to think fear can be that strong."

"Whatever happened to him?"

Uncle Joe swiveled his face toward Joseph's, looking very old, wrinkles swarming his eyes and brow like some fantastic design of ornamental scars. "Not long after, they killed him. People from around here got together. Six men went up, six good men. Old *Hastiin* Keeday, the grandfather we're going to see, he was one of them. Killed the Wolf, then burned him and the hogan and everything up there. Nothing left, I hear. No trace."

A horrible thought occurred to Joseph. "Because you told them—"

"No. It had been building up for a long time, people were scared, something had to be done. I never told anyone what I'd seen, ever. Not even my wife. I never wanted to say it out loud. You are the very first person, Joseph."

That was true, too, Joseph knew, and he felt oddly honored to know his uncle had made such an effort for him. From Uncle Joe's discomfort, he knew this was not just another argument for the old man's late-gained traditionalist worldview. It was an act of deep humility and courage. And, touchingly, affection.

"Why did you tell me, Uncle?"

"Yeah, I'm trying to figure that out. Now I'm so shook up I lost what I was going to say." Uncle Joe looked down at his cigarette, which had burned to the knuckles of his shaking hand and had to be searing him. He flicked it down, ground it out, and stared at his own footprint for a moment.

"After that, I changed. The family put on a Sing for me, and that helped. Mainly, what changed me was I had to think about what it meant to be a man like him, how he got that way. Once, he was probably like anyone else. Then he changed, maybe bit by bit, or maybe all at once, who knows, maybe what's happening to Tommy Keeday happened to him and that's what he became. I don't know. Before that, I was a little fast and loose—in the army, in school. I could talk people into anything, I didn't mind taking their money in ways that weren't so good. And women—that kind of thing. But for years after that, every time I was alone, I saw that . . . thing . . . sitting up off the rocks. It came together in my mind with some bad stuff I'd seen in Korea, too, made me realize that whatever was wrong with that Wolf came from something that's inside every man. Even me. And I decided I didn't want to become anything like that. I couldn't change what I'd seen, but what I would *be*—that much I could control, I could decide."

Uncle Joe had begun drifting back toward the truck, Joseph tagging just behind. "So I guess I thought you should probably think about that. Before we talk to the Keedays. When you're dealing with this boy's problem and the business with Julieta. Today we're coming clean about Julieta's baby, I'll help you however I can. But a thing like this, what you're going to be dealing with, it's going to be very hard. But what you do with it—that you should think about. How you let it change you. How you might choose."

Back in the cab, Uncle Joe didn't start up the truck right away. He sat, slumped with weariness, gazing at the dead-iguana ledge, as if lost in memory. It occurred to Joseph that he hadn't seen his uncle take a drink today, and that he couldn't recall any other time he'd seen him without a bottle close by. He had to be feeling the hard hand of his addiction on him by now. It reinforced his sense that the old man was doing something very heroic for him today.

At last Uncle Joe turned the key and the truck's big engine made a startling roar in the silence.

"Tell you one thing, though," Uncle Joe said finally. He shook his head, as if astonished and grateful for at least one certainty in life. "That Willys was one good little jeep. That was the only time it ever died on me. Only time it ever let me down, and I worked that bastard like a mule."

38

T HE KEEDAY homesite was about four miles off the road they'd come
in on, a driveway consisting of parallel wheel tracks meandering
between rotting buttes and over rolling swells of bare hardpan. Uncle Joe
skillfully navigated the truck over the rough ground, sometimes at no more
than a walking pace. As with most rural Navajos, the various units of the
Keedays' extended family had lived for generations within shouting
distance of each other, so the place was about what Joseph expected: a
scattering of hogans, shacks, sheds, sheep pens spread over a half mile or so.
But the deaths of Tommy's parents and relocations of other kin had left the
grandparents and Tommy alone on the old place, and all but the grandparents' current residence were unused and falling apart.

The old Keedays' home consisted of a small, aluminum-clad trailer
fronted by a tin-roofed, open lean-to. Close by stood a log hogan in good
repair. Between buildings, a little chipboard shed housed a gasoline-
powered electrical generator that radiated wires to the trailer, hogan,
and main sheep shed. Other pole sheds served as summer kitchen, work
spaces, barns. A four-wheeled ATV and a battered white Ford pickup were
parked next to a pair of rust-stained 250-gallon fuel tanks. The extensive
board- and wire-fenced sheep pens were empty now but for two gaunt
horses and maybe a dozen sheep. With the grandparents getting too old to
manage a lot of animals, the family would have moved the main flock to
some other relative's place.

They arrived and sat in the truck with the windows rolled down,
listening to the silence that lay on the land like a heavy physical thing,
wrapping and muffling the whole uneven circle of the horizon. At last the
trailer door opened to reveal Tommy's grandmother, a tiny, wizened
woman wearing a wide dark-brown dress and red wool sweater. They got

out of the truck and made greetings, and after another couple of minutes the old man came out. From what Joseph could see of his face beneath his cowboy hat and black horn-rims, his deeply seamed features seemed carved of aged, smoke-darkened wood. His new-looking blue jeans and crisp checked shirt cinched with a bolo tie suggested he'd dressed up when he'd heard visitors arrive.

When Joseph had first met them at the hospital, their stiff walks, weathered faces, cautious eyes, knobbed hard-worked hands, and the faint sweet stink of lanolin and sheep manure had made them seem rustic and anachronistic, especially set against the sterile tiles of the hospital corridors. In this landscape, though, they seemed stronger, aged but hardy, at home among the brown rocks and dry earth.

But they were also very frightened. However Tommy's condition had developed in the last two days, Joseph knew, what they had seen had been harrowing.

The grandfather was older than Uncle Joe, and Uncle Joe treated him with deference as they made courtesies, mentioned family members who knew family members, remembered veterinary visits from years past, talked about the health of the flock and the price of wool. Watching them, Joseph wondered if even they knew their grandson was adopted. He tried to picture *Hastiin* Keeday as a member of a lynch mob that had murdered an old recluse forty years ago. To his surprise, he found he couldn't muster any judgment against him. Whatever this grave, frail man had done, he'd acted with conscience.

Another sign of eroding certainties, Joseph thought with alarm. *Values, beliefs, all up for grabs.*

The grandparents explained that they'd been wary when they'd heard the truck coming because a Child Protective Services agent had already been there looking for Tommy. When they'd told him that the boy wasn't there, the agent had waved legal papers and warned them that he planned to stop by the houses of Tommy's various aunts and uncles, too.

They were scared of trouble with the authorities, they said, but after what they had seen last night, they were vastly more afraid of the ghost that moved in Tommy and what it meant for their family. Even their hard-bitten dignity couldn't hide that hunted, fearful look.

"What happened?" Joseph asked.

They darted glances at each other, reluctant to speak of it. But *Hastiin* Keeday made a grim face and ground it out: "Our son and our daughter went to the hospital and brought him back here. The Hand-Trembler, Edison Begaye, we had already asked him to be here. We held the divination last night. Tommy seemed better on the way home, and we hoped maybe he was going to be all right. But later, we saw the ghost awaken in him." The old man shut his eyes momentarily as if trying to banish the image. He gestured at a deeply bowed piñon branch among a bundle of kindling: "He bent his back like that, and he spoke in a stranger's voice. For a long time he bent back and forth on the ground, like a grub from the soil. He tore his shirt off and we could see the chindi moving in the muscles in his back. He bit himself. We couldn't stop him. Not even *Hastiin* Begaye, not our son Raymond. We couldn't move our legs or arms to help him."

"What did *Hastiin* Begaye say?" Uncle Joe asked.

The old woman answered: "The chindi of an ancestor has come into him. It's very angry because it was wronged when it was alive." The grandmother bit off the words and then sealed her mouth tight in its radiating wrinkles, growing stern, cutting off any further discussion of the details because the chindi might hear and figure out ways to sabotage the healing rituals. Joseph knew that the old people would need Ways sung, too, having been contaminated by their proximity to Tommy.

With Uncle Joe's tactful probing, they told him that the younger family members had brought the boy up to the summer sheep camp, where they were caring for him in shifts. A young grandson named Eric served as runner between sites, taking up supplies on his ATV. They had already arranged the curing Way with a renowned Singer from Red Rock, and preparations were under way for the ceremony early next week.

Joseph said almost nothing until it was time to bring up his errand. He began his request with a preamble, which the old people waited out, nodding respectfully. But in fact, they needed no persuasion. They answered by praising Uncle Joe's judgment, saying they trusted Joseph and appreciated Julieta. As for the *bilagáana* psychologist, to Joseph's astonishment, they said Tommy had asked them to bring her to him. In one of the few moments when he could speak clearly.

Uncle Joe asked them to remind him how to get to the summer camp, which entailed a lot of gesturing and drawing maps in the sand. It was almost six miles north. The grandfather promised he would tell his daughter and son to expect visitors from Tommy's school tomorrow.

It was almost five o'clock by the time they left. Saying good-bye to the two old people moved Joseph deeply: seeing them standing there, in the last inhabited part of a once-thriving family compound, surrounded by the ruins of hogans whose occupants had died or moved and the remains of defunct sheep operations. A snapshot of two lives approaching their end. Of a bygone era. The old man took his wife's hand and held it against his chest, and they stood motionless, watching the truck pull out as if reluctant to see their visitors go.

The truck bumped and tilted slowly back down the driveway.

Though what the Keedays said about Tommy was deeply troubling, Joseph concluded that the meeting had been very successful. Despite their fear, the old people were facing this family problem with courage. They'd insisted on the old healing ways yet were open-minded about Cree Black. Clearly, Uncle Joe was held in great respect by these people, and he'd done a terrific job, handling everything with perfect tact.

And yet from the pressure he felt in his chest, Joseph knew there was still a lot of unfinished business. The tightening knot in his throat was like a lock, holding back the secrets.

Uncle Joe gripped the wheel hard and said nothing. He seemed burdened, too—sad, preoccupied. Again he had refused Joseph's offer to drive, yet now he seemed shaky. The sweat on his temples gave it away: Whatever else he might be worried about, he was entering alcohol withdrawal.

"You know Margaret's Catholic," Uncle Joe said, out of the blue. "I don't take much stock in it myself, but, boy, does that woman feel better after she goes to confession."

The invitation touched Joseph, but though he ached to tell, he stalled with an uneasy joke: "Why is it I have such a hard time picturing you as a priest, Uncle?"

"Maybe the same reason I have a hard time seeing you as any kind of sinner. Any more than my wife."

"I still haven't told Julieta that I didn't place her baby. That I didn't know where he was or who he was."

Uncle Joe winced with discomfort as his body shook slightly. "So after today, you'll tell her. Blame me if you want, tell her I always refused to tell you. I don't care, got nothing to lose."

"There's something else I never told her. Never told anybody."

Uncle Joe put the truck into low gear to bring it over a particularly uneven shelf of rock.

"I need to tell her. But I'm afraid to for a lot of reasons. One of them is that she's fragile, she has a very strong front, but when she breaks, it's . . . painful."

"She's in for a rough ride, Julieta. Whatever you tell her or don't. Just stand by her, you'll probably fix it up."

"If she lets me. If she'll forgive me. She can get very angry, Uncle. She . . . hurts herself with her own anger. She might not forgive me."

Uncle Joe concentrated on his driving, the sweat beading on his grizzled temples. Joseph wished he'd get stern, get clever, anything that would force it out of him in some way. But of course Uncle Joe wouldn't. It was up to Joseph to tell it, to face it. To let out the pressure that was choking him.

"This was back before the baby was born," he began. "She was six, seven months pregnant, she was living in that apartment in Gallup, she was hiding from Garrett McCarty. I was her only contact with the world. I was the only one who knew what she was going through. She'd been hurt by her husband and then Peter Yellowhorse had left her and gone to California. One time she showed me this letter he'd written, how he'd gotten a job out there, he had another girlfriend, he was going to try out for the movies. That was the only time she'd heard from him. When she wasn't sad, she was furious. She'd risked everything for him, and he'd tossed her aside."

Uncle Joe just drove. Up and down and over the rough track, the endless fields of stone and sand jolting past. The constant rolling and pitching. Joseph gripped the door handle, feeling seasick.

"I knew Peter a little. The three of us got together a few times, clandestine meetings for lunch or at my place, before she got pregnant. I thought he was kind of . . . footloose, but I could see how they felt about each other. They were, what would you call it . . . kindred spirits. They had *chemistry*—sparks flew. And something more, deeper, at least for

Julieta. Maybe for him, too, but it was hard to tell, a guy like that. He was very smart, he could talk like a poet and make jokes and he knew he was good-looking. I heard from people that he had something of a reputation, that women liked him. And he could get away with things without consequences."

"Sounds like me," Uncle Joe put in sadly. "Back whenever."

"But I never told Julieta about that. I thought they should have a chance. I thought maybe he'd change, even he would know he'd never get that lucky again. Not in this life."

"You wanted her."

Early on, Joseph thought, no—not exactly, not yet. At first, it wasn't something he'd let himself think or admit. "They were in love," he said simply. "I liked them both. I wasn't ready, either."

There was a period of silence during which Uncle Joe shifted and accelerated into a smoother stretch. He used the respite from two-handed driving to light a cigarette, the shaking of his hands more pronounced. "Jesus, we've only gone about two miles. I don't know how those old people do it—driveway that takes fifteen minutes, forty minutes to the county road every time."

"So it's winter and she's around seven months pregnant, Peter's been gone six months, she's barely hanging on. Afraid of Garrett, mad as hell at him. Still in love with Peter and so mad she'd throw things when she talked about him. And I'm thinking, How could he do this, how could he leave her? She was so beautiful, Uncle! And by then I wanted her, I wanted her to love me like that. But the last thing I could do was . . . put that in her way. She had enough to deal with as it was." A gout of Uncle Joe's smoke swirled in the cab and Joseph's breath caught on it. He had to cough and clear his throat before going on: "So one night I was at home, I was tired, I'd just come off rotation at the hospital, my first break in a while. This was just before Julieta decided to give up the baby. And I got a phone call."

"Uh-oh."

"Yeah, it was Peter Yellowhorse. He was still in California, he said he'd been trying to reach Julieta for days, but she never answered the phone. He wanted to know if she was all right. He said he was coming back, he was going to catch a bus. Wanted to know if she was still at the old house, or if she wasn't, could I give him her new phone number? This was when she had an unlisted number at her apartment, trying to keep Garrett from finding her. And I'm angry at him, too. I tell him, What the hell do you care? You got her pregnant, left her, broke her heart, you shacked up with some Apache girl! And he tells me he's left that girl because he realizes he can't live without Julieta, he'll do anything for her. Everything he should have known six or seven months earlier."

"So what did you do?" Uncle Joe croaked. His voice was so gravelly and sick that Joseph pulled back from the memory to appraise him with a doctor's eye. He looked alarmingly bad—greenish, clammy, full of tremors.

"When was the last time you had a drink?" Joseph demanded.

"This morning. Just before I got your message on the machine."

Joseph calculated the time and was appalled: almost eight hours. "Why—"

"Because we needed old Keeday's respect. He probably knows I'm a drunk from way back, but he's been a puritan teetotaler since his son got killed drunk driving."

"You can't just quit, Uncle Joe! Going cold turkey, you could have seizures! At your age, you'll have a heart attack!" Joseph yanked open the glove compartment, rummaged through it, found nothing. He checked the door pocket, bent to feel under the seat, twisted to scan the backseat and floor, but there was no bottle anywhere. "Don't you keep something in the truck? You must keep a—"

"*No!* Today is a day of important duties that I want to respect, I don't want to be drunk for!" He gave a terrible glance as Joseph started to argue, and he brought his fist down on the dashboard so hard the sunglasses and cigarette pack there jumped. "*Don't fight with me!* Just finish this business! Today we finish all this business! Tell me what you did. When he asked you where she was."

"I told him he should stay away from her! That he was bad for her. That she was finally starting to get over him, she didn't need him coming back to wreck her life again. That I wouldn't tell him a damned thing and he should stay away!"

"So then what?"

"He hung up on me! And I never told Julieta he'd called. And that was the last time either of us ever heard from him." Joseph continued quickly before he became afraid to go on: "I know what I did, but I don't know why I did it. Did I really do it because I wanted to protect her, because Julieta really would be better off without him? Or did I do it because I wanted to keep him away, so maybe I could be with her myself?"

The truck rode up a sudden incline and at last they could see the slightly smoother track of the dirt road, a quarter mile ahead. Uncle Joe shifted down for the slope and said despondently, "Everybody did something sometime, Joseph."

Joseph knew he meant, *Something they can't forgive themselves for.*

"You were probably right, the kid was no good, he'd've been gone again as soon as the baby was born. You know how a guy like that operates."

"I'm not so sure."

They had come to the end of the Keedays' driveway. Uncle Joe pulled the truck up to the junction, stopped it, and bent to rest his forehead against the steering wheel as if trying to muster enough energy for the rest of the drive. The sun was dipping into a band of haze over the western horizon, turning the desert shadow-black and orange and making the gnarled buttes and rocks point lengthening shadows at them.

"Uncle. Let me drive now."

"No."

"Uncle, you shouldn't be—"

"If your little lecture was enough to discourage him, his heart wasn't in it anyway." Uncle Joe winced with discomfort as he straightened again. "Didn't have the guts."

Joseph felt a wave of nausea come over him, and when he spoke again it was if he were vomiting it out, an expulsive contraction that couldn't be resisted: "You're not seeing what it means! It would have all been different! If I'd given him her number, told him the truth, 'Yeah, she still loves you,' he'd have come back. Even if he'd left her again a couple months later, she'd have kept the baby! You see why I haven't told her?" *You see why I can't be with her?*

Uncle Joe took it like a slap, but then turned to Joseph with eyes that were incredibly sad and old, the lids twitching as alcohol withdrawal wrought havoc inside him. He'd neglected his cigarette and ash had scattered all over his clothes and the seat. Joseph felt fear strike him, that

Uncle Joe was going to collapse or crash the truck. He'd seen withdrawal seizures before, and his uncle was not a good candidate for surviving one.

"Yeah," Uncle Joe wheezed at last. "Well, there's something I haven't told you, too. Another stop we have to make today."

And to Joseph's surprise, the old man turned the truck to the west—not back toward Uncle Joe's home and bottle but toward Highway 666 and Naschitti, into the dull red eye of the sun.

39

CREE WAITED until eleven and the school was quiet before she slipped out of the infirmary. Again the mesa was invisible in the dark beyond the school's lights, but she could feel it there, drawing and repelling her, full of secrets. A strange tremulous calm possessed her, and she wondered if this was what Julieta felt—the abject, willing surrender to whatever had to happen.

Julieta's admission that Tommy was not the first child she'd believed or imagined to be hers was deeply upsetting. Cree had held her for a long wordless moment. There was nothing to say. It was too complex and poignant. It wasn't until they'd started slowly back toward the school, arms around each other's waists, that she began to think about what it meant for the work she was charged with doing.

One clear conclusion was that, whoever Tommy was or wasn't, Julieta McCarty, as a witness caught in the disturbing emotional vortex that often accompanied paranormal events, was in far more fragile psychological shape than Cree had thought. Her perspective on who or what inhabited Tommy was therefore no more reliable than her longing for her lost child.

Just as clearly, her fragility meant that the outcome of this situation would have a profound and enduring effect on Julieta's life. The question, of course, was whether it would prove to be a catastrophic effect or an opportunity for healing.

So far, Cree had been proceeding under the assumption that the recognition Julieta felt, the reason for the entity taking up residence in the boy, had something to do with their genetic relationship and the psychic connections that would inevitably result. It made sense, too, in light of Tommy's state of mind: his desperate curiosity about his forebears, his yearning need for an anchor in the identity of his parents and ancestors.

But what did it mean if it turned out he was not her child? What did it imply about the theory that the entity was a revenant of Garrett McCarty? On balance, Cree thought, it weakened the hypothesis; probably, it increased the likelihood that the entity was the ghost of one of Tommy's actual parents.

The fact was that she didn't have enough information. All she really knew for sure was that she'd experienced an entity or entities out at the mesa, that the mesa had figured in her dreams and Tommy's drawings, and that his problems had begun not long after his visit to the ravine. The convergence of all those elements could not be coincidental. Which meant that the ghost of the mesa remained her only real lead and, until she could spend time with Tommy again, getting to know it her only available course of action.

They had parted at the administration building, Cree going back to the infirmary, Julieta to her duties. Edgar had gone back to Window Rock to compare notes with Joyce and spend the night. Cree had done yoga for an hour and generally tried to stay low-key, charging up for what promised to be a long night.

The most difficult part of the evening had come when Lynn Pierce returned from her day off. They spoke briefly, Cree very aware of the nurse's sliding eyes. Cree had cut short their conversation with the excuse she needed to catch up on her notes and reading; she hadn't yet figured out how to deal with Lynn and her treachery. Yet another problem.

At ten o'clock Julieta had phoned from the admin building to say that Joseph had called. "He said he met with the Keedays. They agreed to allow you and me to see Tommy."

"That's great news!" Cree said. "I'll go first thing in the morning. How can I find the place?"

"He drew a map and faxed it, I have it here. To the grandparents' place, anyway, I guess they'll tell you how to find Tommy when you get there."

"Me, but not you?" Cree was puzzled by her tone as well—the flat, frightened affect that came over the wire.

"I have administrative duties tomorrow. Stuff I can't get out of, a pair of prospective major donors coming to get a tour of the school. It takes the better part of the day, and hundreds of thousands of dollars ride on it. I have to . . . I have to do the charm thing."

"What else, Julieta? What's the matter?"

"The way the grandparents described Tommy, he's losing ground fast." Julieta's voice quavered. "And the way Joseph sounded. He was so *distant*. Like something had happened to him. I asked him what was wrong and he wouldn't tell me. I was so worried I called him back right after we hung up, but he didn't answer the phone. It was only about a minute later, where would—?"

"Julieta. He probably went to bed. You should get some sleep, too. We'll set it all straight tomorrow. You do your work, I'll do mine, okay? That's what I'm here for." Trying to sound reassuring, when in fact, as always, Julieta's frazzled anxiety and aching heart had leapt into her.

The night was cold and crisp, the sky slightly hazy so that only a few stars pricked through the velvet black. Cree had opted against wearing her down jacket because the nylon shell made too much noise. Instead, she'd put on a pair of sweaters, borrowed a denim overcoat from the horse barn, and wore tights under her black jeans. She had brought only a flashlight, a bottle of water, Joyce's can of pepper spray, and a blanket, all tucked into her shoulder pack.

No high-tech tonight. This wasn't about scientific proof anymore; it was about results in starkly human terms, Tommy's survival. Anyway, she wouldn't have dared to ask Edgar for the equipment. He and Joyce would be furious if they knew she was going out alone.

She walked silently along the foot of the mesa, feeling the mounting tension of anticipation. It swelled inside her and made the dark pregnant with latent movement and force. The beauty of the night, its sharp-edged silence, thrilled her. Its fearful glory and clarity exploded joyously in her heart, and she panted with sheer exhilaration. Oh yes, she could die out here or lose her mind and go adrift forever in a lonely cosmos of stars and ghosts. But it was worth the risk. Close to death, you felt your life acutely.

It helped to have seen the area in the daylight. This time, she recognized the ravine before she got to it, an angled slash of deep blue-black against the paler blue of the rock face ahead. Moments later, at its mouth, she found she could now interpret the dim outlines of its sloping floor, the shadowed boulders, the old rock fall, and the forking corridor beyond.

She took a deep breath and one last look around at the bare plain, banished a sudden onslaught of fears that included scorpions and Skin-walkers, and headed up.

Again, she found herself drawn to the area near the rock dam. This time she climbed up and over the tumble of slabs and boulders and stopped just above it, where she had a better view of the cliff faces and shadows of the upper end of the ravine. Again the breeze snaked past her and took her steaming breath with it. Grateful for the stealth her soft clothes allowed, she found a shallow shelf a few feet up from the ground and folded herself into its shadow. It felt strategic and somehow safer than squatting on the ravine floor.

She unfolded her blanket, tucked it around her legs, and put the flashlight where her hand could find it quickly. And then she sat and tried to forget everything. She felt fears and thoughts and discomforts come and go and tried to be transparent to them.

Time passed.

The cold crept relentlessly around her thighs and into her collar. The blue ravine grew darker. More time passed. She felt the gradual onset of the paradoxical state she sought: so alert, yet so near sleep.

Movement startled her. Cree's eyes flicked as she realized that there was someone else in the ravine. Her heart thudded jarringly with the shock of it.

Forty feet farther up, a man crouched in the deep shadow next to a boulder. She could see the silhouette of his head and one shoulder and arm, one sharply bent knee. Motionless. The sight knocked the breath out of her, as if someone had punched her chest. She wanted to run, she wanted to cram deeper into her little shelter, but before she could do either she saw the second man, and she froze in fear. He was thirty or forty feet farther up than the first, just now squatting down in the shadow of a boulder. He tucked his head closer to the rock and all but disappeared.

Above the second, yet another shapeless shadow moved from side to side, coming down. Then it vanished, too.

Cree still hadn't taken a breath when the nearest man crept out of his shelter, slipped closer, and faded into a vertical seam in the cliff. She stared at where he'd been and could just see one long leg, the side of his body, the swell of a shoulder.

He was lit wrong. She could see him too well. Against the dark ravine, his body seemed to glow with a strange luminosity. A tiny, distant rational voice told her he glowed because it was daylight where he was. When he was.

A noise from below roused her from her paralysis and reminded her of her mission. At first she took it for a human voice of alarm, but then she recognized the bleat of a goat. Then the big rustling rumble, hooves and voices, the jangle of harness. She had to get down there, now; she had to find Brother. Warn him back. He shouldn't have gone to retrieve the goats. She shouldn't have gone after him, but she couldn't stop herself, and now it was too late.

Above, someone slipped on rolling gravel. She looked to see two more shapes coming quickly down the ravine and she knew she had to run now or she would lose her resolve and something terrible would happen to Brother.

She leapt down from her shelter and scrambled to the rock dam in confusion, smashing her front into the boulders, then climbing and stumbling and falling among the rocks, bruising her hands. The rocks were all wrong. She rammed both knees into a jagged slab and fell heavily, twisting her body just in time to take the impact on her shoulder. It stunned her, but in an instant she was up again, scrabbling on all fours over the fall and tumbling to the smoother floor of the ravine.

The big noise was there, out on the desert. The evil people were coming. She had to run now. Below, a shape moved out on the sunset-lit desert and she knew it was Brother. And he had caught one of the goats, he was running with it on a rope. She ran out of the ravine mouth to call to him, *Shinaaí, don't go for the goats, come back!* but that was foolish because he had already caught one, he already knew the danger and was running back. Back in the ravine, the men were crying out in alarm and anger.

She had almost reached Brother when part of him broke away, part of his head was gone in an instant and suddenly he was splayed out on the sand and the goat was running away trailing its tether. And then the goat stumbled and rolled, shuddering and kicking its feet in the air as if savaged by an invisible predator. Far away across the ground, she saw the other goat running toward the south and then, panicked, change its mind and turn back. She knelt by Shinaaí and knew that the monster that ate people and took them away had taken him. It was too evil to bear. She stood and ran at it, raging and cursing it, but something bit her leg like a dog or wolf. It tugged just once but so hard she fell to her knees. When she looked down her thigh was open, burst like a shattered gourd. And she shouted up at the horsemen a curse on their lives and clans forever and then her belly and chest burst, too. She fell on the sand and lay as the stamping hooves danced briefly around her and then moved on out of view, toward the ravine. She wanted to turn her head to see what was happening there, but she couldn't move. She lay looking along the ground, out toward the empty desert, a sideways red-lit plane where even the grains of sand were huge and frighteningly vivid. Unable to move her body, she felt her mind and heart fling outward, love and warning and apology snapped like an arrow from a bow, back toward the ravine where the family was. She heard the guns there and then she heard and saw nothing.

She awoke to find herself a hundred yards from the mouth of the ravine, lying facedown on coarse sand. It took her a long moment to regain herself, give herself a name: Lucretia Black. It wasn't sunset, it was deepest night. She sat up quickly and winced as all the pains came at once, the bruised shins and elbows and wrenched shoulder. She straightened and felt every vertebra kink and complain. She got to her feet and swayed for a moment, deeply chilled. After a moment, she thought to push the glow button on her watch, and found that it was after two in the morning.

Two people had died on this spot. She was too battered and numb to examine the experience in detail, but she sensed they were young, a girl of around thirteen and her brother, a little older. The girl had called him *Shinaaí*. He had gone to retrieve the runaway goats against the family's instructions, and she had followed to bring him back, also against orders. They'd been shot by someone the girl thought of as the New People and the Enemy People: men on horses, many of them, enough to make that awful, air-quivering thunder of hooves and motion and manic energy.

She did a quick inventory and admitted that she was beat to crap, that she'd done all she could for now. She absolutely had nothing left, emotionally or physically.

But the *wrong* of it! The lingering sense of the girl's last bitter instant fired her, and she sat back down, suppressed her sobs, and stubbornly ordered herself to stillness. She willed it to come again: demanded that the ghost cycle through its manifestation, commanded herself to find and tolerate the echoes of that life and death. Insisted that the rocks give up their secrets. Whatever, however the hell it worked.

But of course you couldn't force it. You couldn't find it if it wasn't there or if you weren't ready. After fifteen more minutes, she accepted the obvious and got creakily to her feet.

She limped up the ravine to retrieve the backpack and blanket. Climbing over the rock dam again, she thought about the spatiotemporal divergence she'd experienced on her way down, during her urgent rush to warn her brother. The rocks impeding Cree's passage didn't exist in the world of the girl whose final moments she'd experienced; clearly the avalanche that had brought this tumble down hadn't been there when the girl had lived. Her stumbling efforts to clamber over the rocks when half her world didn't contain them brought home just what Tommy must be experiencing when the entity was active in him. It explained the confusion of his labored attempts to climb through the corral fence, or to come down off the examining table: spatiotemporal double vision.

She made it to the niche and stuffed her things into the backpack, then sat for a moment in the dead silence of the night. Not seeking or expecting anything to happen, just scraping together enough energy to walk back to the school.

But something *was* happening.

Ice crystals tingled in her veins: There was a noise. It had started subliminally and grew imperceptibly until it demanded notice and then it was undeniable. At first, a distant mosquito, and now a big, resounding noise, echoing up from the mouth of the ravine.

She tucked herself back into the little hollow, trying to analyze the sound as it swelled and Dopplered between the walls. For a horrible moment she thought she'd slipped back, she'd lost her grip on her self and her present and was being drawn unwillingly back to that murderous past.

But as the noise grew she recognized it. Not horses. A motor.

A bright light panned the south wall of the mouth of the ravine, bouncing, veering, then skidding upward along the south cliff wall toward her. Two close-set, brilliant beams flashed up the cleft, straight into her eyes, and she jerked her head back. For another few seconds the lights stayed motionless, cutting the rock walls nearby into harsh light and shadow. And then they went out. The engine died.

Someone was there. At the mouth of the ravine. On some kind of all-terrain vehicle.

She tipped her head and peered into the darkness below. The blue transparency of the night was gone. Purple blotches and a pair of searing lavender orbs swam in her vision and she couldn't see anything until someone turned on a flashlight, panning it left and right. Somebody was coming up on foot.

Cree slipped the pack straps over her shoulders, waited until the light vanished momentarily, and then jumped down. She landed on all fours and stayed in a deep crouch, where the rockfall below sheltered her from the flashlight's direct beam. She heard the scrape of boots and a rattle of stones as someone moved closer. The beam came up the ravine again, lighting the cliff just over her head.

Staying on all fours, she scrambled as high as the shadows allowed, then froze. The shadows swayed and shifted as the flashlight moved, and then it grew dark where she was. She risked a glance back. Whoever it was had reached the lower side of the rock dam and was pointing the flashlight down. Moving it around, left and right, as if looking for footing.

She took the opportunity to lizard-crawl twenty feet higher. Another ten feet ahead was a fallen sandstone slab big enough to keep her out of view. She leapt for it, stumbled, knocked some loose stones together with a clatter that seemed deafening. She rolled into the embrace of shadow and lay awkwardly half on top of the backpack, cupping her hands over her mouth to muffle her breathing.

Whoever it was had climbed onto the rocks and was shining the flashlight up the ravine, panning it systematically. Looking for the source of the noise! Cree lay unmoving, shaken by her pounding heart, afraid to lift her head to check whether her feet were out of view, afraid to pull her knees up lest the movement attract attention.

After an endlessly suspended moment, the light dipped again. She pulled in her legs, cramming herself behind the canted slab. From the scuffle of boots, it didn't sound as if the person was coming any closer, and at last she dared to tip her head out to look.

Someone was moving around on the rockfall, shining the flashlight down at the jumbled boulders and stones. Cree was only sixty feet away, but all she could see was the brilliant circle of light and the rugged surfaces of the rocks it illuminated. Back and forth. Somebody was looking for something. A very systematic inspection.

She watched for several minutes, trying to decide what she would do if whoever it was came higher. There would be no opportunity to run farther up without being seen, no protection from the light. She could wait behind her slab, leap up, clop whoever with a rock. Or maybe she should use the pepper spray. If she could just get the jump on whoever it was—

The movement of the light changed. The person was coming this way again. Whoever it was came down off the rock dam on the uphill side. Cree groped in the pack for the pepper spray. She brought the can out and positioned her finger on the spray button, mentally rehearsing what she'd have to do.

But the flashlight didn't approach. The person appeared to be inspecting the base of the rockfall, taking time, looking into cracks and gaps. With the glow of the rocks behind it now, she could see the whole black silhouette of the visitor for the first time, and she let slip a gasp of surprise as she recognized the shape. After another few minutes, the light went out and there was silence. Cree saw the flare of a match, quickly extinguished and replaced by the glow of a cigarette. In another moment, the smell of tobacco wafted up. For a time she couldn't see or hear anything, but then she heard the scrape of boots again, up and over the rock dam, fading.

The engine of the ATV cranked and revved, the headlights washed the ravine and panned and disappeared. The retreating wedge of light swept to the right, and the red taillights zipped out of view to the north. The engine noise swelled and faded and was gone.

North, she thought. *The direction from which evil comes.*

She waited for a long time in the darkness, still afraid to move. At long last, she stood and began a limping half walk, half run back to the school and sanity. Her nerves shrieked with tension. She went stealthily, watchfully, ready to dart for cover if there was any indication Donny McCarty's thug, Nick Stephanovic, was coming back.

40

WEDNESDAY MORNING, bright and clear, not yet nine o'clock. Cree had showered, but she hadn't slept and was tired and wired beyond anything she could remember. Earlier, she had called Paul in New Orleans, deliberately dialing his office number so she'd get his answering machine, and left a message saying she'd be out of touch for a few days, don't worry if she didn't call. Then she had called ahead to the Navajo Nation Inn to let Joyce and Edgar know she was coming. It would be a short conference, and they wouldn't like what she had to tell them.

The two of them were already waiting in Edgar's room, where the curtains were pulled wide, filling the room with sunlight. The TV was on with the sound off: some morning news show featuring clips of missiles taking off, then somber talking heads, then some more armaments doing their thing.

"You got a coffeemaker in here?" Cree asked.

"It's already made." Edgar poured her a cup from the little carafe and Cree took it greedily, swigged it, scalded her tongue and was glad for the pain.

"Long night?" Joyce inquired. Deadpan understatement serving as accusation.

"And getting longer by the minute."

"So you haven't slept at all?"

"Let's sit, we've got a lot of ground to cover and then I've got to get going."

They sat reluctantly, giving each other dubious glances.

"Here's the deal. I know where Tommy is, and I have the family's permission to see him. I've got to go, this morning. From what Joseph Tsosie says, he's losing ground fast. The state Child Protective Services people are looking for him, the doctors want to try potentially damaging drug therapies on him, Julieta's going to pieces, and Donny McCarty is eager to make some shit for Julieta and the school for reasons I don't—"

"Cree," Edgar broke in. "Slow down. You're really wound up."

Cree inhaled, counted to three, and went on: "Tommy's aunts and uncles and cousins are on shifts taking care of him, but they may not be able to do much. That . . . paralysis, or whatever the hell it is, is getting stronger—"

"And into the breach steps Cree Black to single-handedly save the day," Joyce said witheringly.

"Don't, Joyce. Don't even bother. I've got to get to him and try to make contact with whatever's in him, and I've got to do it immediately. I'll be leaving here and going to the sheep camp where they've taken him. The grandparents' place is two hours' drive from here, the roads are supposed to be a bitch, and the camp is some miles beyond that. So I can't go back and forth."

"Meaning we're not coming with you," Edgar clarified.

"I can't explain the dynamics right now, Ed! There's cultural stuff, there's racial stuff, there are family issues, it's all very complex territory and we're lucky they're letting even *me* see him. I will certainly ask if you can come, but I doubt they'll go for it. I'd like to put the FMEEG on him as much as you would, but there's no power source for it up there anyway."

She took another breath as they stared at her. She inhaled again and tried to find the brake pedal and put her thoughts in order. Looking down at the half-drunk cup in her hand, she saw the ebony surface shivering with concentric rings as her jangly energy conveyed itself to the liquid. The image teased her memory, and after a second then she placed it: *Jurassic Park*—that glass of water, trembling with the approaching footsteps of *T. Rex.*

"You want to tell us what happened last night?" Ed asked gently. He glanced at her scraped hands and broken nails.

"I went to the mesa, and *don't* bother bitching at me about it! There was an event out there, at least two people died, probably more. Two teenagers, a girl and a boy, trying to retrieve their family's goats. I assume they were Navajos. They were shot by horsemen. I saw it through the girl's eyes. I didn't pick up the brother at all. But the girl called him *Shinaai.*"

"Shot—guns or arrows?" Joyce's legal pad had materialized in her hands.

Seeing that, Cree's momentum stumbled. She looked from Joyce to Ed, saw the concern in their faces and their resigned readiness to support her, and abruptly she loved them so much it hurt. It took her a moment to get her breath.

"Guns," she said.

"Any chance either the boy or the girl is our entity?"

"Not the girl. But the boy or another family member, I'd say a very good chance."

"But . . . what's the link to Tommy?" Ed asked. "What's he got in common with those ghosts?"

"I don't know yet. I need to get something more from Tommy, or I need some historical background that'll steer me. Have you made any headway on the mesa, Joyce?"

Joyce shook her head. "Sorry, Cree. I kept at it after we went to the mine yesterday, but nothing. History teachers up at Diné College and UNM, the people at Gallup Historical Society—nobody knew bupkes about that mesa. I looked at a couple of old maps from the 1800s, but it isn't marked on them. I still have a few leads left to follow up, but I'm not holding my breath."

"Okay. Well, make it top priority today. From what you've learned about the history of the area, do you have any general ideas about what could have happened, or when?"

"Hmm. Horses would mean post-1540 at the least, and probably later. The combination of guns and horses would suggest it's something more recent, closer to the American era, like mid-1800s. Could be an event from intertribal raiding, maybe Utes or Apaches. Or a slave raid by Mexicans, or some U.S. Army action. I don't know."

" 'The New People,' " Cree muttered. " 'The Enemy People.' That's how she thought of them."

Joyce puzzled, made a note.

"What can I do?" Edgar put in. "The electrical system checks out as sound, there's nothing for us to learn there. Nothing that would help you now, in any case. I'd go to the ravine and do some technical work, but we're obviously past that point."

"Help Joyce with the mesa. Somewhere there's got to be a record of what happened there."

Ed nodded. Cree drained her cup, then stood and went to the coffeemaker. She poured the last splash and gulped it, trying to remember what else she needed to tell them.

Joyce looked up from her notes, frowning. "What about the idea of the entity being Garrett McCarty? Is there anything Ed and I can do to verify or exclude that possibility?"

"I don't know how, just now. But I had a disturbing moment yesterday afternoon. Julieta told me she's thought other kids at the school might be hers. That doesn't mean Tommy *isn't* her kid, but from where I sit it shoots a lot of holes in her . . . reliability as a witness. If it turns out he isn't her child, I don't see how the Garrett McCarty idea would hold much water."

"Can we do something to determine, definitively, who Tommy is?" Edgar asked.

"His birth records won't help. I'm hoping I can ask the relatives whether he was adopted. If they'll tell me anything. But we really need to look hard at the Keedays—Tommy's parents, adoptive or otherwise. Have you got any more on that, Joyce?"

Joyce bobbed her head. "A little. Found the medical examiner's report. Thomas and Bernice Keeday, killed in a car crash up near Tuba City. Both had been drinking, but the father's blood alcohol was through the roof, like one point eight, so his last hours and moments would have been pretty cloudy. He was speeding, tried to avoid some cows on the road, drove into a boulder. Death was instantaneous for both of them—severe head injuries."

"Night? Day?"

"Night. Time of death ten fifty-eight P.M."

Cree filed the information away. "Any theories about why one of them would come into Tommy at this point, at this place?"

They both shook their heads.

Cree was pacing aimlessly, frazzled and jittery, but stopped as Edgar stood and took her arm.

"Cree. Before you go blasting out of here. Stop for one second. Stop and tell us, tell yourself, what you've got going for you out there. What you're bringing to the situation in the way of a plan or information. You don't know who the ghost is or what it wants, you don't even know who Tommy Keeday is."

Of course he was right, she wasn't thinking clearly. All she had were a few vague ideas batting around in her head, moths swarming a porch light. But you had to have a battle plan. Ordinarily, an investigation would entail a lot of brainstorming with Ed and Joyce, going over the details, conducting a microanalysis, sifting what they'd learned for clues about the ghost's actions, motivations, historical period, anything. This whole situation had been so headlong from the first moment. They hadn't taken the time.

She dropped onto the bed, bounced, sat, chewed her lips. They watched her.

"If we're thinking the ghost is stuck reliving its last moments, we've got to look at its narrative. That's all I'll have if you guys can't come up with any historical data. What is it trying to do? What is it reliving?"

The entity in Tommy was probably reliving a memory or a fantasy of some action. If a memory, it was most likely one from the period just before and during its death, or a crucial event in its earlier life. Memory or fantasy, knowing it would help Cree discern the ghost's core motivation, its unfulfilled urge.

"What does it do that supports the perseverating narrative idea?" Ed prompted.

Cree tried to recall every moment. "Well, the first night I was there, it went walking. And it seems to attack or . . . fight. There's a period of convulsions every time, too. Some stereotypical movements, too, the arm pushing out and snapping back."

"Is there a predictable sequence to its actions?" Joyce asked.

Cree thought about it, trying to picture it. "Maybe. I don't know. The problem is, you can't tell whether it's the entity or Tommy who's at the wheel at any given moment. You see what I mean? And we don't know how much of what we're seeing is just a . . . a bad fit, a neurological short-circuiting caused by two beings trying to occupy one body. And whatever the ghost is trying to do, it can't very well because Tommy fights it. *We* fight it. We sit on Tommy so he doesn't hurt himself."

"Hmm." Ed turned away, folded his arms across his chest, dropped his head. Turned back. "What would happen if nobody fought it? If you just let it go so you could observe the whole cycle of its actions?"

"I've considered that. So far, I've been too afraid Tommy could hurt himself—walk off a cliff or something. Afraid if we don't interrupt it, it'll take him over completely. But you're right, I'd get a better idea of what's going on if I let it play out. It'd have to be a last resort, though."

Ed nodded. "Okay. So what have we seen that suggests intentional elements?"

"The arm's independent movements. You can't escape the sense that it's acting with self-awareness. Like the entity knows it's 'alive,' it's trying to figure out what's going on. The hand explores, makes gestures, and reacts—when it touched Tommy's hair, it pulled away quickly, as if surprised."

"As if it had expected to feel a different type of hair?" Joyce asked.

Cree shrugged, *maybe*.

"Two ghosts?" Ed hazarded. "*Both* parents? One somehow limited to control of the arm?"

"Seems unlikely. But who knows? It's just so hard to say." Cree's frustration and urgency came back, intolerable. "Again, I don't know who's Tommy and who's his visitor, or when the arm is part of the perseveration and when it's self-aware. I don't know how to figure it out."

Neither of them had any advice to offer.

Cree double-knotted her boots and stood up. "But I'll do my best. *Narrative*. I'll look for the ghost's narrative. I'll look for cycles and sequence. Thanks for keeping me rational. I don't know why this is so emotional for me."

They both looked as if they wanted to say something, but neither did. They just held her eyes gravely.

"Listen, you guys. If I don't . . . if anything happens so that I'm . . . you know, if it gets into me and I can't get it out. You guys find me. You'll bring me back, I know you will. But if you can't, call Dee. If *she* can't, call Mason Ambrose in Geneva. He's the world's worst shit, but he knows a lot about this stuff."

Ed nodded. "One more thing. Take my cell phone. I know you hate to use them, but for this once, I think it's a good idea. Short messages won't screw up your brain irretrievably." He held out the little rectangle. "Please."

Cree took it and put it in her pocket. She stepped toward the door, but paused. Suddenly she felt as if she were about to cry. "Hugs," she mumbled. "Gotta have some hugs here."

They surrounded her, and she drew strength from the nearness of them, their familiar smells and the warmth of their bodies and the glowing, golden aura of their friendship. And then she broke free and left the hotel to begin the drive to the Keedays'.

It wasn't until twenty minutes later, as she turned north onto 666, that she realized she'd forgotten to tell Ed and Joyce about Nick Stephanovic's nighttime visit to the ravine. She turned it over and over in her thoughts. Another convergence on that place, another piece that she couldn't get to fit the puzzle. Finally, aware her circling thoughts were wearing grooves in her brain, she gave up on it. Now it was just time to keep her appointment with the inevitable.

41

THREE HOURS later, Cree finally admitted that she was lost.

Following her AAA Indian Country map and the hand-drawn map Joseph had faxed, she had taken 666 north from Ya-Ta-Hey toward Naschitti. For the first hour, the highway stretched straight into the distance, dividing the world into two completely different halves: on the left, the foothills and massive shoulders of the Chuska Mountains, blue and remote; on the right, the Chuska Valley, a bone-dry plain so vast it gave her vertigo. The dirt here was yellow-brown, parched, bare, and so smooth she could see for what had to be thirty or forty miles. With such long views, she thought at first, finding the Keedays' place would be easy.

But after turning onto the county road and driving sixteen miles on rough gravel, she found the land changing. The vast open spaces gave way to a mysterious country of low, decaying rock formations. The flat-topped, sharp-shouldered little buttes and mesas looked like ancient, abandoned castles. At times she felt as if she were driving the empty streets of some lost city being devoured by the desert. And that was *before* she'd turned off into the labyrinth of lesser tracks and trails that led into the heart of the necropolis.

For the next hour, she'd tried to find the Keedays' driveway. For the last hour, she'd just been trying to find her way back to the county road and start over.

It wasn't Joseph's fault. The map he'd drawn was clear, the landscape features neatly labeled in the most precise handwriting she'd ever seen a physician use. But it was a maze in here—wheel tracks branching and forking again, weaving between buttes and rock formations. Innumerable flat-topped rotting-away buttes all looking the same. No long views to orient by. The fire of urgency that had rocketed her out of the hotel had burned itself out in the frustrating search for the right road, the right rocks, the right direction. Hopelessness began to steal over her.

It was only one o'clock, the sun still searing down, but Cree decided that this was the spookiest country she'd ever been in. It was so dry, so parched, so devoid of plant or animal life that it seemed impossible anyone could live out here. In three hours, even on the so-called county road, she had not encountered a single vehicle or human being. The little buttes were not the lovely, red-hued, sensuous forms of Window Rock, but low, gnarled, close-set islands of mustard yellow shot with streaks of gray and capped by ugly black tops. They stuck up from the desert floor like the stumps of rotting teeth. As she grew tired, the shapes began to frighten her, taking on the look of monsters, gargoyles, corpses, aliens.

You're exhausted, she cautioned herself. *Getting morbid.*

She stopped the truck and looked at her maps with no sense of where she was. Her back and shoulders aching from the hours of tense, tricky driving, she stared at the forking canyons ahead without any idea of which to choose. She took a long swallow from her water bottle and noticed that it was nearly empty.

After ten more minutes of frustration, she gave up on the wheel tracks and decided to look for a way to higher ground, a vantage from which she could get her bearings. It took a while, but at last she found a promising-looking slope and was able to wrestle the truck over gnarled rock and loose gravel to a small promontory thirty feet above the desert floor.

The longer views gave her only a moment of relief. She could see the open plain from here, but she was separated from it by miles of the broken maze, the dead city. The ridge of the Chuskas loomed against the western horizon, but again it was blocked by miles of geological wreckage. There was no human-made thing as far as the eye could see.

She shut off the truck, too tired to go on. *And into the gap charges Cree Black to save the day:* Joyce was right to remind her of her hubris. Quite the rescue operation this was turning out to be.

She took her water bottle and got stiffly out of the truck. The sun was so bright that even through her sunglasses the light seemed to ricochet painfully inside her skull. Surprisingly, though, it wasn't so bad—it scoured her out, bleached her clean. The sun and that cool, perfect breeze, dry and silent. From up here, the ancient rocks all around seemed a little less menacing. She put down the water bottle and began swinging her arms and rolling her shoulders, trying to shake out the tension. Deep breaths of the good air.

Since leaving the motel, she had been dutifully trying to follow Ed's advice: to put her thoughts in order and inventory the usable information at her disposal. But it wasn't much. She had Julieta's theory about Garrett McCarty, which might make sense if Tommy was indeed her child. It was based entirely on Julieta's powerful sense of recognition of Tommy as her son. That odd and often irrational certainty was something she'd learned to trust in herself and others, and from the beginning of this case she'd considered knowing about their biological relationship, and the inevitable dynamic it would create, an important asset.

But given Julieta's state of mind, the validity of that recognition was in doubt.

Okay, so maybe Julieta's thing with Tommy was purely an accident of circumstance, a red herring, made real by Cree's intense empathy with Julieta and reinforced by her own longing to have a child.

She bent at the waist, letting her arms hang loose. Her hair hung down and flipped in the breeze, the blood rushed to her temples. She rolled her neck and felt her vertebrae crackle. After a few moments, she felt somewhat refreshed and stood to take another swig of water and gaze out over the endless badlands.

What else? She had the ghost girl at the ravine and the many ways the mesa seemed to figure in. Maybe the entity was the ghost of the boy named Shinaaí, long anchored at the ravine, that had chanced upon a suitable host environment in Tommy. Why Tommy? Maybe it was, as the Navajos often claimed, an ancestor spirit—maybe Tommy was a lineal descendant of Shinaaí or one of the others killed there. Maybe Tommy's deep yearning to know his ancestors, to overcome his sense of disconnection, had psychically primed him and made him more vulnerable to some rapacious life urge enduring at the ravine. There it was again, the role of biological relationship and recognition, inarguable: *We inherit our forebears' hopes, debts, and errors.*

Which naturally brought up Tommy's most immediate forebears— maybe—Tom and Bernice Keeday. Whether or not they were his biological parents, they'd've had a deep emotional connection. Now that she knew more about the circumstances of their deaths, she was in a better position to compare her experience of the ghost's narrative with their perimortem moments. As for their personalities, their characters, she'd have to ask Tommy and his relatives up at the camp. If she ever found the place.

She tried to feel more hopeful, but objectively her inventory had only served to show her, yet again, how little she knew. Really, she had just about zip that would help identify the ghost and its issues.

The scary thing about her situation was the way it would affect her process. Ordinarily, she relied on external information to augment the often vague impressions she received during empathic contact. Knowing specifics like the ghost's identity and circumstances of death helped pin down what motivated it, what remained unresolved, and which living people might figure in its perseverance and therefore in its alleviation. The absence of information now meant that she'd have to rely more on her ability to share the ghost's experience. She had always tried to set limits on the depth of her communion, sharing a ghost's world dream only with greatest caution. The reason was simple: Without preserving a clear sense of her own, separate identity, she could lose herself in the process. With this entity, a ghost who was an invader, a soul conqueror with a survival impulse that was functionally predatory, it had seemed imperative to keep some distance.

But increasingly it looked as if she'd have to rely on communion to learn what she had to. She'd have to merge with the entity. Surrender to it. She couldn't bear the thought, but neither could she bear the thought of what was happening to Tommy. Maybe she'd absorbed the impulse from Julieta, a mother's protective urge, but here was one other bitter certainty: She would do anything to get the thing out of him.

Desperation came over her again and she began scanning the horizon to the south, looking for some clue as to which way to go. She was squinting against the glare when Edgar's cell phone began vibrating against her thigh.

She dug it out of her pocket and pulled up the antenna with her teeth.

"Cree?" It was Joyce.

"So far, anyway, yeah. I think." She held the phone away from her head, conscious of its emanations.

"Hey, don't joke around. How's reception? I've been trying and trying. You getting me now?"

"Spotty, but yeah, I read you. The country is rough here, breaks up the signal. I'm on a high place now."

"You up at the sheep camp?"

Cree looked around at the wilderness of bare rock and silvery sky and decided not to give Joyce anything to worry about. "I, um, I'm getting there, yeah."

"Well, Ed and I are in St. Michael's. *At* St. Michael's—the priory or church or mission or whatever they call it? We've got something for you on the mesa. The ravine."

"Good timing! I could use something to go on here."

"Well . . . this . . . help." Joyce's words came across interspersed with silence and static.

Cree turned to face south, tugged windblown hair from the corner of her lips and tucked it behind her ear. "Say again?"

"Maybe this will help. The Franciscan brothers who started this place back in the 1800s kept good records. They were working on a Navajo-language dictionary, and they also wrote down observations of Navajo traditions, oral histories, and events in the region? So this guy who lives here, teaches at St. Mike's school, he's a friar or whatever, I don't know my Catholic stuff . . . Father Bryant—Brother Bryant?—he's working on a book, a collection of Navajo personal histories from back then. He half remembered the story when we told him about the lost goats. We went and looked it up in his files."

The phone's radio waves were hurting Cree's mastoid bone, but this could be crucial. She kept it close to her ear, staring out at the distant smooth land to the south. High above, alone in the vast sky, a single puffy cloud floated, serene and mysterious as a cryptic smoke signal.

"You there, Cree?"

"I'm here."

"Okay. So, 1863, Kit Carson and his men are exterminating the Navajos. The ones they can't kill or catch outright, they burn their fields and shoot their livestock, figuring the winter without food will finish them off. This is about six months before they're sent off on the Long Walk. Carson's got detachments of soldiers, some led by *Diné'e'anaí'* guides, rounding up Navajos all over the place—"

"What kind of guides?"

"Oh, *Diné'e'anaí*. Means 'the People Who Are Enemies.' 'The Enemy People'—that's the term you got from your ghost girl, Cree! They were a group of Navajos who allied themselves with the whites. Traitors. Knowing the land, the language, they made it very hard for the other Navajos to escape."

The thought saddened Cree: The division and conflict inside the Navajo soul had been there for a long time. As with every other people.

Joyce insightfully interpreted her silence. "Yeah, it was bad. Everything was falling apart for the Navajos. They . . . it . . . time . . ."

"Joyce, I lost that last part."

"The Navajos called it the Time of Fearing."

Time of fearing: a good description of this moment, too, Cree thought. Of what Tommy and the Keedays, and Julieta, were going through.

"So, this is the story a Navajo survivor told one of the Franciscans, thirty years later. A detachment of soldiers was down in the area where the school is now, and this one family group that lived near there was trying to escape. They're fleeing to the top of the mesa up that ravine, it's the only way up on the northern end. They're driving their goats and sheep with them. Two goats get loose, run back down the ravine. One of the sons goes after them, you can see why, they know they'll need the meat if they're gonna survive. Up on the top of the mesa, the family sees the soldiers coming, so the boy's sister gets scared and goes to call him back. The father and several uncles come down the ravine after *her,* but they're too late, the soldiers are there. There's a fight, both kids get killed, and the father and one uncle. The others got rounded up, sent to the concentration camp. Four years later, the surviving family members moved back to their home turf. They didn't resettle near the ravine, too much sorrow there, bad ghosts. After that they called it Lost Goats Mesa, don't ask me to say it in Navajo, sort of a testament to what had happened. Eventually, the first McCartys came, started mining, bought up the land. People moved away. A few generations later, the story was forgotten."

Despondent, Cree couldn't answer immediately. *Lost Goats.* One little accident, the goats running back. Then tragedy.

"So what can you tell me about them?" she managed at last. "Did they record the family's name?"

"Well, that's complex. It was the children's mother who told the story, thirty years later, right? She was called Yil' Dezbah, and she was of the Waters Run Together clan. Father Bryant says her name means 'Goes to War With,' a pretty common name. I know you'll be wondering if Tommy or Peter Yellowhorse is a descendant of that group, but tracing lineage'll probably be impossible. The clans mix up thoroughly, a lot of names got Anglicized, plus back then it was matrilineal, but for the last couple of generations people mostly use the father's name . . . Maybe the Keedays'll know the genealogy here."

"The boy—how old was the boy?"

"Older than the girl, that's all I know."

"Was his name *Shinaaí*?"

"What? I lost that."

"What was the boy's name?"

"Doesn't say. I asked Father Bryant about *shinaaí*—he says it just means 'my older brother.' Sorry." Joyce blew out a breath. "Think any of this'll help?"

"Absolutely. Great work, Joyce." It wasn't much, but having any data at all was like a tonic. Cree felt exhilaration rising in her. A moment later, her pulse kicked up still further as something flashed between the buttes to the south. Reflected sunlight. She tore off her sunglasses and squinted and after a moment saw what had caused it: about a mile away, the top half of a red pickup truck was just visible, skimming along above an invisible fold of ground. The county road! She'd been this close for the last half hour and hadn't been able to see it. At last she could find her way out of this godforsaken maze.

"Joyce, I have to tell you, you're the greatest!"

"Sorry, I didn't catch that. Say again?"

The phone was killing Cree, and the urgency of her mission had returned like gangbusters. She hurried around to the door of the truck. "I said I love you, and please tell Ed I love him, too."

"Hey, Cree—I don't like the tone of final farewell here."

Cree heard it perfectly but opted to dodge: "What? Sorry, I think we're losing reception. Talk to you soon, okay?"

She shut the phone and slid it back into her pocket.

42

FINALLY GETTING Joseph's map right, she found the Keedays' driveway and drove the dirt track to its end. The grandparents' trailer and hogan were at the far end of a scattering of structures in a canyonlike area between the parched, sun-scoured buttes. The young man waiting for her came to the truck window and introduced himself as Eric, Tommy's brother, although Cree inferred that he was what most Americans would call a cousin. He was a slender Navajo in his late teens wearing jeans, jogging shoes, and a red sweatshirt with a UNM logo. His grandparents were gone, he said, making preparations for the healing ceremony that would be held in a few days. His mother and uncle and brother were taking care of Tommy; they'd had a hard night of it, everybody was very worried.

Eric looked worried, too, Cree thought. No—scared to death.

Cree parked and got out into a silence that stunned her. No wind down here, no long views. The derelict hogans and sheds enhanced the abandoned feeling of what was by far the remotest human habitation she had ever seen.

Eric noticed her reaction and managed a nervous grin. "Compared to this," he warned her, "sheep camp is really out there."

He led her to a four-wheeled all-terrain vehicle. She got on behind him, snugged the straps of her backpack, and put her hands around his flat belly. In another moment they were away, bouncing across the rugged ground. Ahead, the dry soil showed wheel tracks snaking out into dozens of routes through the rock formations.

"So I take it you go to UNM?" Cree called into Eric's ear. It seemed odd to have your legs and arms wrapped around someone about whom you knew nothing.

He half turned his head to answer. "No. Just started at Diné College. Majoring in education."

"Have you seen Tommy since . . . he came back?"

"No. My mother won't let me too near him. That's okay with me."

In a few minutes, Eric had steered them up a rise to a larger plateau topped by gently rolling swells and more vegetation. He accelerated, and the engine noise precluded more talk for a while. The smell of the ATV's exhaust sucked up in the back draft, an oily tang.

When they slowed to navigate through a rockier stretch, Cree thought of another question: "Are you guys close, you and Tommy? You know him pretty well?"

Eric tossed his head. "Ever since he was a baby, yeah. But my folks moved us up to Burnham back when I was a kid, and I'm older, so we went to different schools. He's a real good artist, idn't it?"

Ever since he was a baby: didn't mean anything either way. Of course, Eric might not know. Cree gave up on it. She closed her eyes and just held on, feeling the jolt and sway of the ATV. Trying to charge up her batteries. She almost drowsed despite the jarring motion and the relentless wail of the engine.

The one thing she hadn't taken time to consider was just how she expected to survive. What would keep her intact, herself, when she surrendered to an entity this powerful, charismatic, invasive? What talisman could she hold for protection? It had to be simple and true. *Love, of course, love's the only thing strong enough. Love endures, love perseveres. I know who I am because I love and am loved. Dee and the twins. Mom. Ed, Joyce. Loving Mike and being loved by him. And Pop, of course, my dear poppa. Paul? Not at that point yet. But love, that's what'll bring you back. Bring you home every time.*

Cree caught her head starting to loll and forced her eyes open just in time to be startled by an explosion of movement off to the right. Two ravens had leapt heavily off a small rodent carcass, spreading their wings and flapping resentfully away.

She'd barely caught her breath when Eric pointed up ahead. A low tar-paper roof hunched just behind a rise a half mile away.

"Almost there," he told her.

★   ★   ★

Eric stopped the ATV a hundred yards from the hogan, wishing her a hushed "Good luck." Cree walked the rest of the way, carrying her backpack and a bag of food Eric had brought in the ATV's basket. She was very conscious of the silence here: There was only the crunch of her boots on dry soil, the silvery hiss of her own bloodstream. No sound of voices or human activity.

But she could feel *it* in the hogan. Saturating the silence was the shrill psi buzz she recognized now: the dissonance in Tommy, the radiation of the psychic war inside him. A prickle went up her throat and neck and into her scalp.

Where is everybody? she wondered.

The hogan was low and crude, topped by a rusted stovepipe that canted from a tattered tar-paper roof. Behind it stood some open pole sheds and fenced pens. Beyond, the barren ground stretched away. To the east, boulders and even a few low trees topped the higher swells and bounded the lonely horizon.

She was thirty feet from the door when it opened suddenly and her heart took a slug of adrenaline like a kick in the chest. But it was just a normal-looking human woman. She came out, shut the door quickly behind her, and set its outside hasp.

"*Yá'át'ééh,*" Cree managed breathlessly.

"*Yá'át'ééh,* Dr. Black," the woman said quietly. "I'm Ellen, Tommy's aunt."

They shook hands and Cree handed over the bag of supplies. Ellen was a broad, plump, capable-looking woman in her midfifties, with a square, plain face obviously more accustomed to smiles than to the harrowed look of exhaustion and fear there now. She wore jeans and a brown canvas jacket over a couple of checked shirts. Her hair lay on her shoulder in a dark braid, lightly streaked with gray. Cree liked her instantly.

"I . . . I'm sorry if I looked startled for a second there," Cree stammered. "I was wondering where everybody was."

"My oldest son is over there," Ellen told her, pointing to some sheds. "He got hurt trying to hold Tommy this morning. I think his nose might be broken, but he won't go to have it checked out. My brother Raymond is inside."

"How is Tommy?"

A muffled thump and low voices came from inside the hogan, and Ellen answered with her eyes.

This close to her, Cree could see that her clothes were crusted with spatters of food, and patches of dirt were ground into the fabric at knees, elbows, shoulders. The backs of her hands were scratched, and her lower lip was swollen and split with a line of dried blood. Ellen flinched as another series of thumps came from inside.

"Do you know who the chindi is?" Ellen whispered. "What it wants?"

"No."

Ellen looked at her curiously. "Do you know how to heal him?"

"Not exactly, no."

The look of puzzlement increased. "Do you know why he asks for you?"

More noises came from inside the hogan: sounds of exertion, a clatter. Cree felt the prickle come up her throat again. "I'm not sure. Sorry."

Ellen's eyes searched Cree's face as if she might be missing some hidden message, or looking for clues Cree was joking. Cree could imagine what she saw: some *bilagáana* from the big city, way off her familiar turf, frowsy from lack of sleep, with a scabbed, bruised forehead and scraped-up hands. Not much to inspire confidence.

But a surprising thing happened. Ellen's searching expression gave way to one her face wore much more naturally: a grin, fleeting but radiant.

"Well, you sure tell it like it is, idn't it? Something to be said for that, I guess." Ellen chuckled, sobered quickly, and turned back toward the hogan door.

Cree followed her, marveling at the incredible resilience of this woman's good nature. After what she must have been through in the last thirty-six hours! In the shadow of psychic siege that surrounded this place, it was a bright spark of hopefulness.

It took a moment for Cree's eyes to adapt to the relative darkness inside. The first thing she saw was the single window, a dust-hazed rectangle that cast a Vermeer light on the interior of the eight-sided room. Then she saw Tommy, on hands and knees on the dirt floor. He was struggling through an obstacle course of an overturned table and chairs and a scattering of tin cups and plastic plates.

A middle-aged Navajo man stood motionless on one side of the room, wearing the look of befuddled alertness of someone trying to cross a highway in heavy traffic. It was Ellen's brother, Raymond, a big man dressed in combat pants and a T-shirt that revealed banded workingman's muscles in his arms. His black hair was coiled in a simple bun that lay at the base of his neck.

Tommy's skin was pale and waxy. The face that twisted to look up at Cree was emaciated yet puffy, a sick look exacerbated by the dirt smeared across it. His shirt hung in rags from his shoulders. Scratches bled on his arms. When Cree came in, he looked up with uneven eyes and she saw it react to her presence. A hump writhed through his torso, torquing him, and abruptly he heaved himself up onto two legs like a wounded bear.

For an instant as he rose, Cree had a visual impression of a shape that trailed behind, a phantom being that overlapped Tommy's physical body only incompletely. One whole, vague arm sprang from near the center of his back, the lower part of a leg from his inner thigh. She understood it instantly: *It isn't oriented right in him.*

Tommy swayed on his feet and she lost the image. She stood ten feet away, watching him, not sure how to greet him, trying to find the starting place.

Distantly, she heard Ellen call out, "Ray! Raymond!"

The big man stirred and after a pause glanced over as if startled to see her. "Yeah."

Their voices surprised Cree, too. She realized that she'd been standing there for a time, just inside the half-open door. Hanging in mesmerized indecision as time stretched. And yet now everything was happening too fast. Tommy was walking toward the door. Before he got as far as Cree, Ray had moved in from the side of the room and half blocked him. Tommy twitched violently in alarm but not at Ray. He was looking at Cree as he asked, "What are you doing here?" Ellen answered quickly, "It's Dr. Black!" but Cree wasn't sure it was Tommy who had spoken. His brows had dropped and he gazed from beneath them with that baleful, predatory look. This close, she felt the particular lights of the intertwined beings in him. *Narrative,* she reminded herself vaguely, *find its narrative.* Within the confusion she sensed a strong spark of impul-

328

siveness and behind it a relentless confidence and bottomless determination. *Driven.* Yet there was fear and remorse and anger and impatience, too. She wanted to surprise the entity but now she couldn't remember the word the girl had used for *brother*, and without thinking she called out "Garrett?" Everything was a maelstrom of confusing impressions, and it took her a little while to figure out why: She was down on the dirt floor with Tommy on top of her, pounding at her. His waxy face tossed from side to side above her, screaming. Ellen and Ray seemed to move with lazy, floating motions as they bent to reach for him. Cree fought off his hands. It lasted only a moment and then his efforts became random and he rolled off her and began convulsing on the floor. She twisted away from his humping body and got to her hands and knees, feeling a huge pain throughout her, as if her bones had all exploded and her organs ruptured and her heart split. But that was *his* pain. And still that sense of powerful determination burned, the force of will, the imperious and resistless will, backed by a tangle of feelings from sorrow to tenderness to self-hatred to yearning. As it went on, it veered into a nightmare place of hatred and killing urge. It engulfed her. She vaguely remembered her decision to surrender, but now every instinct of self-preservation screamed in protest against the invasion. Reflexively, she pushed away the foreign being and groped for a life rope, a single certainty, that would pull her free. She found it in the image of Hy and Zoe, wrapping her thoughts around them and clinging to the love between them.

It gave her the strength to get up and lurch a few steps away. Tommy was lying on his back now, Ellen and Ray holding his shoulders with all their weight but unable to restrain his arm from pushing up and snapping back. Slow push, *snap!* back. The chest rolled with its uneven sideways panting and from a long distance Cree heard herself saying, "Watch his breathing! We have to watch his breathing!" Ellen's lip was split again and a line of fresh blood divided her square chin.

Something moved in Cree's peripheral vision and for an instant she didn't recognize it as it hurtled toward her face. Reflexively she shied from it before she saw it was her own hand and arm. It came up and joined her left hand to sweep the hair out of her face and tuck it back behind her ears.

Afterward she held the hand in front of her and wriggled its fingers. They did as they were told. She made a peace sign and a thumbs-up and a fist. It really was her hand and arm, she was in charge. But that half second of unfamiliarity terrified her more than anything she had ever seen or imagined.

43

JULIETA WAS at her wit's end. Joseph wasn't answering his phone. She had called twice and listened to his usual answering machine message that said that if he didn't pick up he was probably at the hospital and that if this was a patient emergency, please call Dr. Irving's office. When she called the hospital, they told her he wasn't on the schedule for today, Dr. Bannock was filling in for him, would she like to have Dr. Bannock paged? She dialed Joseph's cell number only to be forwarded to its answering service, where she got the same message recited by the robotic voice of a stranger.

She had to give up on Joseph for now. She took a last tour of the school to make sure the facility was in order, talked to several key faculty and students, and by the time she was done it was almost eleven, time for the MacPhersons to arrive. Her secretary had taken several calls and left message slips that demanded attention: Donny McCarty, Dr. Corcoran at Ketteridge Hospital, the New Mexico Child Protective Services. But Julieta put them aside. She couldn't do anything about any of it. She had no idea how to respond, and in any case for the next five hours she couldn't let any of it affect her. The major donor ritual had to be done.

The MacPhersons had come all the way from Boston. They were an elderly couple, white haired, tanned, trim, dressed in expensive, ruggedly casual clothes, radiating the robust serenity of the very wealthy enjoying shopping for the appropriate philanthropy. They arrived at eleven in a tremendous Land Rover that they'd rented God knew where; Julieta and the student body president, a senior girl named Rosa Benally, met them with open arms. They went to her office for coffee, where she made them welcome and they chatted for a time. At noon, they went about the sacred fund-raising rite: They joined the students for lunch. They filed through the cafeteria line with the kids, sat at one of the tables with three students and a couple of faculty members. Bright and clean and new, the big room echoed with conversation, the clatter of dishes, the scooting of chairs. The kids were great about the strangers in their midst: curious but too courteous to stare, generally well behaved but as noisy and energetic as ever. Julieta spent the meal introducing students and staff members who passed with their trays and adding occasional comments as Rosa talked about the mural that took up one wall of the long room.

"Way over on the left," Rosa told them, "those are the early Atha-baskan-speaking emigrants, ancestors of today's Navajo and Apache tribes, exploring this region for the first time."

The MacPhersons beamed as Rosa took them through the other panels: the Spanish period, the American colonial period, the Long Walk, the treaty signing, and the handsome Tribal Council chambers in Window Rock, signifying the tribe's growing self-reliance. Sketched but not painted yet, the last panel featured Navajo youths looking toward high-tech professional futures represented by Navajo men and women in lab coats working with microscopes and computers; traditional symbols suggested continuing awareness of cultural heritage.

Julieta explained, "We began it during our second year. The content was chosen by the whole student body, and the drawing was done by our art majors. The painting is being done for art credits by any students who volunteer."

"Very impressive," Mr. MacPherson exclaimed.

"Wait till you see the classrooms!" Rosa told him enthusiastically.

One sharp kid, Julieta thought. With Rosa in charge, the MacPhersons were *toast.* She smiled at the thought, but abruptly she recalled how much Tommy had been looking forward to working on the mural. And that he'd never gotten the chance.

With that, all the worries swarmed over her. She excused herself and went to the hallway outside the girls' bathroom, where she tried Joseph's numbers one more time. Answering machines and forwarding services again.

Joseph, where are you? What's going on? Maybe he was up at the Keedays' with Tommy? But he hadn't said he planned to go today. And why wouldn't he answer his cell phone? Maybe the place was out of service range. She didn't know.

She wanted to run out, dash to her truck, leave the school, go find him. But she didn't know where to look! At home? The hospital? The Keedays'?

The really scary part was that this was not like Joseph. Sometimes he had to go away, or do work he couldn't be disturbed at. But he always let her know in advance. And he would never disappear at a time like this. He knew what she was going through. He wouldn't do this.

Unless something was wrong. Something *was* wrong. She'd heard it in his voice when they'd talked yesterday.

She pecked at the phone one more time, but she misdialed and got computer noises. *Too shook up to even dial right!* She slapped it shut and shoved it into her jacket pocket. She went into the bathroom, where she checked her face and hair, took three deep breaths, and practiced her smile before going back out to the clamor of the cafeteria and the MacPhersons.

Four hours later, the Land Rover pulled out of the parking lot as Julieta and a handful of students waved good-bye. In their last private tête-à-tête, the MacPhersons had talked about four hundred thousand, half to go to the endowment and half to the scholarship fund. It was a whopping gift, and she knew she should feel high as a kite. Instead she felt split like a tree hit by lightning after dividing herself into two utterly disparate beings for five hours. And the fact was, it would take weeks for the MacPhersons' attorneys to conduct the financial audit and for the check to be cut. It left plenty of time for Donny to follow through on his threats and monkey-wrench everything.

Four o'clock. She took one look at the growing stack of messages on her desk and backed out the door, retreated to the refuge of her room in the faculty residence wing. She called Joseph's numbers and got no answer. She called the Navajo Nation Inn to see if Joyce Wu or Dr. Mayfield could give her a cell number for Cree, but they didn't answer their room phones. She called Tommy's aunt's number in Burnham and got no answer.

She stripped off her formal clothes, took a shower, blew her hair dry. She dressed in jeans and a sweatshirt, then sat on the bed, trying to decide what to do.

What she wanted to do was get in the car and drive. To Joseph's house.

Or to the Keedays' place, but that would take two or three hours, it'd be dark before she got there—not possible tonight.

Joseph's, then. Just the thought of seeing him made her feel better. He probably wasn't there, but the decision felt good. She needed to *do* *something*. She got up and scanned the room for her truck keys.

A quiet knock at the door brought her heart to her throat.

But it wasn't Joseph. It was Lynn Pierce, in her nurse's uniform, her silver braid stiff on one shoulder. Julieta stepped back to let her in.

The brilliant blue eyes took in the room before darting at Julieta's face. The bronze fleck sparkled distractingly. "So, how'd it go? Land the big fish?"

"Is there something I can do for you, Lynn? I was just on my way—"

"What do you hear from Tommy? How's he doing?"

"I can't talk with you about Tommy. I know what you did, Lynn. I know you talked to Donny. You and I need to discuss this, but now is not the time."

That brought a widening of the startling eyes, surprise followed by satisfaction. "Gosh, news travels fast out here. What did I say, exactly?"

The disingenuous deadpan awoke a flash of anger in Julieta. "You're fired, Lynn."

"No, I'm not!" Lynn almost laughed at the idea. "Don't be silly!"

"Yes, you are. What you've done is a clear breach of patient confidentiality. Not to mention an outrageous demonstration of disloyalty to this school and everything it stands for. Now if you don't mind—"

"Um, remind me—what does it stand for again? Your desire to pose as some Great White Mother for all the cute little Indian kids? Or just one particular Indian kid?" Lynn paused as if to savor Julieta's stunned expression. "And no, you can't fire me. Because if you do, I will share what I know in additional select circles. It's not a breach of confidentiality, it's an obligation imposed by professional ethics. You wouldn't want the MacPhersons to know you hired a . . . an *exorcist* for a student health problem, would you? Or the people at, say, the Osbourne Trust?"

Julieta's outrage flared and she turned disdainfully for the phone, picked it up, punched Frank Nez's extension. She'd ask him to come escort Lynn off the school grounds. But she had doubts as soon as it began ringing, and before anybody could pick up, she put the receiver back in its cradle. She turned back to face Lynn, anger replaced by heartbreak. In all probability, this was broken beyond fixing. All of it. Lynn, the school, Joseph. Tommy. Her life.

"What did I ever do, Lynn?" she asked softly. "Did I ignore you? Is that it?"

"Don't flatter yourself!" the nurse snapped. But Julieta could see she'd been wounded.

"I didn't know it mattered so much. Really. I would have been a better friend. It's just that doing my job, it takes everything I've got and then some. Sometimes I lose sight of—"

"I have a theory. Want to hear it? It's about you and Joseph."

"He's part of it for you, isn't he? That he and I are close. Is that it? I know you admire him as much as I do. Is that why you hate me? Jealousy?"

Lynn's hands trembled as she took a cigarette pack and a folded foil ashtray from her pocket. She lit a cigarette, drew hard on it, turned her head to blow smoke toward the door. She looked back at Julieta. "You're quite the unusual pair. Lot of history there. Very devoted to each other. So close and yet so far, huh?"

Julieta was surprised at the painful wrench that seized in her chest. *So close and yet so far!* The sense of urgency became intolerable: *Joseph!* She had to find him. She had to leave here. She turned away from Lynn to hide her face as she put on her jacket, found her purse, and checked in it for her keys. "I have to go now, Lynn. Consider this your two weeks' notice. I'll put it in writing tomorrow. I can't tell you how sorry I am that it all blew to pieces for you."

"More accurately, my theory is about you and Joseph and Tommy. The two of you are so deeply *concerned* about Tommy, aren't you. And you're so sure no one knows why. But I think I do. And you know what? I'm not the only one. People have known for a long time."

Julieta lost her breath. She hoped Lynn couldn't see the shock register in her shoulders. She desperately wanted to ask just what she meant by that. But the last thing she should do was show interest or weakness.

"I have no idea what you're implying. But I'm leaving now, and so are you. I'm sorry you lost your husband. You must have loved him a great deal for his death to do this to you. To turn you into this." Julieta turned, saw the damage on Lynn's face, and regretted saying anything. She hadn't meant it cruelly. She went to the door, opened it, and stood aside.

Lynn crossed her arms over her chest and tipped her head forward, a posture at once defensive and defiant. She marched past Julieta and into the hall like that, the cigarette between her fingers trailing a slender banner of smoke.

Julieta followed her down the interminable hall to the side exit, neither of them able to say one more word.

44

"HEY," Cree said. "Hi."

Tommy had surfaced behind the brown eyes. She was very glad to see him.

His bed was a nest of sheepskins and snarled blankets on the dirt floor. Behind the bed and all around the room, the hogan's log walls were hung with tools, coats, sheepskins, chairs, brooms, bundles of kindling, coils of rope. Shelves held cans of food, bottles, flashlights, matchboxes, magazines. Suspended from the sloping, smoke-blackened rafters were several old kerosene lamps and Coleman gas lanterns. At the center of the room, a boxlike woodstove supported a length of rusted pipe.

When Tommy's fit had subsided, they had carried him back to the bed, and now Ellen and Ray stood near the door, watching. Cree knelt at the edge of the blankets, trying to arrange the uncooperative limbs, stuffing folded sheepskins behind him to prop his head up.

Tommy didn't seem to recognize her immediately, but when he did he managed a tiny, quick smile. "Dr. Black," he croaked.

"Think you can eat anything? Your aunt says you haven't been able to keep anything down. You must be starved."

He shook his head and grimaced at the prospect.

"Water?"

"Yeah. Please." His voice cracked, dry and reedy.

Cree took a plastic canteen from the windowsill, held it to his parched lips. He steadied it with his left hand; his right arm hung loose from the shoulder. He was able to drink a fair amount.

"How's the thing?" she asked. She gestured at the limp hand and arm. He frowned at it and seemed about to say something. Then he glanced over at Ellen and Ray, their frightened eyes round in the dark hogan, and clamped his mouth shut.

Cree thought about that for a moment. "Listen, why don't I take the next shift with Tommy, you folks rest up. We'll be all right. We'll call you if we need you, okay?"

They got the message. Ellen gave Tommy a weak smile as she shut the door.

"You must be glad to be up here, huh?"

"Yeah."

"Me, too. It's so quiet. Did you spend much time here when you were a kid?"

He nodded weakly and pointed up at several pieces of yellowing paper tacked to the walls. The drawings were clearly his, a younger hand's rendering of family members, sheep, trucks.

As if exploiting his momentary inattention, the right arm rolled slowly so that the hand lay palm up, and the fingers spread slightly, a sleeping infant's gesture. Tommy's eyes darted at it and quickly away again.

Shit, Cree thought. She hoped it wasn't awakening. She needed some time with Tommy. "Can you tell me what you're feeling?" she whispered.

"Like my head is in two places at once," he mumbled. "Like my eyes are crossed or something, I can't see right."

"Do you know what's the matter with you?"

"*Hastiin* Begaye said there's a chindi in me. Said it's the ghost of an ancestor."

"If it is, do you know who the ancestor might be?"

His shook his head, defeated. As if taking its turn, the ghost rolled the head to the right.

"Could it be your father or mother?"

"Don't think so."

"Why not?"

He shrugged, baffled. "Just doesn't . . . feel like them."

"Tommy, ghosts always *want* something. Do you have any idea what this one wants?"

"*Hastiin* Begaye said it died in an evil way. An unjust way. It wants the injustice to be made right."

"Is that what *you* think it wants?"

338

"All I know is, it wants to . . . come back."

Cree nodded. That much was obvious. "Anything else?"

He started to shake his head again, but hesitated. "It tells, like . . . a story."

Narrative! Cree thought. "What story?"

The hand moved again, that lethargic roll and lazy spreading of fingers. It looked as if it could spring suddenly to vigorous life. Tommy's jaw started vibrating up and down, as if he were chilled to the bone, teeth chattering. But he was able to answer: "Walking. Got to walk a long way in a big hurry. It's cold. Then something bad happens. Like a fight."

"Walking where?"

Before he could answer, a shadow eclipsed the window light. They both startled. Cree looked up to see Raymond through the dusty glass, averting his face, lugging a heavy plastic water carrier. In another second he was gone.

Tommy had lost the train of thought.

"What does it *feel*, Tommy? Do you think it's just angry or is there another feeling there?"

That idea troubled him. "Doesn't always seem angry."

"So what else? Hate? Love? Fear?"

One of his eyes stayed fixed uncertainly on her face while the other spun away as if tracking the flight of an invisible butterfly. He made a deep, guttural noise, *uh-uh-uh-uh,* then muttered something incomprehensible.

Cree waited, but when he didn't say any more, she pressed on: "Do you think I could talk to the chindi? If I did, if you heard me talking to you like you're someone else, you don't ever have to worry. I'm not forgetting about *you,* okay? I'm always on your side. You know that. Can I talk to it?"

He didn't answer. Now she wasn't sure it was Tommy in the eyes. She felt him slipping away and the strange body beast arising with its numbing charisma, its colossal confusions.

"Tommy," she said quickly, "when it's you I'm talking to, you tell me. Okay? Say, 'I'm Tommy.' Can you do that? So I know who you are."

Tommy's eyes took on a sad and distant look, too old for fifteen, and he didn't answer her directly. But he seemed to steady. "I did what you asked," he said.

"What was that?"

"You said I should draw what it felt like."

"Right! Can you show me?"

His left hand gestured weakly at a notebook on the floor against the north wall.

Cree retrieved it, opened it. The renderings were almost too ghastly to look at: painfully labored pencil sketches of what looked like conjoined twins. Too many limbs, multiple deformed heads, bulbous shapes like cancerous growths. She tried to hide her shock.

"It's not so good. I had to do it left-handed." He shut his eyes, exhausted. "You want to know who's Tommy, that's who."

The claim frightened her, even though she wasn't sure just what he meant. There were so many questions. "If I asked you to draw what you *want* to be, what would that look like?"

He looked stricken. Then his face stiffened, a mask intended to keep her out. "I don't know," he mumbled. It was a terrible admission.

He observed her reaction in her face. "I'm Tommy," he managed. Wanting to please her. He looked so worn, ravaged. "Tired now. Got to sleep." He shut his eyes and she thought he was gone until his croaking voice startled her: "Sorry."

She stayed kneeling there for a time, just probing the shifting tides of presence inside him: irregular waves lapping a beach, higher and lower, uneven eddies and flows. When she was sure he was asleep and breathing reliably, she crossed to the other side of the hogan, laid a sheepskin on the floor, and sat on it. At intervals, Tommy's right hand and arm startled her, turning suddenly, flexing, making what looked like abortive movements, and each time her fear spiked at the thought of it coming alive. But so far it hadn't. She tried to relax and get some control of herself. Her body desperately wanted sleep, but she had a lot to consider.

Narrative: So far, she hadn't really glimpsed a story unfolding in the ghost's impulse—no reliving of the period just before death, no crucial memory from earlier times, not even a random visual image of the world the ghost thought it was in. There was its cycle of physical actions, which matched Tommy's description of walking, then maybe fighting. Afterward, there was the repeating sequence of convulsing and the arm pushing up. But she'd learned nothing that would help her identify the entity or determine what motivated it.

But she *had* gotten a tantalizing general sense of its character. This ghost conveyed a sense of vigorous physicality. It also had a burning will, or drive. Determination. Oddly, though, running through all that vigor and drive was *desperation,* as if the vitality were deliberately mustered to overcome resistance. Fatigue, maybe. Or the cold Tommy mentioned. Or sickness.

Or age. Garrett? This ghost's nature was reasonably consistent with a man accustomed to making things happen his way, getting what he wanted. Garrett had been fit for his years but was having to work harder and harder to keep signs of aging from view. Climbing the dragline boom was clearly the act of a man desperate to defy the encroaching limitations of age.

She wished Tommy had been able to tell more about the ghost's affective complex. *Not just angry.* But there *was* anger there at times, rising to murderous rage. And remorse, too, she'd felt it. Of course there was. Most people left life with some measure of regret for things done or left undone; regret and the desire to atone was the engine that animated many revenants. If this was Garrett, homing on Julieta, it could be remorse for the things he'd done—his betrayals and cruelties, the years of feuding. Because Garrett had still felt some love and desire, as Donny had more or less admitted. And, unquestionably, there was a powerful strain of tender longing in this ghost. Also some fire in the belly, lust or desire; Cree was increasingly sure the ghost was male.

Of course, one of the people who died at the ravine could also have had all those characteristics, too. The determination she felt could be their desire to retrieve the goats or to fight off the soldiers; the desperation could be the simple will to survive against long odds.

What about the parents? Could that driven quality be something as mundane as a drunken man's attempt to overcome his alcoholic stupor in order to operate his car? It didn't seem likely. Everything this ghost felt was *sharp,* acute, impassioned, not at all fogged and numbed. And this ghost seemed to be reliving a lengthy pre- or perimortem experience of walking and fighting, utterly inconsistent with the parents' instant death due to massive head trauma.

But it was all speculative. She really couldn't say without a deeper encounter with the entity. *Deeper and deeper.* She had reflexively pulled away during Tommy's last crisis, but she couldn't afford to keep her distance any longer. Tommy was fading away. He was dying. His survival depended on what she could learn directly from her encounters with the entity. She'd have to open herself completely to the ghost. Submit to its invasions.

She shuddered as she recalled that terrifying, incomprehensible strangeness of her own arm, then started as someone rattled the hasp on the door. A crack opened and Ellen's face looked warily inside. Behind her were Raymond and Ellen's eldest son, Dan, a young man in his early twenties with a painful-looking, flaring red nose.

Ellen offered a cautious smile and beckoned to her. "Time for the next shift," she whispered.

45

THEY SAT on the bare ground. The family had set up camp back by the big sheep shed: smoldering fire pit, pots and pans hung on posts, plastic water carrier, rumpled sleeping bags. Cree smelled the coffee before she sat down and her whole being cried out for a dollop of it. Ellen found a pair of tin cups and poured murky coffee from the smoke-blackened percolator.

The afternoon air was cool. Cree sat near the fire where she could pick up a little warmth from the coals, breathing the piñon smoke and burning her lips on the metal rim of the cup. From here, she could see east, past fences to higher land half a mile away, more thickly covered in trees and brush. The sun was lowering to the west, putting the near ground in mixed shadow and sunlight.

"You've done this before?" Ellen asked doubtfully. "Fought with a chindi?"

Cree grinned. "I know I don't look like I know what I'm doing. But the answer is yes. That's what I do. I investigate ghosts and I help people who are troubled by them."

Ellen nodded and blew across her cup.

"Actually, I try not to *fight* it. I have to . . . let it into me a little, so I can know more about it. It's very powerful, isn't it? Don't you feel it, too—the way it sort of hypnotizes you?"

"Oh, yeah." Ellen's big face moved into that warm grin. "I was trying to think what it was like. I keep remembering this one time I went to New York City with my first boyfriend. It was this big thing for us, catching the Greyhound in Farmington, crazy rascal Navajo kids going to take the Big Apple by storm. We got there on a Saturday night and we were so excited, first thing we did was go barhopping with this couple our age we'd met on the bus. We drank way too much. And later on in this one place, I went looking for the bathroom and by mistake I went out the back door into the alley. I stood there in the dark, looking at these brick walls, and I didn't know where I was. I turned around and then I couldn't tell what door I'd come out of, there were three, four dirty gray metal doors, all the same. Middle of the night, and I didn't know what place I was in, or who I was to find myself in such a strange place. Couldn't move. Didn't know what to do. That's what this chindi does to me."

Ellen sipped her coffee with a faraway look in her eyes, but she came out of the pensive mood with a throaty laugh. "It didn't help that there was this sign in Korean or Chinese or something on the other side of the alley—it could have been written in Martian! Luckily, my boyfriend came looking for me. You can bet I didn't drink again for the rest of that trip."

"I had a night like that in Dublin once," Cree admitted. "My husband and me, our first night there. Ouch."

They shared a smile, and Cree felt like sidling over and warming her hands on the glow from the solid, square woman. They both sipped their coffee. The black mud went down hot and stayed burning in Cree's belly, fortifying her. In the deafening silence, they listened for sounds from the hogan and heard nothing alarming.

Ellen's face grew tight again. "I was going to say, that's the scariest thing, but it's not. The way his hand moves when he's asleep—that's the worst."

"What did it do?"

"It did this"—Ellen mimed a beckoning gesture—"and then it kind of spidered around." She made her hand walk along the ground on all five fingers and grope the contours of a rock, then snatched it back as if the sight scared her. Her plump body shuddered involuntarily.

Even in Ellen's imitation of the gestures, Cree couldn't help but see the intentionality of the movements. The hand adapted to what it felt. It seemed to be trying to figure out where it was. There had to be some self-awareness in this ghost, but like everything else about it, it was incomplete, skewed, somehow isolated in the hand and arm of its unwitting host. A blind being lost in time and space. Lost in Tommy's body.

Cree replenished her coffee and poured some into Ellen's cup. "So you folks live up in Burnham now? Eric was telling me."

Ellen looked relieved to put the subject of the hand behind them. "Yes.

We lived on the old place with my parents and Tommy's folks until about ten years ago. First we moved the sheep up there, there's better water and road access. Then I got a job, secretary at the grade school. My husband took a job at the El Paso Gas plant. We still keep a few of our own sheep, but we only help out with the big flock when Ray needs extra hands. We've been after my parents to move closer in, but they won't leave the old place."

Cree nodded. "Were you here for the hand trembling?"

"Oh, yeah. Old *Hastiin* Begaye came up on horseback. Just about killed him, I think, he's eighty-two."

"What do you think of his diagnosis?"

Ellen looked worried again. "All these years, I'd say I didn't believe that stuff but I'd go along. Kind of hedge my bets? And I think the old ceremonies do good for people. But with Tommy this way . . . ." Clearly, Tommy's possession had erased any doubts Ellen might have had. She whispered, "*Hastiin* Begaye, he was scared. He said it's the worst he's ever seen. He tried to look like this was business as usual, but I could tell he was glad to get out of here."

"What ceremony did he prescribe?"

"Two ceremonies. The first will be the Evil Way. That's to get rid of the chindi, to give it what it wants, let it have justice. The second we'll do in a month or so. That's the Beauty Way."

"What does that one do?"

"It's to restore Tommy to harmony and unity. Make him healthy and strong after the ghost goes. *Hastiin* Begaye said Tommy is divided inside, that's what makes him weak and unhappy. He needs to be just one person."

Cree was struck by the insight of the diagnosis. As Joseph had said, he was a boy at odds with himself. Some of it was ordinary teenage stuff—trying to differentiate between himself and his parents or grandparents, loving them yet needing to rebel. But it was amplified by his conflicted sense of what it meant to be Navajo in twenty-first-century America, and by his disconnection from his dead parents, his yearning and resentment, curiosity and confusion. Tommy was divided, not certain which image of his past or future to embrace. Which meant that getting the ghost out was only half the battle. Beauty Way: a way to make him whole. The Hand-

Trembler must be a very perceptive man. Again, it all came down to who Tommy was.

"Ellen, can I ask you about Tommy?"

"If I know the answer."

Cree tried to think of a way to circle in on it. "Your brother—did he have any other children besides Tommy?"

"No. He and his wife, they got kind of a late start. Then they got killed. You know about that?" Ellen looked away, saddened by the memory.

"Yes."

"Tom, my brother, he was a good guy in a lot of ways, but later on he got to drinking and it made him a little crazy. Funny, because Bernice, his wife, she went the other way—when he first brought her home, she was pretty freewheelin'. But then she settled down and was a good mother. A good sister to me. We still miss them both."

Cree nodded. "Does Tommy look like your brother?"

Ellen turned to look at her closely, troubled by the question. "Why do you ask that?"

"Did they adopt Tommy, or—?"

"No!"

"Are you sure? I mean, could they have—"

Ellen burst into laughter again, shaking her head at the crazy *bilagáana* and her outlandish questions. "I'm about as sure as I can get! Tommy was born on the old place, right in my brother's house. Bernice looked like she'd swallowed a watermelon for the last three months. When it was time, she came on fast, one minute she's making fry bread and the next she's got contractions five minutes apart. We couldn't chance putting her in the truck to go to the clinic, she'd never make it. I was the one who caught Tommy from between her legs. I rubbed him until he made his first cry, then I cut his cord myself. That sure enough for you?"

Ellen looked at her with brown eyes that were puzzled, amused, and completely candid. There was no doubting the truth of what she said.

So there it was, at last. Tommy was not Julieta's child.

Cree thought of Julieta and her longing for her lost baby and her deep sense of recognition and all the waiting and yearning over the years: a beautiful, intelligent, dynamic woman who lived and worked so hard while struggling to conceal the deep wound so close to her heart. A weight fell on Cree in a heap, not so much the fatigue of the last week as the sorrows of lifetimes. She knew she should probe Ellen for information about Tommy's mother and father, try to learn more about who they were, what they wanted, how they lived. But right now she was too stunned. She realized yet again how much she had relied on Julieta's connection to Tommy as her one handle on the situation. How much she'd trusted it. How much she'd wanted Julieta to have found her child.

The bitter emptiness was all too familiar. The power she'd given Julieta's supposed connection to Tommy said a lot about where Cree Black was in her own life.

"What?" Ellen asked. "What's the matter?" She watched Cree, worried at the sudden change in her odd guest.

"Nothing," Cree said hoarsely. How would she break it to Julieta? "Nothing. Really."

And that about summed up her progress, Cree thought. Now she was left with nothing. As Julieta was.

46

JULIETA WAS halfway to Window Rock when her cell phone rang. She almost drove the truck off the road as she grabbed it and flipped it open. It was Joseph.

"Where are you?" she shouted. "I've been trying to reach you since last night!"

"I'm at home. I was here. I just had a lot to think about."

"I've been so worried! Are you all right?"

He seemed to consider that. "I was hoping you could come up to my place."

"I'm on my way to your place now!"

"See you shortly, then," he said. And he hung up.

Joseph lived in one of the flat-roofed, sandstone-block houses on the hill in the center of Window Rock. He opened his front door before she reached it. He looked bone tired, but he struck her as handsome and fine as he stood there in T-shirt, khakis, bare feet. When she came up the steps, he put his arms around her and she leaned against him. She wanted to bury herself in him, hold him forever, but the hug he gave her was guarded and brief.

He led her into his living room. As always, she liked the feeling of his place, the mix of tastes. The house was small, just a one-story, two-bedroom shoe box, but well built and charmingly decorated. This living-dining room ran from one end to the other, so windows gave light at both ends, one set offering sweeping vistas to the south and the other shorter views uphill to the red pillars and cliffs of the Chuska bluffs. Over the years, Joseph had bartered his services for the splendid Navajo rugs and other artworks that decorated the place, but he had also hung his walls with framed prints of Miró and Chagall. His bookcase was filled with photo collections, medical texts, biographies, and a collection of comic books, and was topped with a collection of cards and gifts that grateful patients had given him. The Formica dining table and chairs looked as if they were left over from his med school days, but he had invested in a nice calfskin couch and oak coffee table.

The rooms were spotless and fresh, as always, but today there was something different. It took Julieta a moment to realize it was the flowers: a big vase of mixed blooms on the table, another on one of the stereo speakers. Through the door, she saw a cloud of carnations in a clay pot on the kitchen counter.

She caressed the petals of a rose and looked a question at Joseph.

"Well," Joseph said. "I wanted it to be pretty here. When you came. Not much in the way of fresh flowers in Window Rock, but I found these in the cooler down at Basha's."

They stood there for an awkward moment. He looked exhausted and wary, yet somehow at peace with himself. Like a man who had made some decision and had resigned himself to the consequences.

"Thank you for coming. Can I get you something? Coffee, or—"

"Joseph, what's going on? Why are you talking to me like this? I'm not some stranger."

He tossed his shoulders uncomfortably. "Let's sit down."

She let him lead her to the couch. She sat on the edge of it as Joseph took the big chair across the coffee table from her. She waited for him to do whatever it was he intended to.

"I didn't answer your calls because I needed time to think. Before I talked to you. Didn't want to talk to you until I'd figured something out. Figured out a starting place."

"For what? You're scaring me!"

He looked fiercely at her for a moment before springing out of his chair and crossing the room to one of the windows. He leaned against the window frame with one hand and massaged his face with the other. Against the light from the window, he made a trim silhouette, thin at the waist, strong at the shoulder. The muscles in his jaw rippled and rayed from tension.

"Julieta. You see the door to my bedroom?"

She glanced over. A short hallway, the narrow door of a closet, then the door to his room. From this angle she could just see the corner of his bed, covered in a patchwork quilt, and the bookshelf beyond. Another vase of flowers stood on the bookshelf.

"There's a man who lies in that bed every night. And he thinks about you. He wants you to be in there with him. But that's never happened. For a lot of reasons, that's never happened. And that's a big mistake."

Julieta felt heat spread through her: embarrassment, alarm, longing. This was something they'd forbidden of themselves. Why? The taboo had begun, unnoticed, in the months after Peter, and solidified in the time after giving up the baby and the scary period of the divorce. Then for a while they had both been scared of love, of consequences, of mistakes. Later, the taboo had been reinforced by her occasional lovers and his, the distance and tact and accommodation required. Living around it, not looking straight at it, was so habitual that it seemed impossible to face it now. What could she say? *There's a bed like that down at Oak Springs School, too.* True, but such a contrivance. He deserved better.

Before she could find the right words, Joseph turned back. He came across the room to her and sat on the edge of the coffee table. He took her hands and held them as he looked into her eyes. His eyes were deep brown, rimmed with dark lashes, unhesitant and unyielding.

"So what I figured out was, that's the starting place. That's the first thing I had to tell you—I wasn't going to pretend anything different, ever again." He paused to let that sink in: Wherever they were going, there was no going back to where they'd been. "The second thing was, I need to ask you for a promise. There are things I want you to promise me you'll do today. You have to promise you will do all of them, not just some, *no matter what.* I need to talk to you, we need to go for a drive, then we need to come back here and figure something out. After, you can do whatever you need to. Can you promise?"

It can't be happy, she was thinking, *and it can't be easy. Or he wouldn't do it like this.* The thought scared her to death. There was so much to fear right now. But then she thought: *It must be necessary, or he wouldn't do it like this. This must be the only way through.*

"Okay," she said.

"You're sure."

She mouthed the word soundlessly, cleared her throat, and tried again: "Yes."

He held her hands so hard they hurt, still looking into her eyes. Then he got up and pulled her with him. To the door, out to his truck.

Not talking, they headed east on 264 and then north on 666. The mountains loomed on their left, the flat, empty basin of the Chuska Valley yawned to the right. Late-afternoon sunlight washed the land, a chilly white light in the dry air.

Still Joseph didn't talk. In the silence, Julieta's fear grew. She took his hand and held it there on his thigh, making him steer with one hand, too scared to ask him to explain.

This was the way they'd have to go to get to the Keedays' place, but Joseph wasn't saying anything and at last she couldn't stand it any longer. "Are you going to tell me where we're going?"

"Julieta, all these years, I didn't know where your baby went. I wasn't the one who found a home for him. My uncle did. He's the one who knew the family who wanted a child. But he made the same deal I made with you, and he'd never tell me. Sometimes I asked him, and he wouldn't. Even when you were . . . when it was so hard for you not to know. That's why I couldn't tell you anything about Tommy. I didn't know."

"Your uncle Joe Billie?"

"Yes. I know what you're thinking, he's an alcoholic and not to be trusted. But he's more complex than that. He did a wise and compassionate thing back then, for both of us. I believed him when he said he found a good home for your child. And he's helped us a great deal with the Keedays. He's helped me in other ways, too."

She wanted to ask him whether Tommy was her baby, or, if not, whether he knew where her child was now. But there was no point. Joseph had a plan. In her confusion and exhaustion, she found some comfort in knowing he had thought this through. Despite her rising sense of alarm, she felt a desire to surrender to it, to Joseph. She couldn't fight any of this. There was release in relinquishing the fight.

"Okay," she said.

He looked only minutely relieved. Whatever else he had to say, it was hard for him. Without thinking about it, she took her hand back and braced it against the dashboard as if expecting a collision.

"Back when you were pregnant," he began, "I did something that has been a big problem for me. We made a lot of mistakes, both of us, but this was one of the worst for me."

She waited.

"Peter called me. He wanted to know where you were, you weren't answering the phone at the old house."

"What?"

"He said he wanted to come back, he had already broken up with his girlfriend in San Diego, all he wanted was you. But I didn't give him your number. I told him he was no good for you, you were better off without him. He didn't show up. Not long after, you decided to give up the baby."

Julieta heard it, but it didn't connect for a little while. When it did, she crushed herself up against the door, as far as she could get from him, choking on rage. "How *dare* you! How could you have *done* that?"

Joseph didn't flinch. "Because you were falling apart. And because I loved you. I thought I'd be better for you than he would be. I didn't trust him to love you."

She stuttered with indignation as ten thoughts clamored for expression. "How could . . . Jesus Christ, Joseph, what . . . everything I was doing was controlled by *men*, first Garrett and then Peter, and all you could do was control me some more? What you did determined my whole goddamned *life!* You're just as bad as they were!"

He bobbed his head as if he'd expected that. But he didn't look guilty or ashamed. Julieta realized she was looking at a man who'd exhausted his remorse and come out the other side into purpose.

"I thought you deserved a man who showed you some *respect*, Julieta. Okay? And a little goddamned *staying power!*" He shot her a hard look, clearly willing to hurt her if he had to to get his point across. "There are sins of commission, and there are sins of omission. I did that with Peter. But the way I really sinned was what I didn't do. I didn't follow up on it. I didn't come to you in six months or a year or two years and say, 'Julieta, I love you. I want to be with you. Marry me. Have *my* baby.' That's what I didn't do. You want me to feel bad, that's the one that hurts me now."

He was saying all the taboo things, the forbidden things, and yet it was not shocking. They'd both known it, always known it, it had always been there and a source of secret strength and joy. But he had turned Peter away! If she'd known for sure that Peter was coming back, she'd never have given up the baby!

Or would she have?

Julieta's mind was racing. She could see herself back then: seven, eight months pregnant and gaining almost no weight, sacrificing the fat on her limbs to grow her baby. The gray winter seemed endless. She was scared to death by Garrett and Nick Stephanovic and in a rage against them, still in love with Peter and hating him savagely. If Peter had come back, one of two things would have happened. She'd have hit him and scratched him and told him to get out, get lost, how *dare* he leave her and immediately shack up with some Apache slut and then think he could walk back into her life! Or she'd have forgiven him utterly and embraced him and she'd've had the baby and she'd have gotten nothing from the divorce and Peter would have left her because that's who he was, he was a rolling stone and not constituted to stick with a job to pay the bills or wake up at three A.M. to change diapers. And her parents would never have forgiven her for any of it and she'd have turned into another single mother with a half-breed baby, batting around the trailer parks of Gallup.

Still, she couldn't forgive Joseph. She raised her shaking hands to wipe the tears away.

"What else, Joseph? Is that it?" She made her voice hard. "Am I done with my promise yet?"

"No." He had turned gentle again, and that really frightened her. "No, Julieta. I'm sorry. That was the easy part."

It was just another cemetery by the side of the highway, a square of ground separated from the road by a hundred yards of bare earth and rabbitbrush. A little one, lost in the vast sweep of desert, maybe forty graves surrounded by a wire fence with litter caught in the mesh. Some graves were flat earth marked by rectangular headstones, some were knee-high ridges of gravel topped by plastic flowers, bowls of glass beads, photos in plastic frames. A few were surmounted by little wooden crosses; this one was. The photo leaning against the base of the cross had the neutral-colored, motley background of a school portrait. A happy-looking, thin-faced boy of ten or eleven. Black-rimmed glasses and longish hair. Sort of a Navajo Harry Potter.

A little plaque had been laid on the mound. Julieta's eyes flitted at it and darted away. Robert Linn Dodge. That had been his name. Her eyes fled again and came back long enough to see that the birth date was right. And that he'd died almost three years ago.

"A congenital heart defect," Joseph said. "My uncle told me. He got the best care, but it . . . it didn't take."

It was the first time he'd spoken since they'd arrived. Julieta had known immediately what they were there for. They were north of Naschitti when she'd felt the truck slowing. She'd looked up to see the cemetery and had known it all instantly.

It was getting late, the sun was low above the Chuska ridge, the headstones and even the low grave mounds cast pools of shadow. The eastern horizons were impossibly distant and looked chilly. *What a big empty sky. What big open country. Why is the earth where our dead are buried so different? The people in the cars going by don't know anything about this.*

Julieta touched the heat-clouded plastic over the boy's face. She could see herself there: the eyes, she decided, the nose. Peter, too? She couldn't remember Peter. He wasn't anybody anymore. She took her hand away. Here was the truth about her baby. And about Tommy.

And yet when she thought about Tommy, she still felt that belly-deep pull, the sense of recognition. A faraway thought occurred to her: that this terrible fact created another possibility, that Cree Black should know about this, and soon. Or maybe that was just her clinging to her craziness.

Whoever the parents were, they had loved this child: The grave was heaped with colorful trinkets that included sun-faded Power Rangers action figures, plastic statues of Jesus, cat's-eye marbles, cheap jewelry, seashells. Not all were dulled by dust and the bleaching sun; some had been placed recently. They still missed him. He had a such a happy face, despite his illness. He'd been raised in a good home.

I have absolutely no right to grieve, Julieta thought. *It is theirs entirely. How dare I.*

There were the other graves, faded rainbow mounds with stripes of evening shadow along their sides. There was Joseph, standing some distance away. There was that big empty sky. There was his truck, pulled over near the pavement. There was the highway, a station wagon passing slowly, the family inside turning their faces away from the two strangers in the cemetery.

After a while it was time to go.

She went to Joseph, stood in front of him, looking at him, letting him see her face naked with all the feelings. She slapped him once, so hard it smacked like a gunshot, and yet he barely flinched, not even enough to lose eye contact. She panted until she'd caught her breath, glad that part was over. Then she took his face between her hands, stood on tiptoe, and kissed the red blotch on his cheek. She held her lips there tenderly and long, as if it would draw all the hurt out of him. He put his hands on her shoulders, steadying her.

Afterward, she just leaned her forehead against his chest. It didn't feel right, exactly, but really there was no one else. There never had been.

47

THERE WAS a glow in the distance: dangerous like a forest fire in the dark, something malevolent that could rush toward you and surround you and consume you. And there was an irritating insect that buzzed a harsh little song as it drilled into Cree's thigh.

Startled, she brushed and slapped at the bug and half sat up before realizing where she was and what was happening. She was lying in one of the sleeping bags under the roof of the sheep shed. The fire was a tumble of embers. The sunlight was gone but for a dull, colorless brightness in the west, washing the dark landscape in a faint light that turned every feature a monochromatic blue-gray. The silence in all directions was the sound of pure loneliness.

Right. Sheep camp. She had taken a nap. Ellen had lain down, too, but now was gone. With Tommy sleeping and Raymond and Dan taking their shift, Cree had opted to try to rest. She'd drifted off wondering how to tell Julieta about Tommy, her thoughts spinning in slow circles, going nowhere.

The glowing dangerous thing was the battle between Tommy and his invader, always there, an emanation of psychic discord looming just out of view, sixty feet away. And the insect on her thigh was Edgar's cell phone in her pants pocket, ringing and vibrating. Ellen had told her that here on the higher ground, reception wasn't too bad.

She opened it quickly and tugged out the antenna, her heart thudding in her chest.

It was Julieta.

"I was going to call *you*," Cree told her. "Where are you?"

"I'm at Joseph's house. In Window Rock. I called Dr. Mayfield to get your number." Julieta's voice sounded subdued, deliberate. "How are things up there?"

"I'm . . . I was just taking a rest. Tommy's aunt and uncle and cousin are in with him."

"How is he?"

"Not good, Julieta. I'm sorry." Cree's mind was scurrying, wondering how to break the news.

Julieta went on as if she'd planned out what to say. "I called to tell you something I think you should know. Joseph brought me to my child's grave today. He died about three years ago."

Cree's breath went out of her. She couldn't reply immediately.

"Joseph is being very kind. I'm screwed up about it. But I'm coping. I don't deserve to grieve, Cree. Somebody else knew him and loved him every day. I didn't." Julieta's voice was so gentle it seemed disembodied. It faded and swelled as if the breezes over all those miles of desert between them were blowing the signal astray, or lofting out and away some part of her feeling. There was no bitterness or anger in her tone.

"So my first thought was, I was wrong about Tommy. Knowing him that way," Julieta said. "But . . ."

She let the word hang there. Cree understood her reluctance to say the rest: *But maybe I wasn't. Maybe I recognized him because the ghost in him is my son's ghost.*

She couldn't say it because on one hand it could sound like a real neurosis, a delusion that she couldn't let go of no matter what evidence contradicted it.

On the other hand, Cree thought. The theory posed innumerable questions, but it would explain so much. Blood to blood, like to like. If true, it would give them the key to releasing the ghost.

"Julieta, I'm so sorry. I know this is very hard for you. Thank you for letting me know. You're right, it's a very important fact. I understand exactly."

"I knew you would." Very faint.

"Wait, don't hang up! What was his name? How did he die? I don't mean to be so direct, but I . . . I need every bit of information I can get."

"Robert. Robert Linn Dodge. He died of a congenital heart defect. He was sick for most of his life. Apparently he fought back hard. I don't know where he died, or the exact circumstances. I'll try to find out, if you want me to." Julieta stopped, then went on desperately, "Cree, he would have died anyway. Even if I hadn't . . . even if—"

357

"Julieta, you have to come here. The ghost's response to you could be crucial. I need to see you interact. And if you're why it's here, you're the one who has to let it go. Can you come?"

"Of course. When?"

Cree looked around. The rising land to the east was a sweep of deep gray-blue, full of the humped black forms of junipers and boulders. Stars had begun springing out of the night sky. Far too late for anyone to come or go through this wilderness tonight.

"The sooner the better. Tomorrow. Early as possible."

She folded the phone away just as a circle of light edged around the back wall of the shed, bringing Ellen and Ray with it: They'd lit one of the Coleman lanterns. Ellen hung it from a nail and then sat down to stoke the fire. Ray tossed himself down near the fire pit and tipped the coffeepot to see what was left.

"Still sleeping," Ellen said. "Dan's over there, but he's afraid to be inside with him." She looked very worried, and Cree knew why. Tommy hadn't eaten anything for two days. Physical exhaustion would only weaken him, give the ghost the advantage. Even while he slept, it fitted itself more closely to him, a hand working determinedly into a poorly fitting glove.

"I'll go take over now," Cree told them. "I feel a lot better. You folks get some rest, okay? I'll call you if I need you."

"I'm sorry," Ellen said. "My husband and his sister were supposed to come up to help out, but I guess they couldn't get here before it got dark. We're on our own for tonight."

Ray dumped the coffee grounds on the edge of the fire pit and began preparing a new potful. "So I guess we're what you might call a skeleton crew," he joked darkly.

A small scrabbling noise jolted Cree out of her drowse.

She'd been sitting with her back to the far wall of the hogan, keeping vigil on Tommy and the shifting auras and moods that emanated from his sleeping form. Some hours must have passed, but she didn't dare lift her hand to check her watch. The only light was the faint reflected glow from the lantern over at the shed, coming through the window.

It was just enough to see what made the noise: Tommy's right hand.

Tommy lay on his left side, facing her with eyes shut, mouth agape, his breath coming in ragged snores. But the hand was awake. It flexed and stealthily slid along the floor to the leg of the little table beneath the window. When it encountered the leg, it recoiled, then returned to probe the shape of it. That was the scrabbling noise: fingernails against wood.

Cree tried not to react outwardly. Inside, she felt an overpowering revulsion, the sense of the unnatural. A perversion, even by strange standards of the paranormal. The hand moved as though disembodied. It climbed the leg of the table, felt along its edge. When it encountered the corner of Tommy's notebook, it recoiled again.

Tommy shifted in his sleep, rolling slightly so that the arm fell back to the floor. The hand lay palm up and motionless for a moment, like a stunned insect. Tommy's snores snagged and lost their rhythm. His breath seemed snarled in his throat, as if his tongue were choking him. Cree put her hands to the floor and rose to a crouch, ready to spring to his help if his breathing didn't resume.

And, as if it had sensed her in the room, the hand roused itself again.

This time the arm raised toward Cree and the hand made a beckoning gesture with two fingers. It trembled and shook and again seemed to beckon her closer. The movement appalled her. Tommy's head lay canted onto his pillow, his mouth wide and slack, eyes closed. And the thing was alert and beckoning.

Without thinking, Cree took two hesitant steps toward it. *Run!* screamed her instincts. *Surrender,* she commanded herself. She felt time slow and confusion consume the dark room, and knew she must have hesitated because now Tommy's dark silhouette eclipsed the faint rectangle of window. He had risen from his bed.

As he turned, she glimpsed the ghost's body around the outline of his shape, a faintly luminous limb bending momentarily, a shoulder emerging where it shouldn't be and then vanishing again. The dark form moved toward her. The desire to flee became intolerable, yet she still couldn't move.

And then she realized he wasn't coming straight toward her. Tommy went to the door, east-facing as all Navajo doors were, walked face-first into it, groped it with his hands, opened it. Before Cree could react, the doorway was empty.

Her reactions were delayed by indecision. By the time she got to the door, she could barely see his shape in the blue dark, walking east, up the gentle slope toward the higher ground. Cree debated calling for Ellen or Ray, but there was no sound from the sheep shed, and she assumed they were taking some much-needed sleep.

More important, she didn't want to distract the ghost. The freakish intentional hand had given way to the perseverator, and it was living through its narrative now. She had to experience what the ghost was living through and glimpse the world it thought it was in. Instinctively, she sensed she was getting close to identifying it.

She followed Tommy's puppeted body out into the darkness, keeping her physical distance yet extending all her senses toward it. Around them, a wind moved in the sagebrush as if scores of invisible creatures were scurrying furtively through, each suddenly tossing form igniting a fresh jolt of fear. The darkness seemed to flicker and flutter.

The invisible auras of the ghost's moods waxed and waned like an aurora borealis. Fear? Definitely. Or, more accurately, trepidation. But that didn't impede the drive, the burning purpose that kept it moving. What else? Apology or remorse. That cocky self-confidence, too, almost a machismo, a sexualized braggadocio. But so forced, pumped up, so desperate or artificial. *Garrett?*

Confusion and doubt, too, and a childlike *neediness,* seeking consolation or reassurance. And that relentless desire to *overcome.* Maybe a twelve-year-old boy determined to fight off the effects of the badly formed heart that was killing him, frightened, needing comfort?

Robert? Robert Linn Dodge? she called to it in her mind.

Tommy's body stumbled hard on a knee-high rock and went down. Cree's eyes had adjusted to the starlit dark, enough to see that when he got up, his movements were slack and disjointed. Not as if Tommy were fighting the ghost, but as if his body were simply too worn out from the days and nights of warring to obey.

They were getting pretty far from the hogan now. Cree could barely see the building's dark mass, a hundred yards back; the light from the lantern in the shed was mostly eclipsed by intervening junipers. She began having second thoughts about letting the narrative play itself out. It wouldn't be good to go too far in country neither she nor the ghost knew. There were cliffs here. Ellen and Ray might not hear a call for help.

She picked up her pace to close the gap between them.

Always east. Brother would have been heading east as he desperately tried to get back to the ravine. He'd be proud he'd caught one of the goats, maybe that was the cockiness, a young man proving his daring and worthiness. He'd be afraid of the approaching soldiers. He'd be apologetic for disobeying his father's orders not to go back down the ravine.

They were getting too far away. Tommy's movements were weak, but the ghost seemed tireless. Cree couldn't wait any longer for a confrontation. Scrambling in the dark, she flanked the ghost at a distance and came around to head it off. She stopped ten feet away, directly in front of the dark form.

"*Shinaií?*" she called out loud. She conjured in her mind the sense of the girl's mental world, her feeling for her brother.

Tommy took several more toppling steps, stopped, and swayed uncertainly. Now all the ghost felt was doubt and fear. "What are you doing here?" he said breathlessly. Abruptly he put up his hands as if warding off a blow and immediately rage exploded him. He swung his fist at Cree and caught the side of her head. She didn't fall, but it knocked her off balance and rattled her and she tried to dodge him, but it was too late, she was moving too slowly. Tommy lunged again and she had to grab his arms. He growled like an animal, but there was little force in his efforts. They fell over and rolled, Cree turning her face away from the clawing hands, her mouth filling with grit.

"Tommy!" she shouted. "Tommy, stop him!"

Its movements faltered. She tried to push it away and partially succeeded, dragged her upper body out from under. Twisting to look as its fists thudded weakly on her back, she saw that Tommy's body appeared to be fighting with an invisible being. The ghost had drifted askew between worlds. In another few seconds it flailed hugely as pain exploded inside it. Its stomach, its chest, everything bursting. The body began convulsing in regular waves. Cree broke free, scrambled a few feet away, fell down as the pain consumed her. She rolled to look at the Tommy thing. It was fighting for its life. It couldn't seem to breathe.

That thought panicked her and she groped in her pocket for her key ring flashlight. When she put the spot of light on Tommy, she could see the asynchronous breathing rolling his chest side to side, the gaping mouth as the lungs exchanged air. Still she couldn't move. The sense of unrelenting purpose burned in the ghost's mind. It wouldn't surrender. Cree felt its will encompass her, its body spirit irradiate her. The ghost felt itself lying on its back as the ground seemed to rise and fall and shake. It was wounded or sick, dying, yet unwilling to relinquish its life or purpose. It was overpowering her. The ghost or Tommy was looking at her desperately and saying something without breath. She felt the word in her own mouth: *away*. Then one eye fixed on her with enormous effort, and the ghost said it again. This time it sounded more like *awake*. Was the ghost telling her to go away? Was it pleading to awaken? *It wants to come back.* Then the power of it waned a little and she pulled back from the edge. Tommy's body was starting to die as it suffocated.

"Ellen! Ray!" she screamed. "Help me, please!" She looked desperately in the direction of the invisible sheep sheds, waving her tiny light back and forth over her head. The ghost or Tommy was still moving its mouth that way. "Are you saying 'away'?" she asked it. "Are you wanting to wake up? Please tell me!" But the rolling chest had gone still and the staring eye turned fishlike and almost without life. It could no longer move.

She bent and began mouth-to-mouth resuscitation. She shoved on the motionless chest, exhaled into the slack mouth, reared up, shoved again. She screamed and waved the light and this time heard a clank from the darkness and knew immediately that someone had knocked over the coffeepot down at the shed. "Over here!" she yelled. She blew into Tommy's mouth, pushed on his stubborn chest. Waved the tiny flashlight. Heard voices.

It took a while to get him back to the hogan. They waited until his breathing stabilized and until the snapping arm movement had ceased. Ray and Dan kept watch as Tommy slept. Ellen led Cree back to the shed. Neither said anything as Ellen heated some water on the fire and used it to wash the scratches on her face. They weren't severe. When Cree checked her watch, she found it was almost two A.M.

Ellen finished up her face and sat back on her haunches. "Better?"

"Much better. Thank you, Ellen." Cree reached out a hand to touch her brown cheek, cherishing her. She kept her right hand in the pocket of her jacket. She had placed it there carefully with her left to keep it from hanging loose from her shoulder. It wasn't responding. It wasn't *there*. It wasn't actually her arm at all. Her real arm, she was sure, was unaccountably wrapped around behind her, tucked hard along her spine as if she'd slipped her hand deep into the waistband of her jeans and couldn't bring it out. The feeling was so gnarled and knotted it made her nauseous. Some part of the entity's body ghost had entered her. Or she had empathized with it so much she'd inherited its condition. Whatever the mechanics were. It didn't matter, and she didn't want Ellen to worry. They needed to hold out here until morning and hope that Julieta would come and the ghost would reveal itself to her and they could somehow let it go.

No, she decided. Looking at Tommy after they'd laid him among his blankets, she'd seen how the weeks of warring had sapped him. There'd been unceasing doubt and anxiety, and the exertion of the fighting and convulsing. He had nearly suffocated several times. Worst of all, his body had relived someone's act of death innumerable times. There was little left of him, not even physically; even animated by the ghost's preposterous power, his fighting had been feeble. They couldn't wait for Julieta. As soon as daylight allowed, they'd have to get him back to the hospital, where at least his body could be kept alive. Whatever they might do to him there, *this* wasn't working. This couldn't go on.

They sat for a few minutes, warming themselves on the snapping juniper-twig fire Ellen had rekindled. Cree felt crushing disappointment at her inability to enter the ghost's world. To heal Tommy. She had promised Julieta and Tommy, and she had failed them.

Still, as Pop always said, *It ain't over till it's over, and it's never over.* Until morning came, she had to keep trying.

"Ellen," she said hoarsely. "The ghost, or maybe it's Tommy, says things sometimes. Have you heard it?"

"Yeah. Before you came, a couple of times."

"Did you hear it say 'away' or 'awake'?"

"Yeah. Only I thought it was a Navajo word, *awéé'*." Ellen ended the sound with a glottal stop that could almost have served as a *k*.

"That's it exactly! What does it mean?"

"'Baby.'"

"Does that mean anything to you under the circumstances?"

Ellen shook her head. She poked at the fire with a stick as Cree tried to imagine what the word might imply, or who had spoken it. Could it have been Tommy, somehow knowing his possessor was Julieta's child, her baby? Or the chindi itself, understanding its plight and struggling to express the tidal pull toward its mother? It didn't make sense. But if either was true, seeing the ghost with Julieta could well reveal everything. If she got here in time.

But she couldn't let her thoughts be prejudiced by Julieta's longing. There were other possibilities to consider. One of Tommy's parents could have called out for their child at the moment of death. But the death was not at all what Cree would have expected if the entity was one of the parents. The person inhabiting Tommy had been hurt in the stomach and chest, not the head. He—she was sure it was male—hadn't died quickly at all, but had fought off the injury and pain for quite some time. The ghosts at the ravine were probably her strongest candidates; the father had just seen his children killed. He might very well have been calling out to one of his "babies" in his last moment.

She turned to Ellen, who was staring sleepily into the fire. "Are you up for talking anymore?"

"Sure."

"Can I ask what clan your people are?"

"I'm Black Sheep on my mother's side. Towering House on my father's side."

"Are there any Waters Run Together in your ancestry?"

"You're trying to figure which ancestor's in him? Sorry, I don't know. You go back a couple generations, you've got dozens of clans mixed in. Nowadays, people don't know their clans so much."

The impossibility of untangling Tommy's ancestry depressed Cree, but she gave it one more try: "So, Tommy . . . would he be Black Sheep as well?"

"Usually, he'd be 'born to' his mother's clan. We'd say he's 'born for' his father's clan."

"So what was his mother's clan?"

"Bernice? I don't know. She wasn't Diné—she was Jicarilla Apache. She had a lousy family, we never had anything to do with them. She and Tommy's dad met when they both worked at the lumberyard in Farmington."

An alarm went off in Cree's head, a connection being made. Abruptly her heart was pounding and she couldn't seem to catch her breath.

Ellen was looking at her strangely. "You know already, don't you?"

"Know what?"

"About Bernice and my brother. When you first came, asking about whether Tommy looks like his dad, whether he was adopted, all that."

"Tell me about Bernice," Cree said shakily.

"Oh, like I said, she was a wild one. She was already pregnant when she got together with my brother—that's what you figured out, right? My parents never accepted her, called her *aɬjiłnii*—that means, oh . . . like 'loose woman.' But I always figured she was a good match for my brother, he was no saint, either, believe me. And Bernice, she turned out to be the steady one. I was always proud to call her my sister."

"Had she always lived around here?"

"She was born on the Jicarilla rez, that's about maybe seventy-five miles from here. But she'd lived in Farmington and then ran away to California. San Diego. Met some handsome Navajo guy who got her knocked up and then left her high and dry to go back to his true love. She never heard from him again. She came back when she knew she was pregnant. Her family was no good to her, they threw her out. But it worked out okay. When she met my brother, she wasn't showing yet. They fell in love, he didn't seem to mind about her having some other guy's baby, he said he figured he was old enough he should have had some kids by now anyway. And she settled down. They were pretty happy for some years. I always figured, you know, love will find a way." Ellen's face had grown warm with remembrance, but suddenly her lips pursed and turned down. "Unless you do something stupid," she finished sadly. "Like my brother getting drunk that time and getting them both killed."

Love will find a way, Cree was thinking. In Peter Yellowhorse's case, love was still trying to find its way. But he'd done something stupid, and then gotten himself killed.

She wondered how Julieta would handle it when she found out just which ancestor of Tommy's had entered him.

48

T HE ENDLESS night still hadn't given way to dawn when Tommy
started moving again.

They had left the hogan's door open. The predawn stillness stole over
the land with an eerie serenity as gray light filtered into the darkness. Lying
on the floor, Cree could feel chill currents move through the door and
roam the room despite the faint heat of the woodstove.

Just as she rolled over to look at Tommy, the eyes in his gaunt face
popped open and shocked her. When he labored to sit up, she did the
same, struggling to make her arms and legs obey. Her body fit her badly,
like someone else's clothes.

Cree heard muffled movements just outside the door, Ellen and Ray
keeping watch. She had asked them to stay nearby, or follow from a
distance if Tommy still had the strength to walk. Now, watching him as
the darkness paled, she doubted he'd even be able to stand. She
wondered how soon they'd be able to take him down off the plateau,
back to the grandparents' place, and begin the long drive to the nearest
hospital. For a moment, she wondered distantly where Julieta was and
whether she'd arrive in time. She wasn't sure that whenever she might
arrive there'd be enough of Cree or Tommy left to help find the way
through this.

Then she gave up on the problem as the ghost's world engulfed her and
she surrendered herself to it.

Peter's heart surged with joy when he got out of the last car. Just south of
Hunters Point, from here his old house was only a mile ahead. He knew
the land to the east well. Walking it would take a couple of hours longer
than when he used to ride Bird, but going overland cut ten miles off the

distance, and he knew he'd likely have to walk anyway on the seldom-used back roads to Julieta's place.

The bus ride from San Diego to Flagstaff had taken forever, and from there he'd still had two hundred miles to hitchhike. He'd walked back to the highway and had felt lucky when a van pulled over right away. And full of Indians, too. But they weren't Navajos—some Midwest tribe he'd never heard of. They had punched him up a little and taken his last thirty-two dollars, a kind of half-serious mugging, more threat than hurt. The worst part was when they shoved him down the interstate embankment, because the knees of his good jeans burst as he somersaulted down the slope. Looking like some just-dumped rodeo loser, it didn't help get rides. He felt as bad as he looked.

I'm coming to you with nothing, Julieta. But I am coming to you. Back like an echo.

There was poetic justice in his humiliation. Starting again with nothing, from nothing—that felt right, too. All new. Leave the baggage behind. Plus, maybe she'd feel some sympathy for him, it might help ease them over what would probably be a rocky first few minutes.

Return of the prodigal Indian, he'd say to her. *The stuff of which legends are made, yeah?* Standing before her looking like hell, knees torn. Make her laugh.

This was not how he'd imagined it. When he'd first decided to come back, he'd conjured a vision of a tender and heroic homecoming: appearing at her door in crisp new clothes, full of tales of the coast, of dramas in the casting lots, of close brushes with fame and disaster. She'd be angry at first, but she'd see how much he wanted her, she'd be swayed by his passion. She'd forgive him, against her will. She'd be pretty pregnant by now, maybe only three months away, and she'd see how he had changed by how tender he'd be with her. He'd tell her he knew how wrong he'd been, that he'd left Bernice, that he was back for keeps.

The thought of Julieta stirred him and fired his resolve. He remembered her body against his, and it seemed the power of that memory would allow him to overcome anything.

He was close now, maybe eight miles overland. If he hurried he'd get there before dark. He'd ridden Bird this way a dozen times, winding between the hills near the road, then breaking through into the open country beyond. When the land smoothed into the endless miles of rolling swells, he'd let Bird find her own pace and it was always a gallop, that horse loved to run. He'd ride her like the wind in a straight line, shortest distance between two points, the heart line, straight east. He'd fly like an arrow. First he'd see the mesa standing clear of the surrounding land, and that would steer him to the house.

He felt bone tired, bruised and sore, and the closer he got the more nervous he became. She had a lot to be angry about.

But he'd explain. She'd understand. His love would overcome her resistance. She'd see it in him.

Everybody had warned him it was not so easy off the rez, but he'd always dismissed that as the song of losers who didn't have the spark or good looks or willpower to succeed in a world without BIA housing and government handouts. But in fact it *had* been tough. He couldn't get a grip on L.A. at all. Down in San Diego there were more jobs, but coming into Southern California with bronze skin, you came into a labor pool overflowing with Mexicans, and nobody gave a damn whether you were a noble Native American or some newly arrived wetback. And as for having ambitions in broadcasting—hey, who didn't? Plus there was the unrelenting pace of things, and the crowded, controlled feel of the city. Hard rules. No slack. In aggregate, white people were crazy, drank too much coffee. It made them efficient but graceless. He had always looked at the typical Navajo way of doing things with affectionate superiority, but in San Diego he found he missed being around the People, the spacious gracious slow funky chaos of rez life. He missed hearing his own language spoken. On the rez, he'd grown tired of living where everybody was some kind of cousin, too claustrophobic, no privacy, the clan thing with every woman you met. But in white America, it went too far the other way, nobody knew anybody. Being an outsider in San Diego, you went around lonely and empty and unrecognized. Even whites who lived there didn't know each other. He missed Bird and their wild gallops over open land where there was no one to tell him what to do and his spirit took wing.

And most of all, he missed Julieta. Even when he met Bernice and they had a thing for a while, he'd think of Julieta and feel a rat gnawing in his stomach, the sense of missing her and fearing that he'd made a disastrous mistake.

But I'm back. Take two. I'll do it right this time.

Now the walk was taking forever. Early November, after six months on the Coast he wasn't used to the cold. But whenever he bottomed out, he'd picture an image of her: the breathtaking curve of her hip as she shrugged out of her jeans the first time they'd made love. Oh, man. Or the light in her eyes when he'd be at work with the other guys around and couldn't talk to her and she'd look a blue fire of love at him that set him ablaze from thirty feet away. Plenty enough to keep him going.

I'll do it right this time, he promised. *Babies, they're not so bad. People have been having babies, raising families, for years. Decades, even. I'll try it, Julieta.*

Walk, walk, walk. It took three hours to reach the last rise, about a mile from the house. He was aching and tired, but the instant he saw the place, the kinks and pains fell away. The last light of sunset painted its walls, the windows glowed with welcoming yellow. He laughed out loud for joy. He'd made it! There was warmth of every kind inside. There was starting new. Birth and rebirth.

If she forgave him. The thought shivered him. But of course it would be hard at first. He deserved it. He didn't blame Joe Tsosie for not talking to him, trying to keep him away—he'd screwed up royally. She'd be mad because she was hurt and scared. But he'd make it better.

He ran the last half mile.

As he came up to the door, he stood straight and brushed the dust off his clothes. He tugged his hair loose from its ponytail and shook it out over his shoulders, the way she liked it. He tried to catch his breath but couldn't. When he knocked, he was burning. He felt the love light come over him and knew it made him beautiful and strong, irresistible.

Garrett McCarty opened the door.

It was so unexpected that the best Peter could do was stammer, "What are you doing here?"

"What am *I* doing here? I own this house." Garrett McCarty looked him up and down and his eyes narrowed. "I'd ask what you're doing here, but I think I already know."

A big shape moved behind McCarty and Peter saw Stephanovic, the big Irish guy who everybody knew worked as a sort of enforcer type at McCarty mines. He came to the door, looked at Peter without expression, then swept his eyes over the driveway as if checking for cars or other visitors.

Garrett McCarty turned away and made a sharp gesture with one hand. "Nick, invite this kid in, huh? And shut the door, it's cold out there."

One of Stephanovic's huge paws whipped out and came around the back of Peter's neck and yanked him stumbling into the house. Peter cuffed the hand off and stepped away.

McCarty stood belligerently, legs braced wide, face red and full of veins. He was wearing jeans and cowboy boots and a checked shirt opened a couple of buttons to reveal a mat of gray chest hair. "You've got a lot of goddamned balls, don't you. Coming here, knocking on the door. I *knew* she had a brave in the woodpile. I knew it. Is this some macho rite, you want to lock horns with the old buck?" The thought made McCarty laugh. "Or, what—you're the honorable type, looking for *permission* to take my pony for a ride? That it?"

"Don't talk that way about her," Peter snapped.

McCarty threw himself at Peter. He was heavier, but Peter was younger and quicker and his first punch flattened the old man's nose. McCarty reared away, roared, charged again, and they reeled back against the wall, raging and pounding each other. McCarty's nose sprayed blood. Peter felt the power of his own anger, hate brewed from all the things Julieta had told him about the man. He hammered the red face with his forearm and knocked the old man reeling. McCarty staggered into the middle of the room and charged again like a wounded bull. They fell against a coatrack and went to the floor, rolling, tangling in it. Things were breaking, falling from the walls. Peter rolled on top of McCarty and punched the raging face.

Then something hard hit the side of his head, knocking him sprawling on the tiles. Stephanovic aimed another steel-toed kick at him and he barely got his arms up in time to protect his face.

Peter had just gotten to his hands and knees when the big man kicked him in the center of his chest. The force of it lifted him off the floor. He fell on his side and struggled to get his breath. Couldn't inhale. Couldn't move.

Still the rage and ardor burned in him. He wouldn't lose. He wouldn't give up. He would find Julieta.

Stephanovic was standing across the room, giving him a *stay cool* half smile and watching him as he got to his feet. Then McCarty appeared in the living-room doorway holding a kitchen towel against his nose with one hand and a big silver pistol in the other. Stephanovic's eyes went wide and he moved toward his boss, saying, "Whoa, hey, Garrett—" but the gun exploded, sound and flash and impact all at once. Peter felt his insides blow apart. Then another huge noise and another detonation in his gut.

Peter curled around the pain. He felt as if he'd leapt off a cliff and plunged deep underwater. The air was thick and resistant, and the sound of the men's voices was a big rounded booming, slow. One rumbled, *No Navajo punk . . . screw my wife . . . talk to me like that.* The other said, *Didn't have to do that . . . mess to deal with . . . trouble.*

Another man appeared at the inner door. Peter's eyes focused enough to recognize him: Donny McCarty, the old man's son, a pale clerkish nerd who Julieta had always felt sorry for. He swore at his father and boomed, *Never think first . . . could have used it against her . . . cost yourself millions!* Then both McCartys were giving orders. Stephanovic complained but gave in. Donny was already picking up the broken things.

Peter hated them with all his might. He couldn't make sense of anything. He pulled himself down to a secret cave under the water and wrapped himself into a ball. Inside, he found a place of resolve and fire and he knew it could not fail him, it was so strong he knew he could survive anything, find Julieta again.

A kind of empty space and then he noticed he wasn't in the bright lights of the house but outside, under the sky. It was dark and stars. The sharp wild lights gave him strength, too. Stephanovic and Donny McCarty had put him in the open back of Julieta's little workhorse Jeep. The Jeep started and then they were bumping. The metal bed pounded up at him and the pain came in bolts and blasts. Stephanovic was going to kill him, Peter knew, but he was going to surprise him because he had strength inside that no old white businessmen could imagine. He was smart and durable as a coyote. He was strong and young and had fire in him. He had love. Love would win. He'd wait until Stephanovic stopped and he'd kill him and then he'd kill both McCartys and he'd go to Julieta.

The jarring and bumping quit and the night was quiet. Stephanovic was opening the tailgate and lifting Peter out. It hurt. Peter stayed curled around his secret strength, husbanding it. He was barely breathing. He would explode suddenly from his stillness. His love would give him power.

Stephanovic was carrying him between walls of rock, and Peter recognized the ravine that came down near the north end of the mesa. The big man labored on the slope, working his way deeper in and higher up, stumbling and swearing. He dumped Peter onto the ground and then lit a flashlight. Peter opened his eyes into the impossible light, couldn't see Stephanovic but knew he was looking down at him.

"Aw *shit!*" the voice behind the light said. "We thought you were dead. Son of a *bitch!*"

Peter willed his body to move. But he couldn't lash out and he couldn't stand up. All the effort did was bend and straighten him. He was aware that he was writhing on the ground as the big man stood over him. Back and forth, trying to straighten his body, then feeling the unbearable pain and curling back around it.

Stephanovic was grunting and swearing. He didn't want to do this, Peter could tell. Which meant he could be persuaded. Peter tried to find the thing that would convince him to disobey and to help him. He had to find the thing that mattered most in the world. That was Julieta. But he didn't want to say her name. Didn't want to use her to save himself. But she was pregnant, she needed Peter to be father to the baby. He had to be father to the baby. Any man would understand that.

Peter tried to tell him. "Baby," he said. "Baby." Regret tainted the pure clarity of his determination. He hadn't just been stupid, he had been cruel.

He heard Stephanovic's breathless swearing coming closer and thought he'd reached the man, but then a big rock landed next to him, bruising his shoulder.

No, Peter screamed inside. "Baby!" he said out loud. Stephanovic's face was just a white blob in the darkness above him, but he tried to catch his eye, convey his passion. Still the big man didn't understand, so Peter made a gigantic effort: "Don't kill me! I have to take care of her! I have to be with my kid." But his meaning was changing, what mattered most was still deeper. What he really meant was, *Let me live so I can do it right, fix the mistakes. Don't kill me with that undone. Don't kill a man who hasn't undone his cruelties.*

Another rock fell, this one landing directly on his legs. "I don't understand Navajo," Stephanovic said. Then he was gone again. His swearing got distant and then came back.

The effort to shout had tired Peter. He needed to rest, gather his energy.

He found the secret place of strength again and held himself curled there. He'd outwait Stephanovic. If he had to, he could wait forever. He'd curl up and hold himself still and come exploding back. He'd be with Julieta and the kid and set all the mistakes right.

An empty time later, he opened his eyes to find he was covered with rocks. But not entirely. He could see up into the sky in the gaps between them. The rocks were all over him, but they mostly supported each other's weight and weren't that heavy. There was no sound. Stephanovic had gone, left him for dead.

But he wasn't! He was alive, and he could move. One arm was pinned beneath him, but he was able to fight the other arm free. The rocks shifted slightly, allowing him to bring his hand up. He pushed at the big rock that lay just above his chest. It lifted, pivoted, dropped back down. He did it again. He could lift it, but then it just pivoted back and his arm gave way. Again. Again. The rock made a gritting noise as it lifted and a hard, final noise when it fell back. So now he'd rest again. Stephanovic hadn't killed him and hadn't even buried him deeply. He'd get out. He'd find his cousins over near Hunters Point and they'd take him to a doctor and then he'd go to Julieta.

Garrett McCarty would never stop him. Nothing could stop him.

Something was happening up in the sky. No, *near* the sky. Bright light washed over the lip of the ravine sixty feet directly above him. Red boulders and slabs, the crumbling undercut edge, sharply lit against the black sky. The shadows shifted. He heard motor noise. A Jeep up there. Stephanovic had driven around to the south end of the mesa, where the slope was not so steep. The lights eclipsed and shafted bright and the motor labored. Grinding, grating noises. Then all the rocks were moving, the whole section of cliff was falling, gathering other rocks and hurtling down.

49

JULIETA RODE the Keedays' horse as hard as the animal could stand. It was a tall, bony paint gelding, already getting shaggy for winter, out of shape from too much time in the grandparents' corral. She pushed him until he wheezed. The air was a harsh, crisp cold. A hundred feet ahead in the predawn light, Joseph sat behind Tommy's cousin on the ATV. The taillights, so bright when they'd started out, were already dimming as the landscape drew light from the sky.

She hadn't heard from Cree again, but as she'd lain there in Joseph's bed the worry had intruded on the oasis of serenity they'd made together and increasingly she'd sensed it was urgent to get to Tommy. They had left Window Rock at two in the morning and driven the empty roads and wandering wheel tracks for over two hours. They'd awakened Tommy's grandparents and cousin, saddled this horse, and set out.

Once they'd climbed out of the strange canyonlike maze and reached the higher plateau, the going was easier. The horse could sustain a lope for a couple of minutes on end. The ATV bobbed and swerved as the eastern sky turned a bland gray-blue above the dark land.

At last Eric stopped the ATV and let Joseph off, pointing ahead toward a low, dark hogan. Julieta cantered past them, pulled up at the open door, leapt off. The gelding huffed as she dropped the reins and looked through the doorway. A single dull rectangle of window light. Nobody inside.

"Mrs. McCarty?"

She whirled at the voice. A middle-aged Navajo woman stood thirty feet away, looking haggard, blowing puffs of steam into the freezing air. Tommy's aunt, Ellen.

"They're over here. He only got a little way last time. It's good you came. He's starting again. Cree says if he does it again, he'll die."

Julieta's heart clenched at the words. She followed Ellen into an area of rocks and sagebrush, and then spotted the other people: two men, standing some distance apart from two blanket-wrapped forms on the ground. Cree and Tommy.

She hurried to them. Tommy lay twisted among blankets and sheepskins on the bare ground, motionless but not quite asleep. His eyes were open to staring slits in a face that was almost skeletal and greenish in the predawn light. Julieta was seized with worry for him, and with it came that sense of knowing, of resonance, of recognition that she swore she'd forbid herself but that came anyway. She *knew* him. It had to be her child's ghost in Tommy.

"Hey," Cree said amiably. "Good timing."

Julieta was horrified by Cree's appearance. Sitting at Tommy's side, she looked battered and drained. Even with the heavy blanket around her, Julieta could see the hard cant of her head, the tilt of her shoulders. Some of the grotesque half twist of the ghost had come into her.

"Are you all right?" she stammered.

"Fine," Cree panted. "Listen. Not much time. This is going to be hard, Julieta. Hardest thing you ever did. I can't tell you how. Tommy's just about gone. I've only lived through the dying twice. And it's just about done me in. But Tommy's done it dozens of times. And there's the breathing thing. He can't survive another time. You have to let the ghost go. One shot at it. Has to be just right."

Joseph finally joined them. He came to Julieta's side and put his arm around her waist and she put both her hands over his, pressing him against her.

"Hey, Dr. Tsosie," Cree rasped.

"Dr. Black." Joseph bobbed his head. He kept himself outwardly calm, but Julieta knew that his physician's eyes saw the crisis here for what it was.

"Is . . . is it—?" Julieta began.

Tommy moaned and stirred. Behind his slitted eyelids, his eyes were moving wildly. Julieta felt a reprise of that numbing indecision that meant the ghost was awakening.

"You have to go with it," Cree croaked faintly. "With the ghost. It's reliving a memory. Like a recurring dream? There's a place where you can intercept. When he knocks at the door. Don't do it sooner, worlds won't mesh. Don't do it later or it'll too late."

Julieta wasn't sure whether Cree was speaking allegorically. *Knocks at the door—to the real world? To consciousness? To your heart?* Cree's vocabulary mixed poetry and psychology and philosophy, you couldn't always tell.

"What would you like me to do?" Joseph asked.

Cree looked up at him. She started to speak, then seemed to catch something in his face that needed further inspection. After a few more seconds, she almost seemed to smile. "Just keep back a little. With the others."

Joseph nodded, stepped back to join Tommy's family. Tommy's legs began moving in weak, rhythmic thrusts. He was walking while lying down.

Cree had closed her eyes. "Listen, Julieta. At first you won't know what's going on. It'll seem like random thoughts. Like you're making it up. Like a daydream. Just let it happen."

Julieta felt the ghost burgeoning. With its hypnotic aura came that irrational sense of *knowing* again. Panicking, she asked Cree, "What are you going to do?"

"I'll just go with him. Help you find the . . . story. But I'm totally screwed up, Julieta. I'm Tommy, I'm you, I'm me, I'm Peter. I can't—"

"Peter?"

"Tommy's his son." Cree's neck twisted and it seemed to hurt her. "Your best," she choked out. "The person you'd rather be. Got to stack it up right. Like you said."

Julieta wanted to grab her shoulders and shake answers out of her. But Cree's eyes were rolling behind her closed lids. Tommy was moving in his awful parody of walking. Not knowing what else to do, Julieta knelt next to him. She put her hand on his side, felt the trembling effort of his muscles. She shut her eyes.

At first she thought there was nothing she could find. Images popped into her head, but she didn't trust them: fantasy, memory, random subconscious collage, wishful thinking? The effort made her almost sleepy. But some things persisted. She still felt the sense of familiarity, and she let that guide her.

The side of a hill and a horizon. She recognized the land with a shock. Over near Peter's place, the hills along Black Creek. He was walking toward her house. It was chilly out, and the dry hills told her it was autumn. It would have been that fall, when everything fell apart. Yes, it was. He had just come from San Diego. His thoughts embarrassed her. Joseph would hear them. Peter was tired and sore and yet he sparkled and spangled with bright feelings. That *energy:* She knew that energy, the presence that was Peter. Oh, God, it was gorgeous, it was a magnet. Everything was right there, the memory of his hair on the wind as they rode, the corded lean muscle in his thighs against hers. His bronze smooth skin and the brash confidence and innocence in his eyes. Peter was a spark, a wild joyous song. He carried desire like a tightly wound spring in his belly and loins and it commanded her and she commanded it and it gave her great pleasure to know it belonged to her.

Except that it didn't. There was a girl in San Diego. He was coming back but he'd left her and then he must have left the other woman, too, and all he was really doing was following the path of least resistance. He felt and did everything with such certainty, but it was so shallow. So transient.

Julieta wanted to lash out at him. Scream at him. Blithely striding across the rolling swells toward the mesa, so certain he'd be forgiven! But Cree had said wait. Said do your best. No, *be* your best. But what was best?

There was her house, windows glowing in the twilight. Peter was hurrying. He was racing across the ground like a wind-lashed wildfire, heat and light and hunger. Irresistible. The land, the house just the way it was back then, it was all real again.

Peter knocked at the door.

Julieta was dimly aware that Cree had moaned and that Tommy was standing in front of her.

She answered the door with no idea how to respond. She was so hurt inside. She was so angry at him. Yet she felt him so strongly. He was there, he was alive, he had come back, he was afire with longing and contrition. He was a force that bent her.

A ghost's dream, she tried to remind herself. *A woman's memories.*

It didn't help. She was only partly aware that Tommy's body stood before her in the growing light. All she really saw was Peter. The sight of him struck her breathless.

"Birdman," she said softly.

"Julieta!"

He was glorious in his relief and passion. His eyes pleaded with her but he didn't speak again, just stood there, letting his body say everything. His jeans were ripped, his shirt dirty. He was breathing hard. Confused images roiled in his mind: fighting, pain, turmoil. They rumbled and faded away like thunder.

She stepped out to him, cupped his face in her hands. He touched her hands as if to verify they were real, then slid his own hands to her face.

"I came back," he said.

"So I see."

"I was thinking about you the whole time."

"Yes. Me, too," she said. Sadness filled her at the thought.

He hesitated. "I was afraid you'd be too mad at me. But I love you. You have to know that. I always loved you. The whole time."

"I'm not mad anymore. I know you loved me."

"The baby—?"

Another pang of sadness, almost enough to bring her out of the ghost's fragile dream. "The baby is fine. You have a beautiful son."

That confused him even as it eased him. "I was worried. I was afraid—"

"Shhh," she soothed him. "Don't be afraid."

"And I was worried about you."

You hurt me so bad, Birdman, she thought. *So damn bad.* But that was long past, and what she said was, "I'm fine. Everything is okay now. It's all worked out as it should have."

That made him feel much better. He was enormously relieved. A knot released inside him as if the very stuff he was made of unkinked, calmed and smoothed. He was suffused with love for her. His hands moved down her cheeks to her shoulders and down her sides to her waist. They stood together on the edge of the porch that way for a long moment, and then he grinned tentatively.

"I had an unfortunate encounter on the interstate. Now I know what it means to be *rolled*. I didn't want to look like this when you saw me again."

"You're even more handsome than I remembered. Much, much more."

His grin gained confidence. "So . . . you going to invite me in, or what? Freezing out here. Prodigal Indian comes back, yeah? We should celebrate."

Julieta had dimly wondered what would happen at the moment, but when it came there was no hesitation at all. "No, Peter. Things changed while you were . . . gone."

"Uh-oh. Like what?"

"I'm in love with someone else. I've been in love with him for a long time. You can't come back to me."

Peter stiffened in hurt and disappointment, and an image of struggle, fighting, rocks falling flashed through his thoughts. Julieta was vaguely aware that Cree had stirred in her blanket. The dawn light was much stronger now. Tommy held her waist in his thin hands and looked into her face with Peter's eyes, now very confused. He was so weak his legs were trembling with the effort of standing. Peter needed consoling.

"Everything is okay now, my love. I'm happy now. Your son is good. You are free. No diapers, no bills—some relief there, huh?"

Still he looked wounded, but his face admitted there was truth in what she said. *He would never have stayed,* she knew with certainty. *He'd have flown away.*

"Who?" he asked.

"Joseph."

Peter nodded once, not surprised. He looked away from her for the first time. "You're sure this is how it goes?"

"Very sure."

He was coming undone. It was harder to see Peter in the face of the shaky teenager who stood before her clinging to her sides. Julieta suddenly saw the world as Cree must: All the forces that had converged to bring Peter back were starting to slip away. All the longings that had propelled him had been answered or denied by the only person who could. Again the scary horrible dream tumbled in the back of his mind, fighting and guns and falling rocks, but it was remote and irreconcilable with what was happening. This was so much preferable. Still, he felt dismay.

A thought came that had never occurred to her before, and an overwhelming gratitude blossomed in her. "You did something wonderful for me."

He turned back to her. "Oh, yeah? What was that?"

"You showed me how to fly. From that very first day at the mesa. You didn't know it, but you gave me freedom from Garrett. You broke his hold on me."

"Glad I could be of service, ma'am." He was imitating a cowboy, protecting himself with some swagger. But she could see she'd pleased him.

"Can you help me that way again? Would you?"

"You know I would. How?"

"You . . . be free. That makes me free. You fly. Then I can fly."

"Where should I fly?"

"Out there," Julieta said, choking.

She couldn't be sure which landscape she indicated with her gesture. Behind Tommy, the sun still had not risen but was so close to the horizon it gilded the rim of the land with golden fire. Where Peter was, on the front porch of the house in Oak Springs, the stars had come out through the darkening blue and the sky looked deeply domed at the zenith. The shape of the mesa and the rolling swells of sagebrush were magical in the near dark, turning faint as the ghost's world lost conviction.

Peter looked out at it as if he'd just seen something astonishing. He turned back to give her a confiding smile and turned away again. Something like a reflection of light skipped out of Tommy as Peter stepped off the porch.

His foot never touched the ground.

Tommy almost fell, but Julieta caught him in time.

50

I T WAS A strange procession that made its way out of Julieta's corral: three women on horseback, two men walking behind. They didn't hurry. The horses were content to amble, occasionally turning their heads aside to nip mouthfuls of sage. Joyce was having a blast, sitting high astride Breeze with her jet-black hair rippling, eyes sparking; she'd borrowed a cowboy hat from Julieta. Forty feet back, Joseph and Edgar were talking, but Cree couldn't hear what they were saying over the dull clump of hooves. The rhythm of Madie's strides and the movements of her muscular shoulders felt good to Cree, and she wished she wasn't too tired for anything more than a walk.

"Ellen called to invite us to the ceremony. She wanted to make sure you knew you were invited," Julieta said. "It starts on Tuesday. Can you stay till then?"

"I wouldn't miss it," Cree told her. Right now, every bone in her body ached with exhaustion. But a few days of rest would patch her together.

It was Friday afternoon. Behind them, the school was a buzz of activity as the kids milled between buildings. The five yellow buses had parked in front of the dorms and soon most of the students would head home for the weekend. The night had been cold, but the sun had brought warmth and now the air was a mild, cool caress, perfect for riding. To the east, the mesa rose with walls of red-brown.

It looked obscure, Cree thought. Completely anonymous.

"Can I, you know, make him go faster?" Joyce asked.

"Breeze is a mare," Julieta told her. "A female horse. Just tap your heels and make a cluck or kissing noise. First comes a trot, and you have to post—that's support yourself on your legs. Then a canter, what we call a lope, then a gallop."

"What do I do then?"

"You hang on for dear life."

Joyce was already off. Her hair streamed behind her as she cantered off ahead. Her cowboy hat fell back and hung by its cord at her back. Cree smiled, realizing how much she would miss this wide-open land, the dry cleanliness of it.

"I talked to Tommy this morning," Julieta said. "He's doing fine. He's eating. Says his aunt is feeding him big meals, making him drink Gatorade. He's drawing again and wants to come back to school."

The family had taken Tommy to Ellen's house in Burnham until the ceremony. Just the thought of Ellen made Cree smile. "She'll fix him up in no time."

Julieta grinned and then got serious. "Cree. Did Peter . . . did he know he was a ghost?"

"Ordinarily, I'd say no. But I'm never really sure about ghosts' self-awareness. They're usually very confused by the discrepancy between the world they were alive in and our current world. Especially when you intervene in their world dream, they experience a conflict of realities that's fundamentally irreconcilable. Most of Peter's actions were a perseveration, practically just a tape loop replaying his final hours. But whenever his hand moved on its own, I couldn't help feel that it had become the instrument of a conscious being. I have no idea how that would work, Julieta. None. But when I was talking to Ellen about it, she pointed out the parallels with something I should have thought of, the Navajo tradition of hand-trembling. Do you know much about that?"

Julieta shook her head.

"If I've got the traditional explanation right, the Hand-Trembler diagnoses the sick person with the assistance of some helping spirits—not human ones, the four Gila monsters, kind of half gods. They animate the diagnostician's hand and reveal what's wrong with the sick person. At least there's some precedent for the idea of such a selective possession, that . . . isolation of consciousness in one limb. But I don't know how it might work. I just don't know." Cree blew through her lips in frustration. Every case seemed to generate more possibilities and uncertainties than answers. And yet that gave her joy, too: world without end. Infinite mystery. "But I was going to say—at the very end, I did get the sense Peter realized what he was, what was going on. That it was time to let go. That he wanted to do as you asked."

"I think so, too," Julieta said softly. "I'd like to believe that. That he'd be so . . . graceful." She frowned, and Cree knew what she would say next. It was a moment she'd dreaded.

After helping get Tommy to Burnham, they had returned to the school and had talked for a long time. Cree had given Julieta a rough idea of what had happened after Garrett met Peter at the door. The burial in the ravine explained Nick's midnight visit: After Lynn had told Nick and Donny of Cree's interest in the ravine, they had gotten worried that maybe she'd uncovered some evidence. Nick had come back to see if anyone had been digging in the area.

It was a horrible story, and Julieta had taken it hard. But thinking back, she said, there'd been little clues—a word dropped by Garrett or Donny now and again, a smug and cruel look. Even Lynn Pierce seemed to know something about it. Just Wednesday, the nurse had made veiled allusions to Julieta's past, to others knowing her secrets.

What concerned Cree now was Peter's call to Joseph. Julieta would be justified in blaming Joseph for deflecting him toward Garrett's murderous rage. And that would ruin everything.

As if she'd read Cree's mind, Julieta turned to look back at the walking men. "Joseph. He'll blame himself."

"Yeah. But, more important, will *you?*"

Julieta shook her head. "There were so many bad choices that ended up there. All the big ones were *mine*. Trying to be a beauty queen. Marrying Garrett. Not divorcing him the moment I knew what was going on. Getting pregnant. If I'd had my head on my shoulders *one goddamned time—*"

"Hey, Julieta. You want my advice?"

Cree's tough tone startled her, and she looked over wide-eyed.

"My advice is, screw the self-blame. If Garrett had been a halfway decent person, none of it would have happened. Neither of you can take responsibility for what an impulsive, philandering, arrogant, violent man did!"

Julieta stared straight ahead. Cree could only hope she'd get there eventually.

Off to the west, Joyce was bucketing along and whooping for joy. *Who'd have guessed?* Cree asked herself.

"Did Peter know Tommy was his son?" Julieta asked.

"'Know' isn't the right word. I doubt Peter knew he occupied anyone's body. Peter's ghost replayed its memory for fifteen years, there in the ravine, until one day it came across a really compatible environment, a vehicle for the expression of its compulsion. Obviously, there's some kind of natural resonance between kin. Maybe someday we'll figure out how it works. But right now, I don't know."

"But . . . why out at the ravine? Why not back at the house?"

Cree hadn't told her the details, but there was no dodging it now. "He wasn't quite dead when Nick buried him. The rocks Nick knocked down were what finally killed Peter."

Appalled, Julieta sagged. When she straightened again, her lips were pressed tight, white with rage.

This was another close passage for Julieta. If she became obsessed with retribution, no matter how richly deserved, her liberation would not be complete. "I know exactly what you're feeling. But Joyce and Ed and I were talking about that last night. We all agree there's not going to be any evidence of who killed Peter. Not fifteen years later. His bones will show he was murdered, but there won't be any way to pin it on Garrett or Nick."

Cree looked over at Julieta and could see that it wasn't going down easy. She wondered if Julieta could get past this, relinquish her rage over even so great an injustice. There was so much at stake. Julieta was just beginning life as a free person. Cree was certain she and Joseph had already become lovers, but Julieta would have to leave a lot behind if the two of them were to be happy. She could still be deflected back so easily.

But you could give someone only so much advice.

They were not far from the ravine now, and Julieta's small, private duty to the dead. They stopped their horses and waited for the men to catch up.

Joyce was trotting back, cheeks bright with high desert air, stoned absolutely gonzo on so much light and space. "My behind is going to be sore for a week and I won't regret a minute of it!" she sang. Then she remembered their errand and sobered quickly.

★   ★   ★

Julieta and Joseph walked toward the mesa, hand in hand, getting smaller against the cliffs and then disappearing as they went between the walls of the ravine. Cree tethered the horses to a clump of sagebrush and she and Joyce and Edgar sat on the ground. The detailed debriefing would wait until they were back in Seattle, but they took out their canteens and talked about Tommy, about the psychological state and environment that had primed him for the possession. They talked about the independent hand, and what it suggested about the mechanics of possession. They tried to guess at the hypnotic or paralytic effect that surrounded him when the ghost was resurgent; Ed theorized that maybe the antagonism between two different brain frequencies created an electromagnetic field strong enough to affect others. For a while they talked about the role of blood relationship in hauntings, ancestor spirits, the principle of blood to blood and like to like.

Joyce shook her head. "Here I've always bitched about how my mother is trying to live vicariously through me. But she's got nothing on this Peter guy!"

They all laughed at that.

"But what about these ghosts?" Joyce asked, tipping her head toward the ravine. "Here Ed and I did all that work, found out about old Yil' Dezbah and her family, and then we find out they had nothing to do with it. But why did Tommy draw the faces in the cliffs?"

"A period of acute sensitivity, triggered by his sudden invasion by Peter?" Cree proposed. "Or maybe Tommy's something of a natural sensitive and subconsciously picked up on their presence. Or maybe just his . . . hunger to know his parents, his forebears, had a role— primed him, made him more vulnerable." She shrugged. "Personally, I think that's one of the factors that made him receptive to Peter's revenant."

"Which, of course, we'll never know," Edgar muttered.

Joyce sifted soil through her fingers. "So . . . you want to do some work on the ghosts here?"

Cree looked at the mesa, the lonely cleft in the rocks, and shook her head. "I can't, Joyce. I'm too beat. I'm so used up. Julieta says she'll talk to the medicine man about them. Maybe he knows some ceremony that'll lay them to rest. But not me. I'm shot."

They nodded understandingly. But Ed still looked a little downcast: Again, he'd missed the chance to probe the ghost with his instruments. Measuring the electrical activity in Tommy's brain while possessed would have constituted a tremendous advance in parapsychology, mapping the neurological mechanism of possession and quite possibly providing information that would be instructive in other psychiatric maladies. But he'd never had the chance to use the FMEEG. And his inspection of the school's electrical system in pursuit of clues about the flicker phenomenon had produced nothing. Ed sat on the dirt, absentmindedly picking tufts of sage leaf, crushing them between his fingers, sniffing the pungent herb, tossing the crumbs away.

Cree smiled, hoping she could cheer him up. She had saved something for him.

"Ed. I have to tell you about a phenomenon I noticed up at the sheep camp. No electricity up there, right? Just Coleman lanterns, firelight, starlight. So guess what?"

"What?" He looked at her suspiciously from beneath one raised eyebrow.

"We had *flicker!* When Tommy was in full swing, the light appeared to strobe, quite noticeably—natural light, Ed! Kerosene lamps! Meaning it's an optical or neurological phenomenon. Not necessarily electrical!"

"No kidding!" Ed visibly perked up, his eyes changing as the implications hooked him.

"Nope."

"Which would argue for direct neural stimulus. Jeez, that *is* good!" He edged over and put his arm around Cree's shoulder. He squeezed her hard, looking at Joyce. "She's a sweetie, isn't she? Making me feel better." He screwed off the top of his water bottle and raised it in a toast: "To DNS! The future of parapsychology."

They laughed, toasted, then quickly got serious as Julieta and Joseph emerged from the ravine. The two little figures slowly made their way back.

Joyce tipped her head back to observe them thoughtfully. "Think they'll make it?"

Cree looked at them. "I think they already have. I think these two've paid their dues in advance, the good stuff starts now. Like they say: Love will find a way."

"Sometimes it just takes a while," Ed added, getting distant again.

51

"S O GOOD OF you to come all this way to see me," Donny said. His grin was self-satisfied.

"Well, Saturday's your day here. And I sure as heck wasn't driving to Albuquerque at your summons." Julieta's voice stayed level, casual, but she couldn't keep the scorn out of it.

They were on the hill overlooking the mine headquarters, where they'd had their first run-in with Donny. Joyce had joined Julieta and Cree for the ten-mile ride, wearing a cowboy hat again and managing Breeze with the confidence of an old hand. Donny had come up in a company Jeep, accompanied by Nick Stephanovic, who now lounged against the hood thirty feet away. Below, mine operations were in full swing, the machines grinding away, the boom of the distant dragline swinging ponderously. A light plane droned in a slow arc across the cloudless sky to the west.

Saturday afternoon, clear and windless and warm. Five people feigning calm while the tension was thick enough to cut with a knife.

"You sure you want to discuss business with these people here?" Donny said.

"Oh, I think we can trust them."

"Suit yourself. So—I understand you just lost one of your core staff members." Donny's world-weary eyes gloated.

"Lynn Pierce, yes. I had to let her go. But I understand she has a nice position waiting at McCarty Energy."

"Well, we go back a ways," Donny said. "And I'm a big believer in rewarding loyalty. She's a damned good nurse, too. As it happens, we need medical personnel right here in Hunters Point."

"Let's get to it, Donny. I believe you were planning to threaten me?"

"That's an unfortunate way to phrase it. I'd say I wanted to make a trade. Things I know for things you know."

"What do you know?"

"I know you have a boy who's sick and that you're treating it as a supernatural issue. I know Dr. Black is here to exorcise him. I know a medical professional formerly employed at your school who'll testify to how you've handled the situation and who'll be glad to go to the newspapers to make sure the scandal gets good exposure. If that doesn't work, I've got three hundred and seventy-four Navajo employees, which puts me in a great position to informally relay this news to the Navajo community." Donny paused to pull a scrap of paper from his shirt pocket. "*And* I have the names and phone numbers of some people named, let's see . . . MacPherson, in Boston, and an outfit called the Osbourne Trust, and a couple of other philanthropic types known to give money to a certain local school. All of whom, I'm sure, would be very interested. I'd think our keeping quiet would be worth quite a bit to you."

Donny was obviously having a blast. Back at the Jeep, Nick chuckled to himself. Under the circumstances, Cree thought, Julieta was doing a remarkable job of keeping her cool.

"What do you want from me?" Julieta asked through her teeth. "Trade for what?"

"Sending Dr. Black and her friends packing, and then shutting up about whatever the hell you think you know. And then staying out of my hair."

Julieta got a faraway look as she thought about that. After a moment, she turned to Nick. "Hey, Nicko. Did you know that Donny once propositioned me? This was about two years after I divorced his father. I still laugh about it."

"The price is going up, Julieta," Donny said darkly. "Better make a deal now."

Nick eased himself off the Jeep and idled over to stand near Donny. He rolled his shoulders and looked around, enjoying the nice weather.

Joyce had said nothing so far, but now she handed her reins to Cree, slipped off her horse, and stood across from the big man. She'd admitted to Cree that she was hankering for some confrontation with him. Now she looked a little bored, preoccupied with one of her fingernails. Cree knew the signs and they made her nervous. The little airplane snoozed back across the western horizon.

Julieta backed Spence away a couple of steps. "Here's the deal, Donny. What I know is, your father shot Peter Yellowhorse in early November 1986. Garrett's dead and can't get punished. But Nick was the one who finished Peter off by burying him in the ravine near the school. He drove my Jeep to the top of the mesa and pushed rocks over the edge. You helped them, Donny, and you helped conceal the crime."

Donny's jaw dropped. He made a dry croak, shot a glance at Nick. Nick hadn't moved, but his pretense of calm was gone in an instant.

"This is bullshit. Where do you come up with this stuff? Your psychic friend here?"

"We exhumed the bones," Julieta lied. "We identified the remains. His belt buckle was there. It's very distinctive—made by one of his uncles."

"You'll never prove what happened," Nick said.

"Then why were you so worried that you came back to check the ravine Tuesday night?"

That got under Nick's skin. He began to move toward Julieta, but Joyce interposed herself. She didn't look so bored now. She was less than half his weight and came up to his armpit, and Nick looked at her incredulously.

"There's nothing, Nick," Donny cautioned. "Not after sixteen years. She's bluffing us."

"Then there's the in situ uranium plant," Julieta went on. "You're under court injunction not to start building it. But you've been going ahead anyway, over on Area Eighteen. You could get hit for millions in fines and have to tear it all down."

Donny chuckled. "There's no plant. There's no construction. And if you've trespassed on my land to find out different, it's illegally gained information and inadmissible. Fruit of the poisoned tree and all that."

Julieta raised her hand to point to the west. "Yeah, but your airspace is public. Overflight's perfectly legal. And that little Cessna that's been circling for the last half hour? Dr. Edgar Mayfield, Dr. Black's associate, hired it from Gallup. He's up there with a good camera and telephoto lens. He's an engineer and a physicist. Knows what to look for."

Donny whirled to look at the little plane, buzzing sleepily through another slow circle in the distance. Nick looked to him for instructions, but Donny appeared speechless.

"One more thing, Donny. Your source at school is lying. There's no sick boy, and there's no exorcist. There's a consulting clinical psychologist from Seattle, and there's a kid who's fully recovered from a temporary illness. That's all a matter of record. If I hear any suggestion you're spreading rumors to the contrary, I'll have you in court so fast your head will spin."

"What do you want, Julieta?" Donny croaked.

"I want a charitable donation to my school for a million dollars. I want construction on the in situ plant stopped and whatever's there dismantled. And I want Nick turned in to the police with a confession. Afterward, I leave you alone and you leave me alone."

"Not a chance," Donny said derisively. But his expression was anything but confident. He was making that gulping movement in his throat again.

"Fine. We'll see how it shakes out." Julieta brought Spence around and made ready to leave.

"Nick, stop her horse! I need a minute to think this through."

Nick took a step and reached for Spence's bridle, but it was a mistake to take his eyes off Joyce. Cree had seen her use the move in tae kwon do competition: She leapt up, lithe body spinning as her left leg slashed in a savage backward arc. The heel of her boot hit the side of Nick's head with an awful sound. He dropped like a sack of potatoes.

Joyce landed like a ballerina and went to look down at him. Flat on his back, he goggled up at her, eyes wide, mouth moving soundlessly.

Joyce gave him a lascivious smile and asked, "Oh, honey! Was that as good for you as it was for me?"

She turned disdainfully away, took Breeze's reins, boosted herself into the saddle. The three of them urged the horses away.

When Cree glanced back, Nick was still trying to get up. Donny didn't look too happy.

"Sorry," Joyce said ten minutes later. "I couldn't resist." The encounter had put her in a good humor. Cree shook her head, unable to suppress a smile.

Julieta didn't share the mood. She rode with her head tipped down, shoulders slumped. "It's all a bluff, of course. I don't want to exhume Peter's bones, I want to leave him be. And I can't let anyone know about his murder, or about my past, it'll only hurt the school. And you're right, Joyce, after all these years there wouldn't be any evidence to implicate Nick or Donny. Donny's smart enough to figure all that out. He might stop construction on the in situ plant, but he'll never stop hassling me. They'll never have to pay for killing Peter." She rode on and added quietly, "And I don't need the past coming back anymore. I don't want an ongoing feud with Donny. I just want a new life. I have a chance to do things right now. I've already waited long enough."

Cree had no answer. She was glad Julieta saw her own path in the right way. But it was so wrong for them to go unpunished. She felt Julieta's despondency come over her.

They rode in silence for a few minutes.

"You know," Joyce said to no one in particular, "I learned some interesting things while I was out poking around. A lot of stuff on the McCartys and their mines, and some fascinating stuff about Navajo traditions. One of the old ceremonies is called . . . what was it, something like Turning the Basket. It's used if the patient's suffering is inflicted by someone else, like a bad person or a witch. The medicine man turns the evil back on the person who sent it. Rebounds it. It cures the sick person and punishes the wrongdoer in one swell foop. Kind of got me thinking." Maybe it was just the lingering endorphin high from her demolition of Nick Stephanovic, but her small sharklike grin never wavered.

Julieta nodded distractedly. Cree thought about whether such a ceremony might be of symbolic value for Tommy. But he'd been put through a lot of curing, an endless month of fuss and bother. Sometimes you had to let it go, Cree thought. Sometimes justice took the long way around, just like love. Sometimes peace of mind meant relinquishing things. It seemed intolerable to let Nick and Donny get by without consequences, but there wasn't anything anyone could do about it.

Joyce looked over at her thoughtfully, seemed about to say more, but then clammed up for the rest of the ride.

52

SEATTLE. MONDAY, back at the office. Eight A.M. sharp.

Joyce unlocked the door to PRA's suite, turned on the lights, tossed the pile of mail onto her desk. The light on the message machine was blinking and the digital readout told her that there were thirty-two messages waiting. Through the door to Cree's room, she glimpsed the big views of Elliott Bay and the smile of bright blue sky above. She and Ed had arrived Sunday midafternoon, and she'd spent the rest of the day just relaxing and mooning around. She'd done some stretching to ease the soreness in her thighs, then went for a run along the shore of Lake Washington. The rez was great, but it sure felt good to be around a body of water again.

Joyce measured ground Nicaraguan beans into a paper filter, filled the reservoir of the coffee machine, and turned it on. As it perked, she listened to the calls and took notes on pink message slips for Cree and Ed. By the time she was done, the coffee was ready. She poured a mug and took it and the mail into Cree's office, where the Bay and the Sound could keep her company as she went through the week's correspondence.

Between the calls and the letters, there looked to be some promising cases in their future; Ed would be glad to see this stuff when he came in this afternoon. Cree, too, when she got back later in the week and once she got over the exhaustion and existential upheaval that would likely follow the Oak Springs case. Cree was on a perpetual learning curve, rising so steeply Joyce was sure it would one day take her right off the planet. Which day Joyce was determined to forestall as long as possible.

A couple of inquiries had come from people who'd been seeing glowing orbs, one in San Francisco and one right here in Washington, not far from Seattle; Ed would like that, because orb reports were on the increase and the phenomenon promised to be particularly susceptible to physical analysis. There were people troubled by standard-issue phantoms in Florida, Maine, and Minnesota; the person in Maine said hers looked like a druid shaman, like old representations of Merlin. Coincidentally, she claimed to live near one of the supposed pre-Columbian, pre-Viking druidic archaeological sites that occurred throughout the Northeast. Another letter requested help on a poltergeist case in Kentucky and came complete with newspaper clippings with photos of household objects hurtling through the air. Poltergeists always gave Joyce a shiver.

There was even a terse letter from Mason Ambrose in Geneva, accompanied by a check for five grand; the old creep was donating Cree's fee on behalf of Oak Springs School. Trying to redeem himself. Joyce was glad to see the check, because most of the remaining envelopes contained bills and the PRA bank account was, as always, running on fumes.

When she finished sorting and filing, she got herself another cup of coffee, put her feet up on Cree's desk, and stared out the window. She thought back with satisfaction to that last day and night in Oak Springs, which made up for some of the frustrations of the rest of the investigation.

Saturday night, after booking seats for the return flight, she had opted to stay with Cree at the school in the hope that there'd be time in the morning to squeeze in one last horse ride, which she'd decided was easily as good as sex and had fewer risks. Plus there was some other business to see to.

After Julieta had gone back to the faculty residence, she and Cree spent the evening in the big ward room, talking only occasionally. Cree was exhausted and feeling alternately good and then unsettled about the outcome here. They agreed it had been an instructive case, and most of its details had worked out well, but they'd also agreed that a smack upside the head for Nick and some fleeting humiliation for Donny wasn't enough. The absence of justice was a real craw sticker. There certainly was a lot of comeuppance due those two. And due Lynn Pierce, who had done her best to bring the school down. Joyce had been tempted to tell Cree what she'd found and figured out during her research, but Cree was not in a receptive state of mind for such things. And anyway, some details were best kept to yourself.

Cree went on about how she felt only pity for the nurse: perpetually grieving for her long-dead husband, wounded, consumed with envy, fragile, but concealing it all with her coy, insinuating smugness. It wasn't easy to be Lynn Pierce, Cree said, and it couldn't be much fun.

Firing Lynn and throwing some anxiety Donny's way was about as far as it could go for Julieta, Cree said. Julieta had to move on now; she didn't need obsessive concerns for justice or revenge complicating things. It was more important now for her to find the gentleness in herself, to be free from the past and let her love blossom with the good-looking doctor—yaddah, yaddah, all the therapy hooey dear Cree was so prone to.

Actually, Joyce didn't disagree with her in the slightest. But.

Later, when she was sure Cree was asleep, she had gathered up the photocopies she'd made at the newspaper archives, and scanned them again to make sure she had the details right. It was ten-thirty when she went to find the nurse.

Cree and Julieta need never know.

Lynn Pierce wasn't in her bedroom, but Joyce found her in the examining room, tidying up. The silver head bobbed and its thick braid swung as Lynn stooped to pick something up. When she sensed Joyce in the doorway, she straightened and turned quickly, her eyes so wide the bronze speck glinted in the lights.

"Didn't mean to startle you," Joyce said. "I called out from the hallway, but I guess you didn't hear me."

"I'm about to go to bed. Do you need something?"

"I'm just saying good-bye. I have to leave early tomorrow. I understand you'll be leaving soon, too."

"Yes." Tight-lipped, eyes hard and suspicious.

"But I hear you've got another job all lined up."

"Highly skilled medical practitioners and administrators are hard to find out here. I'm fortunate to have professional contacts who respect that fact. I'll be assuming my new position next week."

"Yeah, I saw Donny earlier today. He thinks the world of you. I guess you've worked for him before, right? Up at the Bloomfield mine. Your husband, Vernon, too. I'm sure he'll take good care of you."

"Is there something I can do for you, Ms. Wu?" Lynn Pierce took a paper towel from a dispenser and feigned preoccupation with a smudge on the stainless steel counter.

"No. But there's something I can do for you."

"Oh, that's so kind of you!" Lynn's voice was coy, but when she turned back toward Joyce, her eyes were not. The look confirmed Joyce's sense of her: *This gal is dangerous.*

"Vern, he was a pretty important man in the McCartys' operation?"

Lynn could tell she was being baited, but as Joyce had hoped, she couldn't resist indulging her pride in him. "Vernon was chief explosives engineer at the Bloomfield mine. He was the very best in his field and received numerous commendations for his safety record. He supervised all explosives operations and staff. It's a very important part of coal mining."

"So he probably rubbed shoulders with Garrett McCarty now and again. And Donny."

"Vernon was invaluable, and it's to the McCartys' credit that they knew what they had in him and made a point of treating him well. Vern's office was just down the hall from Donny's in Bloomfield. Vern appreciated their respect and trust."

Joyce nodded. "Do you know what's been going down around here in the last few days? Aside from you telling Donny everything about Tommy Keeday?"

Lynn looked at her speculatively. After a moment, she took a cigarette pack out of her smock, unfolded a little foil ashtray, and lit up. She blew the smoke at the ceiling. "You're kind of a disjointed conversationalist, Ms. Wu, did you know that? Are you going to connect the dots for me, or do I have to guess?"

"Oh, heck," Joyce said, "I'll connect 'em. Why not."

Lynn narrowed her eyes as she sucked hungrily on her cigarette. This time she blew the smoke at Joyce and stared confrontationally at her.

"Your husband once told you something he'd overheard the McCartys talking about, didn't he? Way back, like in 1986, not long before he died. Something very juicy and hush-hush about Julieta. That's how you knew she'd had a lover back then. A Navajo guy. That's why you figured she acted so strangely sometimes—maybe Tommy Keeday was her child."

"Isn't he?"

"What else did Vernon tell you? Did he tell you that Garrett murdered Julieta's lover? Buried him in the ravine over at the north end of the mesa?"

That news clearly caught Lynn by surprise. She said, "No!" and then must have realized it was an admission that Joyce had been right so far. A mask slipped over her face.

"No, of course you didn't know. Because all this time you've been thinking Joseph Tsosie was the father. But he wasn't. A man named Peter Yellowhorse was, and that's who the McCartys killed. And Vern found out. And he made the mistake of letting them know he knew."

"You're thinking you can sour me on Donny McCarty, but I don't believe any of this. And you're not subtle enough."

Joyce tossed photocopies of the *Gallup Independent* articles onto the counter next to Lynn's white, clenching hand. The nurse glanced at them despite herself.

"When did Vern tell you, Lynn? Think back. Because I know when Vern died and how he died."

Lynn tore her eyes away from the photocopies.

" 'Explosives expert killed in coal mine accident,' " Joyce read out loud. "Think about it. Best safety record in New Mexico, but he manages to blow himself up November fifteenth, 1986. A couple of weeks after Peter Yellowhorse was murdered, probably a few days after he overheard Garrett and Nick, or maybe Donny and Nick, talking about it. A few days after he told you the juicy gossip. He knew what they'd done, and it was dangerous knowledge, Lynn. Nick was up at Bloomfield a lot right around then, wasn't he? Really think it's all a coincidence?"

Lynn was holding her cigarette in the V of her fingers, high in front of her, but she had forgotten it. Joyce could see in her eyes that she was thinking back, checking the dates, the details. The tumblers spun and began clicking into place. After a moment, Lynn took a long, long, deep breath. The deadly, metallic look in her eyes chilled Joyce.

Lynn turned back to the counter to stub out her unfinished cigarette. She busied herself with a tray of scalpels. Her hands shook badly at first but then steadied as they moved among the bright blades, putting them one by one into the sterilizer.

"Good-bye, Ms. Wu," Lynn Pierce said expressionlessly.

Joyce left her and went back to the ward room where Cree had been sleeping peacefully. She had felt a little twinge of guilt, knowing Cree probably wouldn't approve. But, hey.

Turning the basket, Joyce thought. She couldn't be one hundred percent sure she was right about Vernon Pierce's death. But those bums deserved it in any case. Donny, Nick, Lynn—the three of them deserved each other, and Lynn was already launched, something like a human heat-seeking missile, coming in under the radar. Oh, it would take a while; she would settle in at the mine and think about how best to do whatever she'd do. But you didn't have to be a Las Vegas bookie to figure the odds on Donny's and Nick's continuing health and happiness were not so good. Joyce made a mental note to check the Albuquerque papers once in a while to see how it turned out.

She finished her coffee, checked her watch and found that she'd been sitting for almost an hour. Still, she felt good and lingered a little longer.

Cree would be back on Thursday. She'd have a lot to think about. She'd done an incredible job with Julieta and the gorgeous Navajo doctor, zeroing right in on the crucial knot that held everything back, kept everything snarled. But Joyce doubted she'd do as good a job when it came to her own love life. Ed hadn't talked about the parallels there, but Joyce was sure he'd noticed them. You'd have to be a major dummy not to. And of course Cree would come back all bent out of shape by it. For more reasons than one. She'd absorbed so much of Julieta McCarty, she probably couldn't even tell whether her feelings toward Ed were truly her own, or some kind of resonance with Julieta's thing with Joseph. Heart-breaking, really.

On one hand, Cree was as ready for a man as anyone Joyce had ever known, but on the other hand, it was complicated. Joyce couldn't decide where the problem lay, exactly. Once, she would have said, Easy—the shadow of her dead husband's hanging over her, her very own ghost. And the cure for that was obvious. She'd told Cree as much last spring, and Cree had wisely gone back to see Paul in New Orleans.

But maybe it was more complex than that, more even than making a choice between Ed and Paul. Seeing Cree out there, riding, walking, the way she expanded into the place, Joyce knew she'd come back in love with the land, the rocks, the big sky, the Navajo medicine men, even the ghosts, as much as with Paul Fitzpatrick or Edgar Mayfield. Cree wasn't all that available because she already had a lover: mystery. Or maybe just *life*. The mystery of life. Whatever.

Joyce honestly had no idea how you could help somebody with a situation like that.

53

T HE OLD Keedays' place was transformed. The Evil Way was not as
large or long a ceremony as others, but it still required substantial
preparation. Tommy's closest aunts, uncles, and cousins had come to
participate and help out, along with a few nonfamily, including Cree,
Julieta, Joseph, and Joseph's uncle. With the medicine man and his two
assistants, there were around two dozen. Pickup trucks and station wagons
were parked haphazardly all around the grandparents' home. The kitchen
stove in the trailer was going, and a couple of fire pits had been set up
outside to help prepare the food needed to nourish the gathering during
the two-day Way. Two sheep had been butchered and now hung from the
branches of a small cottonwood, soon to be roasted.

Cree helped Ellen make piles of fry bread, dropping the dough disks into
smoking oil, spearing them with a fork, rotating them as they bubbled,
flipping them when the underside was golden brown. It was good to see
Ellen again, to bask in her goodwill and good humor.

She met relatives, tried to keep track of their names and connections to
Tommy, gave up, decided it didn't matter. They were all family. They
were here to help him. To heal him. To remind him who he was.

The mood was mixed. In general, the preparations created a festive
atmosphere: people laughing quietly as they worked, exchanging gossip,
chipping in food and money, giving orders to each other, complaining. But
there were no young children present, and an undertone of solemnity and
concern grew as the time for the ceremony itself drew closer. Being
possessed by a spirit was serious and dangerous. Even the inevitable half
dozen dogs seemed restrained and generally stayed out from underfoot.

Ts'aa' Lił'ini, the Singer, was a small, vigorous man in his sixties. He was
dressed in khakis and a white shirt with an antique Pendleton blanket worn

over his shoulders as a robe, and had a serious face. Cree found his dignity and gravity imposing. Ellen and the grandparents introduced her to him, explaining in Navajo her connection to the situation. He nodded his head, his bright, knowing eyes on Cree's, and invited her to participate. Cree thanked him sincerely, explained she'd be more comfortable just helping out on the periphery of things, and let him go about his work.

Cree watched as Ts'aa' Iił'iní and his helpers brought the ceremonial materials from their pickup and laid them out in the appropriate order. Corn pollen, plant materials, colored sand for sand paintings, mountain tobacco, spirit gifts, fire materials: One of the assistants, a chubby man in his late twenties, explained the significance of each and the role it would play in the ceremony. The basket on which offerings would be placed was made of sumac bark, he told her, which gave it its scent. The whole thing was intricate and full of symbolism that was rooted all the way back in the beautiful and complex Navajo creation stories. Cree was aware of standing on the far side of a vast cultural canyon that made real comprehension difficult. After a while, awed and overwhelmed, she excused herself and went to sit over near one of the sheep sheds, where she could take it all in but not get underfoot.

She had done her part. What Tommy needed now, she couldn't help with. He was in the best possible hands.

Julieta and Joseph had come together, made the rounds of introductions, and got right to work with the others. The mutton would be buried in coals, so Joseph and a couple of other men were digging shallow trenches near the fires. Julieta helped bring firewood, lugged cases of soft drinks from trucks, joined Ellen at the fry bread assembly line. Sometimes Joseph paused to watch Julieta. Sometimes she'd turn her head to check on him. When they passed near each other, Cree saw, you could practically see it in the air between them: a shimmer of mutual awareness, fraught with desire and anticipation. The sight was very gratifying.

A tall, very thin Navajo man came toward her from the hogan, cupping a match around a cigarette as he walked. Joseph's uncle, Cree remembered. She'd met him only briefly but had liked him instantly. He was elderly but hale, his nose veined from too much whiskey, fingers stained from too many cigarettes, his suit somewhat out of date but clean and well pressed. He struck her as the kind of guy Pop would have liked.

"Yá'át'ééh," Cree said.

"Hey, you say that pretty well!" Uncle Joe said, looking impressed. He sat down stiffly against the log fence next to her, unconcerned about getting his suit dirty. He spat out a tidbit of tobacco and squinted at the men working near the fire pits. "Know what it means? It's how we say hello, but it means 'It is good.'"

"I didn't know. That's lovely."

"Nice day for this. Perfect weather. That's a good sign for the ceremony." Uncle Joe looked up at the benign sky, then glanced over at her. "Taking a breather?"

"Oh, I was just getting in the way. It looks like it's all under control." She smiled over at him and he returned it. "I'm a little tired," she confessed.

"From what Joseph tells me, you've already done old Ts'aa' Iił'iní's work for him. He should return some of the gifts."

"Not at all. This is just what Tommy needs. This is just right."

Uncle Joe chuckled at himself. "Listen to me! 'Old'? Who am I to talk? The guy's younger than me! Did anyone tell you what his name means— Ts'aa' Iił'iní?"

"Nope. What?"

"'Basket Maker.'"

He gave her a sideways grin and a sharp look as if this information was a gift or surprise for her, and Cree nodded as though she understood. She found him enormously charming and concluded that he must have been quite the lady-killer in his younger years. Like Ellen, he was the kind of person you immediately felt you'd known for a lifetime.

Uncle Joe got serious and narrowed his eyes as he continued watching his nephew. Joseph had taken off his white shirt and was digging in his T-shirt. He had a good build, nice proportions, muscles that moved smoothly in his shoulders as he levered and lifted the shovel. Over near the trailer, Julieta turned her head to admire him briefly. Cree was surprised to feel a little pang of jealousy.

After another moment, Uncle Joe sighed, explained he'd better go help out, and creaked to his feet. Still looking at Joseph and Julieta, he dusted the seat of his pants and straightened his jacket.

"The kids'll be good looking, idn't it?" He tightened his tie while checking his reflection in a hubcap nailed to the shed wall and looked pleased with what he saw. "Runs in the family," he explained.

Later, Julieta took a break and came over to join Cree. She looked ravishing, ten years younger than she had just three days ago. She gathered her big skirt and held it as she crouched down next to Cree. They watched people come and go for a moment in silence.

"They're going to be starting soon. You sure you don't want to be in the hogan?"

"I'm sure, Julieta. I'm just an outsider. I'd rather be over here right now. But I'll go along with the ceremony from here, trust me. If anybody wonders about the strange *bilagáana* sitting out here in lotus position, just tell them I'm weird but harmless."

"It's not a problem. The family's glad to have you. They're grateful." They sat in silence for a moment, and then Julieta turned to Cree again. "Tommy wasn't the only one who was possessed." It was not a question.

"Yeah, well. We've all got our ghosts," Cree said. She remembered vividly the sensation of expulsion, of being emptied, that she'd felt as much in Julieta as in Tommy when Peter had stepped off the porch and into nowhere. Despite all the wrenching emotion and danger, Julieta had handled the whole encounter with admirable grace and strength. She doubted that if Mike appeared to her, returning to her ten years after his death, she'd be able to find the way.

"I have a lot to thank you for, Cree. Joseph and I both do."

"Oh, yeah? Like what?" Cree shot her a mischievous grin. "I want details!"

Julieta looked away, her face reddening, and made her own, private smile. "You're terrible! And you're too observant for your own good, Dr. Black. He is a marvelous man. But I'll leave the details to your imagination."

They sat for another moment.

"Anyway, I wanted to return something of the favor. Or the challenge, however you might look at it. Forgive my presumption, Cree."

Julieta's seriousness stalled Cree in midair.

"You have a . . . boyfriend, right? In New Orleans?"

"There's someone I'm getting to know, yes. I'll be going out there in a couple of weeks. Why?"

"I was wondering. You've known Edgar Mayfield a long time, haven't you? You two seem very close."

Cree felt her serenity fall away, replaced by uneasiness. A feeling of exposure and doubt. When she'd seen Edgar and Joyce off, she'd been reluctant to physically let go of Ed. She'd wished he wasn't so blue, that he'd seen how much he'd helped her even if it wasn't in the technological or scientific sense. She'd resolved to try to tell him when she saw him back in Seattle. Then she'd gotten confused again, thinking about just what she'd say.

Julieta bit her lips. She looked like she wanted to say more, but then must have second-guessed herself. She stood quickly, brushing the dust from her skirt. "I should get back," she said.

Okay, Cree was thinking. *Right, okay. She's right, and I don't want to wait eighteen years to figure out something that important.* She felt close to crying and couldn't figure out just why.

But Tommy had emerged from the grandparents' trailer. He was dressed in new jeans and a bright white shirt, a broad silver-inlaid belt, a heavy turquoise necklace, and a brilliant headband. His red moccasins were exquisite, no doubt lovingly made by one of his aunts. He walked solemnly between his grandfather and his uncle Raymond, looking a little embarrassed at being the center of attention, sobered and intimidated by the seriousness of the ritual. Still, when he saw Cree, he tossed her a quick, shy smile before continuing on to the hogan door.

It was a smile Cree knew she'd remember for a long time, the kind you take out of memory and touch and treasure, like a favorite piece of jewelry from its box.

She watched them go into the hogan, and after a few minutes the compound was empty. It was quiet except for the low voices from inside, muffled by the blanket that hung over the open doorway. She shut her eyes and savored the feel of the event. A soft wind moved through the shallow canyon, past the derelict hogans and sheds, and caressed the cottonwood trees. The clean scent of the desert, tinged with sage, mixed with the smells of roasting mutton and woodsmoke. Cree realized again just how much she'd miss this place, these people. The thought of leaving broke her heart. Everything broke her heart.

She took off her shoes and pulled her feet onto her thighs. She shut her eyes and felt herself drawn into the hogan, the hearthlike place at the center where all those energies converged. The air changed when she heard *Hastiin* Ts'aa' Iił'iní's voice inside, and though she couldn't understand the words she was spellbound by its rhythms, awed by his authority.

Cree intuitively felt what he was doing and tried to find a synesthetic metaphor that would describe it. It was a weaving together, she decided. In daily life, all the energies of living and dead were disparate, often conflicted and chaotic. But the ceremony had invited the living people here as well as the important ghosts and now the medicine man was bringing together all their separate lines. Through the prescribed actions of the ritual, he was gathering the strands of the individual lives and personalities and psyches one by one and guiding them into a beautiful weave of ancient design.

Basket Maker! Cree realized abruptly. Joseph's uncle must be an amazing man, to have known she'd discover the meaning of the medicine man's name.

Eyes shut, feeling like she was floating in the soft desert air, Cree could sense the ceremony, almost see it: Yes, it was like a basket, honoring each strand, giving each participant a purpose, containing and protecting each individual psyche. The People and their ghosts *were* the basket even as they were *in* the basket being woven here. Ts'aa' Iił'iní was gathering the strips in his strong hands, bending them gently, weaving together living and ghosts and past and future into a beautiful thing much more durable than the fleeting present. The troubled ghosts would be acknowledged, included, and calmed. He guided each strand to where it must be, creating the basket that for thousands of years had proved so beautiful, practical, enduring.

Today Tommy would know he was safe in the center of the basket, and, just as important, that he was himself a crucial strand.

Cree just sat, awed and humbled. Stunned. Grateful. Heart wrenched wide open. Still on the verge of tears. There was so much she had to learn.

Yá'át'ééh, she thought. *It is good. Yá'át'ééh.*

AUTHOR'S NOTE

The phenomenon of possession figures in all the world's religions and superstitions and has close parallels in a number of modern medical diagnoses.

The fictional case of Tommy Keeday is a composite drawn from true incidents in Navajo historical literature and from the fascinating, disturbing case of Anna Winsor, which was painstakingly detailed by her physician, Dr. Barrows, between the onset of symptoms in 1860 and her death in 1873. Anna was seized with fits and delirium and then settled into a troubled state in which she experienced her spine as her right arm and her neck as her shoulder; she neither recognized nor retained conscious control of her actual arm. The right arm seemed possessed of a separate, self-aware consciousness of its own and often functioned independently—writing, signing, gesturing—when she was asleep. She feared the alien thing attached to her body and sometimes attacked it in attempts to drive it away. She also spoke in other voices and accents, made prescient pronouncements, and assumed a wide variety of personalities.

Dr. Barrows's original journal is hard to come by, but an account of Anna Winsor's thirteen-year struggle (along with many other cases) can be found in F. W. H. Myers's *Human Personality and Its Survival of Bodily Death,* originally published in 1903, reprinted in 2001 by Hampton Roads Publishing.

The European literature on possession, based largely on Judeo-Christian cosmology, is unusual in that it supposes a purely evil or demonic agent in possession. The great majority of spiritual traditions throughout the world take a broader view, in which the invading entity is just as likely to be neutral or even benign, and include intentional possession among the skills required of practitioners of medical and mystical arts.

ACKNOWLEDGMENTS

I owe a great deal to many people who contributed their support and knowledge to the writing of this book.

First and foremost, I am grateful to my dear friends in the Navajo Nation, Bob Kirk, Ruth Storer, and Ernest Kirk, for sharing their homes and stories, for reviewing drafts, and for setting me straight on many issues. I also owe gratitude to Tamara Martin for our spectacular horse rides and for her grace and generosity, and to Dr. Jim Sielski for advising me about medical administration on the rez. Thanks, too, to Herbert Benally of Diné College—Shiprock; to Dr. Daniel McLaughlin of Diné College—Tsaile; to Dee McCloskey, regional director of NCASC; and to the many others who treated me so kindly during my visits to Dinetah. Please forgive my presumptions, errors, and license.

Special thanks are due John Engles and the Pittsburg and Midland Coal Mining Company, for graciously touring me through P&M's astounding McKinley Mine. Readers should know that P&M's operations in no way resemble the reprehensible practices of the fictional McCarty mine depicted in this book.

Thank you to my wise advance readers, Willow Hecht, Amie Hecht, Stella Hovis, Jean Cannon, Ruth Storer, and Francette Cerulli, whose comments greatly improved this book.

My undying gratitude goes to Karen Rinaldi, Lara Carrigan, Greg Villepique, and Amanda Katz, for being such terrific people to work with, and to my agent, Nicole Aragi.

Finally, once again, thanks to Christine Klaine for coming to me with her wildly improbable notion of writing a fifty-book series of serious supernatural mystery novels!

A NOTE ON THE AUTHOR

Daniel Hecht was a professional guitarist for twenty years. In 1989, he retired from musical performance to take up writing, and he received an M.F.A. from the Iowa Writers' Workshop in 1992. He is the author of three previous novels: *Skull Session, The Babel Effect*, and *City of Masks,* which introduced Cree Black.

A NOTE ON THE TYPE

The text of this book is set in Bembo. This type was first
used in 1495 by the Venetian printer Aldus Manutius for
Cardinal Bembo's *De Aetna,* and was cut for Manutius by
Francesco Griffo. It was one of the types used by Claude
Garamond (1480–1561) as a model for his Romain de
l'Université, and so it was the forerunner of what became
standard European type for the following two centuries.
Its modern form follows the original types and was
designed for Monotype in 1929.